Edgar Wallace was born illegitimately in 1875 in Greenwich and adopted by George Freeman, a porter at Billingsgate fish market. At eleven, Wallace sold newspapers at Ludgate Circus and on leaving school took a job with a printer. He enlisted in the Royal West Kent Regiment, later transferring to the Medical Staff Corps, and was sent to South Africa. In 1898 he published a collection of poems called *The Mission that Failed*, left the army and became a correspondent for Reuters.

Wallace became the South African war correspondent for *The Daily Mail*. His articles were later published as *Unofficial Dispatches* and his outspokenness infuriated Kitchener, who banned him as a war correspondent until the First World War. He edited the *Rand Daily Mail*, but gambled disastrously on the South African Stock Market, returning to England to report on crimes and hanging trials. He became editor of *The Evening News*, then in 1905 founded the Tallis Press, publishing *Smithy*, a collection of soldier stories, and *Four Just Men*. At various times he worked on *The Standard*, *The Star*, *The Week-End Racing Supplement* and *The Story Journal*.

In 1917 he became a Special Constable at Lincoln's Inn and also a special interrogator for the War Office. His first marriage to Ivy Caldecott, daughter of a missionary, had ended in divorce and he married his much younger secretary, Violet King.

The Daily Mail sent Wallace to investigate atrocities in the Belgian Congo, a trip that provided material for his *Sanders of the River* books. In 1923 he became Chairman of the Press Club and in 1931 stood as a Liberal candidate at Blackpool. On being offered a scriptwriting contract at RKO, Wallace went to Hollywood. He died in 1932, on his way to work on the screenplay for *King Kong*.

D0862117

BY THE SAME AUTHOR
ALL PUBLISHED BY HOUSE OF STRATUS

The Black Abbot

HOUSE OF
STRATUS

This edition published in 2001 by House of Stratus, an imprint of
House of Stratus Ltd, Thirsk Industrial Park, York Road, Thirsk,
North Yorkshire, YO7 3BX, UK.

www.houseofstratus.com

Typeset, printed and bound by House of Stratus.

A catalogue record for this book is available from the British Library
and the Library of Congress.

ISBN 1-84232-662-7

We would like to thank the Edgar Wallace Society for all the support they have given
House of Stratus. Enquiries on how to join the Edgar Wallace Society should be addressed to:
The Edgar Wallace Society, c/o Penny Wyrd, 84 Ridgefield Road, Oxford, OX4 3DA.
email: info@edgarwallace.org web: http://www.edgarwallace.org/

TO

THE REV. A V C HORDERN
OF MARKET DRAYTON

A FRIEND OF SOLDIERS

1

"Thomas!"

"Yes, m'lord."

Thomas the footman waited, a look of concentrated interest on his unprepossessing face, whilst the pale man behind the big library desk sorted out a small pile of Treasury notes.

The battered steel box from which they were taken was full to the brim with Bank and Treasury notes of all denominations in hopeless confusion.

"Thomas!" absently.

"Yes, m'lord."

"Put this money in that envelope – not that one, you fool, the grey one. Is it addressed?"

"Yes, m'lord. 'Herr Lubitz, Frankforterstrasse 35, Leipsic,' m'lord."

"Lick it down, take it to the post office and register it. Is Mr Richard in his study?"

"No, m'lord, he went out an hour ago."

Harry Alford, 18th Earl of Chelford, sighed. He was on the right side of thirty, thin of face and pale as students are, his jet-black hair emphasising the pallor of his skin. The library in which he worked was a high-roofed building, the walls bisected by a gallery that ran round three sides of the room and was reached by a circular iron staircase in one corner of the apartment. From the roof to the floor every inch of wall space was covered with bookshelves, with this notable exception. Over the great stone fireplace was a full-length painting of a beautiful woman. None who had seen his lordship could make any mistake as to the relationship which existed between himself and that wild-eyed beauty. It was his mother; she had the same delicate features, the same raven hair and dark, fathomless eyes. Lady Chelford had been the most famous debutante of her time, and her tragic end had been the sensation of the early 'nineties. There was no other picture in the room.

His eyes strayed to the portrait now. To Harry Alford, Fossaway Manor, for all its beauty and charm, was a poor casket for such a jewel.

The footman in his sober black livery, his hair powdered white, lingered.

"Is that all, m'lord?"

"That is all," said his lordship gravely. Yet when the man had moved noiselessly to the door – "Thomas!"

"Yes, m'lord."

"I heard something by accident as you passed my window this morning with Filling the groom – er – ?"

"He was telling me about the Black Abbot, m'lord." The pale face twitched spasmodically. Even in broad daylight, with the sun streaming through the stained windows and marking the parquet with arabesques of crimson and blue and amethyst, the very mention of the Black Abbot set his heart beating faster.

"Any man in my employ who discusses the Black Abbot will be instantly dismissed. Will you tell your fellow-servants that, Thomas? A ghost! Great God! Are you all mad?"

His face was red now, little veins swelled at his temples, and under the stream of anger his dark eyes seemed to recede into his head.

"Not a word! You understand? It is a lie! A mischievous wicked lie to say that Fossaway is haunted! It is a trick played by some of the louts about the place. That will do!"

He waved the bowing man from his presence and resumed his study of the black-lettered book that had arrived from Germany that morning.

Once outside the library door, Thomas could afford to twist his sallow features to a grin. Only for a second, and then he became serious again. There must be nearly a thousand pounds in that cash-box, and Thomas had once served a three-year sentence for a tenth of that sum. Even Mr Richard Alford, who knew most things, was unaware of this interesting fact.

Thomas had a letter to write, for he maintained a lucrative correspondence with one who had an especial interest in Fossaway Manor, but first he had to report the gist of the conversation to Mr Glover, the butler.

"I don't care what his lordship says (and why he should tell a footman and not me, I don't know); there's a ghost, and all sorts of people have seen it! I wouldn't walk down Elm Drive alone at night for fifty million pounds!" This portly man shook a head that the years had silvered.

"And his lordship believes it too. I wish he was married, that's what I wish. He'll be more sensible then!"

"And we'd get rid of Mr Blooming Alford – eh, Mr Glover."

The butler sniffed.

"There's them that likes him and them that don't," said the oracle. "We've never had a cross word, Thomas – there's somebody at the door."

Thomas hurried to the hall entrance and opened the big door. A girl was standing under the portico. She was pretty in a bold way, red of lips and bright of eye and dressed expensively.

Thomas gave her a grin of recognition.

"Good morning, Miss Wenner – this is a bit of a surprise!"

"Is his lordship in, Thomas?"

The footman pursed his lips dubiously.

"He *is* in, miss, but I'm afraid I can't take you in to him. Don't blame me, miss, it's Mr Alford's orders."

"Mr Alford!" she sneered. "Do you mean to tell me that I've come all the way from London and can't see Lord Chelford?"

But Thomas kept his hand on the door. He liked the girl, who, when she had been his lordship's secretary, had never given herself airs (the unpardonable sin of the servants' hall), and who always had a smile for the meanest of the domestic staff. He would gladly have admitted her and felt that his lordship would have been pleased to see her, but in the background somewhere hovered Dick Alford, a man of curt speech, who was not only capable of showing him the door but kicking him through it.

"I'm very sorry, miss; but orders is orders, as you know."

"I see!" she nodded ominously. "I'm to be turned away from what might have been my own door, Thomas."

He tried to look his sympathy and succeeded in assuming an expression of imbecility. She smiled at him, shook hands with him graciously and turned away from the portico.

"Miss Wenner," reported Thomas, "her that Alford fired because he thought his lordship was getting sweet on her – "

The library bell rang at that moment and Thomas hastened to answer the call.

"Who was that lady – I saw her through the window?"

"Miss Wenner, m'lord."

A cloud passed over Harry Alford's face.

"Did you – ask her to come in?"

"No, m'lord; Mr Alford gave orders – "

"Of course – yes. I had forgotten. Perhaps it is just as well. Thank you."

He pulled down the green shade over his eyes, for even in the day he worked by artificial light, such was the gloom of the library, and resumed his study of the book.

Yet his mind was not wholly concentrated on the work. Once he rose and walked up and down the library, his hands clasped before him, his chin on his breast. He stopped before the picture of his mother, sighed and walked back to the writing-table. There was a Press paragraph which he had cut out of a London newspaper, and this he read for the third time, not ill-pleased with the unaccustomed experience of finding himself the subject of newspaper comment, and yet irritated by the subject on which the paragraph was based.

Chelfordbury, a sleepy Sussex village, is engaged in the thrilling sport of ghost-hunting. The Black Abbot of Fossaway has, after a period of quiescence, again made his appearance. The legend

4

is that seven hundred years ago, Hubert of Redruth, Abbot of Chelfordbury, was assassinated by order of the second Earl of Chelford. Since then, from time to time, his "ghost" has been seen. During the past few years horrific stories of an Unseen Being that shrieked and howled demoniacally have been current in the county, but the noisy spook was not actually seen until last week.

Fossaway Manor has other romances besides ghosts. Four hundred years ago a great treasure of gold was, according to legend, hidden somewhere on the estate; so effectively, in fact, that it has never been discovered since, although successive Earls of Chelford have searched diligently for the ancestral hoard.

The present Earl of Chelford, who, by the way, is engaged to be married to Miss Leslie Gine, the only sister of Mr Arthur Gine, the well-known solicitor, informed our local representative that he had no doubt that the apparition of the Black Abbot was a practical joke in very doubtful taste on the part of the foolish youth of the neighbourhood.

He made as though to tear the paper, but thought better of it and put the cutting under a paper-weight.

That reference to the practical jokers of the village was reassuring and might be a comfort when the night came and he needed encouragement.

For Lord Chelford believed in the Black Abbot as religiously as he proclaimed his scepticism.

His restless hand moved to the bell-push on his table.

"Has Mr Richard returned?"

"No, m'lord."

Lord Chelford struck the table pettishly with his palm.

"Where on earth does he get to in the mornings?" he asked querulously.

Thomas, very wisely, pretended not to hear.

2

The reapers had laid low the last of the golden heads, and the sheaves stood like yellow tombstones on Racket Field. Beyond the field was Chelfordbury, where the grey old spire of the church came up from a velvety knoll of trees; beyond again, the green and white downs of Sussex, along the feet of which the railway runs.

Dick Alford sat on a stile on the top of a little hillock and could see across the weald for fifteen miles. He could turn his head and take in the home farm and the green roofs and cupolas of Fossaway Manor, with its broad lawns and its clipped yew hedges. Neither cornfield nor down, manor-house nor pleasaunce, interested him for the moment. His eyes were fixed and his mind centred upon the girl who was walking quickly up the winding path that would bring her presently to where he sat.

She was singing as she walked, the riding crop she carried whirling round and round like a drum-major's baton. His lips twitched to the ghost of a smile. Presently she would see him, and he wondered if she would be annoyed. He had never seen Leslie Gine except in such circumstances that her face was a pleasant mask and her manner conventionally charming. She had been nicely brought up and taught that all things are permissible except one: to make your equal feel foolish.

The song ceased. She had seen him, but she did not check her pace and came quickly up the hill path, slashing at a nettle as she walked.

"Peeping Tom!" she greeted him reproachfully.

She was not so tall as the average English girl, but her slimness gave her height, and the supple movement of her hinted at greater strength than her slight figure suggested. Her face, delicately modelled, had the subtle refinement of her class. Small, beautiful hands and feet, a head finely poised, eyes of a deep grey, and a red mouth that smiled easily, Leslie Gine in rags would have been unmistakably a beautiful lady.

Dick had seen her riding; she gripped the withers with her knees, jockey fashion, and was part of the horse. He had seen her on the polished dancing floor; there was lissom grace in every line. When he danced with her, he held in his arms a fragrant something that had more substance and character than he had thought. The hand on his shoulder was definitely placed, the body which his arm encircled was firm; he could feel the tiny muscles ripple under his hand.

She stood now, her little black riding hat askew, her figure clad in neat black relieved by the lawn collar. Her neatly booted legs were planted stubbornly apart, one gloved hand holding her waist, the other swinging the crop. In her grey eyes was an imp of mischief that gleamed and danced all the merrier for the studied solemnity of every other feature.

Dick Alford, from his vantage place on the top rail of the stile, chewed a blade of toddy grass between his white teeth and surveyed her approvingly.

"Been riding, Leslie?"

"I have been riding," she said gravely, and added: "a horse."

He looked round innocently.

"Where is the favoured animal?" he demanded.

She looked at him suspiciously, but not a muscle of the tanned, lean face so much as twitched.

"I dismounted to pick wild flowers and the beastie ran away. You saw him!" she accused.

"I saw something that looked like a horse running towards Willow House," he confessed calmly. "I thought he had thrown you."

She nodded.

"For that prevarication you can go and find him – I'll wait here," she said, and, when he got down from the stile with a groan: "I meant you to do that, anyway. The moment I saw you I said to myself:

'There's a lazy man who wants exercise!' Sisters-in-law-to-be have privileges."

He winced a little at this. She may have noticed the cloud that came momentarily to his face, for she put out her hand and checked him.

"One of the grooms can find him, Dick. He is such a hungry pig that he is certain to make for his stable. No, I *don't* mean the groom. Sit down; I want to talk to you."

She swung up to the stile and took the place he had vacated.

"Richard Alford, I don't think you are enjoying the prospect of my being the mistress of Fossaway House?"

"Manor," he corrected.

"Don't quibble – are you?"

"I count the days," he said lightly.

"Are you?"

He took a battered silver case from his hip pocket, selected a cigarette and lit it.

"My dear Leslie – " he began, but she shook her head. She was very serious now.

"You think I will – interfere with things? With the management of the estate – I know poor Harry couldn't manage a small holding – with – oh, with all sorts of things, but I think you are wrong."

He blew three smoke rings into the air before he answered.

"I wish you would manage the estate," he said quietly. "It would be a blessing to me. No, I'm not worried about that. With your money – forgive the brutality – the estate will not count. A bailiff could manage it as well as any second son!"

3

He spoke without bitterness, without a hint of self-pity, and she was silent. He was a child of a second marriage, and that had made it worse for him. When old Lord Chelford followed Dick's mother to the grave, the second son's portion was his. The estate, the title, the very car he had used as his own, passed from him. A tiny estate in Hertfordshire that brought two hundred a year, some old jewellery of his mother's and a thousand pounds came the way of the second son. And the thousand pounds had never been paid. In some mysterious fashion it had been swallowed up.

Mr Arthur Gine had settled the estate. In all the circumstances Dick felt happier when he did not think of that thousand pounds. Yet, for some reason or other, he thought of it now, and as though she read his thoughts dimly, and associated his reserve with her brother, she asked:

"You don't like Arthur, do you?"

"What makes you say that?" he said, in genuine surprise. He had never betrayed his aversion to the dandified lawyer.

"I know," she nodded wisely. "He exasperates me sometimes, and I can well imagine that a man like you would hate him."

Dick smiled.

"Harry doesn't hate him anyway, and he is the person who counts."

She looked round at him, swinging the crop idly.

"It doesn't seem real to me that I'm to be married at all – it was such a funny proposal, Dick, so polite, so formal, so – unreal! I think if it had come in any other way – " She shook her head.

Dick wondered a little drearily how his brother would propose. Harry was something of a novice at the love game; once he had had a pretty secretary, and on a warm June afternoon Dick had interrupted what was tantamount to a proposal from the enterprising young lady. And the flustered Harry would have agreed to her matrimonial suggestions, only Dick had happened along – and the calculating Miss Wenner had left Fossaway Manor rather hurriedly. He remembered this happening.

"I suppose if he had proposed in the conventional way you wouldn't have accepted him?"

"I don't know," she said dubiously. "But it was quaint and – queer. I like Harry awfully. I have often wondered if he would like me if – " She did not finish her sentence.

"If you weren't so horribly rich?" smiled Dick. "You're not paying him a very high compliment." She held out her arms and he lifted her down, though there seemed no necessity for it, as she was a very agile young person as a rule.

"Dick," she said, as he crossed the stile and they walked side by side towards the main road, "what am I to do?"

"About what?" he asked.

"About Harry and everything."

He had no answer to this.

"Arthur is very keen on my marrying him," she said. "And really, I'm not averse – at least, I don't think so."

"That is the worst of being a great heiress," he bantered.

"I wonder?" Her brow wrinkled in a frown. "And am I a great heiress?"

He stopped and looked at her in surprise.

"Aren't you?"

He seemed so shocked that she laughed.

"I don't know; my uncle left me a lot of money years and years ago. I don't know how much – Arthur has managed my estate for years. I have all the money I need."

"Then don't grouse!" he said crudely, and she laughed again.

"I suppose most girls in my position have their marriages arranged in the way mine has been arranged, and until quite recently I have accepted the idea as part of the inevitable."

"And why have you changed your mind now?" he asked bluntly, and saw the pink come into her face.

"I don't know."

Her answer was very short, almost brusque.

And then she saw the look in his eyes – the infinite yearning, the hopelessness of them. And in a flash there came to her a knowledge of herself.

For some reason which she could not understand she became of a sudden breathless, and almost found a difficulty in speaking. She felt that the thump and thud of her heart must be audible to his ears, and strove desperately to recover her balance. Vividly before her eyes came the picture of her fiancé, the thin, irritable young man – the weakling with all that man needed in his hands, save manhood. A pitiable, nerve-racked creature, now pleading, now bullying – oblivious of the impression he made on the woman who was to share his life. And from this mental figure of him her eyes moved mechanically to the man by her side; calm, serene, radiant in his strength and self-reliance.

Ten minutes later she was walking back to Willow House, and in her heart she struggled with a problem that seemed well-nigh insoluble.

Dick Alford, making his slow progress homeward, saw the lank figure of his brother waiting at the end of the elm drive.

The wind flapped the skirts of his long frock-coat; standing, he stooped slightly and had a trick of thrusting forward his head, which gave him the appearance of a big, ungainly bird. His face was dark with anger, Dick saw as he came up with him.

"I deputise many duties to you, Richard, but I'll do my own love-making, understand that!"

The blood came into Dick Alford's face, but he showed no other sign of his hurt or anger.

"I will not have it – you understand?" Lord Chelford's voice was shrill with childish fury. "I will not have you interfering in my private affairs. You sent one girl away from me, you shall not take Leslie!"

"I am not – " began his brother hotly.

"You are – you are! You don't want me to marry! I am not a fool, Dick! You stand next in the line of succession! I am going to marry Leslie Gine – understand that! You shall not break that engagement."

For a moment the brutality, the injustice of the accusation, left the younger man white and shaking, and then, with a supreme effort, he laughed. Scenes such as this were of almost daily occurrence, but never before had Harry Alford gone so far. In ten minutes the storm would pass, and Harry would be his old lovable self, but for the moment it was bitterly hard to bear.

"Why do you say such horrible things?" he said. "I got rid of Wenner because she was not the wife for you – "

"You didn't want me to marry! You are waiting for my shoes, a dead man's shoes!" almost screamed the elder son. "The last thing in the world you want to see is a new Countess of Chelford. You know it, you know it!"

Dick Alford was silent. God knew his brother spoke the truth! It would be a woeful day for him when Harry Alford brought a wife to this great house to share the dreadful secret which hung like a cloud over Fossaway Manor.

4

Dick Alford was in the little study where he usually worked, a business-like room filled with filing cabinets and deed-boxes. The French windows giving to the lawn were open, for though it was September the night was warm, and he was working in his shirt-sleeves, a pipe gripped between his teeth, his eyes protected from the overhead light by a big green shade that he wore affixed by a band to his head. If there was a resemblance between Lord Chelford and his mother, not even the keenest observer could trace in Dick Alford the slightest likeness to his half-brother. He was a creature of the open, a six-foot athlete, broad of shoulder and slim of flank, and his tanned face spoke of a life spent on the windy downs. His blue eyes surveyed the footman with a quizzical smile as he pushed his battered old typewriter aside, relit his pipe and stretched himself.

"Black Abbot? Good lord! Have you seen him, Thomas?"

"No, sir, I have not seen him. But Mr Cartwright, the grocer down in Chelford village – "

He gave a graphic narrative of Mr Cartwright's horror, amazement and confusion.

"They telephoned up from the 'Red Lion' to ask if his lordship had heard anything about it." Even Thomas, who believed in nothing except Thomas, shivered. "It is the first time he has been seen for years according to all accounts, though he has been heard howling and moaning. Nobody knows who set fire to the vicarage when the parson was away at the seaside – "

"That will do, Thomas. As to Cartwright, he was drunk," said Dick cheerily, "or else he saw a shadow."

He glanced out at the lawn, bathed in the blue-white rays of a full moon.

"You can see things in the moonlight that never were on land or sea. I understood that his lordship said that the Black Abbot was not to be discussed?"

"Yes, sir."

"Then shut up!" said Dick.

Pipe in mouth, he strolled across the hall into the dimly lit library.

The three electroliers that hung from the roof were dark. Only the two green-shaded reading-lamps that flanked each side of the desk were alight, and these intensified the gloom. Dick closed the door behind him and lounged over towards the desk, pulling a chair behind him.

Chelford frowned at the sight of his brother.

"Really, Dick," he said irritably. "I wish to heaven you wouldn't loaf about the place in shirt and breeches. It looks fearfully bad."

"It feels fearfully cool," said Dick, sitting down. "Will your nerves sustain the smell of a bit of honest 'baccy?"

Lord Chelford moved uncomfortably in his chair. Then, reaching out his hand, he snicked open a gold box and took out a cigarette.

"My pipe against your stinkers for a hundred pounds!" said Dick, with a cheery smile. "Cigarettes I can stand, but scented cigarettes – "

"If you don't like them, Dick, you can go out," grumbled his lordship fretfully. And then in his abrupt way: "Did you see this newspaper cutting?"

He pulled the paper from under the crystal weight and Dick skimmed the lines.

"We are getting into the public eye, Harry," he said, "but there is nothing about me, which is unkind."

"Don't be stupid. How did that get into the papers?"

"How does anything get into the papers?" asked Dick lazily. "Our spook is almost as useful as a Press agent."

Harry snapped round on him.

"Can't you take this seriously? Don't you see that it is worrying me to death? You know the state of my nerves – you have no sympathy, Dick, you're just as hard as rock! Everybody seems to hate the sight of you."

Dick pulled at his pipe glumly.

"That is my unfortunate character. I am afraid I am getting efficient. That is the only way I can account for my unpopularity. It keeps me awake at nights – "

"Don't fool, for heaven's sake!"

"I'm serious now," murmured Dick, closing his eyes; "try me with a hymn!"

Harry Chelford turned away with a gesture of utter weariness, fingered the manuscript at his hand and gazed from his brother to the door. It was a gesture of dismissal and Dick rose.

"Don't you think you've done enough work for tonight, Harry?" Dick asked gently. "You look absolutely all in."

"I never felt better in my life," said the other emphatically.

Dick slewed round his head to read the printed page from which his elder brother had been copying, and saw at once that his effort was in vain; the book was written in Old German, and Dick's linguistic abilities ended at a mastery of restaurant French. Lord Chelford put down the book with a sigh and sat back in his padded chair.

"I suppose you think I'm a fool wasting my time on this" – he raised his hand towards the serried shelves – "when I could be having a very amusing time with Leslie?"

Dick nodded.

"Yes, I think you might be more profitably employed out of doors. Really, for a bridegroom-to-be, you're the worst slacker I've ever struck."

There was a superiority in Harry Chelford's smile.

"Happily, Leslie knows she is marrying a bookworm and not an athlete," he said, and, rising, walked over to where Dick was sitting and dropped his hand on his shoulder. "What would you say if I told you that I was halfway to discovering the real Chelford treasure?"

Dick knew exactly what he would say, but replied diplomatically.

"I should say you were three parts on the way to discovering the philosopher's stone," he said.

But his brother was serious. He paced up and down the long library, his hands behind him, his chin on his breast.

"I expected you to say that," he said. "I should have been rather surprised if you hadn't. But the Chelford treasure has an existence, Dick, and somewhere with it is the greatest treasure of all!"

His brother listened patiently. He knew by heart the story of the thousand bars of pure gold, each bar weighing thirty-five pounds. The legend of the Chelford treasure was inseparable from the Chelford estate.

Harry walked quickly to his desk, pulled open a drawer and took out a small vellum-covered book. The pages were yellow with age and covered with writing that had faded to a pale green.

"Listen," he said, and began reading.

"On the fifteenth of the month, the same being the feast day of St James, came Sir Walter Hythe Kt from his cruise in the Spanish seas, for the cost of which I raised first three thousand eight hundred pounds and eight thousand pounds from Bellitti the Lombard, and Sir Walter Hythe brought with him on ten wagons one thousand ingots of gold each of thirty-five pounds weight which he had taken from the two Spanish ships *Esperanza* and *Escurial*, and these ingots he shall put away in the safe place if yet the weather be dry and the drought continue, though rain is near at hand, to judge by the portents, deeming it wise not to inform my lord Burleigh of the gold because of the Queen's Majesty and her covetousness. Also he brought the crystal flask of Life Water which was given to Don Cortes by the priest of the Aztec people, a drop of which upon the tongue will revive even the dead, this being sworn to by Fra Pedro of Sevilla. This I shall hide with great care in the secret place where the gold will be stored. To Sir Walter Hythe Kt I had given permission that he keep for himself one hundred bars of like weight, and this he did, thanking me civilly and sailed off from Chichester in his ship the *Good Father*, which ship was wrecked on the Kentish coast, Sir Walter Hythe, his shipmaster and all his company perishing. Such was his terrible misfortune. As for myself, being in some danger because of the part I have taken in promoting the welfare of my true sovereign lady, Mary – "

Lord Chelford looked up and met the steady eyes of his brother.

"The writing ends there," he said. "I am certain that he was not interrupted by the arrival of Elizabeth's soldiers to arrest him for his share in the conspiracy to put Mary on the throne. He must have had time to secrete the treasure. Where is the crystal flask?"

"Where rather is the gold?" asked the practical Dick. "If I know anything about Queen Elizabeth, she bagged it! Nobody ever found it – for four hundred years our respected forefathers have been searching for this gold – "

Lord Chelford made an angry gesture.

"Gold – gold – gold! You think of nothing else! Curse the gold! Find it and keep it. It is the flask I want!" His voice sank to a whisper, his face had grown suddenly moist. "Dick, I'm afraid of death! God! You don't know how afraid! The fear of it haunts me day and night – I sit here counting the hours, wondering at which my spirit will go from me! You'll laugh – at that – laugh, laugh!"

But Dick Alford's face was set, unsmiling.

"I do not laugh – but can't you see, Harry, that such a thing as an elixir of life is preposterous?"

"Why?" Lord Chelford's eyes were shining. "Why shouldn't this discovery have been made by the ancient civilisations? Why is it more wonderful than wireless telegraphy or the disintegration of atoms? Thirty years ago flying was regarded as a miracle. The flask – I want the flask of Life Water! The gold – throw it into the road – let the poor devils take it who want it. I want life – do you understand? – life and the end of fear."

He dropped heavily into his chair and wiped his streaming forehead.

"The End of Fear!" he muttered.

Dick listened, his eyes never leaving his brother's face. And this was to be Leslie Gine's husband. He shivered at the thought.

5

If the Honourable Richard Fallington Alford had been regarded by the compilers of such volumes as being sufficiently important to have his biography enshrined in a popular work of reference, his life's work, his hobby and his recreation would be described as "looking after the Chelford estate." His bailiffs said he knew every blade of grass; the tenant farmers swore he could price a standing crop to the last penny of its worth. He knew Fossaway Manor, its strength and weakness, better than the estate architect – could point out where the foundations were scamped by the Elizabethan builders. He could trace the walls of the old castle which Richard of York had burnt and razed, beheading the fourth earl for his treachery under the great archway, one crumbling pier of which still showed its grey and battered head above the roses that now surrounded it. He gave to the broad lands of Chelford a loyal and passionate devotion which any mistress might envy.

In the chill of an autumnal morning, when mist blanketed the hollows and a pale sun was struggling through thin clouds, he strolled across the park towards the abbey ruins. There was little of them left. A truncated tower wrecked by lightning; a high, arched space where an oriel window had once flamed; mounds of scattered stones left where Cromwell's soldiers had overturned them; and, under the carpet of grass, a "feel" of solid pavement.

He drew at his pipe as he stepped out, and the tobacco smelt sweet and wholesome in the cold air.

He was on his way to the home farm, and his errand was a prosaic one. A cow had died in the night, and his cowman had reported symptoms of cattle fever.

The familiar ruins showed up ahead, the half-arch, like a huge question mark, arrested his eye and raised again the well-argued problem of restoration. Some day, when the Chelford ship came home; when that coal vein was proved, or when Harry had a rich wife.

This was an unpleasant thought. His lips curled in a grimace of distaste.

He stopped suddenly.

A figure was walking amongst the ruins – a woman. Her back was towards him and she was obviously unaware of his presence. Something about her figure seemed familiar – Dick turned from the path and walked towards her.

Evidently she did not hear him, for when he spoke she started, uttered a little scream and turned a frightened face to him.

"Good morning, Miss Wenner," he said politely. "You are up and about very early."

There was no need for him to wonder whether this girl had ever forgiven him for the very painful interview that had preceded her retirement. Recognising him, her eyes blazed with hate.

"Good morning, Mr Alford." She was civil enough. "I'm staying in the village and I thought I would like to come up and see the old place."

He nodded gravely.

"You had a similar thought yesterday," he said, "and tried to see my brother."

"Well?" defiantly.

"I gave you to understand, Miss Wenner, that we should all be much happier if you never again passed the lodge gates," he said quietly. "I hate saying this to any woman, but you ought to be the first to recognise how very uncomfortable you make me feel. I thought you would apprehend this."

"Apprehend" was a stilted word, but he could think of no other.

"Is that so?" The colour had deepened in her face. "Is – that – so?"

"That is so," he nodded.

She looked at him for a while and her lips curved.

"I'm sorry I've annoyed the family chaperon," she sneered.

He could admire, in a detached way, her wholesome good looks; could even admire her courage. Her wrathful eyes were fixed on his, the break in her voice betrayed the fury she strove to conceal. As for Dick Alford, he felt a brute.

"I'm extremely sorry if you don't like my calling," she said, her voice razor-sharp and tremulous, "but I think the least Lord Chelford could have done was to see me, considering I've worked for him for three years, and after all that has passed between us – "

"The only thing that passed between you, Miss Wenner, was your weekly wages," said Dick, with maddening calmness.

But now he had taxed her to the limit of endurance.

"He asked me to marry him, and I *would* have married him if you hadn't put your spoke in!" she said shrilly. "I could get thousands and thousands out of him for breach of promise if I wasn't a lady! You second sons and hangers-on poisoned his mind against me! You ought to be downright ashamed of yourself, you good-for-nothing penniless pauper!"

Dick was faintly amused at the redundancy.

"You've wrecked and ruined my life," the pretty virago went on, "with your interference, and after all the work I've done! After all them – I mean those hours I've spent with his lordship workin' at the Treasure, an' he told me I was the most helpful secretary he'd ever had – "

He let her talk herself to a sobbing incoherence.

"All this may be true," he said soothingly, "and probably is. The point is, your presence here is a little – indelicate."

Seeing her look round over her shoulder as she was talking, he had taken a quick survey of the ruins, expecting to discover that she had a companion. But there was nobody in sight. The ground sloped steeply from where he stood to the little Ravensrill, the broad brook which had for a thousand years marked the boundary of the manor.

Unless somebody was concealed behind the fallen masonry she was alone.

"I suppose you want me to clear out now," she gulped, and he inclined his head.

"I will walk with you to Fontwell Cutting – that is the nearest way to the village," he said, and she was too much occupied with her manufactured misery to resent his offer.

What had she been doing in the abbey ruins so early in the morning? He knew that it was useless to ask her.

As they passed down the steep path to the road she spoke over her shoulder.

"I wouldn't marry him for a million pounds!" she said viciously. "He is going to marry Leslie Gine, isn't he? I wish him joy!"

"I will convey your kind message," he said ironically, an indiscreet rejoinder, for it roused the devil in her.

"Mind he doesn't lose her, that's all!" she screamed. "I know! Everybody knows! You want her money too – the second son's in love with her – that's a nice look-out for Harry Alford!"

He sat swinging his legs over the edge of the bluff, watching her till she was out of sight.

Everybody knew that he loved Leslie Gine! And he only knew it himself at that moment!

6

In all the city of London there was perhaps no office more elegant than that in which Mr Arthur Gine spent his leisurely business hours. It was a large room, panelled in white wood, with pink-shaded wall brackets of frosted silver. Its floor was covered with a deep rose carpet into which the feet sank as into an old lawn; and such furnishing as the room held was of the most costly description. Visitors and clients who had business with this dainty lawyer were warned not to smoke in his sacred presence. The windows were doubled to keep out the noises of Holborn; there were exterior sun-blinds to exclude the fugitive rays of pale sunlight which occasionally bathed the City; and long velvet curtains, in harmony with the carpet, to shut out the horrid world that roared and palpitated outside Mr Gine's exquisite chamber. In this room was a faint aroma of roses – he was partial to the more expensive varieties of perfume, and had a standing order with the best of the Grasse houses.

He was a fair man with an unblemished skin and a small yellow moustache; a credit to his hosier and shirt-maker. His wasp-waisted morning coat fitted him without the suspicion of a wrinkle; his grey waistcoat, the severe dark trousers with the thinnest of white stripes, the patent shoes, the exact cravat, were all parts of a sartorial symmetry.

Mr Gine seldom appeared in the courts. His head clerk, a grey hard man of fifty, who was generally supposed by Mr Gine's brother solicitors to be the brains of the business, prepared most of the briefs, interviewed the majority of clients, leaving to his employer the most important.

On a bright morning in the early days of September, Mr Gine's big Rolls glided noiselessly to the kerb, the youthful footman seated by the side of the driver sprang out and opened the door, and Arthur Gine stepped daintily forth. There was a small white rose in his buttonhole, and the passer-by who saw him, noting the perfect shine of his silk hat, the glitter of his patent shoes, and the ebony stick that he carried in his gloved hand, thought he was a bridegroom stopping on his way to church.

He entered the tiny electric lift and was whisked up to the first floor. A porter opened his door with a little bow and Arthur walked in, followed by the servitor, who took his hat, gloves and cane, and disappeared with them to an inner room. Mr Gine sat down at his desk, glanced at the letters that had been left opened for his inspection, and pushed them aside. He pressed an onyx bell-push twice, and in a few seconds his hard-faced managing clerk came in, carrying a wad of papers in his hand.

"Close the door, Gilder. What are these?"

Gilder threw the papers on the polished table.

"Mostly writs," he said curtly.

"For me?"

Gilder nodded, and Arthur Gine turned over the papers idly.

"There is going to be trouble if they give judgment against you for some of these," said Gilder. "Up to now I've managed to keep them out of court, but there are at least three of these which must be paid. I haven't had a chance of speaking to you since I came back from my holidays. Did you lose much at Goodwood?"

"Eight or nine thousand," said Arthur Gine lightly. "It may have been more or less."

"That means you don't know because you haven't paid," said Gilder bluntly.

"I paid a few – the more pressing," the other hastened to assure him. "What are these?"

He fingered the writs again with his beautifully manicured hand.

"One of them is very serious indeed," said Gilder, picking it out from the rest. "The trustees of the Wellman estate are suing you for three thousand pounds – the loan you had from Wellman."

"Can't you fix them?"

Gilder shook his head.

"I can't fix trustees – you know that. This is going to look ugly if it comes into court."

Arthur Gine shrugged his shoulders.

"There is nothing ugly about a loan – "

"You were Wellman's lawyer," interrupted Gilder.

"And he was not capable of managing his affairs. I tell you that will look ugly, and the Law Society will be asking questions. You'll have to raise money to settle this case out of court."

"What are the others?" asked Arthur Gine sulkily.

"There's one for twelve hundred pounds, furniture supplied to Willow House, and another from the vendor of Willow House for balance of purchase-money unpaid."

Arthur Gine leaned back in his chair, took out a gold toothpick and chewed it.

"What is the full amount?"

"About six thousand pounds," said Gilder, gathering up the writs. "Can't you raise it?"

His employer shook his head.

"A bill?"

"Who is going to back it?" asked the lawyer, looking up.

Gilder scratched his chin.

"What about Lord Chelford?" he asked.

7

Arthur Gine laughed softly.

"And what do you imagine Chelford would say if I went to him with such a proposal? You seem to forget, my dear fellow, that to Chelford I am the brother of a young lady who on her twenty-fifth birthday inherits the greater part of a million pounds. I'm not only the brother, but I am her trustee. Besides which, I am managing his mother's estate. What would he think if I tried? Chelford's a fool, but he's not such a fool as that, and I would remind you that all his business affairs are in the hands of the Second Son."

"You mean Alford – why do you call him that?"

"He's always been known as the Second Son since he was a child," said the other impatiently. "He is a shrewd devil, never forget that, Gilder. I don't know whether or not he suspects that I'm a fake, and that Leslie's fortune is a myth, but there have been times when he has asked some deucedly uncomfortable questions."

"Is the fortune a myth?" asked Gilder, and his companion looked at him slyly.

"You ought to know, my friend," he said. "We have been living on it for eight years! The croupiers of Monte Carlo have raked into their treasury quite a lot of it – various bookmakers I could mention have built handsome villas out of it. A myth. It wasn't a myth ten years ago. It was two hundred thousand pounds short of a myth? But today – "

He spread out his hands and eyed the writs with a whimsical smile.

"What do you expect to get from Chelford – he has no money?" asked Gilder.

Mr Gine chuckled.

"You may be sure that before I went to the expense and trouble of buying – or nearly buying – a house adjoining Chelford's place, and before I took the trouble to bring Leslie and him into touch, I took the elementary precaution of sizing up his position. He is comparatively poor, because that brother of his will sell none of the estates. He has the family obsession – their motto is 'Hold Fast.' Harry Chelford is realisable at a quarter of a million – apart from the buried treasure!"

They both laughed at this.

"You've been lucky up to a point," said Gilder seriously. "It was luck to inherit his legal business – "

A clerk came in with some letters to sign at this moment, and, after he was gone: "Does your sister still think she is an heiress?" asked Gilder.

"She has that illusion," replied the other coolly. "Of course she thinks so! You don't imagine Leslie would lend herself to that kind of ramp, do you?"

He took a pen from the silver tray before him, dipped it into the ink, and, drawing a sheet of paper towards him, scribbled down the figures.

"Six thousand pounds is a lot of money," he said. "I lost three times that amount when Black Satin was beaten a short head in the Drayton Handicap. The only thing to do is to rush the wedding."

"What about the Yorkshire property?" suggested the managing clerk.

Arthur Gine made a little grimace.

"I put a man in to buy it. I could have made twenty thousand profit on that. There's coal in abundance; that I have proved. But the Second Son was on the job, damn him!"

There was a long silence.

"What are you going to do?" asked Gilder.

"I don't know. I'm at my wits' end." Arthur Gine threw down the pen. "The position is exquisite torture to a man of my sensibility. Can't you suggest anything?"

"Give me five minutes," said Gilder, and went out.

As Gilder was making his way to his own office, a clerk handed him a letter. It was addressed to him personally, in an illiterate hand. Behind the door of his office bureau he opened the envelope.

The letter began without any preliminary.

His lordship is still working on the Treasure. He had an old book sent to him from Germany last Tuesday, written by a German who was in this country hundreds of years ago. I cannot read the title because of the funny printing, which is like Old English. His lordship has also had a plan sent to him from a London bookseller of Fossaway Manor. His lordship's brother, Mr Alford, has sold Red Farm to Mr Leonard for £3500 (here Mr Gilder smiled). Miss Gine came to tea yesterday with his lordship and Mr Alford, and afterwards Miss Gine and his lordship went for a walk in the home park. There is some talk about the Black Abbot having been seen near the old abbey. He was seen by Thomas Elwin, the half-witted son of Elwin, his lordship's cowman, but nobody takes any notice of this. He has now been seen by Mr Cartwright, the grocer. His lordship has had an offer for his Yorkshire estate, but I heard Mr Alford advise him not to sell, as he was sure there was coal on it.

Gilder nodded, understanding just how his employer's plan had fallen through.

…When I was taking tea into the library I heard his lordship say that he wanted the wedding to take place in October, but Miss Gine said she would like it after Christmas. His lordship said that he didn't mind because he was so busy. Mr Alford said he thought that the marriage settlement should be fixed by Sampson & Howard, who were the old Lord Chelford's solicitors, but his lordship said that he thought the settlement had better be in Mr Gine's hands. I did not hear any more because Mr Alford told me to get out. Miss Wenner, who used to be his lordship's secretary, came down from London yesterday, but Mr Alford has given orders that she is not to be admitted. His lordship did not see her –

Mr Fabrian Gilder's spy reported other minor matters which were less interesting. He read the letter again, put it in his pocket and was busy at his desk for five minutes.

He came back to find his employer leaning over his desk, his head between his hands, and laid a slip of paper before him.

"What is this?" asked Gine, startled.

"A six-months bill for seven thousand pounds. I've put an extra thousand in for luck," said Gilder coolly.

Gine read the document quickly. It was a bill, and required only his signature and that of Harry, Earl of Chelford, to make it convertible into solid cash.

"I dare not do it – I simply dare not do it!"

"Why tell him it's a bill at all?" asked Gilder. "You can get him by himself, spin a yarn – you have a fertile imagination – but I suggest to you that you tell him you need his signature to release some of your sister's property, and once his name is on the back of the bill – "

Arthur Gine looked up sharply. Was it a coincidence that this excuse should be suggested? There was nothing in the head clerk's face to suggest otherwise.

"But when it comes due?" he asked irresolutely, as he turned the document over and over in his hands.

"In six months' time he'll be married, and if things aren't better with you, he'll either have to meet the bill or hush the matter up."

The eyes of the two men met.

"You're on the edge of ruin, my young friend," said Gilder, "and I'm rather concerned. If you go down, my livelihood disappears."

How true this was, Arthur learnt one bitter day.

"You make a deuced sight more out of it than I do," he grumbled, as he wrote the name of a bank across the face of the bill.

"I spend less than you, and when I get money I know how to keep it."

"You might even raise the sum yourself," said his employer, with a feeble attempt at jocularity.

"I might," said Gilder grimly, "but, as I said before, I know how to take care of my own, and lending money to you is not my notion of a good investment."

He had been out of the room only a few minutes when he came back and, closing the door carefully behind him: "Do you know a Miss Wenner?" he asked.

Mr Gine frowned.

"Yes. What does she want?"

"She says she must see you on an urgent personal matter. Is she one of your – friends?"

Arthur shook his head.

"N–no – I have met her. She was Chelford's secretary. Can't you find out what she wants?"

"I've tried, but it is a matter personal to you. Do you want to see her? – I can easily stall her."

Arthur thought for a while. She might have something important to tell him.

"Ask her to come in," he said.

A few minutes later Mary Wenner came into the room and greeted him with a familiar nod.

"Well, my dear, this is an unexpected pleasure. You are getting prettier every time I see you."

She accepted the flattery as her right, and sat on the edge of his desk.

"I've been down to Fossaway, Arthur," she said.

"Silly girl," he smiled. "But I thought that affair was all over and done with. You've got to be good, Mary. Chelford is going to marry my sister."

"Isn't that grand! And I'm not surprised. I saw you working when I was at Fossaway."

She slipped down from the desk and dropped both her hands on his shoulders.

"Arthur, I'm tired of stenogging! And I want like sin to get back on that cold-blooded hound Dick Alford. I've been fired out once for proposing to a man – I'm going to take a second chance. We've been good pals, Arthur."

He murmured something in his alarm.

"Listen – don't turn down a good thing. You can marry me and I'll bring you a bigger dowry than your sister will take to Harry Alford."

He stared at her.

"You? Dowry?" he stammered.

She nodded slowly.

"Marry me, and I'll take you to the place where you can lay your hands on fifteen tons of Spanish gold – the Chelford treasure! Two and a half million pounds!"

8

Fifteen tons of gold! Two and a half millions sterling!

Arthur Gine stared at the girl incredulously. But she was making no idle statement, and that she at least believed what she said was clear from her flushed face and shining eyes. For a second he was speechless.

"Fifteen tons of gold?" He frowned and smiled at the same time. "You're mad, Mary!"

"Mad, am I?" She nodded vigorously. "Oh, indeed, I daresay you think so, but you won't be thinking that very long! I have found the Chelford treasure, I tell you."

He sat down heavily in his chair, his startled eyes still fixed upon hers. He was for the moment inarticulate.

"Rubbish!" he managed to say at last. "There is no Chelford treasure! Living so long in the same house with Harry Alford has made you as mad as he!"

She walked slowly to the desk and, with her palms on the ledge, leant down over him.

"You think that, do you?" she asked in a steady voice. "I was three years Lord Chelford's secretary, and it's true I had this treasure stuff dinned into me from morning till night. The sight of a black-lettered book makes me ill even now, and the plans of Fossaway Manor that I've studied – well, I don't like to think of them! I've lived with this treasure for three years, Arthur, and there have been times when I could have screamed when it was mentioned. I got so that I came to like Dick Alford just because he never spoke to me about it. And then one day there came a bundle of plans from London – Harry had a standing order with an old bookseller to send him anything he could find about Chelfordbury or Fossaway Manor. Harry had gone up to town that morning and I had no other work to do, so I went through these dusty old sheets to index them. And on the third sheet I found something that made me open my eyes."

"What was it?" asked Arthur carelessly.

She looked at him with a quiet smile.

"A lot has to happen before I tell you that," she said. "Arthur, if I give you this, or your share of this, will you marry me?"

Arthur looked at her steadily.

"If you can put me next to a million, or half a million," he said slowly, "I would marry you if you were the plainest woman on the face of the earth! instead of being the bonniest, prettiest little angel – "

"You can keep that stuff for later," she said practically. She opened her handbag and took out a paper, and he watched with fascinated interest. If he expected the secret of the Chelford treasure to be laid before him in writing, he was to be disappointed.

"I'm not much of a lawyer," said Mary, as she smoothed out the paper and laid it on his blotting-pad, "but I think this is binding on both sides."

He took up the paper with a wry face and read it.

In consideration of receiving one-half of the Chelford treasure, I, Arthur Gine, of Willow House, Chelfordbury, Sussex, agree to bind myself to Mary Agnes Wenner in the bonds of holy matrimony within one month of the treasure being found and divided.

"Is that in order?" she asked, watching his face.

He put the paper down.

"My dear girl – " he began, in his suavest manner.

"Listen, Arthur." She perched herself on the edge of the desk. "This is the time for 'yes's' and 'no's,' for 'I will's' and 'I won't's'! I'm not in love with you and you're not in love with me. But I want a home and a position. I may not be a lady, but I am ladylike, and I have lived long enough with swagger people to make no mistakes. Is it yes or is it no?"

Arthur looked at the paper again.

"Does it strike you," he said, "that the Chelford treasure is not yours or mine to divide? That it belongs to Lord Chelford, his heirs and his successors?"

"It is treasure trove," she said startlingly. "I know the law of the country, because I've talked this thing over with Harry times without number. Treasure found hidden after hundreds of years has to be divided between the State and the finder."

He shook his head with a smile.

"Our Mary is a lawyer!" he bantered. "You're wrong, my dear. That is only the case if the owner of the money cannot be found. In the present instance there is no doubt whatever that the treasure would belong to Chelford."

He saw her face fall and went on.

"I don't know that that is going to inconvenience us seriously," he said, looking her straight in the eyes. "You cannot lose what you never had, eh?"

She drew a deep sigh of relief.

"It is Harry's, I suppose, but after the way he has treated me, and all that I've done for him – "

"Yes, yes," he said soothingly. "We needn't worry about Harry. The only question is, have you found the treasure?"

She nodded.

"You've actually seen it?"

"No," she hesitated, "I haven't seen it. I hadn't time. But I saw the boxes through the grating. The door was locked, and I was so excited that I had to come out and walk around. And then Dick Alford saw me."

Arthur was puzzled. He knew this girl well enough; they had been good friends in the days when she was Chelford's secretary, and she had been a most useful agent of his.

"Now let's get down to brass tacks," he said brusquely. "Where did you see this treasure and when?"

"I'll tell you when. I saw it two days ago," she said, to his surprise, for he had thought she was talking about some experience she had had when she was an inmate of Fossaway Manor.

"Two days ago?" he gasped.

"Two days ago," she affirmed. "And as to where, well, there's another matter to be settled before we get as far as that, Arthur. Will you sign that agreement?"

He looked at the paper again. His training in the law, his natural instincts against putting his name under any document which bound him, urged him to temporise.

"It is yes or no," she said, as though she read his mind. "I'm not going to fool around with you unless you mean business. I'll take it to Harry, and maybe, if I put him in possession of this gold, he'll do the right thing by me."

And, seeing that he made no move, she took up the paper, folded it determinedly and put it in her little satchel.

"What's the hurry?" he said, in alarm. "Mary, you're mad to expect me to take a big decision like this without giving the matter a moment's thought. Don't you realise what you're asking me to do? You're proposing an act of sheer robbery and you're asking me to become an accomplice. After all – " He shrugged his shoulders.

"If your conscience is hurting you," she said, "we'll leave it. I'm not the sort of girl who'd throw herself at any man's head. I'll take it along to Harry and see if his conscience is busy."

She turned to go, but before she reached the door he had intercepted her.

"Don't be silly and don't be unreasonable." He was more than a little agitated. "It's a big thing you're asking – "

"It's a big thing I'm giving," she said impatiently. "Two million and a half pounds – there's nothing mean about that."

He took her by the arm and forcibly drew her back. "Sit down and don't be a fool," he said. "I've told you already I'll marry you tomorrow, and I'll go farther and say that there never was a time when money was sweeter to me than it is at the moment."

"Will you sign that note?"

He skimmed it through quickly, making sure that he was under no obligation if the treasure did not materialise, and, picking up a pen, he made a little correction, she watching suspiciously, and signed with a flourish.

"What is that you've put into the paper?" she demanded.

"An exit for Arthur Gine," he said with a whimsical smile. "The document reads, 'In consideration of receiving on behalf of my client, Lord Chelford,' etcetera, etcetera."

At first she did not understand, and then a slow smile dawned on her face.

"I see," she nodded. "That means that if anything comes out, you're acting for him and not for yourself. Arthur, there are times when I think you're clever!"

Arthur Gine smiled as he put his arm about her and led her to the window. Below, thick streams of road traffic were passing east and west. A great lorry was under his eyes; he saw an inscription on its side, "5 tons." It would require three such lorries to move the Chelford treasure, he thought, and for a moment his head reeled.

"I'll tell you how clever I am when I handle the first bar of the Chelford treasure. And you'll know how clever you are when I've dealt with the last. There's two millions in this. Now tell me, where is this gold?"

She looked at him for a second, and then, lowering her voice:

"In the vaults of Chelford Abbey," she said.

For a second neither spoke, and then: "Will you see your sister, Mr Gine? She has just arrived."

Arthur Gine spun round, an oath on his lips. Gilder had come noiselessly into the room, his inscrutable eyes fixed upon his employer. Not a muscle of his face betrayed whether or not he had overheard the last words.

9

Leslie Gine's occupations at Willow House were well defined. Though her brother did not maintain a very expensive or elaborate establishment, he lived in a style consonant with the position he held in the county. There were little dinner-parties, an occasional dance, and, in the winter, Arthur, who was a good man to hounds and was ambitious to be master of the local pack, entertained on a lavish scale the more prominent members of the Hunt. In these amenities Leslie acted as hostess for her brother, and at all times was the real housekeeper of the establishment. For all his extravagance he was a careful and grudging house-master, required that the necessities of life should be bought in the cheapest markets, that the best at the lowest price should be found upon his table.

The resolve to go to town that morning had been born of a sudden impulse. The day was her own and she could do as she liked with it. For some reason the idea of lunching alone did not appeal to her. She had a wild thought of going on to Fossaway Manor, but remembered that Wednesday was a day that Dick Alford gave up entirely to visiting his tenant farmers. She did not attempt to explain to herself why the prospect of lunching *tête-à-tête* with her fiancé was even more distasteful than lunching alone. She had got beyond the point of finding excuses for herself; she felt a certain recklessness; was conscious that her manner and attitude of mind were defiant. Against what and whom?

With a lift of her pretty shoulders she shrugged the matter out of consideration. All that she knew was that the preoccupation of Dick

Alford and the unlikelihood of seeing him made a visit to Fossaway Manor not only undesirable but out of the question.

She would go to town: the decision was taken in an instant, and she went upstairs and dressed hurriedly, whilst the gardener wheeled her little two-seater to the drive before the house. Five minutes later she was spinning along the straight road towards the railway station. She had plenty of time; indeed there was a certainty that she would arrive at the station at least half an hour before the train left, even if it was punctual.

As she entered Fontwell Cutting she thought she saw a familiar form crossing the field towards the road a quarter of a mile away, and her heart jumped for no known reason. The high walls of the cut road shut out her view, but when she emerged and slid down the steep little hill to the village road, she discovered that she had not been mistaken, and brought her car to a halt as Dick Alford opened a field gate and came out.

He greeted her with a wave of his hand and a smile, and, to her consternation, would have passed on had she not called him back.

"You are very jumpy and cross this morning," she said, and to her surprise he admitted that fault, though she had seen nothing in his manner to deserve the challenge she had made.

"I am very annoyed indeed. If there is one thing I don't want to see, it is our good farms turned into little residential estates for the City gentry! I sold Red Farm to Mr Leonard last week, under the impression that the old" – he checked a naughty word – "gentleman wanted to extend his holding, though why on earth he should want to buy Red Farm, which is the poorest land around here, I couldn't guess."

"And what has he done?"

Dick was indeed very much annoyed, she noticed now, and was secretly amused. She had a woman's satisfaction in seeing the man she liked thrown momentarily off his balance and revealing himself in a light that was new to her.

"And what has the old – gentleman done?" she mocked him.

"He has resold the farm to a wretched man in London – though the purchaser is not aware that such a sale is invalid without my signature."

"A stranger?" she asked.

"Yes; though he has been living in the neighbourhood all summer. He has a cottage somewhere about here."

"On the Ravensrill?" she asked, in surprise.

"That is the fellow," he nodded. "I've never seen him, but I understood he was only staying here for a few months. And now I find that the beggar's bought Red Farm and intends putting up something in stucco with bow windows! And I daresay he will dig an artificial pond, start a rosery, and turn God's productive acres into a forcing house for sickly flowers!"

"Why shouldn't he?" she asked coolly, and he stared at her. "After all, you said this was the poorest land round here, and if it cannot be useful it may as well be beautiful. I rather like artificial ponds and roseries."

In spite of his annoyance he laughed.

"Then probably you'll go to Mr Gilder's house-warming," he said. She started.

"Who?" she asked.

"Mr Gilder. He's something in the City – probably a deuce of a swell in his own way, but I wish he'd gone somewhere else. And as to Leonard, I've already told him that I shall not go to his funeral."

"Dick, you ought to be ashamed of yourself!" she said indignantly. "Poor old man!" Then, in a different voice: "You don't know his Christian name?"

"Whose – Leonard's?"

"Don't be stupid – Mr Gilder's."

Dick frowned.

"Fabrian," he said at last. "What a name! It sounds like a secret society!"

She wondered if Arthur knew of this enterprise of his clerk: it was hardly likely that Mr Gilder would buy property in the neighbourhood without consulting his chief. For the moment she deemed it prudent to turn the subject.

"If you were nice and kind and brotherly," she said, "you would come along with me to the station and garage my car like a nice man."

He stood irresolutely, and for a moment she went hot at the implied rebuff. And then: "I'm wasting my master's time," he said, "but there are occasions when pleasure must interfere with duty, and this is one of them. Do you mind if I drive? I have no faith in women drivers."

"You are very rude," she said, but nevertheless moved aside to let him take the wheel.

"How is Harry this morning?"

"Fine," he said sardonically. And then, heartily ashamed of himself: "Harry is trying a new patent medicine. You've never been in his bedroom? That is an indelicate question to ask, but have you?"

She shook her head, the hint of laughter in her eyes.

"There are about eight hundred and forty-five varieties of patent medicines in Harry's bedroom," he said grimly. "Once every three months we have a spring-clean and chuck 'em out! Really there isn't very much wrong with Harry, and if he did not read patent medicine advertisements he would be a happier man. Just now he's trying something for his nerves, and if there's anything left in the bottle at the end of the week I shall take it myself."

"Poor Harry!" she said softly.

"Yes, I'm a brute to grouse," he said, almost gruffly, and seemed to imply in some subtle fashion that she was a provocative party to his brutality.

It occurred to her as strange that he never spoke about the time when she would be mistress of Fossaway Manor. It would have been natural in him to say, "When you're married I hope you'll cure Harry of that nonsense," but he had made no such reference. That was the strange thing about Dick, that he never even suggested or hinted of a coming time when she would be Countess of Chelford. In one way she was glad he did not – especially now.

They wound slowly through the leafy lanes, passed a little wood, all olive, russet and purple with the decay of autumn, and came to the station ten minutes ahead of time.

"You have had no further visit from your Black Abbot?" she asked, as they strolled on to the station platform.

He shook his head.

"No; the police came last night to make inquiries. I don't suppose it will go much farther. You read about it in the newspaper, of course?"

She shook her head.

"Servants talk," she said.

"I really don't believe in this Black Abbot," he went on. "It is queer that Harry is scared of this spook. He never goes outside the house when the old Abbot is reported in the neighbourhood."

"You don't believe either?"

He pursed his lips.

"When I see a ghost I shall believe it. Until then I am politely sceptical."

As the train drew out of the station she put her head out of the window and looked back. He was standing stock-still upon the platform where she had left him; and although she could not see his face, she felt that he was gazing after her, and thought she detected a certain tenseness in his very attitude – all of which was very pleasing to Miss Leslie Gine.

10

Strange as it may seem, she had never visited her brother's office in High Holborn before she left her taxi at the door and came up in the elevator to his magnificent suite. Her appearance had a prosaic cause. She had left the country without a penny: a fact she did not realise till the ticket collector, working through the train, came into her compartment and aroused her from a daydream to the realisation that she had neither ticket nor money to pay for it. She gave the man her card, and a taxi brought her to Holborn.

She was to have another novel experience. A tall, thickset man, with iron-grey hair and a strong, attractive face, had come into the waiting-room to meet her. She remembered him as the solitary fisherman who had sat fishing for hours on the bank of Ravensrill without, apparently, catching anything. So this was the redoubtable Mr Gilder of whom Arthur had so often spoken. She was not especially curious about him. He was a head clerk, and, by Arthur's account, a clever man at his work; but now that she saw him she was impressed. He was distinctive – outside of type. The average of humanity you may pass in the street without noticing. It would be impossible to have seen Fabrian Gilder once without recognising him instantly after the passage of years. The jaw was almost square, his big mouth was so tightly drawn that he seemed to be lipless; a powerful nose, a pair of penetrating grey eyes, under straggly, uneven eyebrows; this, and the breadth of his shoulders, conveyed an imponderable impression of power.

"You are Miss Gine, of course?" he said. "I would have recognised your relationship with your brother even if I had not known your name."

It was a little shock to Leslie that she in any way resembled Arthur, for Arthur's good looks were of a variety which she neither envied nor admired.

"He is engaged at the moment. If you'll sit down I'll go along and tell him."

His eyes did not leave her face. She had often seen in stories the word "devour" applied to an intensity of gaze, and she thought that fictional characters must look somehow as Mr Gilder was looking. He was not staring; it was the concentration, the probing investigation of those bright grey eyes, that made her writhe inside. If he had been impertinent it would have been an easy matter to have dealt with him, but he was respect itself. His attitude was deferential, his general manner was friendly. He was dressed very well and carefully, she thought, and wondered whether Arthur's preciosity in the matter of clothing influenced his staff. The grey homespun, the rather solid shoes, were set off by the expensiveness of his linen. With a woman's eye she saw that in his way this man was something of a dandy too.

"I hear you are going to live near us, Mr Gilder?" she said, and he was obviously taken aback.

"Why – yes," he said awkwardly. "I've bought a little place near your house. I love that part of the country."

"We shall be neighbours," she said with a smile, but felt no pleasure in the prospect.

"Er – yes. I suppose we shall be, Miss Gine," he agreed.

"It will be very nice for Arthur. I suppose it was his suggestion that you should come down?"

He had a nervous little trick of stroking an invisible moustache, for he was clean-shaven.

"Well – no," he said. "I haven't told Mr Gine yet that I have bought the property. I thought another time would be more opportune. I bought it for a song – thirty-five hundred pounds."

She looked up quickly.

"That is an expensive song," she said, before she realised an error of taste.

This time he was visibly disconcerted.

"Yes; I borrowed the money," he said.

She had a feeling that he was going to ask her a favour, and guessed what the favour would be: Leslie had the uncanny gift of reading people's minds and gathering their surface thoughts, and in those moments when Fabrian Gilder dropped his mask he was rather easy. He opened his lips to speak, thought better of it, meeting perhaps the chill atmosphere of a refusal before it was given, and then: "I'll see if your brother is disengaged," he said, and went into the room to Arthur Gine, his head reeling with the vision which had emerged through the grey fog of his drab life.

Day after day he had watched her, and she had never known. He had left his rod and line to steal behind trees that he might see her pass. She was romance *in excelsis* – the perfect realisation of thirty years of dreaming.

It took him a second to compose himself before he turned the handle and walked in, and then he stood stricken dumb by the words that came to him.

11

"My sister?" said Arthur quickly. He looked from Gilder to Mary Wenner. "Come and see me later," he said in a lower voice. "Gilder, show Miss Wenner out through the side door."

Gilder opened the private door and followed the girl into the corridor.

"Where are you living?" he asked.

There was such a note of authority in his voice that for the moment the girl was taken off her guard.

"37, Cranston Mansions. Why?" she asked, with a certain archness that indicated resentment but invited a further offence.

"Because I want to see you," said Gilder. "May I come round to your flat some evening?"

Miss Wenner was shocked a little at this. There were moments when her sense of propriety was easily outraged. She was curious too: so far from resenting his commanding address, she rather liked it.

"Yes, any evening you wish, if you will let me know that you are coming. I will ask a young lady friend to keep me company."

Gilder's hard lips curled.

"Unless you particularly want a chaperone don't get one," he said. "I have much to say to you that I don't want anybody else to hear."

He accompanied her to the elevator, and on the way extracted a promise to receive him alone. Miss Wenner was almost as curious to know the object of that visit as Mr Gilder was to discover what was behind the amazing statement he had heard. He passed the closed door of Arthur's room and heard voices. He would have given a lot for an excuse to interrupt brother and sister, but something told him that it would be wiser if he kept out of his employer's way until he was absolutely certain that the girl had not betrayed the very carefully hidden transaction which had made him the proprietor of Red Farm.

"You're a little goose to come up to town without money," said Arthur, as he skinned three notes from his pocket-book. "Here is enough to keep you happy for the rest of your life."

"Would fifteen pounds do that?" she laughed, and was going, when she remembered.

Arthur listened in amazement to the news she had to give.

"Gilder has bought a house at Chelfordbury? Impossible!" he said. "He would have told me. Why the dickens does he want a house? – besides, he has no money."

"Hasn't he?" she asked, in surprise.

Arthur scratched his chin irritably.

"I suppose the beggar has; but a house at Chelfordbury – that is extraordinary! I wasn't even aware that he knew the place."

"He is the man who has been staying at Ravensrill Cottage all the summer," she said.

"The fisherman!" He whistled. "What a close bird he is! Of course," he went on quickly, "there is nothing wrong in a man wanting to live at Chelfordbury, and there's no reason in life why he shouldn't buy a house. But what a sly old fox!"

He was troubled; she saw that he was trying to hide it behind a flippancy which was transparent to her.

"I knew, of course, that somebody had rented the fisherman's cottage, as they call it, and to think that he's been down all these months and never once given himself away!"

"He has a car, if he's the same man who was living at the cottage," she nodded. "Dick Alford is furious!"

Arthur chuckled.

"Poor old Dick!" he said good-humouredly. "He loathes this residential idea, and when I put forward a scheme to cut up one of his northern estates into residential properties, he nearly bit my head off.

Harry would have done it like a shot, and I hope, my dear, when you're married you'll persuade him – "

He waited expectantly.

"Yes – when I am married," she said, and her tone made him glance at her keenly. But he was wise enough to skim over that subject.

"Dick, of course, is a fool," he said, with good-natured contempt. "He has a blind faith in the future of agriculture in this country, and grudges every acre that's taken out of cultivation. And yet, if you were to put up a scheme to build huge blocks of cottages to relieve the slum congestion, or something equally quixotic and unprofitable, he would jump at the idea. I can well understand that the mere thought of a successful lawyer's clerk setting himself up as a country gentleman would make Dick foam at the mouth!"

"He wasn't foaming when I left him," she said dryly.

"When you left him?" He was quick to take a point. "Yes, he came down to the station with me." And she could not account for her momentary feeling of embarrassment.

He was still searching her face, and then, laying his hands on her shoulders, he shook her gently.

"Old girl," he said, "keep your mind off the second son! He's a good-looking fellow, and side by side with his brother there's no question of choice! But he's a second son, which means that he's next door to being broke. And you can't live on good looks or – "

She raised her eyes slowly to his.

"What do you mean – I can't live on good looks?" she said deliberately. "Why do you emphasise the fact that Dick Alford is poor? Aren't I an heiress?"

He did not speak, and then, with a little laugh, dropped his hands.

"Why, of course, chick!" he said lightly. "Only – well, I want you to do something for yourself. Make a name in the country. It will be something to have the position which Harry can offer you. Dick is quite a good fellow – one of the best, although he doesn't get on very well with me. But there's nothing to it with him, Leslie. You might as well marry some poverty-stricken gentleman farmer – "

He stopped under the steady gaze that met him.

" 'Poverty-stricken' again, Arthur. Without suggesting that I would rather marry Dick Alford, I wonder why the question of his poverty interests you so much. If you had called him a commoner and a nobody, I could have understood, but you insist upon the question of my possible fiancé's wealth, and that seems strange to me."

He laughed long and loudly, but his merriment seemed, to her sensitive ear, lacking in sincerity.

"You ought to be a lawyer, Leslie! Upon my word, I've a good mind to have you coached for an examination! You'd look simply topping in a wig and gown! And now, my little girl, you must run away, because I've a tremendous lot of work to do."

He put his arm round her shoulders and walked with her to the door, and breathed a sigh of relief when he heard the whine of the elevator carrying her down. Closing the door behind him, he rang the bell, and, to the clerk who came:

"Ask Mr Gilder to come in, will you, please?"

12

When Gilder had this message he knew that the girl had told her brother; and although he had his fair share of moral courage, it needed a conscious effort on his part to answer the summons.

"Gilder, what is this story of you buying Red Farm?" asked Arthur sharply.

"Why should I not buy Red Farm?" replied Gilder coolly.

"There is no reason in the world why you shouldn't," said Arthur, after a moment's thought; "but it is rather curious you never told me."

"I thought you might object," said Gilder. "Business men hate their workaday associates living anywhere near them. It was stupid of me not to tell you. I've been living in a cottage at Chelfordbury for three months − was that in itself objectionable? You will forgive me for saying so, but although I have always regarded you with the respect that is due to an employer, I have never quite looked upon you as my feudal lord!"

Arthur grinned for a second.

"Once or twice I thought of coming over to see you," Gilder went on, "but I've always had what I think to be a natural reluctance to intrude myself in a social capacity upon my chief. If you had ever invited me to come and stay a weekend at your place I would have come, and you would have known all about my presence in the neighbourhood. As it was, I felt very much in the position of a servant enjoying himself in his own independent way and feeling no need to consult his employer as to how he should employ his spare time − and money."

"And money," repeated Arthur. "I didn't know you were so well off, Gilder?"

Mr Gilder inclined his head.

"I have already hinted to you that I have made considerable sums. There, again, it has never seemed necessary that I should keep you acquainted with my bank balance."

"You have had a moderate salary," said Arthur significantly. "Not a generous amount, I agree; certainly not an amount from which a man could save a sum sufficient to buy and rebuild Red Farm and maintain it."

For answer Gilder put his hand in his pocket and, taking out a little Russia-leather note-case, laid it on the table. The name in gold letters upon the cover was that of a bookmaker who carried one of his employer's biggest accounts. With this firm Arthur had lost his largest bets, for Trumans had offered him facilities which other houses had denied to him.

"Truman?" He frowned. "What has that to do with it? Have you been backing horses?"

Gilder shook his head.

"No," he said simply. "I am Truman."

Arthur Gine gaped at him. Truman! The bookmaker to whom for weeks in succession he had been paying thousands upon thousands of pounds!

"Then the money you have – is my money!" he gasped.

"Your money?" said the other quietly. "If Trumans had not taken it, some other bookmaker would have done so. When you won you were paid – have you any complaints?"

"My money!" muttered Arthur.

Gilder replaced the book in his pocket.

"You remember five years ago complaining to me that you couldn't find bookmakers who would take big bets by telegram within a few minutes of the race? That little talk gave me an idea. I knew you lost steadily, that you were one of those – unfortunate people – "

"Say 'fools' – that was the word on your lips."

" 'Mug' was the word," said Mr Gilder, with great calmness. "I knew you were one of those people who couldn't stop betting. So Trumans came into existence. Their book of rules was sent to you, featuring the important concession that you could wire big sums of money up to within a few minutes of a race. Do you know how much you've lost in the last five years?"

Arthur was pale with fury, but, mastering himself, shook his head.

"You have lost sixty-three thousand pounds to Truman alone," said the other slowly. "And I have won it!"

The colour came and went in Arthur Gine's face. He knew all the time that his rage and resentment were unreasonable. Hitherto Truman had been a name on a telegraph form, an address somewhere in the West End to which his unprofitable telegrams were sent. Who they were he neither knew nor cared; they might have been people infinitely more objectionable than Gilder.

But there was a suggestion of duplicity in the man's confession. Arthur Gine felt that be bad been tricked by a servant he trusted, and he was helpless in face of sixty-three thousand facts, all of which balanced on the side of the hard-faced man before him.

"You are not Rathburn & Co., I suppose?" he asked, mentioning another bookmaking firm that had drawn heavily upon his resources.

To his amazement, Gilder nodded.

"I am Rathburn & Company. I am also Burton & Smith. I am, in fact, the three bookmakers to whom you have been losing money at the rate of thirty thousand a year for the past five years. There is no sense in looking like that, Gine. I have been guilty of no crime. On the few occasions when you have won money, you have been paid. Your losses would not have been so distasteful if they had been made to an unknown man. I took the risk – my luck against yours. When I started, I staked my little fortune – three thousand pounds, won through the years by scrimping and saving. If you had been lucky, I should have been ruined."

"Instead of which you were lucky – and I am ruined," said Arthur Gine huskily. He was shaken from his accustomed calm. "You are quite right, though it is a little – bewildering."

He looked curiously at the inscrutable face of his managing clerk, striving to readjust his estimate of a man whom he had looked upon as little more than a superior servant. Then the humour of the position struck him and he laughed.

"If I'm not careful I shall be sorry for myself, and I should hate that, Gilder! So you're a rich man, eh? What are you going to do with your money?"

Gilder's eyes did not leave his face.

"I am going to settle down in the country," he said, "and I am going to marry."

"Splendid!" There was a note of irony in Arthur Gine's tone. "And who is the fortunate lady?"

It was a long time before the other replied. He stared open-eyed at his sometime master, and then, very deliberately and slowly: "It is my desire and intention to marry Miss Leslie Gine," he said.

Not a muscle of Arthur Gine's face moved; his colour did not change. But into his eyes came a glare which was malign and devilish. For a second the imperturbable Gilder was scared. Had he gone too far? Both men were learning something that day. Gilder had a momentary view of something that was very ugly and menacing, and then the curtains were drawn and the inner self of Arthur Gine vanished in an enigmatic smile.

"That is very interesting and very – enterprising of you, Gilder! Unfortunately, I have other plans."

He rose leisurely from his chair, walked round the desk and confronted the other, his hands thrust into his pockets.

"What are you prepared to pay for the privilege of being my brother-in-law?" he bantered.

Fabrian Gilder took up the challenge.

"The return of half your betting losses for the past five years," he said.

Arthur shook his head.

"Not enough," he smiled.

"The cancellation of four bills," said Gilder deliberately, "drawn and accepted by Lord Chelford, the acceptance in each case being forged by you."

Arthur Gine staggered back to his desk, his face white and drawn, and Gilder pursued the advantage.

"You didn't think it was an accident that I suggested you should get Chelford to back a bill for you, did you? Seventy-five thousand pounds isn't enough for you, eh? I'll give you this alternative: five years in Dartmoor!"

13

Leslie had spent rather a boring afternoon, and not once but many times she regretted that she had promised to return to Arthur's office. He was driving her down to Willow House, and but for this arrangement she would have returned to Chelfordbury by an early train, for her shopping did not occupy more than an hour.

She rang up her brother to suggest this plan, never doubting that he would agree, but, to her surprise: "I think you'd better return with me, girl. Come along to the office about half past four instead of five. By the way, Gilder wants us to go home to his flat to tea. You don't mind, do you?"

"Mr Gilder?" she said, in surprise, and he went on hastily:

"We ought to be civil to him. He's going to be a neighbour of ours, and he — he's not a bad sort of fellow."

Her inclination was to plead a headache and be excused an experience which, to state the matter mildly, was not wholly to her taste. But Arthur seldom asked a favour of her, and it was apparent from his tone that he was anxious she should show this act of civility to his head clerk; somewhat unwillingly she agreed.

If he detected her reluctance he made no comment upon it and seemed in a hurry to ring off. There was no reason in the world why the projected call should make her uneasy, and yet, for some obscure reason, this coming experience hung like a cloud over her for the rest of the afternoon. This time, when she returned to the office, she entered by Arthur's private door. He was alone, sitting at his desk in a familiar attitude, his head between his hands, his gloomy eyes fixed upon the blotting-pad. She thought his face had less colour than usual; and in his eyes there was a haggard, hunted expression which was startling. He forced a smile to greet her, but she was not deceived.

"Aren't you well, Arthur?" she asked anxiously.

"Fit as a fiddle," he laughed; "only I have had a pretty heavy day. I suppose I look a little washed out."

He did not seem very anxious to discuss himself, but plunged straight into the subject of the surprising call they were to make.

"Gilder has a flat off Regent's Park," he said. "Be as nice to him as you can, Leslie. He's been a pretty useful man. By the way," he said awkwardly, "he is a bachelor."

She smiled at this; in her wildest dreams she would not have imagined that this statement had any particular interest for herself.

"I had no idea he was such a – that he was so prosperous," she said. "No, I don't mean that bachelorhood is a sign of poverty, but his estate at Chelfordbury, and his flat in Regent's Park, are not exactly what one would have expected."

"He isn't a bad fellow," repeated Arthur, as he rang the bell. "I think you'll like him: he is rather – amusing."

"Amusing" was not the word he would have used in all truth, but it was the only word he could think of at the moment. As though he were waiting for this summons, Mr Gilder came in answer to the bell. He carried a light coat over his arm and a spotless grey felt hat in his hand. Again Leslie was uncomfortably conscious of the man's scrutiny.

"You know Mr Gilder, Leslie?"

His uneasiness and apprehension were communicating themselves to her. Try as she did, she could not succeed in shaking off her sensation of disquietude. The atmosphere was electric; she would have been dull indeed if she had not responded to the strain.

Throughout the journey Mr Gilder talked almost without interruption. He had a deep but pleasant voice, and was an easy conversationalist. Arthur was beginning to know something about the man with whom he had worked side by side all these years, and to regard him in a new light. Hitherto Gilder had been a cipher – a familiar figure that had appeared from heaven knew where in the morning and had disappeared at the end of a day's work into the blue. As though unconscious of his employer's wonder and speculation, Gilder chatted on.

Afterwards, Leslie catalogued the subjects which were discussed so one-sidedly during that drive. He talked of aviation, of wireless, of books he had read – Dumas was his favourite – of the war, of Russia, of Italy's renaissance, of American writers, of the weather, polo – of almost every subject that occupied public attention. She knew that he was trying to impress her, and saw in this no more than the natural desire of a man to look well in the eyes of a woman.

The flat was bigger than she had expected, and was one of many in the most exclusive apartment house on the Outer Circle. Arthur viewed its expensive appointments with a glum face. One black week of his at Ascot must have furnished three such flats as this, he thought, and the little devil of resentment and loathing grew stronger in his heart.

Tea was served by two trimly uniformed maids, and Mr Gilder acted the part of host to perfection. He had a library of rare old books which she must see, and he took them to a room the walls of which were fitted with bookshelves and reminded Leslie, though there was no resemblance between the two apartments, of the hall wherein her fiancé spent most of his time.

Gilder was showing the girl a rare first edition when a surprising thing happened.

"Do you mind if I run out for five minutes, Leslie? I want to see a fellow who lives on the other side of the Park."

Arthur Gine's voice was husky, his assumption of ease a miserable failure. The girl looked at him in astonishment, and then examined the face of the little watch on her wrist.

"If you want to be back at Willow House in time for dinner – " she began.

"I shan't be gone more than a quarter of an hour," he said desperately. "If you don't mind – "

Before she could utter a word he had vanished. It was all so unexpected, so strange, that she could not quite realise what had happened, and the last thought in the world she could have had, was that Arthur was deliberately leaving her alone with this grey man.

On one point her mind was made up: she did not like Mr Gilder, and was fairly certain that her antipathy was shared by her brother. His strange manner in the presence of the man, his awkwardness, and, most convincing proof of all, his silence, puzzled her. Arthur was intensely selfish, would not go a step out of his way either for courtesy's sake or to save the feelings of those whom he regarded as his dependents. And this sudden desire to oblige his head clerk was contradictory to her knowledge of him. Yet she felt neither alarm nor annoyance, finding herself in that little library alone with this square-jawed clerk.

As the door closed upon her brother, Fabrian Gilder carefully replaced on the shelf the book he had been examining.

"I shall be in my new home by the spring," he said, "and I hope I shall see more of you, Miss Gine."

She made a conventionally polite reply.

"My ambition has always been to settle in the country and to follow my two hobbies, which are fishing and reading," he went on. "Happily, I am in the position of being able to retire from my profession – your brother has probably told you that I am a fairly wealthy man."

Something in his tone focussed her attention. Her heart beat a little faster, and for the first time she was conscious of being alone with him.

"I am not an old man – fifty I regard as the prime of life – and I think I have the capacity for making any woman happy."

She met his eyes steadily.

"I hope we shall have the pleasure of meeting your wife," she said.

He made no reply to this, and she grew hot and cold under the scrutiny of those merciless grey eyes. And then, before she realised what was happening, his two big hands had closed about her arms and he was holding her away from him, peering into her face.

"There is one woman in the world for me," he said, and his voice was husky with emotion; "one face that fills my eyes day and night! Leslie, all these months you have not been out of my sight or mind!"

"Let me go!" she cried, struggling to free herself.

"I want you! I've worked for you, I've schemed for you! Leslie, I love you as you will never be loved again! I want you – I want you!"

He was drawing her nearer and nearer, his eyes like coals of fire; fascinating her to a queer listlessness that was almost quiescence. She found no reserve to combat him, and could only stare helplessly at the hard face.

There was a knock at the door. He pushed her aside, his face convulsed with rage.

"Who is that?" he asked harshly, and the voice of the maid replied:

"Mr Richard Alford to see you, sir!"

14

Dick Alford, waiting in the pretty drawing-room and wondering exactly how he should introduce what promised to be a very unpleasant discussion, saw the door flung open and a white-faced girl run in.

"Oh, Dick, Dick!" she sobbed.

In a moment she was in his arms, her face against his breast.

"For God's sake, what has happened? How did you come here?" he asked, bewildered.

Before she could reply, the big figure of Fabrian Gilder filled the doorway. The man did not speak, but the smouldering rage in his eyes was eloquent.

"Well, what do you want?" he boomed.

Dick put the girl gently from him.

"Why are you here, Leslie?"

"Arthur brought me," she gasped. "I'm awfully sorry to make such a fool of myself, but – "

Dick looked from the girl to the man in the doorway and began dimly to understand.

"Arthur brought you here?" he said slowly. "And left you alone – with this man?"

She nodded.

"Is he a friend of yours?"

She shook her head.

"I only met him today."

Gradually the explanation of her distress was beginning to dawn upon him, and a cold rage filled his heart. An unfortunate moment for Arthur Gine to return. Dick heard the tinkle of a bell, quick footsteps in the hall, and saw the white face of the lawyer, made hideous by the smile he forced.

"Hullo, old girl! What's the trouble?" he asked.

He did not look at his host, Dick noticed with gathering fury.

"I think you had better take Leslie home," he said. "I have a little business to do with Mr Gilder."

Gilder had recovered something of his command of himself and his feelings; the situation, awkward as it was, had brought him violently into the circle about which so far he had revolved. It were better to be considered as an undesirable suitor than to be denied consideration as a factor at all in Leslie Gine's life.

"May I ask by what right you dispose of my guests?" he demanded, but Dick took no notice of him.

"Look after your sister, Gine," he said, and there was a scarcely veiled menace in the words. "I will give myself the pleasure of calling on you this evening."

He took the girl's hand in his; she was still white and shaking, but smiled into his face.

"I've made myself rather ridiculous, haven't I?" she said, in a low tone that only he could hear. "Dicky – perhaps I'm getting a little jumpy, and I may have taken offence – "

He patted her hand gently and walked with her past Gilder into the hall, Arthur following. It was Dick who opened the door, and stood patiently until they had gone, then he turned to face the enraged owner of the flat.

"I had some real business to do with you, Gilder, but that can wait. First of all, I would like to ask, what have you said to Miss Gine?"

"That is entirely my business," said Gilder. His gaze was steady; again he was completely master of himself, if not of the situation.

"My business also," said Dick, without heat. "You are aware that Miss Gine is engaged to my brother?"

Gilder licked his dry lips.

"That doesn't really interest me," he said. And then, after a second's thought: "I'm going to be frank with you, Alford – we may as well clear the air. I have asked Miss Gine to be my wife."

"Oh, indeed?" said Dick softly. "And what had Miss Gine to say to that?"

"You didn't give her an opportunity of replying," said the other, "but I rather think that there will be no difficulty in the matter."

Dick did not conceal his smile. A shrewd judge of men, he had rightly understood the situation when he had seen Arthur's face on his return to the flat.

"You mean there will be no difficulty so far as Mr Gine is concerned? I admit you have an historical precedent. You are not the first lawyer who wished to marry into his master's family."

If Dick had not been angry he would not have said this; immediately the words were out he was sorry. But Gilder took up the point quickly.

"I am not an Uriah Heep," he said, with a grim smile. "I am neither humble nor lowly."

"I'm sorry, but really I don't think that matters very much, Gilder. Whatever Mr Gine's attitude may be, there will be a considerable difficulty in respect to Miss Gine – and to me."

"To you?" Gilder's eyebrows went up and his lips curled. "Are you the lady's – er – "

"I am not engaged to Miss Gine, but my brother is," said Dick evenly. "But that is not the point. I am a friend of Leslie Gine's, and even if she changed her mind about marrying into my family, that would not affect the issue."

Gilder was about to speak, but Dick went on: "I don't know what pull you have with Gine, or what dire threats you are holding over his head."

He saw the man start, and laughed.

"That went very near the mark?" he said. "But whatever influence you have, Gilder, you are not going to marry Leslie Gine."

Gilder's eyes narrowed.

"Is that a threat?" he asked.

"You can take it as a threat or as a pleasant compliment, or any old way you choose," said Dick, with that impish smile of his. "And now, if you don't mind, we'll come to business. You've bought a property of ours – Red Farm. You've paid thirty-five hundred pounds to Leonard. I have come to ask you to call off your bargain and to take five hundred profit."

"In other words, you want to buy it back, eh? Well, there's nothing doing!" said Gilder harshly. "I intend living at Red Farm, and there isn't a law in the land that can stop me. You may not like my presence, but that is neither here nor there. I am not living at Chelfordbury for the pleasure of seeing you every day of my life."

Dick nodded.

"I wondered why you wanted to live there at all, but now I think I understand," he said. "The offer I have made to you is without prejudice to any action I may take. Unfortunately for you, Leonard has no power to retransfer the property without my brother's consent – which means my consent, for I hold his power of attorney. Leonard may hold the property, but you cannot. You're a lawyer and it is not necessary for me to explain the intricacies of a copyhold lease, and that was all Leonard was buying. If you decide to fight the case, I'll take you into court, and you know that I shall get a verdict against you. I am offering you a chance of settling the matter amicably."

"Which I refuse," said the other promptly.

Dick inclined his head.

"Very good. You will probably, on considering the matter in a calmer atmosphere, take a different view."

He walked from the room, swinging his hat. In the doorway he turned.

"As for Miss Leslie Gine, you will be well advised to reconsider that question also."

"And suppose I don't?"

Again that unfathomable smile.

"You are going to be sorry," said Dick cryptically.

15

Not a word did Leslie say about her interview with Gilder, and her brother seemed just as anxious to avoid the topic as she. They drove down from town, and all the time he kept up a ceaseless flow of talk about affairs which he thought might interest her. He was nervous, and once, when she woke him from a reverie with a question, he started and turned red.

"Sorry!" he stammered. "I was thinking of something."

"And something unpleasant, Arthur," she said gently.

He was staring straight ahead of him.

"Yes, something damnably unpleasant!"

They were nearing Chelfordbury now, and she put the question that had trembled on her lips throughout that long journey.

"Arthur, do you know what Mr Gilder asked me?" And, when he did not reply: "He proposed to me," she said.

Still he avoided her eyes.

"Did he?" he asked awkwardly. "Well, that's an extraordinary thing for him to do!"

"Arthur, did you know he was going to propose to me when you left us alone?"

"He isn't a bad fellow," said Arthur Gine lamely. "Of course the idea is preposterous. But, after all, it is no sin for a fellow to fall in love with a girl and want to marry her – I mean, one can see his point of view."

Leslie was a little shocked; she was more than a little angry. But she kept a tight rein on her tongue.

"But, Arthur, you wouldn't agree to that? You know I am engaged to Harry. Why, you told me that it was the dream of your life to see me wearing a coronet! Not that I want to wear the beastly thing, but that was what you said."

Ordinarily, Arthur Gine was possessed of a ready tongue and a nimble wit. He had lied his way out of many an embarrassing situation with more worldly-wise people than Leslie. But, somehow, in her presence his brain refused to function, and his witticisms were banal and vulgar even to himself.

"My dear little girl," he said, with an attempt at cheerfulness, "it really doesn't matter to me whom you marry so long as you're happy. Gilder is a very solid man; he has a considerable private fortune."

This time she swung round on her seat and faced him.

"Arthur, why do you insist upon the fortune? Where is my money?"

The question came point-blank and was not to be fenced with. He roused himself to meet a situation which had never before arisen.

"Your money? Why, invested, of course!"

He tried very hard, but he could not produce that convincing note which was so necessary.

"Your fortune is in all sorts of shares and bonds. What a queer question to ask me, girlie!"

"How much money have I?" she demanded ruthlessly.

"About a quarter of a million – a little more or a little less. For goodness' sake don't talk about money, my dear."

"But I *will* talk about it," she said. "Arthur, have I any at all?"

His laughter did not carry conviction. And usually people accepted his word. Harry Chelford had asked him only a week before in what stocks his late mother's fortune was invested. And Arthur had replied glibly enough. It was the Miriam Chelford Trust that had occupied his mind through the journey. Something must be done there. Dick Alford had started to ask questions, and Dick had a memory like a recording machine. As for Leslie and her tiresome questions: "What a silly kid you are! Of course you've got money! I wish to heaven I had half your wad! You're a very rich little girl, and you ought to be a very happy little girl."

She shook her head.

"I don't think I have a penny," she said, and his heart sank.

With a tremendous effort of will he met her questioning eyes.

"Why do you say that?"

She shook her head.

"I don't know – in a way I hope I'm poor. I know I had money left me, because you showed me the will a long time ago. But you've been handling it, Arthur, and I've an idea that things haven't been going too well with you."

"Do you mean I've stolen your fortune?" he asked loudly, and she smiled.

"I wouldn't accuse you of that. I think it is possible you may have invested my fortune – unwisely! And it is quite possible that that quarter of a million has dwindled and dwindled until it has disappeared. Is that so?"

He did not answer.

"Is that so?"

"I wish to God you wouldn't ask such stupid questions," he said irritably. "Of course it isn't so!"

For one wild moment he had the impulse to tell her the truth; but vanity, a shrinking from the possible effect the news would have upon the one person in the world for whom he had a grain of affection, inhibited the confession.

Back he came naturally to the one thought present in his mind as he chattered and as he brooded. His last hope lay in the discovery of the Chelford treasure. If that were found, he could snap his fingers at Gilder, could restore the wasted fortune of his sister, and establish himself beyond assail. Gilder would never dare bring his story of the four bills to a court of law, and if he did, backed by the Chelford fortune Arthur could face the storm, confident that, if he made restitution to the man he had robbed, no evil consequences would follow. He was grasping at a straw, and knew it. But Mary Wenner was a shrewd little devil, not the kind of girl who, for the sake of making a sensation, would come to him with a cock-and-bull story. She might have been mistaken; on the other hand, she was so brimful of confidence that he could not believe the story was altogether without foundation.

The road to Willow House skirted the grounds of Fossaway Manor, and he saw the crumbling arch, red in the setting sun, standing like a fiery question mark that attuned with his mood of doubt and hope.

Arrived at his home, he went up to his room to bath and change before dinner, and it was with a positive sense of freedom that he found himself alone. He was a fool not to have told her the truth, he thought. After dinner he would get her in a softer mood, and make a clean breast of it. And then, at the tail of this decision, came the recollection of his interview with Mary Wenner. Suppose she had told the truth? Suppose he found these millions of pounds that had lain for centuries in the ground? He formed yet another plan.

16

To his unspeakable relief, Leslie was in her most cheerful mood throughout dinner, and the thought of Fabrian Gilder seemed to have been effectively banished.

"Leslie," he asked, after the coffee had been served, "I want you to do me a great favour."

She looked at him across the table, doubt in her eyes.

"Do you remember Mary Wenner, who used to be Harry's secretary?"

She nodded.

"Yes. Dick doesn't like her very much; he was telling me the other day – "

"Never mind what Dick likes or dislikes," he said testily. "Great heavens! are our lives to be run according to his fancies? I'm very sorry," he apologised with a laugh, "but you'll have to forgive me – I'm rather nervy tonight."

"What about Mary Wenner?" she asked.

"I was wondering whether you would like to ask her down here to stay a weekend? I shall have a lot of work to do, and she's a very excellent stenographer. But I'll be perfectly frank with you, and tell you that that is not the only reason I'd like you to invite her. She's been in some kind of scrape and I want to help her through."

Leslie Gine was not curious, or she might have questioned him more about this mythical trouble.

"I don't know why she shouldn't come," she said. "If you'll give me her address I will write to her. I rather fancy that Dick's main objection to her is that she had some sort of attachment for Harry."

"She's almost forgotten Harry," smiled her brother. "To be perfectly candid, I like the girl. She's not a lady, of course, but 'lady' nowadays is a vague and meaningless term. And there was really nothing in her affair with Harry. I mean it was not serious."

"I've never thought so," said the girl, and thereupon the question of Mary Wenner was dismissed.

He had, he said, some work to do that night, and left her alone in the drawing-room, and for once she did not find time hanging very heavily upon her hands. Ordinarily the prospect of an evening spent alone would have seemed intolerably dull, but she had so much to think about, so many perspectives to adjust, that she rather welcomed her solitude.

Even at so short a distance of time, her experience with Fabrian Gilder seemed grotesquely unreal. Perhaps she was still numb from the shock of it, for, going over that unpleasant feature incident by incident, she could be neither angry nor amused. Perhaps she was a little afraid – she still felt the pressure of his strong hands upon her, still saw the grey fires that burnt in his eyes. And Dick! how natural it had been to go to him – how safe she had felt! Would it have been the same if Harry Chelford had providentially arrived? She was sure in her mind that she would not have run to Harry, or found comfort in his encircling arms.

She looked at the clock; it was ten minutes past nine. Dick would be back at Fossaway Manor by now, and she went out into the hall and, taking off the receiver of the telephone, gave a number.

Arthur's study door opened into the hall, and he came out.

"To whom are you telephoning?" he asked suspiciously.

"I'm calling up Fossaway Manor," she said.

"You're not going to invite Dick Alford over, are you?" he demanded resentfully.

Before she could reply, he heard the ring of a bell in the servants' quarters and she ran to the door. Through the glass panel she saw the gleam of a white shirt-front on the unlighted porch, and switched on the lights. It was Dick, and, with an oath, Arthur Gine flung back into his room and slammed the door. He had hoped that Dick had forgotten his threat to call that night.

"Enter Richard of Chelford!" said the girl dramatically, as she threw open the door. "I was just phoning to you. I'm bored to extinction and I want amusing."

Which was not true.

"I don't feel at all amusing," said Dick, as he closed the door and hung up his cap on the hat-rack.

She took him by the arm and led him into the drawing-room.

"Arthur is invisible tonight; he is working very hard. He doesn't approve of you, and you hardly approve of him, so we shan't be interrupted. Dick, it was lovely of you to arrive as you did this afternoon."

"Gilder proposed to you, I understand?" said Dick quietly.

"Did he tell you?" She fetched a long sigh. "Yes; I was amazed. I suppose it was very complimentary, but why did he do it in such a great hurry, do you think?"

Dick took a cigarette from the box she offered him and lit it before he replied.

"That is exactly what I've come to discover," he said. "I feel rather like a grand inquisitor, but I must know."

"And I can't tell you."

She was acting. He knew that her one object was to turn him from an interview with her brother, and she in turn knew that her efforts would be in vain.

"You had no hint of this precious proposal in advance? Arthur told you nothing?"

"No; Arthur couldn't possibly have known. He told me that Mr Gilder wanted us to see his new flat, and although it was a great bore going out to tea with somebody one doesn't know, I went – "

"To oblige Arthur, of course?"

"No," she insisted; "you must credit me with a reasonable amount of feminine curiosity. Bachelors' establishments intrigue me. Your one drawback, from my point of view, is that you've only a poky little office and, I presume, a wretched little servant's bedroom."

"For a second son I'm rather well off," said Dick with a quizzical smile. "You are sure Arthur didn't give you any forewarning of this proposal?"

"Absolutely sure. He was as much astonished as I was."

"Have you discussed it with him?" he asked quickly.

She hesitated.

"Yes, I spoke about it in the car on the way down, and Arthur was rather – astonished."

"Only astonished – not furious?"

"He may have been furious too. Arthur doesn't carry his heart on his sleeve."

"I should imagine not," said Dick dryly, and then: "Will you ask him if I can see him for five minutes?"

She looked at him with troubled eyes.

"You're not going to quarrel, are you, Dick?"

He shook his head.

"No, I'm going to ask him a question or two. You realise that I'm entitled to know."

"Why are you 'entitled'?"

"Don't you think I am?" he asked gently.

Her eyes went up to his for a second, and then dropped, as she read something there that thrilled and hurt her. Without a word she went out into the hall and knocked at Arthur's door.

"What does he want? I can't be bothered tonight," said Arthur Gine fretfully. "What a fellow he is for interrupting people when they're busy!"

"I think you'd better see him, Arthur," she said, and added: "And get it over."

He shot a quick glance at her.

"What do you mean – get what over?" he asked.

"Whatever there is to get over," said Leslie quietly.

Arthur looked down at the picturesque confusion of papers that covered his library table.

"All right, shoot him in," he said ungraciously.

17

He did not attempt to rise from his chair when Dick entered, closing the door behind him.

"Sit down, will you, Alford? Leslie tells me you want to see me."

"Leslie need not have given you that message. I'd already told you this afternoon that I would come to you for an explanation."

"Of what?"

"Of the unpleasant happening at Gilder's flat. This man proposed to your sister – you know that?"

"Leslie told me," said the other, after a moment's silence.

"And you were annoyed, one supposes? You will dismiss this clerk of yours tomorrow?"

The other leaned back in his chair.

"I don't see why I should," he said coolly. "After all, it's no crime for any man to propose to a pretty girl. Of course he's not the sort of fellow I should choose for a brother-in-law, but if brothers had to choose husbands for their sisters, you know, Alford, there would be some very queer marriages!"

"What is his pull?" asked Dick quietly.

"I don't – "

"What is his hold on you?"

"What the devil do you mean?"

"Just what I say. You would never tolerate a man like Gilder paying attentions to your sister, apart from the insult he offered to a prospective Countess of Chelford, unless he had such a grip on you that all your natural indignation was crushed by the fear of some consequence he held over your head."

Arthur Gine found it difficult to control his voice.

"My dear fellow, how very melodramatic!" he scoffed. "'Hold over me!' You must have been studying the latest Drury Lane play! Naturally I would rather see Leslie married to your brother, but I certainly would put no obstacle in her way if her heart was set elsewhere."

"On Gilder, in fact?"

"On Gilder," nodded Arthur gravely, as though the matter had been the subject of deep thought and much self-communion.

And then Dick Alford asked a question that brought the man to his feet, white and shaking.

"Is it the question of the bills?"

"The – the what?" faltered the lawyer.

"The four bills which were supposed to be backed by my brother – the signatures being forgeries. I thought you knew that I had seen them. They were shown to me at the bank, and fortunately I did not disclaim them – fortunately for you, I mean. When I went to see them again they were taken up. I presume Mr Fabrian Gilder redeemed them. That would have cost him a little overm five thousand pounds, and I presume he did not do that out of sheer altruism."

Arthur Gine's mouth was dry; he could scarcely articulate.

"I didn't know until today," he muttered. "Harry was ill at the time. The money was due to me for – for – legal costs. I went down to the bank to take them up and found they had been honoured."

"Was that the pull?"

He did not meet the steady gaze that was fixed on him.

"Yes, that was the pull, if you want to know. You don't suppose I'd allow Leslie to marry a swine like Gilder unless – unless he had something on me, do you? Can't you understand my position, Alford? I'm ruined! That fellow could send me to gaol – he still can."

Dick shook his head.

"Fire him tomorrow," he said. "If he produces the bills I will undertake that Harry will acknowledge the signatures."

The pink came back to the colourless face of the lawyer. "You'll do this?" he said eagerly. "My God! you don't know what a weight you've lifted off my mind. You're a brick, by Jove! I'll fire him tomorrow."

He held out an eager hand, and Dick took it with some hesitation. At the best of times Arthur Gine did not impress him; at this moment, almost incoherent with relief, he seemed a pitiful coward.

"I will pay Harry every penny. I have something on the stocks now that will bring me in a fortune, that will wipe out all my debts and put me on my feet again."

There was humour in the situation; for the thing which was to rehabilitate his fortunes was no less than the barefaced robbery of Harry Chelford's inheritance! But Arthur was not conscious of the irony of the position. He would deal with Gilder in the morning. Thank God he had not gone still deeper into the mire! The knowledge that in his pocket-book was another bill as yet unuttered did not cool the glow of virtue he was experiencing. Henceforth he would walk the straight way.

"There's one thing you could do for me, Alford – hurry along that marriage. Fix it for next month if you can. Leslie is just a foolish girl, she is trying to put off the inevitable, but that's natural, isn't it? Can't you buck up Harry – "

Dick Alford looked at him steadily.

"The matter must be left entirely to Leslie," he said, and there was something very definite and final in those words.

They came out of the library together; Leslie, waiting, a little fearful, saw the smile on her brother's face and breathed a sigh of thankfulness.

"You're not going?" Dick was reaching for his cap.

"I have to get back to the house," he said, and, seeing her look of disappointment, he stood irresolutely.

"Come along in and play mah-jong. I am in a mah-jong mood," said Arthur, almost jovially.

If there was one thing that Dick could not endure that night it was to sit *vis-à-vis* with Arthur Gine. He would like to have stayed with the girl, but for the moment her brother seemed an inevitable third.

And he was terribly informative. Arthur was in his most expansive mood.

"Here is something that will interest you!"

He pointed to the wall. Hanging against a dark wooden shield was an iron dagger – black and sinister, the handle worn smooth, the long blade notched and jagged. Dick had seen it before.

"That should be at your place, Alford. The veritable dagger of the veritable Black Abbot's slayer – Hubert of Redruth! Look at his arms on the hilt."

"I have seen it," said Dick shortly. "Put on your coat and come for a walk, Leslie," he suggested, and the obliging Arthur, who would have been agreeable to any scheme he propounded, seconded the suggestion.

18

The night was cool and dark. There was a full moon, visible at intervals through the drift of the clouds. Leslie slipped her arm through his as they walked down the dark avenue towards the road.

"Did you quarrel?" she asked.

"N-no, we didn't quarrel," said Dick. "There was a little plain speaking, but I think it cleared the air, and, after all, that was what I came for. He is dismissing Gilder tomorrow."

She was silent at this, and did not speak again until they were on the road.

"Is that wise?" she asked. "I'm a little afraid of the man. I feel he would be a very bad enemy."

She heard his soft laugh and felt reassured.

"He's that all right," said Dick; "the worst enemy any man could have, I should imagine. But an enemy is only dangerous in ratio to his hurting power. I don't think Mr Gilder will hurt anybody."

"Not Arthur?" she asked. "Not Arthur, and certainly not you."

She squeezed his arm in hers. "You'd be a wonderful brother," she said.

"I am," he said curtly, and she smiled in the darkness.

"Your handsome relative asked me to persuade you to marry next month, and I told him point-blank that I would do nothing of the kind. Leslie, do you know that you never see Harry from one weekend to another?"

She had realised that for a long time, and it was a constant subject for self-reproach that she had less and less desire for her fiancé's society.

"He is really not interested in me, Dick," she said. "Harry is so absorbed in his treasure hunt and his queer chase after the elixir of life – "

"He's told you that, has he?" asked Dick quickly. "Why, of course!" she scoffed. "Do you know, Dick, he has almost convinced me that there is something in his idea?"

She waited for him to reply.

"Don't you think so?"

"In the Life Water – perhaps there is."

"And in the treasure?" she asked.

"Maybe. Generations of Chelfords have hunted for that wretched gold, and I suppose in the past four hundred years almost as much money has been spent in the search as the treasure is worth! I'm perfectly sure in my own mind that Good Queen Bess of pious memory bagged every bar of it!"

"And I'm perfectly sure she didn't," was the surprising reply. "I've been reading Elizabethan history very carefully, and the year that your ancestor hid his gold was the year that the Queen was so hard pressed for money that she had to borrow from the Lombards."

He stopped.

"Is that so?" incredulously.

"Absolutely. And if you weren't such a sceptic and would read a little more, you would know what any schoolchild could tell you, that in 1582 the Queen was broke. Do you object to that vulgar word?"

"It is a familiar one, at any rate," he laughed.

They had reached the deep cutting, and he turned to the left, opened a gate, and they walked up a little path towards the ruins of Chelford Abbey.

The moon was showing through a rift in the clouds.

"You ought to see the abbey by moonlight, if you've never seen it. It's rather beautiful," he said, as he gave her a hand to assist her up the steep path.

As they came in sight of the broken walls and towers of this ancient place of peace, something of the solemnity of the scene entered her heart, and she stood still, looking spellbound upon the wreckage of a once great abbey. The abbey ruins stood on the broadest surface of what was locally known as "The Mound" – the high embankment which ran almost from Fossaway Manor to the road, following the course of the little Ravensrill. Here, if tradition spoke the truth, a place of sacrifice had stood, before the English church had risen in flint, before the Norman monks laid chisel to stone on their great abbey.

The moon softened and idealised the broken stonework, and in her mind she went back through the years to those ancient times when the black-robed figures of the monks moved where she now stood. Below, to the left, she could see the fret of sparkling silver where the moon was reflected in the Ravensrill. Here they had sat, these ancient men, with their fishing-rods, discussing the little events of their narrow world. They had passed into dust, and this great abbey, the pride of their eyes and the work of their hands, was crumbling rapidly into like nothingness.

"It is wonderful!" she breathed.

Were her eyes deceiving her? She could have sworn she saw something moving in the shadow of the old tower. He heard the quick intake of her breath.

"What is it?" he asked.

"I don't know – my imagination, I think. I thought I saw somebody moving there."

He followed the direction of her eyes.

"There would be nobody here at this time of the night, unless it is the Black Abbot," he said jocularly, "and we're not scared of him, are we?"

"I'm not for one," she said, with a firmness that she was far from feeling.

At that moment she heard something – something that turned her blood to water. It was a low moan of anguish, a sobbing diminuendo of sound that began on a high note and wailed down the scale until it was inaudible.

"What was that?" she asked, grasping his arm.

He did not speak; he was straining his eyes towards the shadows.

Again the sound, this time a wail that ended in a scream. He caught the girl by the shoulder. At that moment he had seen a figure moving away from the abbey towards the river. A tall, black figure that showed clearly in the moonlight. She saw it too.

"Don't leave me, Dick!" she begged, as she felt him strain away from her.

Then of a sudden she felt his tension relax.

"Let him go," he said, half to himself.

She clung to him desperately, frantically, as the figure stumbled and staggered towards the trees that would presently engulf him. The dreadful Thing ran on, stopping now and again to turn and gibber and mouth at the man and the woman who stood motionless on the edge of the cutting. Waving wild arms, now howling in dreadful glee, now screaming in senseless fear, it vanished in the dark of the wood – an obscene, uncleanly thing that belonged to bad dreams and the horrid imaginings of madness. Far away in the distance came the howl of him, and then the night swallowed him up.

"How dreadful!"

And then her knees gave under her and she remembered no more.

19

Leslie opened her eyes and frowned up into the face that was bent over her. She was lying on the verge of the road, for Dick had carried her down into the cutting and a hundred yards towards Willow House.

"Oh, how awful!" she shuddered, and closed her eyes. "It was the Black Abbot?"

Dick Alford did not reply for a while. His anxiety for the girl was such that all other interests had passed from his mind.

"I am all right now," she said, and, with his assistance, stood shakily on her feet. "I told you I was a fool. This is my crazy day! Dick, what was it?"

"He was too far away from me to see," said Dick; "probably one of our stupid villagers under the influence of drink."

She shook her head.

"No, it was not that, Dick! It was – " She shuddered again. "I think I'd better go home."

"I think you'd be wise," he said gravely. "I wish I hadn't brought you out now."

She laughed a little shakily and clung to him tighter.

"In a way I'm glad you did," she said, as they walked slowly towards her home. "Dick, I had all sorts of queer dreams: just before I woke up I felt somebody kiss me. It was so convincing that I can still feel the lips on my cheek."

"I kissed you," he said, without shame. "I thought the shock would bring you to life!"

Her laughter was almost hysterical, for Leslie's nerves were jangled and on edge.

"You might at least have denied that," she said. "Dick, you have no subtlety!"

As they walked slowly towards the house, she noticed that he looked back once or twice.

"You're not expecting that – that thing to follow us, are you?" she asked, her teeth chattering.

"No, I thought I heard a car" (which was true). "I'll swear I saw a haze of light over the crest of the road, but I must have been mistaken."

He was not mistaken, and knew it. A car had been following them, had been slowly ascending the hill to the cutting; he had seen the reflected rays from the lamps distinctly, and had heard the soft purr of the engine. What was more certain than anything else, the car could not have turned in that narrow road, so that the only explanation was that the unknown driver had switched off his lights and stopped his machine.

"Let me look at you." He turned her to the moonlight and lifted her face. "I don't know whether you're horribly pale or whether it's a trick of the moon," he said, "but you look mighty ill! You had better go straight to bed, preferably without seeing your brother."

"Why?" she asked, in surprise.

"I don't want this spook story to get around, for one thing," he said. "And for another – oh, well, the other doesn't matter."

Leslie realised that she was walking at a much slower pace than her physical weakness justified. She was still a little shaky, but in every sense had recovered from the shock. Too sane to believe in ghosts, she had nevertheless been shaken by the terrible experience. She leaned heavily on Dick's arm as they paced up the avenue to the house, turning on to the grass so that Arthur should not hear their footsteps and come out to give them a boisterous welcome. Presently, with a sigh, she dropped his arm.

"I'm glad I went out," she said, in a low voice. "And I'm rather glad – " She did not finish the sentence.

The silence that followed was a little disturbing for both of them. Suddenly she faced him.

"Dick, do you want me to marry your brother?"

He did not answer.

"Do you – really?"

She heard his sigh in the dark. She could not see his face, for they stood in the shadow of a great cedar immediately before the house.

"I don't know," he said. There was a bleakness in his voice she had heard once before. "It isn't a question of my liking. I can offer you no reason why you should not marry him. You must do what you want, Leslie. The decision must rest entirely with you – and if I were a praying man, I would spend the night praying that you did right."

"Do you wish me to marry him?" she asked again.

"I cannot tell you." His voice was hard, and there swept over her a wave of unreasonable anger and resentment against his detachment.

"I won't ask you that question again," she said, her voice trembling. "Good night, Dick."

She ran into the hall and up to her room, and long after she had gone, he stood where she had left him, looking wistfully at the door which had closed upon her.

With something like despair at his heart, Dick Alford walked quickly along the road towards Fontwell Cutting. He had something to distract his mind for the moment.

There was no sign of the car, and, instead of passing through the cutting gates, he continued over the brow of the hill.

When he went out at night he invariably carried a small flash-lamp (he kept a stock of them at the house, for his electric supply had a trick of failing at inconvenient moments), and this he took from his pocket, and, switching it on, threw the light on the road, sweeping the beam from side to side. This was not a main thoroughfare, and, except for his own and Gine's car, and an occasional tradesman's Ford, there was little traffic. He saw the diamond-shaped impress of Arthur Gine's Rolls, could pick out his own little machine, and presently he saw a new track: the track of tyres with an arrow-shaped tread. He could distinguish the exact spot at which it had stopped. Apparently the driver had made no attempt to turn, but had gone backwards some distance. He followed the trail till it curved round, apparently into an open field. The wagon gate was closed, but on the loamy earth the mark of wheels was very apparent.

Red Farm, thought Dick, and, opening the gate, he went into the field. His search was a very short one, for the deserted car was parked close under the hedge parallel with the road. All the lights were out, but the radiator was still hot. He examined the machine carefully; it bore a London number and was new; an American touring car, replete with all the gadgets of its kind. He made a careful note of the number and, walking back to the gate, sat on the top rail and waited.

His vigil was not a protracted one. From where he sat he could see over the swelling hill the top curve of the abbey arch, and five minutes after he had taken up his position he saw a figure silhouetted against the skyline cross the brow and descend the hill towards him.

Fossaway Park was enclosed in a large-meshed wire-net fence, which offered no obstacle to any person who wished to surmount it; but the stranger had evidently not reconnoitred the ground very thoroughly, for Dick heard the clang of the wire as some heavy object struck against it, a curse, and presently he could discern a figure climbing over the wide mesh and dropping into the road.

For a few seconds it was out of sight, and then he saw it again, silhouetted against the white of the road. Nearer and nearer it came.

"Good-evening, Mr Gilder," said Dick politely. "Are you seeing the sights of Chelfordbury?"

Gilder started violently and almost dropped the heavy stick he was carrying.

"Hullo!" he stammered. "Who the dickens are you?"

A beam of light shot suddenly from his hand and focussed the questioner.

"Oh, you!" said Gilder, taking a long breath. "Gosh! you scared me! I was just admiring your old ruins by moonlight. They're rather fine."

"On behalf of the ruins I thank you," said Dick, with elaborate courtesy. "Any nice things that you can say about Chelford Abbey are deeply appreciated by its present owner."

The man was disconcerted and obviously ill at ease.

"I left my car in the field; I thought it might get in the way of traffic – " he began.

"The traffic around here between ten and midnight is not very numerous," said Dick; "but if you have the illusion that Red Farm is your property, it is quite understandable that your car should be parked there. What is the game, Gilder?"

He was conscious that the man's eyes were peering at him.

"I don't know what you mean by 'game.' Is it unlawful to admire a moonlight view?"

"It is unlawful to trespass on my brother's property," said Dick. "May I repeat my question: what is the game?"

"I don't understand you. Do you mind letting me get through that gate? I am going home."

Dick Alford descended from the gate slowly and pushed it open.

"You are a suspicious character, Gilder."

The man snapped round at him.

"What the devil do you mean?"

"Just what I say. You are a suspicious character. It is very suspicious to find you loafing around Fossaway Park at this hour of the night, particularly after certain things which have happened recently."

"Do you think I am the Black Abbot?" sneered the man, and Dick's chuckle came from the darkness.

"There are many interesting possibilities about you, Gilder. What did you expect to find in the abbey?"

"I tell you I was merely admiring the view by moonlight. If that is an offence you can bring me before a bench of magistrates."

Dick, his hands in his pockets, stood watching the man as he switched on the lights of the car and started her up.

"The place to admire the ruins is from the crest of the hill, not from the ruin itself," he said. "If you had been a normal admirer you would never have been out of sight. May I also suggest that it wasn't necessary to switch off your lights or to hide your car – the best view of the abbey is from the upper road. Gilder, you had better be careful."

"Is that a threat?"

"It is a warning," said Dick. "And a man as clever as you would not lightly despise such a warning. By the way, my solicitors are starting an action tomorrow to set aside your agreement with Farmer Leonard. I am hoping that you will not involve yourself in the expense of defending the action."

"That is a matter that I shall discuss with your lawyers," said Gilder, as he started the car.

Dick watched the machine as it waddled over the furrows and turned on to the road, and followed it out, closing the gate behind it.

"Do you know anything about racing, Gilder?"

Gilder turned with a jerk. Was this man privy to his secrets?

"I know a little – why?"

"Do you know what a warning-off notice is?"

Gilder stared at him open-mouthed.

"Yes, it is a notice issued by the Jockey Club warning people off Newmarket Heath."

"Splendid!" said Dick. "Will you take a warning-off notice from me? I warn you off Willow House and all that is contained therein!"

"And if I don't accept the warning?"

"You'll be sorry, as I've remarked before," said Dick.

Gilder jammed in his clutch and the car jerked forward with a whine, and soon its tail lights had disappeared round the bend of the road.

20

The second son climbed the fence, though the gate was near enough, and, passing the abbey ruins, walked briskly towards Fossaway Manor. His way brought him past the wing of the house in which his brother's library was situated. One of the big leaded windows was open and he caught a glimpse of Harry at his desk, sitting in the half-light, his head on his hands, a book before him. Dick sighed and continued on his way.

Thomas, the footman, answered the bell he rang.

"Get me some coffee and biscuits. I shall be working late," he said.

When the man had gone, he went to his desk and unlocked the post-bag that had come up from the station that night and shook out a heap of letters. He sorted them over carefully, and, selecting one, opened it. The letter bore the Royal crest and the plain address "New Scotland Yard," and was from an old school friend of his.

DEAR DICK,

Thank you for your rather extraordinary letter, but I am afraid we can do nothing for you officially. Private detectives, of course, are punk for your purpose, and the best I can do for you is as follows. We have a detective sergeant at headquarters named Puttler – you may have seen his name in connection with the Hatton Garden robbery. He's a very efficient man and marked for promotion, but rather a weird-looking bird. At the Yard we call him 'Monkey Puttler,' though he is universally liked in spite of this unflattering sobriquet. Puttler never takes any kind of holiday, and is generally supposed to spend his spare time in criminal investigation and to sleep in an odd corner of the Yard. He is entitled to six weeks' holiday leave. Of course, in ordinary circumstances he would never dream of taking six minutes, but I have had a talk with him, and with the complete approval of our chief (it was necessary to tell him what you wanted) Puttler will spend his holiday at Fossaway Manor. As I said before, he is rather a queer-looking creature, a rabid teetotaller, a strong churchman, with violent views on church music. You can rely absolutely upon his discretion. I've told him that you will pay him ten pounds a week and all his expenses. I only wish I could let you have him permanently, but I trust that in six weeks your trouble will be cleared up.

Dick put the letter carefully in his inside pocket, and walking across the hall, went into the library. Lord Chelford heard the door close and looked up.

"Hullo, Dick!" he said, quite amiably. "What is the news?"

Before he answered, Dick Alford walked to the window through which he had seen his brother, pulled it close and fastened the lock.

"What is wrong?" growled Chelford.

"Our monkish friend has been seen," he said, "and I think it advisable that your window should be kept closed."

Harry Chelford's hand went up to his lips.

"Can't we do anything with that fellow?" he asked fretfully. "Where are the police? What do we pay them for? It's monstrous that the countryside should be terrified by – Really, Dick, couldn't you do something?"

"I'm getting a man down tomorrow to make a few investigations," said Dick.

He charged his pipe carefully and lit it with a match which he took from a silver container on Harry's table.

"I've been over to see Leslie," he said. "Put away that infernal book and talk."

With evident reluctance Lord Chelford closed the thick tome over which he had been poring and leaned back in his chair with an air of resignation.

"Leslie? I don't see very much of her," he said. "She's a very intelligent girl and knows how busy I am. Not every woman would show so much understanding. Did you see Arthur?"

Dick nodded.

"I had a phone message saying that he was coming over in the morning. He wants me to sign some documents in connection with Leslie's estate. Good fellow, Arthur."

"Very," said Dick, without a trace of sarcasm in his voice.

"Yes, I owe a lot to Arthur." Harry looked up through his horn-rimmed spectacles and nodded as he spoke. "I shouldn't have met Leslie, and certainly I shouldn't have had any idea of marrying," he went on naïvely, "but Arthur was very keen to get a husband for her who wasn't a fortune-hunter. And, of course, the money will be useful."

Dick listened patiently to this disjointed excuse for the forth-coming marriage. He had heard it before in identically the same terms.

"Why do you want to marry money at all?" he asked. "We're not paupers."

Harry Chelford shrugged his thin shoulders.

"I suppose we're not," he said indifferently. "I never bother about the money side. You're such a clever old bird, Dick, that I'm spared that. By heavens, I don't know where I should be if it wasn't for you. Do you get all you want yourself, Dicky?"

Dick Alford nodded.

"A nice girl," his brother went on, "and, as I say, a sensible girl. I wish you'd get her over to dinner one night; there are several things I want to talk about to Arthur. There's the Doncaster estate, for example. I had a letter from somebody the other day, saying that they were willing to pay a very big price for Creethorpes. I don't see any reason in the world why we shouldn't sell."

"But I do," said Dick, puffing slowly at his pipe. "I also have had the offer, and when I get one that approximates in my eyes as being near the Creethorpes value, we may sell. But the price that has been offered is ludicrous."

"A hundred and twenty thousand pounds?" murmured Lord Chelford, shaking his head disparagingly. "I don't see how you can improve on that, Dick."

"We can try," said Dick.

His eyes were roaming the desk, and after a while he saw a book which was seldom far away from his brother's hand, and, getting up, he reached over and took it, Chelford watching with a triumphant smile.

"It's got you, has it, old man?" he asked. "I thought it would sooner or later. You're too sensible to dismiss the Chelford treasure as a myth."

Dick turned the old pages covered with pale writing: the diary of that Lord of Chelford who had suffered for his disloyalty at the hands of the common headsman.

The idea had come to him in the middle of the previous night, and all that day the old diary had been in and out of his mind at odd and incongruous moments. Whilst it was not true that he had been won over to his brother's faith in the existence of the treasure, his curiosity had been piqued by a vague recollection of one line in the diary. He turned it up now and read:

These ingots he shall put away in the safe place if yet the weather be dry and the drought continue, though rain is near at hand.

"I am only wondering," he said, as he handed back the book, "what effect the drought had upon the hiding place; why rain would have spoilt his plan, as apparently it would."

"Ha, ha!" said his lordship, almost boisterously. "The poison is working, Richard! You will become as ardent a treasure-hunter as I. Shall I tell you where the gold was hidden?" He leaned forward, his elbows on the table, his eyes gleaming. "In a cave, or an underground chamber of some kind. There are three references in this diary to a chesil." He turned the pages rapidly. "Listen, here is one," he said, and read:

"This day Tom Goodman brought me the chesil from Brighthelmstone."

"Which is Brighton, I presume?" asked Dick.
His brother nodded, turning the pages.
"Here is another reference," he said.

"The new chesil has come. I have left it near the place, and those dull wights who see it will know little of its value to me."

Dick smiled.
"It must have been something remarkable in the way of chesils," he said. "It doesn't mention its size or its shape."
"Nowhere; I have searched the diary for that."
There came a tap at the door; it was Thomas.
"Will you have your coffee here, sir?"
"No, put it in my room."
"Are you working tonight, Dick?" asked Chelford.
"After you've gone to bed, Harry," said Dick, with a laugh, "and I think it is about time you went. One of these days you'll have a break-down and I'll have to call in your pet abomination."
"Ugh!" shivered Chelford. "Never bring a doctor into this house – I loathe them!"
He got up, stretched himself with a yawn, and Dick followed him out of the room.
"I shall sleep well tonight," said his lordship, pushing back his long black hair with a characteristic gesture. "If I'd only known of that stuff before!"
"What stuff is this?" asked Dick good-humouredly.
Never a day passed that some new patent medicine did not come into the house, some cure-all, accompanied by pages of closely printed

literature. Lord Chelford's patent medicine habit was a vicious circle. The literature of one cure-all revealed symptoms of which he had never been conscious before. No sooner had he settled upon a miraculous nostrum than it was superseded by one even more dazzling in its promises.

Dick followed him up the stairs into the long room where he spent the few hours he could tear himself away from his library. A four-poster bed, an old dressing-chest, a deep closet in which his scanty wardrobe hung, and a very long table, the surface of which was literally covered with bottles and small boxes, comprised the furniture of his room, with the exception of a battered armchair before the fireplace. There must have been over a hundred boxes and packages on the table. Some of these came in consequence of standing orders given years before, and never countermanded: these had never been opened. There were cures for asthma, for bronchitis, for rheumatism, marvellous liniments, amazing sleep-inducers, nerve tonics – every disease to which the human system is liable had its antidote in that collection.

By the side of his bed on a small table was a jug of hot water and a glass. Chelford opened a tin chosen from the medley of bottles and boxes, took out two small white pellets and dropped them into a glass, covering them with water. He stirred them till they were dissolved, Dick watching, half amused, half pitiful.

"Ah!" Chelford put down the glass. "That's the stuff! No drugs, Dick – just a mixture of natural elements that bring rest to the tired brain and sleep to weary eyes!"

"I guess you're quoting the label," said Dick, with a laugh. "Even cocaine is a natural element. And there's nothing nearer to nature than morphia. You're an old goop, Harry, and if I had my way I'd take all these infernal bottles and dump them into the round pond."

"I should probably be dead in a month," said Harry with a smile, as he began to undress, "and you'd have to stand your trial for wilful murder!"

Dick closed the door behind him, waited till he heard the bolt shot home, then went downstairs to his own room. His coffee was waiting and he began his three-hour task: the opening and answering of letters, the examination of leaflets and the inspection of bills. There were cheques to be signed, envelopes to be addressed, and it was nearly three o'clock before he rose stiffly, and, pushing open the door of the French windows, walked out upon the lawn.

21

There was a sign of dawn in the sky. The air was sweet and pure and he drew great breaths of nature's champagne before he lit his pipe and strolled noiselessly along the lawn, keeping parallel with the face of the house.

He had never felt less sleepy, and he was debating in his mind whether he should take a cold bath and go on with some work that he had left unfinished on the previous day, when he saw, only for a second, a pin-point of light in the distance. It was a white, star-like flicker that dawned and disappeared almost instantly.

"If that isn't a flash-lamp I'm a Dutchman," he muttered, went back into his room, and, taking down a shotgun, slipped a handful of cartridges into the pocket of his dinner jacket.

There had been a number of poaching affrays in the neighbourhood, and the unknown poachers were a desperate gang who had never hesitated to shoot. Dick felt it best to be on the safe side, and, with the gun under his arm and two shells rammed home into the breech, he strolled across to where he had seen the light.

It is a fact that Dick Alford had no constitutional objection to poachers. His views on the subject had shocked many a hoary-headed country justice, for Dick held to the line that it was pardonable for any man to "shoot for the cooking-pot," and to him poaching was a mild joke.

The house and surrounding trees obstructed his view, but a five minutes' walk brought him through a thin plantation to the Priory fields. Now he saw, unless his judgement was at fault, that the light must have come from the direction of the abbey ruins. He stood for ten minutes in the shadow of a wood, but no light showed. And then, as his foot was raised to walk forward, he saw it again – just a momentary flicker, and this time there was no doubt that it came from the abbey. No intelligent poacher would waste five minutes on that part of the estate, though there were trout in the Ravensrill, and the burrows of a few rabbits in its banks.

He moved forward steadily up the slope of the Mound, and soon he could distinguish the chaos of stone and crumbling walls. The intruder was no expert burglar, for again the light flickered. Was it Gilder, he wondered, as he followed the course of the little river. Had that sinister man returned to admire the view of the abbey by moonlight? The east was turning grey; the cold morning wind had freshened; but though he wore only a thin dinner suit, Dick did not feel the cold. Stealthily he climbed to the top of the Mound, pausing to take observation.

Again the light, this time not fifty yards away, and he could make out the figure of a man moving slowly amidst the broken walls. He was searching the ground diligently, his lamp waving to and fro.

"Lost anything?" asked Dick.

The visitor spun round with a startled cry.

"Hullo! Who are you?" he asked hoarsely, and Dick recognised the voice.

It was Arthur Gine!

A painful and embarrassing moment for Arthur Gine!

"Hullo!" he said awkwardly. "I couldn't sleep."

"Were you looking for an opiate?" asked Dick politely. "You should have come up to the house; my brother has a small drug store, and we might have been able to find something for your insomnia."

"Don't be amusing," growled Arthur, thrown off his balance. "What I meant was, I couldn't sleep, so I came out for a walk. This place interests me."

"I did not know you were an archaeologist, and a midnight archaeologist at that! The country simply swarms with 'em!" said the ironical young man. "Or perhaps you're a moth-hunter? Or did you come out to hear the nightingale? It's rather late in the season."

"See here, Alford, I don't want you to get funny at my expense. I tell you I came out for a walk. You're not going to suggest I'm trespassing, are you? If it comes to that, what are *you* doing here?"

He heard Dick chuckle and went hot under the collar.

"I am attached to the estate: I thought you knew that," said Dick at last; "and one of my jobs is to challenge suspicious-looking individuals at whatever hour they show themselves or their flash-lamps."

"Oh, you saw the light, did you? I thought somebody would." Arthur was himself again. "The truth is, Dick, I had a horrible dream that woke me up. I dreamt I saw that wretched Black Abbot, and the dream was so vivid that I resolved to come along and have a look at the place. It was on the edge of the cutting that he was last seen."

"Oh, a ghost-hunter!" murmured Dick. "That, of course, explains everything. You came armed, I see? Very wise!"

Arthur had been praying that this objectionable man would not notice the steel crowbar he carried, but the eyes of the other were peculiarly sharp, and there was just enough dawn light to reveal the nature of the instrument he carried.

"You didn't see the Black Abbot, I suppose?" said Dick, in his polite conversational way. "No? I shouldn't imagine you would. It's rather late for him. Our family ghosts keep early hours. They are a respectable lot, and the Abbot, as you probably know, was a highly respectable and even a religious man, though not, I believe, untouched by the horrid voice of scandal."

He was walking by Arthur's side to the cut road as he spoke, and the light was not good enough for him to see the dull flush that came to that good-looking man's face, but he could guess it.

"I don't want to quarrel with you, Alford, but I have the greatest objection to your being sarcastic at my expense. I don't know why I should explain anything to you, but you've been a good friend of mine tonight and I'm telling you the truth. And, really, it's hardly playing the game to doubt my word."

Dick said nothing to this, but poised himself watchfully on the edge of the cutting until the ruffled man had disappeared from sight. What was the meaning of all this? he wondered. What attraction had the abbey ruins for these strangely assorted people? First Mary Wenner, then Gilder, and now Arthur Gine. What was there about these ancient stones which would bring the fastidious lawyer from his bed to make an early morning search? He knew Arthur rather well, much better, in fact, than he guessed. He hated discomfort of all sorts, but here he was, at four o'clock in the morning, absurdly but suitably attired in a golf suit of irreproachable pattern, a crowbar in one hand and an electric torch in the other, turning over the rubbish of the abbey and seeking – what? The treasure!

Not till that moment did the solution flash upon Dick Alford, and he was so overcome that he sat down on the nearest sandstone block and laughed till the tears came into his eyes.

The treasure! Harry had infected these prosaic people with his obsession. But how? Obviously, Mary Wenner was the connecting link. There was a time, he remembered, when she was an enthusiastic seconder to Harry's efforts, and believed as implicitly in the existence of this mythical gold as did her employer. Arthur was a friend of hers: he had heard them "Arthur" and "Mary" one another; and, through Arthur, Gilder must have come into the knowledge. So that was the explanation! And the Chelford treasure was obviously the windfall that Arthur Gine expected.

He was smiling to himself all the way back to the house, until a thought came into his mind that turned the joke of it. Suppose they were right and he was wrong? Suppose there was a treasure to be found? No sooner did the thought occur than he had laughed it out of his mind. These people merely reflected Harry's enthusiasm and faith.

He fastened the door of his study and went up to the room that overlooked the gardens of Fossaway Manor. Immediately opposite his door was a narrow passageway ending in stairs as narrow that led to the servants' quarters. As his step sounded on the grand stairway, a shadowy figure that had been prowling about the corridor slipped into the narrow entrance and crouched down. Thomas, the footman, saw Dick go into his room and close the door, and he breathed more freely. He waited, but he could hear no movement.

Silence reigned in Fossaway Manor. No sound came from the world outside. In five minutes Dick was lying in a profound slumber. He had drawn down the blinds that the light should not break his rest, and the room was in almost complete darkness.

Ordinarily he would have heard a sound, the sound of the floor-boards creaking outside his door, and would have been awake instantly. Twice the planks creaked under a heavy weight, but he did not stir. And then the handle of his door turned slowly and the door itself moved the fraction of an inch. The thing outside listened, showing its white teeth in a grin. The sound of Dick Alford's regular breathing came out to him and he pushed the door open a little farther, and, crouching, moved stealthily towards the bed, feeling for the brass rail at the foot.

Not a sound came from the intruder, and yet he was shaking with laughter. He fumbled in his pocket and took out a long-bladed clasp knife and opened it carefully, testing the edge with his thumb. Then, slowly, his long fingers went out to locate the position of the body. The Angel of Death hovered in that second above the sleeping man.

From the hall below came a woman's voice – distraught – beside herself with fear.

"Dick – Dick, for God's sake!"

Dick turned uneasily in his sleep and half opened his eyes.

22

"Dick!"

It was a girl's voice, sharp with fear, that came from the hall below. "Dick!"

The thing with the knife dropped the weapon and, cringing back towards the door, hesitated a second, and slipped out.

"Dick!"

Again the voice, and Dick woke. Was he dreaming? Slipping out of bed, he threw open the door and walked on to the landing.

"Who's calling?" he asked, husky with sleep.

"It is I – Leslie! Dick, I want you."

He went back to his bedroom, pulled a dressing-gown from a hook and raced down the stairs, dressing as he went. She was standing in the gloom of the hall, a slim figure. She had no hat; her bare feet were thrust into slippers, and she wore an overcoat over what was evidently a hastily assumed skirt.

"What is the matter, dear?"

He pushed open the door of his study and led her in. She was trembling from head to foot.

"I don't know. Something dreadful has happened," she gasped. "I thought my car would wake you – didn't you hear it?"

"Something dreadful has happened? What?" he asked quickly.

"I don't know. I suppose I've got everything out of proportion – I saw Arthur fighting with a man on the lawn. It was dreadful. I thought I must have been mistaken and went to his room, but the bed was empty and had not been slept in. By the time I could get downstairs on to the lawn, they had disappeared. Oh, Dick, what can have happened?"

"Fighting?" He was incredulous. "I saw Arthur – I don't know how long ago; it may have been an hour or two. I don't know how long I've been sleeping."

It was daylight now; the clock over the mantelpiece showed it to be a quarter past five.

"Just wait a moment. I'll be with you in a jiffy."

He ran up the stairs and in five minutes rejoined her, dressed, and, lifting her into the car, he sent the little machine flying down the drive.

"How did you get into the house?"

"I came through your study. I rang the bell at the door, but nobody answered me. And then I tried your French windows and they were open."

"I'm always forgetting to lock them. I'm glad I did. And they will never be locked in the future," said Dick. "Now just tell me what happened?"

She told her story coherently. Her very association with this man had restored her failing courage. And as she grew calmer she became penitent.

"What a scare-cat you will think I am!" she said ruefully. "I don't know what time it was – about half an hour ago, I think – but I was sleeping when I heard voices. I went to the window and looked out. It was still rather dark; there are an awful lot of trees before the house; but I could see two men, and I wouldn't have known one of them was Arthur, only I heard him speaking angrily."

"Did you hear anything he said?"

"No, they were too far away. They were near the laurels that hide the house from the road. And then I saw Arthur strike the man, and they began to struggle, and that is all I saw. By the time I'd got downstairs they had disappeared."

"But you say you saw him? How could you?"

Dick gave a version of his encounter with the lawyer that was more flattering to Arthur than was deserved.

"But that couldn't be true!" she said, in perplexity. "He hadn't been to bed at all. What is the meaning of it, Dick?"

"The Lord knows!" said Dick piously. "I wish my friend Puttler was here."

The car ran through the cutting and took the long, straight road to Willow House; they were turning into the drive when Dick saw a man walking in front of him.

"There's your Arthur," he said, and she uttered a little cry of thankfulness.

It was Arthur with a difference. His nose had been bleeding, one of his eyes was slightly discoloured. In other circumstances Dick would have laughed, but the girl was so concerned with her brother's injuries that it would have been brutal even to find anything amusing in the discomfiture of this dandified young lawyer.

"It was nothing," he said gruffly. "I met a poacher and had a slight argument with him."

The knees of his new golfing knickers were soiled and torn; the knuckles of his hand were red and bleeding. Dick felt that it was not the moment to ask him questions, and followed the brother and sister into the house, an interested and cautious observer of events.

The servants had been roused and one of them brought some coffee, and Dick, who had been half dead from sleepiness, accepted the steaming cup gratefully.

"What do you think has happened, Dick?" she asked, when Arthur had gone up to his room to treat his injuries, having refused all the assistance she offered.

"I think he has told us what has happened. He had trouble with a poacher. In other words, he had a vulgar fight. It is one of those distressing happenings that the best of men cannot always avoid."

She shot a suspicious glance at him.

"You don't mean that, Dick. And it couldn't have been a poacher. I'm perfectly sure it was Mr Gilder."

Dick was not prepared to contest this point of view. The probability of Arthur's assailant being his head clerk was one that had occurred to him. But why should Gilder be in the vicinity of Willow

House at that hour of the morning? At a suitable opportunity he would ask Arthur Gine for the truth.

He was conscious that she was looking at him, and, meeting her eyes, he saw something that made him catch his breath.

"What shall I ever do without you?" she asked, with a gesture of helplessness. "I run to you crying every time I am hurt, and you appear by magic whenever I'm in trouble! Dick, one of these days I'm going to be a disgrace to my sex!"

"I hope not, Leslie," he smiled. "What particularly outrageous thing have you in mind?"

She nodded wisely.

"You will see," she said. "I also can be mysterious!"

He declined the loan of her car and returned on foot to the house. Unless Harry's sleeping draught had taken effect, he would have heard the car, for his room faced the drive. But no sound came from the King's Chamber, as his sleeping apartment was magniloquently termed, and Dick went to his room and took off his clothes.

He was getting into bed when his foot touched something hard and shiny, and, stooping, he picked it up.

"Moses!" said Dick under his breath, and switched on the light.

The knife was a new one, its edge razor-sharp. He turned it over and over in his hand and frowned. Then, walking to the door, he locked it; and Dick did not usually sleep behind a locked door. But he realised that the twenty-four hours through which he was passing were pregnant with unpleasant possibilities.

23

The office of Gine & Gine was thrown into some disorder the next morning by a most unexpected occurrence. Mr Fabrian Gilder, for the first time in his twenty-five years' association with the business, did not put in an appearance. Instead came a note to the senior clerk, asking that a certain drawer in his desk should be opened and the contents thereof sent by special messenger to Mr Gilder's house in Regent's Park. There was a postscript to the note.

It is unlikely that I shall return to the business. I have handed my resignation to Mr Gine, and intend to devote my time to the development of my private affairs.

A wire from Arthur Gine appointed the senior clerk to take the place of the retired Gilder: an arrangement not altogether to the satisfaction of the senior clerk, for there were unpleasant whisperings about Gine & Gine, hints of dire developments to come that made the older members of the staff quake in their shoes.

Arthur did not appear that day, nor the next, and the mystery of Gilder's resignation remained unsolved, for the confidential messenger who carried his papers to his flat, and who expected to hear from him the reason for his sudden departure, was not admitted. Mr Gilder was in bed; he had come up from the country early in the morning and had met with a slight accident whilst getting out of his car. Apparently he had remained awake long enough to write his letter to the office, but was now sleeping, so the servant said. And she spoke the truth,

101

though he did not sleep as soundly as he might have done had his lips not been cut and his shoulder slightly strained. You cannot indulge in fisticuffs in the uncertain light of dawn without incurring a certain amount of damage.

Curiosity was not the besetting vice of Dick Alford; even if it had been, he would not have spared the time to make a call at Gine & Gine's to discover the extent of Mr Gilder's damage. He had his bath and shaved just before lunch, and came downstairs to find that the noon train had brought him a visitor.

Sergeant Puttler he recognised, though he had never seen him before, from the description that his friend had sent him. He was a tall, gaunt man of forty. The tired-looking brown eyes that gazed with gentle melancholy from their deep sockets reminded Dick of a sick and sorrowful chimpanzee he had once seen. His forehead was low, his upper lip long, and his arms reached almost to his knees. These features, added to a constitutional stoop, contributed to his unprepossessing appearance. Poor Mr Puttler was not unaware of the simian mould in which his frame was cast, and it was, apparently, a matter which alternately depressed and pleased him.

"Well, sir, how do you like me?" he said without a smile, though there was a twinkle of malicious joy in his brown eyes. "I've known people to faint the first time they've seen me, especially romantical people."

"I shan't faint," smiled Dick, "possibly because I'm not romantical."

The footman came in at that moment, and evidently romance tinged his soul, for at the sight of the strange, long-armed man he visibly staggered and blinked.

"Take Mr Puttler up to his room. Afterwards, Puttler, come and dine and I have something to tell you."

The dazed Thomas led the way up the stairs to a room next door to that occupied by Dick. The housekeeper had been warned of his coming and the room was ready. He deposited his suitcase and took stock of his rather handsome surroundings.

"Is there anything further I can do, sir?" asked Thomas.

Sergeant Puttler blinked at him.

"Nothing, thank you." And, as Thomas was going: "What do you call yourself now?"

"Me, sir – my name is Thomas Luck."

Puttler shook his head sadly.

"Thomas Bad Luck," he said; "William Hard Lines or Henry Too Bad. Does your master know that your name is Sleisser and that you've done a stretch in Dartmoor?"

"No," said the man sullenly.

"He will, Thomas – he will," said the detective gently, and with murder in his eyes the footman slunk out of the room.

Mr Puttler came downstairs purring with satisfaction.

"Are you sure that is my room, Mr Alford?" he asked. "Not expecting the Prince of Wales, are you? I've always been ambitious to sleep in a four-poster bed. Now, Mr Alford."

"First of all, I must introduce you to my brother. By the way, he is rather of a nervous disposition, and I've told him that you're a member of an accountancy firm who has come down to help me with my books."

Mr Puttler expressed his agreement with this mild form of deception. He was taken to the big library and formally introduced. Harry Chelford was so used to the advent of Dick's extraordinary guests that he saw nothing unusual in the appearance of the simian Puttler. Happily, he was near-sighted, and though it was a startling experience to find himself shaking hands across a very broad desk, which an ordinary man could not have spanned, he did not realise the cause of the phenomenon.

Dick entertained accountants, land agents, an occasional bailiff or two, so that there was no novelty in the invitation. Learned-looking strangers came to his table from time to time and were introduced and passed out of his mind.

"He will be staying six weeks," Dick had told him, "and you mustn't object to his prowling round the place, because I want to get a true valuation of the estate, and he has his own peculiar methods."

"You might get him to price the Black Abbot," said Harry, half dourly, half amused. "What we want, Dick, is not so much a valuer as a good policeman."

Dick Alford thought that the guest might fulfil both functions, but he did not say so.

He ushered his visitor back to his own little office, carefully closed the door and sat down at his desk.

"Now make yourself comfortable. Do you smoke?"

Mr Puttler fumbled in his pocket and produced a black pipe.

"It's not very aristocratic," he apologised, "but I prefer 'bacca to cigars and cigarettes."

"I'll join you," said Dick.

His study had two doors: one that opened into the hall and one into a side corridor running back to the housekeeper's room. The two men had been talking for ten minutes, though, as far as Mr Puttler was concerned, his contribution to the discourse was limited to an occasional question, when Thomas came noiselessly down the side corridor, peeped into the hall and walked back to the study door. There was a look of apprehension upon his lean and shapeless face which was not without cause. Stooping, he put his eye to the keyhole. He could just see the end of the settee and the head and shoulders of the strange visitor. He was holding something in his hand – a white-handled knife – and was examining it with curiosity. Thomas bent his head and pressed his ear against the hole.

Dick's back was to the door and he was speaking in a lower tone than usual, and this reacted to the disadvantage of the eavesdropper, for only a few distinct and intelligible sentences came to him.

"…might have been somebody admitted to the house by one of the servants," was the first thing he heard. A few minutes later, Mr Puttler, whose voice was distinct, asked: "Was the window in the library open?" And he heard Dick say "Yes," and add something which he could not catch.

The soles and heels of Thomas' boots were of rubber. He passed into the hall and made another reconnaissance, then returned to his listening post, in time to hear Dick say: "My brother hasn't an enemy in the world. I am afraid I can't say the same – "

Once the listener caught the word "treasure," and once he heard the name of "Arthur Gine," but in what association he could not learn. Again Thomas visited the hall. He could not take the risk of being seen listening at the door. He was free from observation so far as he knew. The old Chelford butler was in the servants' hall. Dick and his brother did not lunch till two, an unholy hour from the point of view of servants, but very suitable for Dick and his peculiar occupation.

He squinted through the keyhole again. The detective still had the knife in his hand and was looking at it intently. He heard him say, "This is new," and then Dick entered upon a long and apparently explanatory statement, not a word of which came to the disgusted man who was listening. He was most anxious to hear some reference to himself, but, if it was made, he did not overhear his name.

Soon after, however, a familiar phrase caught his ear. Dick Alford was talking about the Black Abbot, and he heard rather a sketchy description of that spook. Then his voice dropped again, and coincident with this Thomas heard the stately footsteps of the butler, slipped back to the housekeeper's room and was busy in the pantry when the stout Mr Glover found him.

24

The luncheon was not a genial meal. Harry had acquired the disgraceful habit of bringing a book to his meals, and he was utterly absorbed in the volume, and left Dick and his visitor to carry on a conversation as though he were not present.

Mr Puttler, who was a man of wide experience, was neither embarrassed by his magnificent surroundings – for Lord Chelford lived in a princely style, three footmen and a butler waiting upon them – nor did he feel it necessary to live up to the state in which he found himself. He was altogether unaffected, had a fund of anecdotes and could tell funny stories without apparently enjoying them himself, which is the art of amusement. Only once did Dick interrupt his brother's reading.

"Leslie is coming to tea," he said. "She phoned over just before lunch."

Harry Alford looked up and his face fell.

"That is very unfortunate," he said. "I had promised myself an uninterrupted afternoon with Fra Hiekler. I've just had a facsimile edition sent to me from Leipzig. Hiekler, you remember, Dick, was a cloistered monk in the days of Elizabeth, our abbey being one of the few that was not interfered with by Henry the Eighth or by Elizabeth either; partly, I think, because our particular order of monks were antagonistic to the Jesuits."

Dick listened patiently, and when his brother had exhausted the history of the Black Fathers of Chelfordbury:"You'll have to be civil and come to tea, and after that I've no doubt Leslie will not object to your going back to Fra Hiekler, who was a German, I presume?"

"He was a German," said Harry gravely. "And the circumstances which brought him to Chelfordbury were rather peculiar."

"The best German I ever read about" – it was Mr Puttler who interrupted – "was Robinson Crusoe."

Dick thought it was a crude jest on the part of his guest, but, if it was so, Mr Puttler was unconscious of his humour. Harry stared at the "accountant." He took such statements as these very seriously indeed.

"I am not well acquainted with Robinson Crusoe," he said, "but surely you are wrong in saying that he was a German? I have always regarded such characters as typically English."

"He was a German," said Mr Puttler firmly, "though few people are aware of the fact. If you look at the first page of the story you'll see these words: 'My father was a merchant of Bremen,' and Bremen's in Germany, or I'm a Dutchman. And if his father was a German, he was a German, because there was no such thing as naturalisation in those days."

Having dropped his literary thunderbolt, Puttler was prepared to take up the subject which Dick had interrupted by his question.

"The trouble with church music, Mr Alford, is that it's a little too sugary. It appeals to the senses. I've had many an argument with my brother churchwardens – "

"Are you a churchwarden?" asked Dick, in surprise.

Again the gleam of laughter in the man's deep-set eyes.

It's hard to believe," he said modestly, "but I am."

Soon after this, Harry left the table, and was gone five minutes, when he returned with a fat volume under his arm.

"You're right, Mr – "

"Puttler," suggested Dick.

"You're right about Robinson Crusoe. What an extraordinary fact, to think that one has lived all one's life under such a mistaken impression!"

This evidence of literary skill on the part of the visitor brought a remarkable change in Harry's attitude. Before, Puttler might have had no existence. He was one with the milkman, the grocer and the village postman.

He took Puttler affectionately by the arm, and led him into the library, and there Dick left them, knowing exactly the course of instruction that Mr Puttler would receive; for Harry's first act was to unlock his desk and take out the Diary. Dick was relieved to have Puttler off his hands for an hour or two. That day he was experiencing a sense of unbelievable relief. A great burden had been lifted from his shoulders, and one of his more pressing and secret troubles had been half dissipated.

He ran halfway down the drive to meet Leslie's car, and leapt on the running-board while the car was moving.

"Practising for a tram-conductor," he said cheerily. "I've decided on my profession, when you arrive at Fossaway Manor, mistress of all these demesnes."

"When will that be, Dick?" she asked, looking steadily ahead.

"Never, I hope."

In his lightness of heart he had not kept that usual guard on his tongue, and the words were out before he could stop them. Twice he had been taken off his guard, and he would have given anything to unsay his words.

Apparently she did not attach any great significance to them, for she did not turn her head, sending the car spinning to the broad gravelled place before the old porch. He jumped down when she stopped the machine and helped her alight.

"I have to prepare you for a curious bird," he said, and described Mr Puttler with more truth than flattery.

"What is he, Dick?"

"He's an accountant," said Dick glibly. "He's also quite an amusing fellow and full of weird information. I'm going to try a little on you. Do you know that Robinson Crusoe was a German?"

"Why, of course, his father lived in Bremen," she said, and he was still laughing when he took her into the library.

In the presence of his fiancée Lord Chelford exhibited a nervousness and a *gaucherie* which might have been understandable if he were meeting her for the first time. He had never quite overcome the novelty of his engagement, and his attitude towards her was one of awe rather than of reverence.

"How do you do, Leslie?"

He had never kissed her in his life; now he held her hand for a fraction of a second and dropped it as though it burnt him.

"Do you know Mr Tuttler?"

"Puttler," said the other, and Leslie looked into the melancholy eyes and read something in them that Dick had missed, and possibly Mr Puttler's closest associate had not seen.

She did not pay him the poor compliment of feeling sorry for him, though she read in those quick-lighting deeps a craving for woman's sympathy which Nature, by her cruel handiwork, had repelled in advance.

"Glad to know you, Miss Gine. I know your brother – Mr Arthur Gine, the solicitor, isn't it? I thought so."

"Has Arthur come?" asked Harry.

"No," said Dick. "We're going to have tea in the drawing-room. Will you come along, Harry?"

"Surely, surely," he said hastily. "You'll excuse me, dear." It was an effort to employ even so banal an expression of affection.

When they reached the beautiful drawing-room, with its windows open to the terrace, and a riot of gorgeous sulphur chrysanthemums showing above the stone balustrade, they found they were alone. Mr Puttler had melted away as they were passing through the hall. He explained afterwards that he wanted to stroll through the gardens, but the girl knew that the man's uncanny instinct had told him that, of all the people in the world, these two were satisfied best with one another's company.

"Did you sleep?" she asked.

He nodded.

"I didn't get up till lunch time," he said. "And you?"

She shook her head.

"No, I couldn't sleep. Poor Arthur!"

"Did you try beefsteak?" he asked brutally. "Really, the most incongruous company I can imagine is a black eye and Arthur Gine!"

"He is awfully shaken," she said seriously. "I have never known him to be so upset. It was Mr Gilder."

"I knew," said Dick, "or, at least, I guessed. Did you find out the cause of the quarrel?"

She hesitated.

"I don't know; I think it was something to do with me."

"What was Gilder doing at your house?"

"Arthur didn't tell me," she replied. "From what he said I gather that Mr Gilder had been watching Arthur and had followed him somewhere."

"To the abbey ruins – yes, that is quite possible. And of course your brother objected to that, naturally. Why are they watching one another?"

"Is Arthur watching Gilder?" she asked in surprise.

"It almost looks like it. Leslie, I want to tell you something that nobody else knows, not even Harry. It may bring a little ease to your mind in the dark hours of the night. Puttler is a detective, a Scotland Yard man."

She stared at him.

"A detective? Why on earth – "

"Things have been happening that I don't very much like," said Dick. "I've been worried nearly sick about them, and though I'm quite capable of dealing with most contingencies, the Lord has ordained that I should take seven hours' rest in every twenty-four, and there must be somebody awake when I'm asleep."

"The Black Abbot – is that what is worrying you?"

He bit his lip thoughtfully.

"Yes and no. Some aspects of the Black Abbot's activities trouble me more than I should like to confess. Leslie, do you believe in the treasure?"

"The Chelford treasure?" she asked, in surprise. "And what do you mean by believing in it? It is true that the gold was brought to Fossaway Manor in olden times, isn't it?"

"Perfectly true," said Dick, "and perfectly true, I should imagine, that it was taken away. But do you believe that it has any existence, that it can be found? Suppose one dug up every square inch of the park, pulled down this old house of ours, probed into the bowels of the earth, do you think it is possible that the gold could be found? Because, if you don't, there are other people who do besides Harry."

"Do you believe?" she challenged.

He heaved a deep sigh.

"Heaven knows, I'm ready to believe anything! And I thought I should never drag down my lofty intelligence to such deeps. But, Leslie, my dear, I am getting – " He paused for a word.

"Convinced?"

"Not exactly convinced, but shaken in my obstinacy. I've become a doubter of my own scepticism, and that's the worst mental condition a man can reach – or almost the worst," he added.

"Does Harry know you are a convert?" Her fine eyes twinkled with mischief.

"He suspects me," said Dick gloomily. "If I thought the money was here – "

She regarded him steadily.

"Would it make a big difference to you, Dick?" she asked.

"Me personally?" He shook his head. "Lord, no! It would make a difference to the – " He paused. "To Harry. I was going to say the estate. The estate, to me, is something distinct from any personality. It stands for the agglomeration of dead men's efforts, the cumulative sum of all their strivings."

She looked at him for a long time in wonder. She loved him in this serious mood of his.

"You've made rather a fetish of Fossaway Manor and the Chelford estates, haven't you?"

"Have I?" He was genuinely surprised. "I wonder – " And then he laughed. "It isn't a bad line for a second son to exalt the estates to which he will never succeed, above the personality of the man who will get them! It makes him rather superior to the real heir. Put my fetish worship down to vanity, for the Lord knows I have my share of that."

"I doubt it," she said quietly. "Come out on to the terrace. Your flowers are lovely."

"Everything in the garden – " he began, but she checked him with a warning finger.

"If you get vulgar I shall go in and find Puttler."

25

She leaned on the grey stone balustrade and looked down upon the wind-stirred tresses of great golden chrysanthemums, each as big as a large-sized saucer. They were not all gold; there were deep red blooms and snowy white and flaming orange, and beyond them a huge bed of late-flowering roses; even from this distance she could sniff the delicate fragrance of them.

"It's a beautiful old place," she said in a hushed voice. "I don't wonder that you love it. How long has your family owned this estate, Dick?"

"Eight hundred years," he said. "The first of the Chelfords sliced off the head of the original owner and stole the property. Successive generations of Chelfords, whose own heads were cut off with monotonous regularity, enclosed a few thousand acres of common-land belonging to the people – and there you are!"

She laughed softly.

"You have very few illusions, have you?"

"None," was his curt reply, and somehow the answer hurt her.

They had to send twice for Harry before he put in an appearance, and he seemed disappointed to find that Puttler was not there.

"That is quite an intelligent fellow, Dick," he said, delicately spearing a cucumber sandwich. "He has an extraordinary knowledge of history, particularly English history. Unfortunately, he doesn't read German" (Harry read German as well as he read English, French or Italian), "but I have persuaded him to take up the study. Have you everything you want, Leslie?"

He had helped her to nothing, and was happy to find that her requirements had been supplied. Only twice he spoke to her: once to ask about Arthur, and the other time when he made an oblique reference to his forthcoming marriage.

"Marriage ceremonies and the pomp of them are a little indelicate, I think. It is a barbarous custom, these veils and bridesmaids and barbaric orange-blossoms. Now in America I am told that it is quite the usual thing to be married in a drawing-room. I'm sure that could be arranged, couldn't it, Dick? The bishop is quite an obliging old gentleman."

"Turn Puttler on him: he's an authority on church ritual," said Dick.

"The man is an authority on most things," said Harry, with unaccustomed enthusiasm. "He was telling me that possibly there was some cryptogram in existence which would give a direct clue as to the treasure." And then, seeing the half-smile on the girl's face, he gave one of his rare boyish laughs. "We are still chasing shadows, Leslie, but it is a very substantial shadow, believe me. Now, Puttler thinks – "

They listened without comment to Puttler's views, which in this case were neither informative nor particularly brilliant.

"Puttler's mind apparently runs to dungeons, and there are dungeons to this place," said Harry vigorously. "I am going to have a look round tomorrow. There are probably secret places under the floor which might be profitably examined."

"The dungeons, as you call them, are wine-cellars," said Dick ominously; "and if Puttler goes fooling around my port there will be trouble! Besides which, Harry, I don't suppose there has been a single ancestor of ours who hasn't dug up the floor of that unfortunate dungeon – one of them in the days of the Regency had the walls stripped, and the beggar never replaced the stone. It cost our father the best part of a thousand pounds to repair the damage done by this old gold-hound!"

Dick noticed that whilst Harry was present the girl's manner was just a little strained and unreal, and she was nervous too, started when she was addressed and was content to listen without including herself in the conversation. It was not until Harry had gone, with a lame apology, back to the library that she became her real self again, and the old Leslie crept forth from its hiding-place. Once, whilst Dick and his brother were discussing the affair of the dungeons, she had walked on to the terrace, and out of the corner of his eye he saw her in profile, a slim, frail-looking girl, with her delicate face and her glorious hair, and in the setting she looked almost ethereal. It was as though some old masterpiece of Botticelli had come to life.

When the door had closed on Harry she came back and sat down with a little grimace.

"Was it very rude of me to go out? Dicky, I can't work up any interest in the things that really fascinate Harry! Whatever will he talk about when the treasure is found?"

"The treasure? Oh, you mean the gold? He will probably talk about you."

She made a little *moue*.

"I'm too young to be interesting to Harry, three hundred years too young," she said. "Now tell me about your detective. I liked what I saw of him. He is to be your little guardian angel? And, Dick, will he have a beat – is that the word? Because, if he has, I do hope he'll take in Willow House. I'll even lend him my car."

"Are you really frightened?"

She thought for a while before she replied.

"I think I am," she said. "When I was a child the first air-raids fascinated me, the second were interesting, but after the third or fourth they became – just air-raids. And the Black Abbot – well, he's very picturesque, Dick, but he's rather terrifying. Didn't you tell me that Harry feared him?"

"He does a little."

"Why, I wonder?"

"Harry is naturally of a nervous temperament," said Dick. "People are born that way, and it is absurd to talk of 'cowardice' where they are concerned. Now I was born without the knowledge of nerves, and I daresay if you saw me chasing the Black Abbot you would think I was terribly brave. As a matter of fact, it is simply because I've no imagination."

"That isn't true," she said. "Why do you always belittle yourself?"

"Because I am by nature excessively modest," he said gravely, and at that moment they caught sight of Mr Puttler strolling through the long lines of rose trees that ran parallel with the eastern wing. Together they went down the terrace steps and intercepted him.

"It is a lovely place," said Mr Puttler, shaking his head in admiration. "I've never seen so many roses together in my life, except at Covent Garden market, and they're not roses, they're just merchandise."

"I've told Miss Gine that you're a detective, Puttler."

Puttler frowned at this.

"You know Miss Gine better than I do," he said good-humouredly. "Speaking for myself, I find that life is much easier to live if you keep your mouth shut. Not," he added hastily, "that I want to be offensive. That's only my way of reasoning and my way of talking. There used to be an officer in our division who rose from the rank of plain police constable to superintendent by the simple process of never saying anything to anybody. If he was asked for his opinion on a matter he used to shake his head and say there was much to be said on both sides, but he had his own private opinion, and even when he was called into a case he'd say nothing, but listen to what everybody else said and smile. That smile was worth a thousand a year to him."

They crossed the rose garden and were strolling across the lawn. Under a huge elm Mr Puttler stopped to continue a story which was fated never to be finished.

"One day the superintendent said to this man, whose name was Carter, 'Carter,' he said, 'I can't understand – ' "

Crack!

A bullet snicked past the detective's face, struck the bole of the tree and sent the bark splintering. From a clump of rhododendron bushes two hundred yards away floated a pale blue cloud.

"Down on your face!" said Dick hoarsely, and dragged the girl to the ground, only just in time.

Crack!

The second bullet struck a little lower. A splinter of bark hummed past the girl's ear.

"There's someone in those bushes who doesn't like me," said Mr Puttler.

Pulling a long-barrelled Browning from his pocket, and bending low, he sprinted towards the bushes, zigzagging as he ran.

A third shot rang out and the running man pitched forward on his face and lay still.

26

Dick flew forward to the prostrate figure, and, kneeling by his side, turned him on his back. His eyelids were working spasmodically, but there was no sign of injury, except a bruise on the side of his face which had been caused by his coming violently into contact with the ground. And then Dick saw the man's right boot. The sole had been ripped off and there was a patch of blood showing on the toe of the sock. At the sound of a rustling skirt Dick turned his head. The girl was coming towards them.

"Go back behind that tree and don't move," he shouted authoritatively, but for once she did not obey him.

She was rather pale, but there was no other evidence of fear as she knelt by his side and began to unfasten the collar of the stricken man.

"He's stunned. I don't think it's anything worse than that," said Dick. "I thought at first he was finished – look at his boot!"

He was pulling it off gingerly, and the operation must have hurt a little, because the detective winced and opened his eyes.

"Hullo! What has happened?" he asked, looking round. "Did that bird shoot me?"

"I don't think he's hurt you very much." Dick was looking at the foot. The bullet had ricocheted, cutting a shallow gash on the man's instep, but there was no other injury.

"Do you feel fit enough to look after Miss Gine?" said Dick.

The detective reached round for the gun he had dropped and humped himself to his feet. Without another word, Dick raced across the grassland to the bushes, and the girl watched him in terror, expecting every second to hear the fourth and the fatal shot.

After five minutes he emerged from the bushes, holding something in his hand which he was examining curiously as he walked towards them.

"A Lee-Enfield rifle, Army pattern," he said. "I found these cases."

He put them into the detective's hand. Puttler examined the exploded cartridges carefully.

"You didn't see him, of course?" he said.

"No, I think he must have got round to the back of the house. The bushes run practically from the west wing of Fossaway Manor to the end of the Mound. He might, of course, be still hidden in the bushes, but the probability is that he made his escape as soon as he saw you fall," said Dick. "I think we'd better go inside and I will find you a pair of shoes, unless you have a spare supply."

They were halfway to the house when they met Lord Chelford.

"Who was that shooting?" he asked irritably. "Dick, I told you that I did not want rabbit shooting or any other kind of shooting within half a mile of the house. It gets on my nerves terribly. Really, I think, you must show a little more consideration."

The girl had opened her lips to explain when Dick caught her eye, and with splendid mendacity she invented a hurried but effective excuse.

"My fault, Harry. I saw a stoat, and I hate stoats." The fact that they had not so much as an air-gun between the three of them was unnoticed by Harry.

"Well, of course." He was obviously taken aback by her championship. "If that's the case it can't be helped. Only in future, Dick, old boy – "

He walked rapidly back to the house.

"Why shouldn't he be told?" asked Leslie; then, realising the foolishness of the question, she was all penitence. "There is no reason why he should be, of course. I was silly to suggest it. But, Dick, who did such a terrible thing? It couldn't have been an accident."

"It wasn't an accident: of that I can assure you," said Mr Puttler, nursing his injury. "The first two shots that were fired hit the tree within three inches of one another. Are you going to notify the local police, Mr Alford?"

Dick thought for a moment, then decided against that course, and to Leslie's surprise the detective approved.

"I think you're right," said Puttler. "Where is the nearest rifle range?"

"About fifteen miles away," said Dick sardonically. "You needn't follow that line of thought."

"I'm not following any line of thought," said the detective. "I'm only foreseeing possible alibis. I spend my life standing in front of alibis and waving a red flag."

Through the tan, Dick's face was grey. He seemed suddenly to have gone old, and Leslie looked at him anxiously.

"Dick, at whom were they shooting?"

"I don't know that they were shooting at anybody," he said wearily. "They just loosed off a few rounds to scare us."

And then he laughed; it was a fierce, hard little laugh, and she winced at the sound of it.

"I am thinking of Harry and his nerves, and the stoat and every damned ridiculous – I beg your pardon, Leslie; I'm afraid I'm getting rattled."

She smiled at this.

"Dick, will you say goodbye to Harry for me? I promised my brother I would come home early. No, really, you need not take me. I'm not at all afraid of being held up by armed desperadoes!"

"Neither am I," said Dick, "but I don't fancy you overmuch as a driver."

And in her annoyance at this false accusation she forgot to resist his escort.

By the time he had returned to the house, Puttler had secured a dressing for his foot. The injury was so slight that he could resume his shoes, and pooh-poohed the suggestion that he had better lie up that night.

"It was a narrow escape," he said, "but I'm rather glad I got that bullet, and that it didn't go where it was intended."

Dick looked at him steadily.

"For whom was it intended?" he asked.

Without hesitation came the reply.

"For Miss Leslie Gine: I thought you knew that."

Dick could find no answer, but in his heart of hearts he knew that Puttler was speaking the truth.

27

Mr Fabrian Gilder sometime head clerk to the firm of Gine & Gine, and now a gentleman of leisure, was in one sense a hard man. He did not forgive even slight injuries, and in the past had gone a long way out of his path to get even with those who had the misfortune to affront him. And Arthur Gine had offended beyond hope of forgiveness. A few days before, Gilder would have thought it a very simple matter to be revenged upon his enemy; but now the simple process of laying an information and of preferring a charge of forgery was contingent upon four bills which were in his possession being repudiated by the man who was alleged to have backed them.

He could do no more than present those interesting documents, and this he did through his bank. Dick had already made arrangements for their redemption. It was not entirely an act of philanthropy on his part, for he was a business man, and took over from the frankly reluctant Mr Gine the choice of a number of unsaleable shares which Dick regarded as having a certain value. The bills which had been renewed from time to time were met, and that ended Mr Gilder's chance of carrying his threat into execution.

He was the type of man who thrived on opposition. Though it would be true to say that he had fallen in love with Leslie Gine the first time he had seen her, which was months before that unpleasant scene at his flat, his desire for her grew as his chance of winning her receded farther and farther into the background.

On the night that Dick had found him examining the ruins of the abbey, Mr Gilder had returned to the cut road when he thought the coast was clear and had discovered yet another in quest of the treasure. He had witnessed the interview between the two men and had followed Arthur back to Willow House with no other intention than to offer his help, for a consideration, in discovering this mythical fortune. For Mr Gilder had heard quite enough, that day he surprised his employer with Mary Wenner, to know that somewhere under the abbey lay either the fortune or its key. He had overtaken Arthur on the drive, and Arthur was in an unpleasant mood; hot with the man at the interruption of his search, smarting under the sting of Dick Alford's sarcasm.

At first, startled by the unexpected apparition of his head clerk, Arthur had snarled round on him, and there and then discharged him from his service and defied him to do his worst. It was Gilder who had struck the first blow.

When Arthur was in his more unpleasant moods he said things that no self-respecting man could endure, and the black eye which the lawyer nursed was an advertisement of his indiscretion.

Gilder might be a bookmaker, but he was not a thief. At least, "thief" was rather an extravagant description of his duplicity. He came back to London half crazy with rage, but a day in bed restored his mental equilibrium and he sat down to plan how best he could frustrate any plans which his late employer had formed for gaining possession of the treasure. By this time Gilder too was convinced: his last doubts were removed. He had been sceptical as to the treasure's existence, but he knew such things had happened, and he had a natural desire to be in any scheme which produced immediately and without great labour a vast, undreamed-of sum.

His cut lip healed in a few hours, though it was still swollen, and towards the evening of the second day after his retirement from the firm of Gine & Gine, he dressed himself with great care, and, calling a taxi, drove to an address he had once scribbled on his white shirt-cuff.

Mary Wenner occupied a tiny flat, every compartment of which might have been contained in one large-sized room. It was perched on the top floor of a block near Baker Street. She enjoyed an uninterrupted view of the Metropolitan Railway and such shunting operations as are carried out in that busy centre, and she was as a rule free from callers; for there were no elevators in the block, and to climb up four steep flights of stairs was something of an undertaking.

Mr Gilder was not strong for physical exertion and cursed the parsimonious builder who had neglected to put in this easy method of transportation. Nevertheless he climbed, and presently was ringing at the polished bell of No. 37.

Mary had a daily servant, who was a charwoman in the morning, a parlourmaid in the afternoon and her own natural self after six, at which hour she left for the night. This aged woman, with her dingy white cap askew, opened the door and took the card in to her mistress, leaving Mr Gilder on the mat. She came back with an ingratiating smile, and pointed to the room where Mary was to be found.

"This is an unexpected pleasure, Mr Gilder," said Miss Wenner conventionally. "I'm sure I never thought that you would be as good as your word. Sit down, won't you?"

She really was pretty, he observed; in her plain house dress she was prettier than in a more elaborate attire. The flat, though small, was well but not expensively furnished. It left him with the impression that she had bought everything with her own money, and he had rather a nice feeling towards her in consequence. For Fabrian Gilder was a queer mixture of Puritan and adventurer. Later, Mary had her flat to thank for certain pleasant developments.

There was only one chair on which be could sit, and this he took.

"You'd like a cup of tea? I'm just going to have mine," said Miss Wenner. "I've been out all day shopping and everything."

"Are you – er – working?" asked Gilder delicately.

"No, I'm not in business," replied Miss Wenner, more correctly. "Only common people 'work': the gentility "go to business."

She went out, disappearing in a mysterious cupboard, which had just enough room for a tiny kitchen table and a gas-stove, and he heard the rattle of cup against saucer, the "plomp!" of a gas ring being lighted, and after a while she came back, a little flushed and apologetic.

"Maids are so stupid, aren't they?" she asked. "You can never trust these common daily people. I had an awfully nice maid, but she went away and got married, the stupid child!"

She received very few visitors, she told him. Her "sewing woman" came twice a week. She had a very dear friend – a girl, she hastened to assure him – who spent Tuesday evenings with her and sometimes slept in the flat. But a male visitor was the rarest of phenomena.

"You can't be too careful," said Miss Wenner primly. "A girl's character is her principal asset – don't you agree, Mr Gilder?"

Mr Gilder agreed.

"That is what I have always said about my work with Harry – excuse me, I mean Lord Chelford, only we were such awfully good friends that I've never dreamt of calling him by anything but his Christian name."

"And did you call Richard Alford by his Christian name?" asked Mr Gilder, not without malice.

Her nose went up in the air.

"Him!" she said contemptuously. "I don't take any more notice of him than I do of any of the other upper servants! He's educated and all that – went to Eton and Harrow" (even Mr Gilder winced at this), "but you judge a man by his manners and not by his education. There's no doubt at all that Dick Alford has the manners of a pig!"

She said this with feeling and no little vehemence. Mr Gilder, who knew something of the circumstances, understood and almost sympathised.

"I was going to say that down at Fossaway I often felt that it wasn't right to be in that big house with no lady there except the housekeeper, who, of course, is a servant, and – Oh! here you are, Gladys!"

28

She rose as Gladys brought in the tea-tray and laid it carefully on the table. Gladys was sixty, toothless and more or less chinless. She wore most of her hair in a bun, which overflowed, drooping over her neck in picturesque confusion. Gladys had the smile of one who enjoyed the privilege of entertaining a visitor. She smiled at the girl, smiled at Mr Gilder and smiled herself out of the room. Fabrian Gilder thought he had never seen a more ghastly exhibition.

"You're a good friend of Gine's, aren't you?" he asked, as he sipped his tea.

She dropped her eyes in maidenly embarrassment.

"We are rather good friends, but no more. We may be something closer – who knows? He has always behaved like a perfect gentleman and treated me like a lady. I must say that for Arthur. But he's a little trying; don't you find him so?" she asked, with a girlish naïveté that was a little overdone.

"I have left him," said Mr Gilder briefly. "He and I disagreed over a question of policy and I retired. In fact, we had a very bad row and came to blows – I tell you this because you'll probably learn the facts from him sooner or later."

Mary was shocked; and when Mary was shocked she covered her rather generous mouth with her two small, white hands.

"You don't tell me!" she said in a hushed voice. "Blows! Is that it?" She nodded her head to his lip.

"That's it," said Gilder shortly.

"Blows!" repeated Mary Wenner. "How perfectly disgusting and vulgar!"

"I wanted to talk to you about Arthur Gine," Gilder broke in upon her horrified wonder. "We're not good friends, but that doesn't mean I bear him any malice. But naturally, as we are parted, I don't feel called upon to protect him and stand between him and his dupes" – he emphasised the last word – "as I have done in the past. You know him as well as I do," he went on, as she was about to speak. "You know his vanity; you know how perfectly unreliable and insincere he is; you know too that he'd get out of any promise he ever made, even if it was in black and white."

He was watching her narrowly all the time he spoke, and now he saw her eyebrows arch.

"Indeed?" she said coldly. "I don't know anything about the law, but I can't see how a gentleman, or a common man for the matter of that, could get out of – what is the expression – legal obligations?"

"Then you don't know Arthur Gine as well as I do," he said. "But that is beside the point. I haven't come here to blackguard him or to make him look smaller in your eyes. Not that I could," he said, anticipating her protest a little ambiguously. "But I believe in a girl having a square deal, especially a working girl who may have nobody in the world to look after her interests. And I tell you that that fellow couldn't go straight if he was fired from a gun. Now what about the Chelford treasure?"

At the words she sat bolt upright, and a look of blank astonishment came to her face.

"Do you know?" she gasped.

"Of course I know! You're going to help him find the gold, and in return – " He paused.

That was exactly what he had come to find out. What obligation had Arthur undertaken in return for the information she would give him? And he was pretty sure of his ground. He knew the girl; had had some dealings with her when she was with Chelford; and since he lived on his knowledge of human beings, he had analysed her with more or less accuracy. He knew her vanity, her ambition; had heard something of her summary discharge from Fossaway Manor. There was only one reward that Arthur Gine could offer.

"He has promised to marry you," he said, and he was not altogether drawing a bow at a venture.

"Did he tell you that?" she said, with a little catch in her voice. "I hope you don't think, Mr Gilder, that I've thrown myself at his head? That I wouldn't do for the best man in the world." She looked at him thoughtfully, and added: "Old or young. I trust Arthur as a gentleman to fulfil any promise he has made. I am going to do something for him that will make all the difference in the world – "

"When is he going to marry you? After the treasure is discovered, I suppose?"

She nodded.

"He will have to marry me then," she said.

"I realise that. You're a girl that has to make her way in the world without influence, and possibly without friends." Mr Gilder knew he was on the right tack here. "He can offer you a position and you can offer him money. After all, that is exactly what his sister is doing, and nobody thinks any worse of her for that."

"Exactly," murmured Miss Wenner, who had never seen the matter in that light before.

"The point I want to make is this," he went on. "What bond has he given you?"

"His word of honour," said Miss Wenner dramatically.

"I daresay. But what valuable bond has he given you?"

"I'll show you."

She went into the next room, which was evidently her bedroom, and, returning with her bag, placed it on her knee, opened the flap and took out, amongst other things, a slip of paper, which she passed across to Mr Gilder. He read it at a glance, noted the careful emendation which Arthur had made, and passed it back.

"That is valueless," he said, and her face fell. "What is to prevent his going to Chelford and striking a bargain with him? Where do you come in then? Besides, this is what is known in law as a promise under duress – that is to say, under compulsion. If he is acting in the interests of his client, he can plead that he had to make this promise in order to secure information which you were illegally withholding."

She stared at him.

"It's not illegal to know and not to tell?"

He nodded.

"To know of the existence of hidden treasure and to withhold your information is a crime in some countries, and I daresay it is in England. But that's beside the point. Where do you come in, Miss Wenner?"

She bit her lip thoughtfully.

"I never saw it in that way," she confessed. "What can I do, Mr Gilder?"

"Get him to marry you first." He felt inclined to offer the obvious solution, but changed his mind. Mary Wenner married would be a useless ally.

At the back of his mind he was certain that this rather vulgar girl – for he had a nice and finicking taste in the matter of women – had discovered the Chelford millions. If he had not had this belief he would not have made his call. He believed that by some accident, or by reason of her close association with Harry Alford, she had unveiled the mystery of the lost gold; and his object now was to discover how far his theory was justified by facts.

"Is there no way of making that agreement more binding, Mr Gilder?" she asked. "You're a lawyer – couldn't you draw up something he wouldn't wriggle out of? Naturally, I'm too much of a lady to want any man to marry me if he doesn't want to marry me. If he just hinted as much I should tell him to go – I should simply say, 'Oh, very well, I'm not at all anxious to marry, thank you very much.' I think a girl who throws herself at a man's head is despicable, don't you, Mr Gilder?"

He did not answer this query.

"I could draw you up an agreement that would be legally binding, but I doubt if even that would help you. Why trust him at all?" he asked bluntly.

She dropped her eyes at this.

"Who, or whom, could I trust?" she asked, and took an invisible crumb off her dress. "This is such an awful world, and men are so very deceitful, Mr Gilder. The young ones are the worst, of course, but they haven't experience. I do think that a man isn't in the prime of life till he's about forty-five." She waited. "Or fifty. He's sort of settled down and sowed his wild oats, and he doesn't want to go out at nights and all that. And I'll admit that Arthur is flighty. I wouldn't tell it to anybody but you, but he tried to kiss me any number of times, and he once said the most terrible thing to me at Fossaway Manor. I said to him: 'Arthur, you seem to forget that you're speaking to a lady,' and he just curled up and died, if you understand me. I don't mean that he actually perished – "

"I understand what you mean," said Gilder, and went on to make his most startling revelation. "Now listen, Miss Wenner. You're a sensible girl and I can talk to you as I could talk to very few people."

This cliché of intensive flattery, which so seldom fails even when employed upon intelligent people, produced in Miss Wenner the strained attentiveness which was called for.

"Suppose I tell you," said Fabrian Gilder darkly, "that Gine is already trying to anticipate your discovery?"

"I beg your pardon?" Mary Wenner was not very strong on the more flowery expressions of speech.

"Suppose he's trying to get ahead of you – trying to find the gold without your assistance?"

"He wouldn't dare!" she gasped.

Mr Gilder nodded very slowly, very deliberately.

"He has already tried," he said. "Two nights ago I was watching him, suspecting his plan. He went at three o'clock in the morning to the ruins of Chelford Abbey, and he took with him a crowbar – "

Whilst he was speaking, the red in her face deepened and the wide-opened eyes grew brighter.

"The hound!" she breathed. "The twisting, double-faced monkey!"

It was not a ladylike expression, but for the moment she was superior to sham.

"The dirty, thieving, twisting sneak! To the abbey, with a crowbar? I'll take my oath on a Bible that I never breathed a word of where it was hid – I mean hidden. Let him go with his crowbar – ha, ha!" She laughed shrilly, but gave no other evidence of supreme amusement. "I'll crowbar him! Let him search and scrape and dig and see what he can find."

He tried to soothe her, but for the moment her soul was breaking in tumultuous waves upon the muddy flats of Arthur's duplicity.

"He has deceived me! I don't mean in an unladylike way – I mean – you know what I mean, Mr Gilder? I trusted that man. I gave him all my heart." The sob came naturally, but it was largely due to intensified annoyance. "I gave him all that a woman could give a man – information I mean, Mr Gilder – I don't want you to get any wrong ideas about me, because I've always behaved like a lady, and nobody can point their fingers of scorn at me."

She grew calm after a while.

"Who can you trust?" she asked bitterly. "Who – can – you – trust?"

"You can trust me." Fabrian Gilder's voice was very gentle, almost pleading.

He was rather a good-looking man, she observed; his grey hair gave him distinction.

"You wouldn't want a legal document from me."

"Yes, I would," she said obstinately. "I don't trust men."

"You shall have any document you wish. I will even go as far as compromising myself hopelessly."

She coughed.

"I don't think I should go quite as far as that," she said, misunderstanding him.

"I mean that I would take the risk of detection, without safeguarding myself as Arthur Gine has done."

She dabbed her eyes with her pocket-handkerchief.

"Of course, Mr Gilder, I don't know you very well, but I'm not going to say that I don't like you. I've always said to Agatha – my Tuesday friend, as I call her – 'Mr Gilder's a perfect gentleman.' In fact, I'm – Mr Gilder, what is your Christian name?"

"Fabrian," he said.

She lingered tenderly over the word and smiled, a wistful sideways smile.

"I should call you Fabe, I suppose? It's a perfectly lovely name. As I was saying, I don't want to throw myself at any man's head."

"Let us go down tonight."

Her face changed.

"To the abbey – tonight?"

He nodded.

"My car will get us down in an hour and a half, and we can wait till it's dark; and unless there's a lot of digging to be done – "

"There is no digging," she said. "But tonight?"

"Why not?" he demanded. "My cottage is less than a mile from the abbey. If the gold is there and reachable, we could get away with enough to make us rich for life."

She pondered this, and then:

"I know you'll think it horrid of me, Mr Gilder – Fabe – that does sound familiar, doesn't it? – but I would like something in black and white."

There and then Mr Fabrian Gilder produced a document that was enough, as he observed jocularly, to hang him, and, reading it, even Mary Wenner, with her keen instinct for safeguards, was impressed. He wrote the agreement with his own fountain pen, on paper which he provided, and he had brought along that pen in his pocket with a view to such a contingency. It was a new pen, filled with an ink that he had purchased at a novelty store in Wardour Street, and which was guaranteed to fade within six hours of writing.

Miss Wenner read it through, folded it and put it into her bag, and disappeared into her bedroom. She came back with the bag, but he guessed that the agreement was disposed in some safe place.

"Now, Fabe, what time do you want to start?"

"At nine-thirty?" he suggested, and she nodded.

"And don't trouble to bring a crowbar," she said a little viciously, as she remembered Arthur Gine's rank treachery. "I'll carry all the tools we want in my bag."

29

The weather had changed that afternoon. Big black clouds had come up from the west; a steady drizzle of rain had set in when Fabrian Gilder brought his car to the rendezvous in Marylebone Road. He had pulled up the hood, and, as a matter of precaution, he had cleared out every portable thing from the tonneau. If there was gold he must find room for it, and he made a careful calculation as to the weight he could carry on each journey.

He was surprised at himself that he had accepted as a fact so readily that there was gold to be taken. From the girl he learned for the first time the extent of the treasure. He had inquired casually of his garage man the amount of strain the back axle would stand. That was unnecessary, for he had once driven four fairly heavy men a considerable journey. Supposing they weighed 170 pounds, that would be the equivalent of twenty bars of gold.

It was nearly ten before the girl appeared. She was wearing a long raincoat and stepped into the seat by his side with a voluble apology.

"I nearly didn't come," she said. "I only just remembered after you'd gone that awful Black Abbot."

He was a little amused.

"You don't believe in that kind of hokum, do you?" he asked, as the car went swiftly down Baker Street.

"I don't know." She was dubious. "He did appear once or twice when I was at the Manor, but we used to believe that these were villagers' stories. According to the newspapers they've seen more of him lately – ugh!" She shivered.

He tapped his pocket significantly with his hand.

"I've got something here that's mighty bad for abbots black or white!" he said. "Don't you worry, little girl."

"No, Fabe," she said meekly.

Very delicately he suggested that she might call him by the Christian name his parents had given him. There was no diminutive, he explained, and excused his correction by telling her that there was a possibility that she might address him and he would not know to whom she was speaking.

"I don't believe in long engagements, do you?" she went off at a tangent.

"No, I don't. They should be short – and sweet!"

They both laughed together, and were in excellent humour by the time they reached the deserted streets of Dorking.

"I only have one anxiety," he told her. "Mr Richard Alford has got a habit of prowling round at odd hours. On a night like this he'll hardly leave his comfortable apartment."

"Comfortable apartment!" she scoffed. "Why, he's only got a tiny little office, and his bedroom's not much bigger than mine. I simply detest the man. He gives himself more airs in a day than dear Harry gives himself in ten years – you don't mind me saying dear Harry? You're not jealous, are you?"

He assured her he was not at all jealous.

"I should have married Harry if it hadn't been for him. Harry was simply crazy about me, but Dick hated me – how that man hated me! Mind you, I've always snubbed him when he got a little too fresh. I don't say that he was chasing me – I hate girls who think every man is after them – but he was certainly very attentive once or twice. After lunch or dinner he'd get up and open the door for me, and that's a thing that Harry never did. But of course I saw through it. It was all deceit and artfulness."

She chattered at rare intervals, except during the five miles of driving rain that forced its way under the cover and lashed her face.

"It's a horrible night," she complained.

"On the contrary, it's one of the best nights I could have chosen even if I had the ordering of the weather," said Mr Gilder.

When they reached the secondary road that led to Chelfordbury he proceeded with greater caution, extinguishing the flaming head-lamps and relying upon the two small lights that were placed on the front mudguard. He knew the road so well that there was no danger of mishap; his chief anxiety was that he should not, by the reflected rays of the bigger headlights, be recognised.

A mile from Fossaway Manor he switched out the remaining two lights, for he had a shrewd idea that this section of the road was visible from Lord Chelford's house. To the nervous girl riding at his side, it seemed that they were in imminent danger every minute of colliding with one of the telegraph posts which ran along the side of the road. Happily she was not aware that the smaller lamps had been extinguished.

"Don't worry," he assured her. "I know every inch of this road; I've driven up it a hundred times. My cottage lies just beyond Willow House."

The car, which had been moving silently and smoothly, began to slow as it went up the hill that led to Fontwell Cutting. He switched off the engine, and, jamming on the brakes, got out and opened the gate into Red Farm field. Then, walking alongside the car, he released the brakes and guided it to the place where Dick had found the machine a few nights before.

"Here we are," he said.

He took her arm; she was shivering, and when she spoke he heard the chatter of her teeth.

"I wish I hadn't come," she said, started, and pointed into the dark. "What is that over there?" she whispered fearfully.

"A pollard willow," he said. "Really there's nothing to be afraid of – Mary."

"I don't know about that," she quavered. "Don't let go of my arm, will you? Have you got a pistol?"

He assured her that he had.

Through the little gate, which he knew was unlocked, up the steep and slippery slope, and immediately ahead of them in the darkness were the solemn ruins.

"I'd rather not show a light," he said in a low voice. "That was how Gine was discovered. Do you know your way?"

"If I can see the tower," she suggested.

Stooping down to get an artificial skyline, he saw the bulk of the ruined tower and guided her forward. Once she stumbled over a heap of stones, and would have screamed if his hand had not covered her mouth.

"For God's sake be careful!" he urged. "Now how do we get to the vault?"

"Wait." She released his arm and went towards the wall of the tower. He saw her once more, when she was groping her way round. Presently she whispered: "Come along."

He followed her, and reaching out her hand she took his.

"There's a step down," she whispered.

They were going into the tower, although he did not remember having seen any opening. He heard a rusty squeak.

"It's very narrow; you'll have to squeeze through."

The opening, he judged, was about a foot wide, and he had some trouble to pass the obstacle.

"It's a big corner stone," she said, in a low voice. "It swings round and opens like a door. It's the way the old Abbot used to go out when he carried on with Lady Chelford – you've beard that bit of scandal, I suppose?"

The "bit of scandal" was some eight hundred years old and was news to him.

"If you've got a lamp you can put it on."

He pulled out his torch and turned the switch. They were in a tiny stone chamber at the top of a circular flight of moss-grown stairs. Above was a vaulted roof, which seemed to be cut out of one piece of stone, as it might well be, for the interior measurements of the tower could not have been much more than four by five. The thickness of the walls he could judge; they had been built in the days when walls had other functions than to support a roof.

"Come along." She led the way, stepping gingerly on the slithery moss.

He counted twenty-five steps, and then they were in a large stone chamber, so weather-worn that it seemed to be a natural cave. Walls and roof had lost their symmetry, and only the square of it told him that it was the work of man's hands.

"Have you got the key?"

He nodded. Many years before, Gine & Gine had defended a famous burglar and had secured his acquittal on a technical error in the indictment. In reward he had presented to his lawyer a key which he claimed would open any door, big or small. It was a curious contrivance, consisting of a steel rod into the end of which strangely shaped projections could be screwed. Arthur had given it to his head clerk as a souvenir, having no interest in such matters himself, and rather scandalised that the firm was engaged in so discreditable a business as defending a burglar. This souvenir had now become an instrument of providence.

"Here is the place." She still spoke in a whisper, though it was hardly likely they could be overheard.

In each corner of the room, facing them as they turned from the foot of the stairs, was a small, narrow door, deeply recessed. They reminded Mr Gilder of the cell doors in Dartmoor, and there was a further likeness in another respect. Near the top of the left-hand door was a tiny iron grille, consisting of three rusted bars.

"Look!" she whispered.

He flashed the light of the lamp inside, where a deep, narrow cavern showed, along two sides of which ran a stone bench, and on the bench were innumerable cylinders of significant shape. He inspected the nearest; there was a curious seal at one end.

Fabrian Gilder's heart beat faster. The girl's hand that held his arm tightly was trembling.

"I'm so frightened," she whimpered.

"What are you frightened about?"

"I'm so afraid of that awful Black Abbot." She was on the verge of hysterical breakdown. He must work quickly.

He was fitting one of the accessories to the rod, and he pushed it in the big keyhole and turned. There was a grind and a click, but when he pulled the door it was fast. Again he tried, fitting another steel accessory, and on the third attempt the key turned with a horrible squeak, and he pulled the door open.

As he did so, the girl gripped his arm frenziedly.

"Look! Oh, my God! Look!" she screamed, and he turned.

Standing at the foot of the stairs was a figure in black, his face hidden under a long cowl. Two eyes they saw, gleaming feverishly upon them. Terrible, menacing, the Black Abbot was coldly surveying them!

30

With an oath, Gilder whipped a pistol from his pocket, but in doing so the beam of his lamp fell for a second. When he brought it up again, pistol extended, the figure had vanished.

"Don't go, don't go!" she shrieked, gripping his arm. "Oh, Mr Gilder! Oh, Fabrian, don't leave me!"

He thrust her aside and ran to the foot of the winding stairs and went cautiously up. He heard the sobbing breath of the girl coming behind him.

"Don't leave me! Don't leave me in the dark!" she sobbed.

Higher, higher, cautious, watchful, but no sign of a black habit. The little room above was as they had left it; the tiny slit of a door was open.

Brushing past him, the girl stumbled and staggered into the open air and collapsed on to her knees.

"Take me away! Take me away!" she raved. "I wish I had never come!"

Gilder turned with a curse and swung the stone door closed, then, half-carrying, half-dragging her, beside himself with fury, in which was mingled no little fear, he brought her to the road and to the car.

The rain was pouring down. He pushed back the hood of the car savagely, so that the full force of the storm should beat upon her – he dare not allow himself to be burdened with a fainting girl. He would take her back to her flat and leave her – there would be plenty of time for him to return and investigate those cylinders.

As for the Black Abbot – He breathed a little more quickly when he thought of that terrifying appearance. Whoever it was – and that it was human he did not doubt – they would live to regret their interference. By the time they reached Horsham, the girl, drenched to the skin, cold and shivering, had got back a little of her balance. Her teeth were chattering, but not with fear. She was inclined to be garrulous, but he answered in monosyllables or not at all.

"I wonder I didn't die," she said. "I've never seen anything so perfectly horribly ghastly! Did you see the way his eyes glared? They looked as if they were alight, didn't they, Fabe?"

"Fabrian," he snapped.

"I never saw anything like it, not even in the pictures," said Miss Wenner. "Couldn't we have the hood up, Fabe – Fabrian?"

He stopped the car with a jerk, pulled up the hood and fastened it.

"What are you going to do?"

"I'm taking you home. We'll make another attempt tomorrow night. By the way, how did you get that stone corner piece to turn?"

"I can't tell you that, Fabrian," she said firmly and truly. "That's my only hold over you."

"Don't be stupid. You used a bodkin or something, didn't you? I noticed there was a space between two stones which looked to be artificial."

"A pair of scissors," she said. "There's an iron catch inside that slit – I only found it by accident."

He knew all he wanted to know now; could dispense with her for the rest of the night, for ever, as it happened. He declined her invitation to come upstairs for a drink and no sooner was she out of sight than he was flying back into Sussex.

Halfway between Dorking and Leatherhead, his petrol gave out, and he had to wait on the charity of a passing motorist, and it was not a night when traffic was very thick. At last he found a Good Samaritan who gave him enough to take the machine to the nearest filling station, and at Dorking, with his tank replenished and a few extra tins against emergency, he went on confidently.

Two o'clock showed on the illuminated dial of his watch when he backed the car into the field and mounted the slope to the ruins. From here onward he moved noiselessly, one step at a time, stopping every few paces to listen. But there was no sign or sound of the masked man.

He found the corner of the tower, with his penknife pressed back the catch, and, pulling at the rough stone, the edges of which crumbled in his hand, he opened the door.

Stopping only to examine the upper chamber, he went slowly down the stairs, his pistol in one hand, his lamp in the other. There was no sign of the intruder, but –

The door of the treasure-house was closed. He pulled, and it swung open. Flashing his lamp into the long, narrow cell, he saw something that sent the blood from his face. The "ingots" had disappeared, every one of them! Neither the bench to the left nor right held a single cylinder. Beads of perspiration were running down his face as he turned, and it would have been death to any human spook who opposed him, for his heart was bitter against whoever it was had checked his enterprise.

He made another inspection of the underground chamber. Unlike its fellow, the second door in the opposite corner of the room was solid. Neither peep-hole nor grating gave a view into the room it guarded. He guessed that behind the nail-studded portal was a similar room to that in which the cylinders had been stored. Trying his key on the lock, he could produce no result. He put his shoulder to the oaken face, but the door did not budge by so much as a fraction of an inch.

Before this room the flooring consisted of a long slab of stone that ran without a break to the centre of the apartment, and was the exact width of the narrow doorway. Had this any significance? Kneeling, he examined the stone carefully. It was different from the rest of the paving. The broken stones that formed the floor of the room were worn smooth by the passage of generations of men; this oblong strip was rough-dressed, more like the underside of a paving-stone than its chiselled surface. He stamped on one end and felt it give ever so slightly; stamped on the other end and had a like experience. In the middle ran a staple, balancing the stone, and beneath there was a hollow space. Some day or night he would come along and conduct a more careful inspection.

He came into the upper room to confront a more urgent problem. Just as he was about to extinguish his lamp preparatory to passing through the opening, he saw the stone move. Before he could spring forward it had thudded into its place. From somewhere outside he heard an unearthly chuckle of laughter.

Trapped! He pushed at the door, but it was inflexible. Inch by inch he examined its surface. There must be an opening somewhere, he thought. He remembered the story of the amorous Abbot and his clandestine excursions. It was certain that a means existed for opening the door from the inside.

He searched the wall; nothing appeared. And then it occurred to him to send his light slowly along the floor, which was made up of broken flagstones. One, smaller than the others, attracted his attention, because it lay at a truer level than the rest, and he tugged at its end, and, with great effort, pulled it up. Beneath he saw a great iron ring, so rusted that it was almost razor-thin. With his handkerchief he gripped it and pulled. It gave a little, and, as it did so, he saw the door move. Again he strained at the handle, and slowly it came up; although the door had moved only an inch he knew it was clear of the invisible catch which held it. Running to the stone, he pressed with all his might. It swung open and he came staggering out into the eerie light of dawn.

The storm had passed; overhead, the stars were shining in the paling sky. Far away to his left a wisp of smoke curled up from the twisted chimneys of Fossaway Manor. Fabrian Gilder wiped his hot face and strove to overcome the bitterness of his defeat. And then, at his feet, he saw something and, stooping with a cry, picked it up. It was one of the cylinders, heavy and laden, that had been dropped by those who had cleared the vault. It was not heavy enough for gold. He knew that at once. The cover was of lead. He tore away the seal, expecting to find an opening, but the cylinder had been sealed at both ends. He carried it quickly down the slope, and in the shelter of the cut road he took out his knife and slit the thin lead end, and pulled out a tightly rolled sheet of parchment. He opened it and stared. It was an ancient missal, beautifully painted and, as a work of art, priceless, but a poor substitute for thirty-five pounds weight of solid gold!

31

And that was all the other cylinders contained, he thought, with a gleam of satisfaction. Whoever had watched him – and he suspected Arthur Gine naturally – had had the same disappointment.

It was in this room that the old monks had stored their ancient music; there was a certain grim humour in the thought of how he had spent his night and the reward for it.

He crossed the road, opened the gate and went into the field where he had left his car, and stood stockstill, petrified with amazement. The car had disappeared!

The tracks were plainly visible. They led through the cutting, along the road towards Willow House. There was nothing to do but to tramp after them. A mile beyond Arthur Gine's residence was Ravensrill Cottage, his own property, he thought with some satisfaction, and a snug retreat where a man could get a hot bath in an hour and a steaming cup of tea in a quarter. The prospect was cheering, for he was wet through, weary and footsore.

The tracks passed the entrance of Willow House and continued on the way to the cottage; and when at last he turned the bend of the road that brought his little country home into view, he saw the car standing before the door. There was no sign of any living creature. He went round the house, searched the tiny plantation to the left, and even descended to the banks of the stream, before he opened the door of his cottage and went in.

He put the key in the lock and, to his surprise, on the pressure of his hand, the door opened. The door which opened into his little dining-room yielded to his pressure before he could turn the key. He gazed, stricken dumb with amazement. A small fire was burning in the grate, on which a kettle was steaming. An open teapot was on the hearth, and somebody had broken open a tin of biscuits. He heard a footstep in the next room and swung round to meet the intruder; and at the sight of him he dropped the point of his levelled Browning.

"Thomas!" he said, unable to believe his eyes. "What the devil are you doing here?"

"Fired this morning," said the ex-footman curtly.

"This morning? Why, it's hardly daylight!"

Thomas nodded.

"Alford found me wandering about the house when I ought to have been in bed and asleep," he said, "and he hoofed me out."

"But why?"

The man was uncomfortable.

"How do I know why?" he demanded. "That dog never liked me. I think he suspected me of writing to you."

Gilder knew that this story was a lie, designed to show him under an obligation to this ex-servant. Thomas had been a useful correspondent of his: all that went on at Fossaway Manor had been faithfully recorded for his information.

"You are in trouble. What have you been doing?"

The man pursed his lips.

"Well," he hesitated, "I may as well tell you the truth. Have you ever heard of Monkey Puttler? Wait a minute, I'll make the tea."

He picked up the steaming kettle and filled the pot, and not till he had put it back on the hob did he continue his narrative.

"Monkey Puttler's a 'busy.' Every crook in London knows him, and I know him as well as anybody because he got me three years for a job I did at the Westinghouse Hotel."

"Burglary?" asked the other, to whom this was news. "An inside job," said Thomas tersely. "You can call it burglary if it gives you any pleasure. Anyway, Monkey caught me and pushed me over the Alps for three long and weary ones. When I came out I got this job. There were pickings to it too. Chelford isn't a man who counts his change, and

Alford doesn't dare ask him what he's done with his money when he comes for more."

"An ex-convict, eh?" Gilder was slightly shocked and regarded the man from a new angle. "I didn't know that or I should never have employed you!"

"I had to kid a bit," confessed Thomas, with a grin. "You kidded me all right!" replied Gilder. "Well, I didn't exactly kid you," said the other, amused. "But that day when I went to your office and you started cross-examining me about how things were at the Manor with Gine, I didn't see why I shouldn't earn a few honest dollars."

"Well? Go on about your friend Monkey – what is his name?"

"Puttler. He came yesterday."

"To Chelford's house?" asked Gilder in surprise.

"Yes," nodded Thomas. "Alford pretended he is an accountant, but he's a busy all right; I knew him the moment I saw him, and, what's worse, he knew me. I'd come to Chelford's service on a false character and I knew my number was up as soon as I saw his ugly phiz. Sure enough, last night Alford gave me notice, told me to clear out today. I'll catch that bird one of these days," he said, with an ugly look in his face.

"But why this morning?" asked Gilder.

"I was going to tell you," said the other impatiently. "Chelford keeps a cash-box in his library; it's in the second left-hand drawer, and he's generally got a wad of stuff there. He's childish in the matter of money. I knew if I could get my hooks into the stuff I could lift enough to be happy, and leave enough behind so that Chelford couldn't swear whether I'd had it or not. I got into the library about four this morning, and was going upstairs when Alford spotted me, told me to go up and dress and clear, which I did. He's got something on his mind, that fellow, he never sleeps!"

"He caught you with the money?" asked Gilder in disgust.

"Not he – I shoved that out of the library window as soon as I got it. I picked it up later."

"What was Mr Alford doing, wandering about the house at that hour?"

The man made a grimace.

"You never know when that bird is around," he said. "He's not human; I tell you he doesn't want sleep!"

Though Gilder was certain he was telling the truth, yet he was equally sure that the man was concealing something. There seemed to him to be gaps in his story, which he bridged readily enough. Wisely he decided that it was not the moment to cross-examine him. On one point he made up his mind. This man and he must part company, and soon.

"Why did you come here?"

"Thought you were in London," said the other coolly. "I've been here before to see you, and I didn't think you'd mind my using your house for a day or two – maybe a week or two," he added, his eyes fixed on the other's face.

Gilder scratched his chin thoughtfully.

"I don't know that it will do me much good if it's known that you're an ex-convict."

"They needn't know; why should they?" said the other.

"Did you bring my car here?"

Thomas nodded.

"I was going over to Red Farm first; there's a groom there who's a friend of mine. Then I saw your car and thought something had happened to you. I waited for a time, and when you didn't turn up I brought it along."

"Did anybody see you?"

"Nobody. It was nearly dark."

What was the man concealing? The impression that Gilder had – and he was a skilful reader of minds – was that Thomas was bursting with some vital information. Once or twice it had been at the end of his tongue, and he had inhibited the sensation.

"You can stay here if you like; I'm going to town. If I get a letter from the local police saying you're living in the house, I shall write saying that you have no authority. You understand that I must protect myself?"

"I can understand that, guv'nor."

Again his lips moved to speak, and again he checked himself.

"What do you want to tell me?"

"It's too big to tell. I am going to keep it. Maybe if you come down later I'll spin you a story that's worth a million dollars."

Thomas had once spent twelve months in a Canadian penitentiary, and it was his favourite pose that he was an American crook.

"A million dollars – yep!"

32

Gilder poured out the tea, helped himself to biscuits, and, his hunger appeased, went into his room, and from a bureau took a complete change of clothes. The water was too cold for a bath, and he had a rub down with a rough towel as a substitute. He felt another man when shaved and clean and warm. He came back to Thomas, who was smoking a short briar pipe, peering into the fire.

"When you've decided to talk, you had better send me a wire – not from Chelfordbury, but from Horsham."

He wrote his address on a page of his notebook, tore it out and gave it to the man, then, cranking up his car, he went back through the dull morning to London.

At ten o'clock he was roused from a heavy sleep to answer the telephone. It was Mary Wenner, and he cursed her under his breath.

"Is that you, Fabe? I've been so worried about you all night, my dear. You didn't go back to that awful place?"

"I'll come and see you this afternoon," he interrupted. "Don't talk on the telephone: people can hear."

"Fabe, dear" – there was a note of real anxiety in her voice – "you didn't go back and get any of that gold, did you? I know you're awfully brave, but I wouldn't have you risk your life for the world."

"No, I didn't get any gold," he said.

"Oh!" she replied, and in that "Oh!" was disappointment and annoyance. "It wasn't so bad for you, a man," she said, with some asperity in her tone. "Here I've been laying in bed all night thinking of you, and worrying about you – "

"I will see you this afternoon," he rasped, and hung up the receiver.

He had no intention of seeing her that afternoon or any other afternoon, but in this matter his will was not the determining factor. Soon after tea, when he was preparing to go out, she walked into his dining-room unannounced. What she had told his servants, he shuddered to think. She passed swiftly across to him, stooped and kissed him chastely on the brow, and then seated herself by his side.

"Dear," she said, and he closed his eyes patiently, "do you mind if I do something that seems a teeny-weeny bit deceitful?"

"I don't mind—" he began.

"But this is something which affects your honour, dear." Her sober eyes were fixed on his. "You must never think I'm not faithful to you and all that sort of thing, but he's written to me such a pleading letter—"

"Who has written?" he asked, suddenly interested.

"Arthur. I've also had a letter from his sister; she wants me to go down and spend the weekend with them, and of course I'd much rather stay up here with you. But I feel I ought to have it out with Arthur and let him know that my affections are no longer his. After all, even if we didn't get the fortune, I know that I'm dealing with a gentleman who doesn't want me for my money alone. And you're not exactly a pauper, are you, dear? I went and asked a young gentleman I know at Stubbs' Agency, and they told me that you were worth at least a hundred thousand pounds."

Gilder groaned.

"And I have your promise, in writing."

"Yes, you've got everything, my dear Mary," he said wearily.

"And, Fabe, dear, such a curious thing happened about that paper. When I took it from under my pillow this morning, what do you think? All the writing had disappeared! You could have knocked me down with a feather."

He stirred uneasily in his chair.

"That is most extraordinary," he found words to say. "I was so upset about it that I took it to a gentleman friend of mine, who's in the conjuring business. You've probably seen him: he takes rabbits out of paper bags, and he says that you must have used invisible ink, and he showed me how to bring the writing back and make it permanent."

"And did you?" asked Gilder hollowly.

"Why, of course I did, dear. You just squeeze a lemon, rub it over the paper and hold it in front of the fire."

Gilder's head reeled. All he could say was "Oh!" This was awkward – very awkward; but it was a difficulty that might easily be surmounted. At the worst he could buy her off for a thousand, and the promise of marriage was contingent. Still, it was a very unpleasant document to be produced even in a breach of promise case; for, strong in the faith of the invisible quality of his ink, he had made an agreement which was very damaging to himself.

"Are you going to stay with the Gines?"

"I think so, dear." The hesitation was assumed, he knew; she had already made up her mind. "I really think that I ought to go. Arthur, of course, is a very old friend, and although he's nothing to me, any more than the dirt beneath my feet, and I should no more think of throwing myself at his head than I should of flying to the moon, well, I feel I ought to go."

"Then for heaven's sake go!" he said curtly, and she murmured her thanks, and would have lingered on, but he accompanied her to the door and opened it very pointedly.

He gathered that, whilst she held him to his promise, she had not altogether lost hope of bringing Arthur Gine to heel.

She had hardly left the place before a telegraph boy arrived. Gilder was expecting a wire from one of his bookmaking businesses, now in process of liquidation, since their only client had passed from active operations. The telegram was addressed from a village five miles from Chelfordbury and ran:

Get down here as fast as you can. Big news for you.

It was signed "T."
Would Thomas talk? And what had he to say?

33

The groom who brought Dick Alford's horse to the door had a report to make.

"That fellow was seen last night, sir."

"Which fellow is this?" asked Dick, as he swung into the saddle.

"The Black Abbot, sir. Gill, the gamekeeper up at Long Meadow Cottage, saw him at four o'clock this morning walking through the Long Meadow. By the time Gill got his gun he'd vanished."

"And what was the Black Abbot doing in the Long Meadow?" asked Dick sardonically. "Picking buttercups?"

"It's rather late for buttercups, sir," said the unimaginative groom. "But Gill says that if he'd had his gun he'd have taken a pot at him."

"And there would have been an inquest, and the best Gill could hope for would be a verdict of justifiable homicide. You can tell Gill from me that the Black Abbot is to be tackled – by hand! A live ghost will tell us a lot, but a dead ghost is practically useless as an information bureau."

He cantered through the home meadows, behind the house, and, avoiding the abbey ruins, rejoined the winding Ravensrill. Setting his horse at a walk, he followed the bank of the stream, his mind so completely occupied by the events of the past twenty-four hours that he would have passed unnoticed the girl who was lying face downward on the opposite bank.

It was a glorious morning, warm and sunny. The sky was an unblemished blue, the world was bathed in yellow radiance.

Overhead, a flight of migratory birds were moving southward, and the faint chatter of them came down to him.

"Good morning, Sir Galahad!"

He reined in his horse and looked round in bewilderment. Presently he saw her.

"Good morning, Guinevere!" he said, and, turning his horse's head to the stream, he came gingerly down the slope and sent the reluctant hack into the water.

"Be careful!"

"There's a ford here," he said. "In fact," as he emerged with his horse's girth dripping, "this is the original Chelford. Knights in armour, and probably Britons in feathers and woad, have crossed Ravensrill at this spot. What on earth are you doing?"

He slipped to the ground, dropping the reins, and allowed his mount to forage at will. She was lying now at full length, but resting on her elbows. Immediately beneath her face was a slab of rock in the centre of which a hole some eighteen inches in diameter had been worn. When he saw this he laughed softly.

"Leslie, what questions have you to ask the Wishing Well?"

Why it was called the Wishing Well he had never learnt – no water had ever risen from that deep cavity, which, by some freak of nature, extended to unplumbed depths. Yet here, generations of country swains had come to prostrate themselves and bellow into the cavity the burden of their hearts' desire. And tradition had it that the well answered them clearly and intelligibly.

"I'm asking about me." Her face was pink, probably from her unusual posture.

"And what said the well?" he mocked.

She scrambled to her knees and pushed back the hair from her forehead.

"I'll not tell you – ask something!"

With a growl and a groan he stretched himself on the warm grass and, hollowing his hands, roared into the crevice: "What is going to happen to Leslie?"

They waited, and then the echo came back, queerly distorted yet distinct.

"Marry her!"

They laughed together. It was the trick of some hollow place below that through the ages had sent back the same reply to every question.

He got up to his feet.

"I wish you wouldn't wander around without my escort," he said seriously, and she laughed.

Never had he seen her looking more beautiful than that morning. She was a thing of air and sunlight, a baffling unreality that did not belong to the sordid world in which he was living.

"I got up early and was bored, so I went walking, and then I thought of the well and wondered whether it had learnt any new tricks. Arthur's very conscious of his eye and he won't go out until his face is normal. Poor Arthur!" She hesitated, looking at him. "You haven't found – " She did not finish the sentence.

"The gentleman who did the shooting? No, but we have a pretty shrewd idea. By the way, I have fired Thomas. You remember that hangdog footman who was always near at hand when he shouldn't have been."

"What has he done?" she asked.

"Nothing particular. He is an ex-convict: Puttler recognised him as soon as he arrived; and I found him at three o'clock this morning coming out of the library and made him turn out his pockets. He had no very considerable sum of money in his possession, but the chances are that he had cashed it. Poor old Harry is such a slacker in the matter of keeping accounts that it will be almost impossible to secure a conviction. Of course, Thomas swore the money I found – not a large amount – was his, and as it meant a fuss in waking up Harry, who I am perfectly sure could have given me no information, I allowed the brute to get away with it."

"Where is he now?"

"Thomas? I expect he caught the first train for London. I don't suppose he'll be applying for a job in the neighbourhood, but to be on the safe side you had better tell your brother."

There was a moment of silence, then she asked: "Did you find the rifle?"

He shook his head.

"It was an Army rifle, but there isn't such a thing at Fossaway Manor, though there are plenty in the village. In fact, nearly a dozen of our people working on the estate are Territorials. Puttler says that a poacher's gang was responsible."

Dick was a poor liar, but Leslie suspected nothing and did not question this theory. If she had, she might have pointed out that poachers use shotguns and snares, and that the rifle as an instrument for the destruction of game was about as valuable as a steam-hammer for tacking down carpets.

They walked across the field towards Willow House, Dick leading his horse.

"I want you to make me a promise, Leslie," he said. "What is it?" she asked, knowing before he spoke what it would be.

"I want you to promise me not to take these early morning walks, to use your car and to keep to the roads."

Her eyebrows rose.

"Why? Surely there is no danger? You're not afraid of the Black Abbot?"

But he did not answer her smile.

"No," he said, "I'm not afraid especially of the Black Abbot, but I'm very much afraid of the something that is behind the Black Abbot."

She knew that he did not wish to be questioned further, and changed the subject. She had a visitor coming, she told him, and only when she told him who it was did his eyes twinkle.

"Good Lord! That lady? I suppose you realise you're harbouring a dangerous rival?"

"Don't be horrid, Dick. The poor girl was very fond of Harry, and in the letter she wrote to me she told me that she hoped I wouldn't be embarrassed by her coming – "

"She would say that," said Dick grimly.

" – and that she had almost forgotten Harry's stupid infatuation."
Dick stopped to laugh.

"Can you beat that?" he asked, with tears in his eyes. "Jumping
snakes! 'Harry's stupid infatuation!' Well, I won't be ungenerous."

"Don't," she warned him. "I'm rather sorry for the girl."

"Don't," he mimicked. "You need never be sorry for Mary. If you
keep her off the subject of me, you'll have a very pleasant weekend.
But in the matter of Richard Alford she is a fanatic. I won't tell you
the horrid things she says of me, because it would prejudice
you against her."

"How do you know?" she challenged. "Quite a number of people
say horrid things about Richard Alford."

"Not to you," he said quietly, and she flushed, and again changed
the subject.

"I don't know why I'm up so early; I didn't go to bed till two."

"It was ten minutes past two when your light went out," he said
promptly, and she stared at him.

"How do you know?"

"I happened to be passing your house."

He was in such a hurry to explain that she was suspicious.

"The Black Abbot was about last night. Puttler and I did a little
ghost-hunting."

"Did you see him?"

He shook his head.

"Nobody saw him except a terrified gamekeeper."

Suddenly she turned to him with a little gasp of surprise.

"It *was* you!" she accused.

"What was me?"

"I am sure I saw somebody at the lower end of the drive. You were
smoking a cigar: I could see the little red glow; and at first I thought
it was Harry, and this morning I found the end of the cigar near the
lodge gates. Richard Alford, do you ever sleep?"

"Frequently," he said, with a smile, and put his arm round her shoulder. "I'm being brotherly: take no alarm," he mocked her. "Leslie, dear, will you promise?"

"What?" she asked.

"Not to wander through the fields at odd hours. I don't want to alarm you – I feel a brute as it is – but there may be real danger for the next day or two. Please don't ask me what it is, because I can't tell you; I'm not so sure that I know."

She turned this over in her mind for a long time.

"Has it to do with the Chelford treasure?" she asked, and, to her surprise, he nodded.

34

In sight of her house he left her, and, remounting his horse, cantered away. She watched him until a bend of the road hid him from view, and then with a little sigh she walked slowly towards her home.

What was the mystery? She had never taken the Black Abbot very seriously, believing that the apparition had its origin in a stupid practical joke carried out by a villager with an histrionic bent. The legend she knew: Dick had told her, and Harry, who kept alive all the legends of the family, had described in detail the eight-hundred-year-old murder. But how was the Black Abbot affecting her? And what was the meaning of this close guard that Dick Alford was keeping on her? She had no doubt that it was he who was watching the house in the early hours of the morning.

In the night she had reached a momentous decision. It had been made after long thought and heart-searching, and she would have given everything to have had the courage to have told Dick that morning. But in that bright, sunlit world she was averse from hurting him. But would he be hurt? Her life's future hung on that question.

She had been dimly conscious that a man was standing before the gate of Willow House. She had seen him when she was some distance away, and now, as she drew near, she had a feeling that he was waiting to speak to her. He was tall and wearing an ill-fitting grey suit and a golf cap; from his lips drooped a limp cigarette. He took his hands out of his pockets as she came near and touched his cap, and then she recognised the ill-favoured Thomas, the ex-footman.

"Good morning, miss," he said.

"Good morning, Thomas."

She viewed with more interest than she had done heretofore the lank, awkwardly made man.

"I wonder if I can have a word with you, miss?"

She hesitated.

"I am afraid I can do nothing for you, Thomas," she said. "Mr Alford tells me he has discharged you."

He forced a grin.

"Mr Alford never did like me, miss," he said. "I've been falsely accused, and I'm going to see my lawyer when I get to town. One minute, miss," he said hastily, as she was opening the gate. "I could tell you something that would be worth a lot to you."

Her grey eyes fixed him in a steady stare.

"You can tell me nothing that would be of the slightest value, Thomas – " she began.

"Oh, couldn't I!" His head went up and down in a succession of nods. He was ludicrously like a nodding mandarin she had on her writing-table. "You don't know what I know. I could tell you something, and I could tell Mr Gine something, that nobody don't know. People talk about the Chelford treasure – "

"I don't want to hear any more," she said, and, turning, walked up the drive.

For a moment he glared after her as though he contemplated following, but thought better of it, and, lighting the cigarette, which had gone out, he slouched back to his borrowed home. And then an idea occurred to him. Beyond the low wooden fence was a thick belt of laurels. If one of his plans were carried out and he had to make a quick exit from Chelfordbury, it might be worth while to reconnoitre this house. He jumped over the fence and made a cautious progress through the bushes.

"Who's that you were speaking to, Leslie?" Arthur Gline was lying in a deck chair on the lawn, his eye covered with a piece of white lint.

"Thomas," she said.

"The footman from Fossaway? What did he bring – a message?"

"No, he's been discharged," she said as she passed him. "Dick suspects him of stealing, and he sent him about his business this morning."

"Have you seen Dick, then?" he asked in surprise.

"Yes, I met him; he was riding over to see the miller." She lingered at the back of the chair.

"You always seem to be meeting that fellow," he mused, with a frown. "It is 'Dick this' and 'Dick that.' Do you think it's wise, Leslie, playing with fire and all that sort of thing? You never tell me you meet Harry."

"Harry never comes out of his library," she said with a smile, "and it's difficult to miss Dick if you're out of doors. Not that I've ever tried to miss him."

He took out his cigarette and looked at it thoughtfully, his lips pursed.

"Dick's a good fellow," he said again, "but it is unnecessary for me to remind you that he is a second son, and as poor as a church mouse. Yes, Leslie, I'm going to insist on that poverty. After all, you're not marrying a pauper in Harry. And I tell you frankly that it is necessary that you should marry a rich man!"

The truth was coming – she braced herself to meet it. "Who will also take my fortune on trust," she said quietly. "If I married Dick, who is a business man, he might ask to see my bonds and shares."

A tense moment of silence, then: "There are no bonds or shares!"

He had to set his teeth to make his confession. He could not see her face; he dared not look round or meet her eyes.

"There are no bonds or shares?" she repeated slowly. "Then what I said in the car was right? I am penniless!"

35

The truth was out. Leslie stood rigidly behind her brother, looking down on him.

"I am penniless?" she asked.

He had to wet his dry lips before he could speak. "I've been trying to work up courage to tell you this for a long time," he said. "I'm a coward – a cur! You have a few thousand pounds that I couldn't handle, but every other penny of your fortune I have spent." His voice was hoarse, scarcely recognisable. "You'll have to know this sooner or later; you might as well know it now. I don't know what you'll think of me. I'd like to say that I didn't care, but that wouldn't be the truth. I've gambled away a quarter of a million, and I'm as near to bankruptcy and ruin as makes no difference."

He pulled the lint bandage from his eye and got up and faced her. Save for the discoloration of his cheek, he was white as chalk.

"I'd no intention of telling you," he said in a low voice, "but you piqued me into it, and I'm glad it's over."

Raising his eyes to hers, he did not see the look of condemnation he expected. There was neither contempt nor consternation in her face. The red lips were curved in a half-smile, and in her eyes was nothing but kindliness and pity.

"Thank God!" she said in a low voice, and he could not understand her.

"This means, of course, that Chelford will have to take you without a fortune," he said.

She shook her head.

"I have already written to Harry, breaking off my engagement," she answered him. And then her arm slipped through his. "Let us go in to breakfast," she said. "This is one of the happiest days of my life."

The letter came to Harry Alford, Earl of Chelford, with two or three other personal letters; his main correspondence was with London booksellers, for he was a restless collector of ancient tomes. He looked at the letter, recognising the handwriting, frowned and turned it over. Then, with some evidence of annoyance, he slit the flap.

DEAR HARRY,

I have thought for a long time that we have so little in common that a marriage between us could not possibly lead to happiness for either of us. I suppose the correct thing to do would be to send back my engagement ring, but fortunately, or unfortunately, you forgot to present me with this token! I wish you every happiness, and I hope that we shall still be good friends.

Harry read the letter, rubbed his forehead in perplexity, then, rising from his chair, almost ran from the library. Dick was on the lawn, playing with his dog, when his brother burst into the little study.

"I say, look at this! What do you think of it?"

Dick read the letter with a troubled face.

"I'm sorry," he said.

"Sorry!" said Harry shrilly. "It's disgraceful! I shall look a perfect fool! Leslie's treated me very badly indeed – but that reference to the engagement ring is in shocking bad taste."

"I thought you'd given her one," said the patient Dick. "Didn't you?"

"It is a barbarous and stupid practice. I never dreamt of giving her a ring. Why should I? She had a ring, a beautiful one. You must have seen it – a diamond that she always wears. What is the sense of it? The reference is in very bad taste – shocking!"

And yet, in spite of his agitation and anger, Dick thought he detected relief in his brother's voice. But his vanity had been hurt, and that is a sore place with many men of greater calibre than Lord Chelford.

"Without any warning. She was here yesterday, but said not a word about it!"

"You hardly gave her a chance," said Dick. "You scarcely spoke to her, and really, Harry, you took no trouble to entertain her. Be reasonable."

Harry fondled his chin and glared through the thick lenses of his horn-rimmed spectacles.

"I suppose not," he said, with sudden mildness. "But really, I'm not a marrying man. I want no more than my books and my mission. But I'm going to look a fool over this business, Dick." His anger was rising again. "Everybody in the county knows we're engaged, and they'll come prying around to discover what is wrong. We shall have those beastly newspaper men sitting on the front step, and that is more than I can endure!"

"Then let them come to me," said Dick. "I'll give them all the explanation they need, and they'll be sorry they asked. As for newspaper men, I eat 'em alive!"

Still his brother was not wholly mollified.

"What made her do it? Do you think she's found somebody else she likes better?" He peered at Dick in his short-sighted way. "That would make it even worse. I'm very annoyed with Arthur Gine. He threw this girl at me."

"Don't let us talk about it," said Dick sharply. "It isn't a very dignified attitude to take."

His brother looked at the letter dubiously.

"What am I to do?"

"Write a charming letter, freeing her," said Dick. "You can do no less."

"But do you think she's got another man in her eye?" demanded Harry.

"She has probably a dozen," said the other brutally. "Do as I tell you, Harry."

And Harry Alford went grumbling back to the library.

So she had done it! Dick hardly knew whether to be elated or depressed. A week ago he would have been the happiest man in England; today – he shrugged his broad shoulders, pulled his pipe from his pocket and savagely stuffed tobacco into the bowl. This would mean a break, for a time at any rate, between the Gines and Harry, and there arose an alarming thought. Suppose Harry transferred his legal business to another firm? That would mean ruin for Arthur Gine. Dick had so far been able to cover up the defalcations of Leslie Gine's brother, and in a few months he could have obliterated all trace without hurt to the estate. But at this stage, if Harry insisted –

"His lordship would like to see you, sir." The second footman had come up unnoticed behind him.

Dick steeled himself for the interview and went in. His brother was sitting at his desk, his head in his hands, his hair rumpled and an angry frown puckering the white skin of his forehead.

"Dick, I'm going to cut out these Gines," he said. "I want you to ask your lawyers to take over from Arthur, and tell them to be deuced careful and check every item. That fellow handles my mother's estate, and roughly I think he must have nearly fifty thousand pounds in securities. If there's a penny missing, Dick, I'll prosecute the fellow – I will, by God! He's made a fool of me before all the county, and if I get half a chance I'm going to get back on him."

Dick's heart sank.

"What lawyers do you suggest?"

"Sampson & Howard. They're good people and they're not too friendly with Arthur. Will you take that in hand, Dick?"

Dick Alford nodded. As soon as he could escape from his brother's presence, he went round to the garage and, taking out his car, drove to Willow House. Arthur was still on the lawn, walking up and down, and from his attitude of depression Dick gathered that something unusual had happened. Possibly he had been told about the breaking off of the engagement. But here he attributed the wrong cause.

"I want to see you, Gine."

Arthur Gline started and turned at the sound of the voice.

"Hullo!" he said awkwardly. "Does Harry know?"

Dick nodded.

"And he's very angry, I suppose?"

"He is rather furious. That's what I've come to see you about. Where is Leslie?"

"She's in the house. Do you want her?"

"No," said Dick quietly. "I want to talk with you. Come for a walk with me."

They strolled out of all possibility of earshot from the house, and then: "Harry has decided to take the legal management of the estate out of your hands, Gine," he said. "He spoke to me this morning of some funds that you're handling – about fifty thousand pounds' worth of stock from the late Lady Chelford's estate. Is that money intact?"

Arthur did not answer.

"Is that money intact?" asked Dick again.

"No," said the other huskily; "not a penny of it."

Dick stared at the man in horror.

"You mean the money is lost?"

Arthur nodded.

"Yes, I was persuaded to put it into an oilfield in Texas. The shares are not worth two cents a thousand."

Dick groaned.

"Oh, you fool, you cussed fool!" he muttered. "Don't you realise what this means? I can't cover you up now, not even for Leslie's sake. You madman!"

Arthur Gline passed his hand wearily over his eyes.

"What is the use of ragging me?" he asked plaintively. "I've been expecting this trouble, and have lived under the shadow of it for years. I'll have to take my medicine."

"And Leslie?" asked Dick sternly. "What of her? Has she to take your medicine too?"

The man's pallid face was distorted painfully.

"Don't talk about Leslie, for God's sake!" he said. "That's the worst of it. I'm not scared of Dartmoor or bankruptcy or anything. Leslie's the only fear I have."

"Can you raise the money?"

Arthur gave a harsh little laugh.

"Raise it? How do you think I can raise fifty thousand?"

"You have no friends?"

The lawyer's lips curled.

"Not fifty thousand pounds' worth," he said curtly. "No, I'm afraid, Alford, I've got to go through with it. I've been a blackguard, a vain, stupid fool – I've asked for all that is coming to me and I shall not squeal."

Dick was silent, going over the problem that this horrible situation presented. Arthur could go to prison and stay there for the rest of his life, for all he cared; but Leslie: this would break her heart.

"There is one thing I want you to promise me," he began, as he foresaw one possible solution which might present itself to Arthur's mind.

The lawyer smiled and nodded.

"You can trust me," he said. "I've got some sort of religion tucked away inside my system. Self-destruction is not my idea of a gentleman's solution. I tell you I'll stand up to anything that comes, and I'm not going to blow my brains out and leave a coroner's jury of yokels and carpenters to discuss my private affairs and probe into my iniquities. When will the transfer take place?"

"We've got a week yet," said Dick. "I can hold it up for that long; but once the papers are in the hands of the other lawyers, nothing can save you."

A week! Arthur Gine pinched his lower lip in meditation. Seven days. So far as he was concerned, if he had seven years to make reparation he could not see daylight.

"And get out of your mind that you're going to find the Chelford treasure," said Dick, and the shock made the man jump.

"Why, how do you know – " he stammered.

"I know all about that. I tell you that you can cut it out. That isn't a solution. It's only robbing Peter to pay Peter; for if there is any gold – and heaven knows I doubt it – it belongs to Harry, and must go to

Harry. What about Leslie's fortune? Of course that is non-existent. Does she know?"

"I told her this morning," said the man, and now Dick understood his depression. "She took it like a brick; in fact, she seemed almost happy about it. And why, I can't for the life of me understand. Women are queer things."

"I know one woman who is the most wonderful thing in the world," said Dick softly.

He did not wait to see Leslie, but left as hurriedly as he came, and the man who had been lying at full length beneath the laurel bushes waited till the two men had disappeared, and then crawled painfully and carefully back to the road, mounted the wall and stepped out for the nearest telegraph office to send his news.

36

Mr Gilder arrived at his cottage in the evening and found his "tenant" sitting on the doorstep smoking a pipe. Fortunately, the cottage was in the middle of a thin plantation of trees, and the river at the back made an approach from that direction impossible. Nevertheless, Mr Gilder was alarmed at the lack of precaution the man showed.

"If you're going to stay here you've got to keep inside the house. I tell you I don't want people to know that you're living here. Now, what is the big news?"

"Come inside," said Thomas, with a grin, and his host felt that the invitation into his own house was a little superfluous.

Thomas was not a good story-teller, and it was with many "You see what I means," and at inordinate length, that he unravelled his tangled narrative.

"I'd been hanging round the house all the morning. I wanted to have a talk with the young lady."

"What about?" demanded the other.

"About a certain thing."

"Now see here, Thomas: you're not to speak to Miss Gine – do you understand? You're not to approach her, and you're not to go anywhere near the house."

"Well, it's not a bad thing that I was there this morning," grinned Thomas. "Because I heard something that will make you jump!"

It took half an hour for him to repeat, with more or less accuracy, the conversation he had heard on the lawn. When he came to the vital point, Mr Gilder whistled.

Arthur Gine had managed the Chelford estate without his assistance, and Gilder was as ignorant of the particulars of the property as if it were in some other office.

"Fifty thousand, eh?" he mused. "Well, that's more than Arthur Gine will collect in a hurry."

"That's what he said himself," said Thomas. "He said to Alford: 'Friends? Well, I haven't got fifty thousand pounds' worth' – those were his very words. He said, 'I'll go to Dartmoor, and that doesn't worry me. What worries me is Leslie.'"

"Did you hear when the transfer was to be complete – I mean, when the stocks were to be handed over to the other lawyers?"

"In a week," said Thomas. "Mr Alford said, 'I can hold it up for a week, but I can't keep it any longer. And once those papers are in the other bloke's hands, your name is mud.'"

Fifty thousand pounds! Gilder paced up and down the narrow room, his hands behind him.

"You say that the engagement with his lordship is broken off?"

"He didn't say so," said the man, "but that's how I took it. He said, 'Was Harry very annoyed?' That's his lordship. And Alford said, 'Yes, and he's going to change his lawyers.' And he said, 'What about Leslie's fortune?'"

"Call her Miss Gine, will you?" interrupted Gilder roughly.

"He didn't say Miss Gine, he said 'Leslie.' But to oblige you I'll say Miss Gine," said Thomas. "He said, 'What about Miss Gine's fortune? Is that gone?' And Gine said, 'Yes, every penny.'"

This was no news to Gilder – Arthur had told him as much.

"And here, Mr Gilder – the Black Abbot was around last night. I've got an idea about him! His lordship's scared to death of the Black Abbot. Did you know that?"

"Don't talk to me about the Black Abbot!" snapped the man. He wanted to work this thing out, and the chatter of his guest disturbed him. "You keep inside and out of sight. I think you'd better go to London tonight. You've got money?"

"I've got a bit of money. I was a fool! There's an old-fashioned diary in that library that his lordship would give a couple of thousand pounds to get back, and I had it in my hand! That is the thing I ought to have pinched."

"And if it was found on you, you'd have been in prison. As it was, you had taken money and you got away with it."

This point of view had not struck the ex-convict before.

"That's true," he agreed. "Lord! what a headpiece you've got, Mr Gilder! If I had your brains – "

But Mr Gilder was not in a mood for flattery.

"I've got an idea," Thomas went on, unconscious of the distraction he was causing. "Let me go up to London tonight and come down tomorrow."

But Gilder did not hear him. Fifty thousand pounds! And for that price he could buy – Leslie Gine! His pulse quickened at the thought. There were no "ifs" or "buts." She would gladly make that sacrifice for her brother's sake. This time he had them all in the hollow of his hand: Leslie, Arthur Gine, and last, but not least in dislike, Dick Alford.

Mentally he reviewed his financial position. He had considerably over a hundred thousand pounds in gilt-edged securities, which were easily realisable – or transferable. He had house property in the north of London, and a fairly large fluid balance at the bank. And he was fifty. There were fifteen years of life ahead of him – fifteen happy years. How could he better use his money than in buying happiness? The life companionship of that fragrant thing, and afterwards a will whereby she lost all interest in his property if she married again – Mr Gilder thought a long way ahead. And his marriage would be a knife in the heart of the second son, for he guessed Dick Alford's secret.

He saw his way now; the plan was fool-proof and invincible. Nothing stood between him and the realisation of what had once been a wild and foolish hope.

"A week? You're sure of that?"

Thomas nodded. His cunning eyes had not left Gilder's face. Unconscious of the curious scrutiny, Fabrian asked: "Why do you think this news is interesting to me?"

The man grinned and closed his right eye in a significant wink.

"Didn't you ask me to tell you how often the young lady went to Fossaway Manor? Didn't you tell me to write everything that happened between her and his lordship?"

Gilder was silent.

It was not a comfortable thought that he had employed such a man as this to watch the girl he loved.

"You'd better keep close here," he said. "I don't want you to be seen by the villagers or by the people from Fossaway Manor. Does anybody know you're here?"

"No, sir. Not even Miss Gine: she never asked – "

Gilder interrupted him brusquely.

"If you're going to town, go by night, and come back by night. I'm not so sure that it won't be a good idea to stay here after all."

He got back to London late in the evening and spent the night in a strict examination of his finances. He had dismissed from his mind all thoughts of the Chelford treasure. Mary Wenner had certainly justification for her confidence. He himself had been deceived when he had looked through the grating and seen those cylinders neatly arranged on the stone bench. Who had moved them – the Black Abbot? There must be some explanation for him. But he had his own ideas on the subject, and the moment had not yet arrived when he could test his theory.

The next morning he spent in the City and at Somerset House, examining the will of the late Lady Chelford. Her legacies were set forth in detail, and the character of the shares and stocks with which Arthur Gine had been entrusted were particularised, and John Henry Gine, Arthur's uncle, named as trustee. A search of the court files failed to reveal any successor to Arthur's uncle, and apparently no trustee had been appointed, the stocks being left in Arthur's care. He would, of course, have authority to sell and reinvest, and there would be no trouble if shares of a corresponding value were handed over to Harry Alford's new solicitors.

Arthur Gline had spent a very busy day in the seclusion of his study. His task was not a pleasant one: he was putting in order the chaos of his affairs, and as the list of his liabilities grew, he himself seemed to grow older.

He had only interrupted his work to lunch with his sister, and Leslie, who thought that the cause of his distress was her vanished fortune, did her best to cheer him. His first act had been to gather on paper the remnants of her vanished quarter of a million, and the remnant was pitiably small, amounting to less than two thousand pounds. He told her this at lunch.

"But that's really a much larger amount than I expected, Arthur," she smiled. "We shall be able to live for two years on that."

It was in his mind to say that he would possibly be living for five years on less, but he wanted to avert that news until it was inevitable that she should know.

At five o'clock she was having tea in solitary state when the maid brought her a card. She had not heard the arrival of the visitor's motorcar, for the drawing-room was at the back of the house. She took the card and read it.

"I don't think I want to see this gentleman," she said. "Will you ask Mr Gine – "

And then she remembered the struggle on the lawn and Arthur's damaged eye.

"Yes, I'll see him," she said. "Ask him to come in."

Gilder was dressed as for an official visit. He carried a glossy silk hat, an incongruous sight in the country, in his gloved hand; his morning coat sported a large yellow rose; his patent shoes shone violently. Before he came to Willow House he had called at his own cottage to refresh his memory on one or two points, but the house was empty. Thomas had evidently gone up to town, as he had said he would. At first he was annoyed, but later he was glad that the man was not there. After all, he knew enough, more than enough for the comfort of Leslie Gine.

She met him with a distant little bow.

"I'm afraid you will not regard me as a welcome visitor, Miss Gine," he said; "but I have a little business to discuss with you, and I should be grateful if you would give me a few minutes of your time."

"Will you sit down, please?" she said coldly.

He was gazing at her with that queer, hungry look she had seen in his face before.

"I understand your engagement with Lord Chelford is broken off?" And, when she did not answer: "It was partly that which brought me here, and partly something much more serious; something," he said, with distinct deliberation, "which affects you very closely, Miss Gline."

He paused, expecting a reply, but received none. She sat bolt upright in one of the deep chairs that abounded in the room, her hands folded lightly on her lap, her gaze fixed on his.

"I was, as you probably know, for many years your brother's right-hand man. In consequence, I have a very intimate knowledge of his affairs; and not only his affairs, but the affairs of his clients. I know, for example, that your large fortune is mythical."

If he had expected to shock her he was disappointed. She nodded slightly.

"I know that also, Mr Gilder," she said. "I hope you haven't made this long journey to tell me this?"

For a second he was staggered. He had expected his announcement to be the first of two tremendous sensations; she saw the disappointment in his face and could have smiled.

"There is another matter," he said, recovering himself, "which does not directly affect you. Your brother administered the estate of the late Lady Chelford, in the sense that he had in his charge stocks and bonds to the value of fifty-one thousand pounds. That is quite usual in an old-fashioned lawyer's business, but today, of course, the stocks would be in the hands of the bank, and the dividends automatically credited."

Her heart nearly stopped beating. He saw the colour fade from her face and was very sure of himself.

"My brother has – that money?" she said.

"He *had* it." He emphasised the word. "I understand that the present Lord Chelford is changing his lawyers, and in a week's time those stocks are to be handed over to another firm."

She was speechless, knowing that he was telling the truth, understanding only too well just all that this narrative implied.

"Fifty thousand pounds is a lot of money," Gilder went on suavely; "a very difficult sum to raise in a week. And in a week that money must be in your brother's hands."

She raised her eyes, and, seeing the pain in them, he was almost sorry for her.

"You mean – that the money – that Arthur hasn't those stocks to transfer?"

He nodded.

"Are you sure of this?"

"Absolutely sure."

A long silence, when the ticking of the little French clock came so loudly to their ears that instinctively both glanced at the mantelpiece together.

"Why do you tell me all this?"

He cleared his voice.

"A few days ago I told you, rather uncouthly, I am afraid, that I loved you," he said. "You may not credit me with the – the affectionate reverence I have for you – but I love you! There is nothing in the world I would not do for you, no price that I would not pay."

Her eyes did not waver; she seemed to be reading his very soul.

"Even to the extent of providing fifty thousand pounds in a week?" she said in a low voice.

"Even to that extent," he answered.

She rose slowly to her feet.

"Will you write down your address?"

So calm was her voice that she might have been discussing an ordinary matter of business.

"I know where you live, but I have forgotten the name of the building and the number."

He wrote it down with an unsteady hand and left the paper where she had placed it.

"I must know tomorrow," he said, "yes or no."

She dropped her head.

"You shall know tomorrow," she said. "If I tell you I will marry you, you can make the arrangement about the money – I will not fail you."

Without another word, he walked to the door, turned and favoured her with a deep bow, and went out into the hall. She heard the whirr of his car grow fainter and fainter. But still she did not move.

37

The door opened. It was Arthur.

"Was that Gilder who came?" he asked, and, when she nodded: "The brute! Why didn't you send for me?"

He saw her face, and, quickly:

"Is anything wrong, Leslie?"

"Yes," she said, and marvelled herself at the evenness of her tone. "He came about some money that was in your care – a part of the estate of Lady Chelford."

She saw from the quick change in his face that all that Gilder had said was true; but then, she had never doubted that.

"Does Dick know?" she asked.

"Yes, he knows. I wonder what you think of me?" he asked huskily. She shook her head.

"Does it matter, Arthur, what I think? What will happen if the money isn't found?"

"I've got a week yet," he said. "How did he come to know?"

"Can you get the money?"

It was a useless question.

"Dick said he will do his best."

"Nothing can be done with Harry, I suppose?" she asked. "No, that's too impossible to think about. What will happen when the truth comes out?"

He drew a deep breath.

"I don't know; imprisonment, I suppose. It's horribly rough on you, Leslie. I've said that before, but words mean very little, and I am at the end of words."

His voice broke for a second, but he caught hold of his weakness in time, and, seeing the fight he was making, there came a look of admiration to her eyes.

"You poor soul!" she said softly.

Another long pause.

"What did Gilder want – just to tell you that?"

"Partly that."

"And to make you an offer?" There was just a hint of eagerness in his tone; the drowning man was gripping hard on a straw. It made her heart ache to think that, even at that moment, when he knew he deserved nothing but her loathing, he could contemplate yet another sacrifice upon her part without protest.

"He made me an offer – yes," she said. "And I don't know what I shall do. I'm going to see Dick."

"Is that necessary?" he asked anxiously.

She nodded.

"I'm going to see Dick," she said. "I will phone him."

She moved to the instrument and lifted the receiver from the hook, when he caught her arm.

"I shouldn't be guided – too much by Dick," he said breathlessly. "Gilder's a brute, but you might be happier with him than with Harry."

She shook off his arm and gave a number. The servant who replied told her that Dick was out, that he had gone to London that afternoon, and would not be back until late at night. She hung up the instrument, went back to the drawing-room, and took up the paper on which Gilder had written his address.

"You have six days, Arthur," she said. "I have less than twenty-four hours. I don't know whose case is the worse, but I rather fancy it is mine."

He heard her go up to her room, and after a while followed and tried the door. It was locked.

"Leslie!" he called anxiously, but she did not hear him.

With her face buried in the pillow, she was saying goodbye to Dick Alford, and her heart was breaking.

38

Passing down Wardour Street that afternoon, Dick Alford had seen a familiar face. A man came out of a shop with a bundle under his arm, and, recognising the young man, turned on his tracks and walked rapidly away. Dick grinned; there was no mistaking Thomas, and he wondered what was the nature of his purchase.

He glanced at the window of the store and was puzzled; for Thomas did not seem the kind of man who would indulge in the frivolities which were exhibited behind the plate-glass.

Dick was not in any very good spirits. He had made two calls, and on each occasion had suffered a gentle rebuff. He was going now to see his last hope. The big City bank was closed when he arrived, but a porter admitted him to the presence of the old man who had been his father's best friend. The war had turned plain Mr Jarvis, a country banker of the eighties, into Lord Clanfield, the head of the greatest banking corporation in Europe.

He gave Dick a hearty welcome, for the boy had been a favourite of his.

"Sit ye down, Dick. What has brought you to this square mile of trouble?"

Plainly and briefly Dick stated his business, and Lord Clanfield frowned.

"Fifty thousand pounds, my dear boy! Do you want it for yourself?"

"No, I want it for a very dear friend of mine." It required an effort to describe Arthur in these flattering terms. "He has got into a scrape."

His lordship shook his head.

"It couldn't be done, Dick. If it was for you, to get you out of a scrape – but then, you're not the kind of lad who'd ever get into one – I'd give it to you out of my own pocket."

"You couldn't lend it to me on my personal security?"

The banker smiled.

"Lending it to you, Dick, would be giving it to you! What chance have you of repaying fifty thousand pounds? A second son! Harry is marrying this year, and there will be an heir to the estate next year! No, no, old boy, it would be impossible."

Then, in his desperation, Dick Alford told the story, suppressing only the names. The old man listened with a grave face.

"He has got to go through with it, Dick," he said. "If you get him out of this trouble he'll probably get into worse. The poor little girl – I'm sorry for her. Of course you're speaking about Gine? No, no, you needn't be afraid, I shan't say a word. But I've had my suspicions for a long time. Let him take his medicine, Dick, and do what you can for the girl. Once that fellow is behind bars and the whole wretched trouble is at an end, come to me for any money you want – for the girl. I knew her father and her uncle, and the great-uncle who left her a lot of money, which I suppose has gone up in smoke with the rest, and I'm willing to go a long way to help her. But you mustn't pledge your credit, Dick, for that worthless man."

Dick came away from the City weary and sick at heart, too dispirited even to interview the fourth man he had intended seeing. His only hope now was his brother, and he knew Harry's obstinacy too well to expect help from that quarter, which could not even be asked for, except by betraying as the borrower the man for whom he had conceived an unreasoning hatred.

Monkey Puttler met him at the station, and had a piece of news to impart.

"That bird Thomas is still in the neighbourhood," he said. "He's been living in Gilder's cottage."

"Indeed?" said Dick. He was really not concerned with Thomas or Gilder or anything in the wide world except the heartbreak that awaited Leslie Gine.

"Gilder's been down today. Ascot's all over, isn't it? Anyway, he was dressed like a doctor in new clothes – top hat and everything."

"Where has he been?" asked Dick, with sudden interest.

"I don't know. I guess he went to call on Mr Gine. I saw his car coming out of the drive, and he looked very pleased with himself. And I've found the rifle."

"Where did you find it?" asked Dick quickly.

"Up against the river. Someone must have thrown it in, but didn't throw hard enough. There were three or four cartridges still in the magazine – a sporting Lee-Enfield. They've tried the knife and they've tried the gun; I wonder what new one they'll put out on us."

"Have you seen Harry?"

"Saw him this afternoon," said the cheerful Puttler. "He worked that chesil gag on me, but I didn't give him my views."

In spite of his anxiety, Dick smiled.

"Have you any views on chesils?"

"Yes, sir," said the other confidently. "He thinks chesil is an instrument. He doesn't seem to realise that in Elizabethan times 'chesil' meant 'gravel' or 'shingle.' "

Dick stopped and stared at him.

"Is that so?" he asked.

"Ever heard of a place called Chelsea?" said the informative Mr Puttler. "Do you know what 'Chelsea' means? It means 'Chesil Ey' or Shingle Island. Why, the word isn't even obsolete; you'll find it in any dictionary. The new 'chesil' that is spoken of in the diary is a load of shingle he got from Brighthelstone. That's Brighton. Now why did the old bird want shingle? Obviously to put in some kind of concrete or mortar."

"For heaven's sake don't start on the treasure, or I shall go mad!" groaned Dick. "At any rate, you don't believe in its existence, thank goodness!"

"I do," said the surprising man emphatically. "I'm as sure that those thousand bars of gold are in existence as I'm certain you and I are walking up this road. Your brother's got a book down that shows all Queen Elizabeth's private accounts; there's the million she stole from the Spanish ships that put into an English port when they were on their way to Holland; there's the money she got from Drake and the other seagoing burglars; but there's not a hint of the Chelford gold."

"Then where is it?" asked Dick in exasperation.

"Ask me before I go," replied the other cryptically.

39

A dozen letters were written and burnt in the fireplace of her bedroom before Leslie composed the one that was eventually placed in an envelope and addressed to "Fabrian Gilder, Esq., 35, Regency Mansions, London."

> DEAR MR GILDER, *she wrote*, I agree to your terms. The money or equivalent shares must be deposited in the Horsham branch of the Southern & Midland Bank, in the name of Leslie Gilder, so that I may have control of the account from the moment I am married. I do not expect you to trust the word of one of my family, and I presume that you will wish the marriage to take place in the next few days. Will you please make arrangements for the ceremony, and tell me when and where I am to meet you? I expect it to be at a registrar's office by special licence. I can only say that, although this marriage is not of my seeking, you may trust me to be a loyal wife.
>
> Very sincerely,
> LESLIE GINE.

The last post was collected by a motor-cyclist postman at ten o'clock from a little wall box not a hundred yards from the house. There was an earlier collection, but somehow she could not bring herself to post the letter until the very last moment. Ten o'clock was an unusually late hour for a country collection, but it was the last box on the postman's route and was an especially convenient arrangement, not only for the inhabitants of Fossaway Manor, but for the tenant farmers who wished to notify their daily consignments.

She saw Arthur at dinner after the letter was written, but beyond the exchange of a few commonplaces they did not speak. He went back to his study, carrying his coffee with him, and she was left alone to the contemplation of the dark future. She wished she had seen Dick before she wrote, but it was too late now. Gilder had asked her to give him his answer that night, and she had promised.

What would Dick say? She screwed up her eyes tightly as though to hide the vision of him, and her lips trembled.

"No weakness, Danton!" It was a favourite quotation of her childhood, and had been the slogan at all moments when tears were near at hand.

She took the letter from her bag and looked at it. Stamped, addressed, she had but to drop this into the little letter box, and thereafter the angle of life was twisted to a new prospect: the bleakest, dreariest prospect that any woman had faced.

And it had to be done. The hands of the clock moved slowly and inexorably round. Nine o'clock – a quarter past – twenty minutes to ten; she set her teeth and got up from the little table where she had been trying in vain to concentrate her mind upon a game of patience, went upstairs and put on her hat and coat, and, with the letter tightly gripped in her hand, stole down across the hall, opened the door and went out.

It was very dark; she could scarcely see her way down the drive. Clear of the overhanging trees, her eyes, grown accustomed to the darkness, made out the road. She thought that she saw somebody on the road ahead and heard footsteps, but she was nervy, she told herself. Nevertheless, she stopped and listened. She heard nothing and went on.

A few minutes' walk brought her to the pillar box, and here she waited. A big spot of rain fell upon her hand; she heard the sough of the wind through the trees; and then, far away, she saw a tiny star of light and heard the faint clank of the postman's cycle. She thrust the letter into the box and turned to retrace her steps.

Then it occurred to her that the postman would pass her, and she did not wish to see him. Which way should she go? Her heart and inclination beckoned to Fossaway Manor. Dick – she must see Dick. She fought against the madness; the postman's light grew brighter. Then she ran, down towards the cut road, through the gate and up the slope to the abbey. There she sat down to recover her breath, and presently she saw the reflection of a lamp, heard the thunder of the postman's motor cycle as it passed.

There went fate, on that dark road, noisily, bumpily. The red light faded from sight, and she got up, walked leisurely past the abbey ruins, without one thought of ghosts or haunting spirits, and took the lower and shorter path to the Manor.

She was halfway across the Long Meadow when she stopped. Fear was clutching at her heart; she could feel the flesh creep on her neck, and, turning, looked back. Somebody was following her. Consciously she had heard no sound, but to her heart flashed a warning signal that set it racing. She could see nobody. It must be her imagination, she told herself; yet here, reason and instinct were at variance, and instinct won. She *knew* there was somebody immediately behind her, less than twenty yards away.

She could intercept the long drive to Fossaway Manor before she could reach the house. She decided to make the longer journey, and, turning abruptly, walked with quick strides across the velvety grassland in the direction of the elms which flanked the drive. Once she looked back, and thought she saw a moving shape. She quickened her steps, broke into a gentle run. She must not allow blind panic to overcome her, she told herself.

Again she looked back but saw nothing, and, ashamed of her fear, she slowed to a walk and reached the elms and the drive with heartfelt thankfulness. Exactly how she should break in upon Dick she did not know. She hoped he would be in his study, and that she could call him out from the lawn.

Nearer and nearer she came to the house, and then, of a sudden, she whipped round. Somebody was behind her: she was sure of it now. She heard their feet upon the gravelled road.

"Who is there?" she called.

There was no answer, but the footsteps stopped. They might be walking on the grassy verge, she thought, and, turning, ran up the drive. Whoever followed was running too. She heard a sibilant whisper and her blood turned cold. Then, as she emerged from the trees, she saw a figure against the grey sheen of the round pond, saw the shape of it – the long habit and the heavy cowl. With a scream she flew.

The drive continuing past the window would bring her to Dick's study. She saw with a gasp of relief that the door was open and a light shining inside. Over her shoulder she saw the queer shape again, and screamed. In an instant Dick was out of the study and had caught her in his arms.

He listened to her breathless story, then almost carrying her to his room, he put her in a chair and ran out into the night. In a few minutes he came back.

"I saw nothing," he said. "It was the Black Abbot, you say?"

"I don't know; something in a cowl and habit: I'm sure of that."

It was a bad introduction to the story she had to tell; indeed, in her terror, she almost forgot the object of her visit.

"Did Arthur come with you?"

She shook her head.

"Dick, I know," were the first words she said when she had recovered her breath.

"You know what?"

"About Lady Chelford's money."

She saw his face change.

"Did he tell you?" he asked, the red coming into his face.

"Not Arthur, no. It was Gilder."

"Mr Gilder told you? I knew he had been and I knew he had called. Was that why he came?"

She nodded.

"For nothing else?"

"Yes; he came to offer me the money."

She saw his eyes narrow.

"He did? At a price, of course?"

She nodded.

"And you — what did you say?"

She found a difficulty in breathing; speech for the moment was impossible without making a fool of herself.

"You agreed?"

She nodded again.

"I have just posted the letter to him," she said.

She saw him bite his lip, and a red spot of blood showed. If he had stormed at her, cursed her, she could have borne it; but he did no more than look at her. There was nothing in his gaze that was uncharitable.

"Oh, Dick, Dick!" She was sobbing on his breast and his arms were about her, comforting her.

"You can't do it, my dear. Anything is better than that."

She shook her head, incapable of speech.

"I tell you anything is better than that." His voice was hard, uncompromising. "Better Arthur go down for five years than that you should live in hell all your life! I know that man — I know his kind — it isn't his years, it's his mind and his evil heart. If he were twenty I would say, 'No, you can't do it, Leslie.' "

She pushed herself gently away from him and dried her eyes.

"I must, Dick; I have given my word. I cannot trick him. The last thing I said to him was, 'If I tell you I will marry you, you can make the arrangements about the money — I will not fail you.' I cannot fail him; I cannot fail myself."

His face was drawn and haggard.

"This can't be!" he said. "Something will happen. I don't know what — "

He stopped.

"What's that?" she gasped, terrified.

From somewhere in the grounds came a shrill shriek that was hardly human. Again it came: a sobbing, blubbering shriek that turned her heart to ice.

"Stay here," said Dick, as he made for the open window, but she flung herself upon him.

"You shan't go! You mustn't go!" she cried wildly. "Dick, something dreadful is happening. Oh, God! listen, Dick!"

This time the shriek was shriller, and died away into a thin wail of sound.

He pushed her aside and ran out on to the lawn.

"From which way did it come, do you think?"

"Over there." She pointed ahead to the drive.

"Let me come with you – do, please do!" she begged. "I dare not be left alone."

He hesitated.

"Come," he said roughly, and took her arm with a grip that made her wince.

Together they ran towards Elm Drive, and then he stopped.

"Go back and get my hand-lamp. It's on my writing-table," he said. "I will wait here for you."

She fled back to the room, took up the lamp with fingers that trembled so violently that she could scarcely hold it, and rejoined him.

"It was over there. I heard something a second ago. If I hadn't promised to wait – "

He turned on the light, swinging its rays over the ground before him, and going ahead of her. Presently she saw him stop, and a circle of light focussed on something brown that lay huddled on the grass.

"Stay where you are," he commanded, "and turn your back."

A voice hailed him in the distance: it was Puttler, and, guided by the lamp, he came on the scene.

"Who is it?" he asked.

"I don't know," said Dick in a low voice.

At his feet was the huddled figure of a man. He was lying on his face, and was attired from head to foot in a long black habit around which a rope was girdled.

"The Black Abbot?" said Puttler incredulously. "Is he dead?"

"Look," said Dick, and pointed to the wet shoulder and the horror of the throat.

Puttler knelt down, and, putting his arms under the figure, turned it on its back.

The face was covered by a black cowl, and this he gently raised.

"Merciful God!" said Dick, in a hushed voice. He was looking into the grey face of Thomas, the footman.

40

"Thomas – the Black Abbot!"

Dick looked at the pitiable thing, bewildered; and then he remembered the girl and, with a low word of instruction to Puttler, went back to her.

"Is he – dead?" she asked fearfully.

"Yes, I'm afraid he is."

"Who – who is it?"

"One of the servants," he said evasively.

"Not Thomas?"

Why she should think it was Thomas she could not for the life of her tell.

"Yes – Thomas."

She made no further inquiries, and they walked back without a word to his room. He rang the bell, and, to the footman who answered: "Ask Mr Glover to come to me," he said.

The old butler came apprehensively. All the servants had heard the scream in the park.

"Where is his lordship?"

"He went up to bed about five minutes ago, Mr Alford."

"Had he heard – anything?"

"No, sir. He's so particular about our talking of the Black Abbot – "

"How do you know it was the Black Abbot?" asked Dick sharply, and the butler explained that somebody had seen the figure in the grounds.

"He was trying to open a window. One of the maids looking out of her window saw him walking on the paved path below, and raised an alarm. Has he hurt anybody, Mr Richard?"

"No, he has hurt nobody," said Dick.

He drew the butler out into the hall and closed the door behind him.

"A man has been found in the grounds in the dress of a black abbot – and he is dead – murdered!"

"Good Lord, sir!" said the startled servant. "Is it anybody we know?"

"Thomas," said Dick laconically, and the old man staggered back against the panelled wall.

"Not our Thomas? Thomas Luck, the man who was dismissed?"

Dick nodded.

"Get the servants to bed. Tell them that the scream came from somebody who was skylarking and that we caught him – anything you like." Then, catching a glimpse of the man's ashen face: "First of all you'd better go down into the dining-room and help yourself to a good stiff glass of brandy and water; you look a corpse, man!"

"Thomas!" muttered the old man. "It's terrible! Do you think – "

Dick cut short his question.

"Do as I tell you; get the servants to bed. The police will be up here soon enough, but I'll arrange that your staff are not questioned till the morning."

He went back to the girl.

"As for you, young lady," he said, with a grim smile, "I seem to spend my life taking you back to your home."

"Couldn't I stay?" she asked timidly.

Dick shook his head.

"We shall have to call in the police, and I want to keep your name out of the business. Arthur is at home?"

"Yes, Arthur is at home," she said listlessly.

At that moment the telephone bell rang and he took up the instrument.

"Is that Lord Chelford's house?" said an unfamiliar voice.

"Yes," said Dick shortly.

"I'm speaking from the sub post-office. That isn't Lord Chelford speaking?"

"No, it's Mr Alford," said Dick.

"Well, listen, Mr Alford. Have you sent anything very important from the local postbox?"

"Why?" asked Dick quickly.

"Because our roundsman reported that the box had been tampered with. He couldn't get in his key, so the letters that had been posted between six and ten have not yet been collected."

Dick uttered an exclamation.

"Right! When it's cleared, will you ask the postman to bring the letters up to the Manor? There are one or two that I want to withdraw."

The man at the other end of the wire hesitated.

"Why, in the special circumstances, yes," he said, and Dick hung up the receiver and turned slowly to the girl.

"The letter box hasn't been cleared."

Slowly the significance of the words dawned upon her.

"What shall I do?" she whispered.

"Give me authority to withdraw your letter to Gilder. There are six more days."

She held her breath. For a second a vision of her brother in convict's garb came to her eyes, and then she looked at the man before her. Something of his vitality, his confidence, passed to her soul.

"I will do as you tell me," she said, in a voice little above a whisper. "But, Dick, what will happen?"

"I am going to do my duty," said Dick.

And all that sleepless night, as she tossed from side to side in her bed, she pondered those words but could find no solution to their mystery.

41

Puttler, unshaven and weary-eyed, dragged himself to the study and poured out a large cup of tea that the butler had brought in, and drank it at a gulp.

"Scotland Yard has given me charge of this case, for which you may thank your stars!" he said. "Considering we've had to do all our work between eleven and four, I think I've set up a record in investigation. Thomas' monkish attire was hired, as you thought, from a theatrical costumier's in Wardour Street – "

"I saw him coming out with a bundle under his arm, and wondered what use he could find for fancy dress," interrupted Dick.

"That is fact No. 1," counted Puttler. "Fact No. 2 is that he was making ready for an escape. He even tried to open your local letter box, probably earlier in the evening. Do you send money by post?"

"My brother does, frequently. It's a habit I've tried to cure, without success."

"That is fact No. 2," said Puttler. "He couldn't open the box, but we found the key on him. He had moved everything of value from Gilder's house. I found his portmanteau packed and cached in the field where you say Gilder parks his car. And obviously he was coming to relieve your brother of any loose cash he might find in the library. I found his tools scattered on the flower bed under one of the library windows."

"How was he killed?" asked Dick.

Puttler scratched his head.

"By a regiment of soldiers, to judge from the appearance of him!"

They talked till the sleepy-eyed Mr Glover staggered in and asked permission to go to bed, and then they walked out into the cold morning and joined the party of police that were searching the grounds.

"I suppose the best thing we can do is to go to bed also," said Dick, and at that instant Puttler stooped and picked something from the long grass.

It was a long dagger, its steel hilt black with age, the blade coated with something that was still wet. They looked at one another.

"Do you know this?"

Dick nodded mutely.

"What is it?" asked Puttler.

"It is the dagger that once belonged to Hubert of Redruth – the Black Abbot!" said Dick.

The man's jaw dropped.

"Where does it come from?"

Dick shook his head.

"The last time I saw it," he said slowly, "it was hanging in the hall of Arthur Gine's homuse."

42

"Curiouser and curiouser," said Puttler, who had literary leanings.

Dick heard his name shouted in an agitated voice, and, looking round, saw the butler running towards him, no longer sleepy-eyed, but very alert and white.

"What is the matter, Glover?"

"The maid – foolish girl only just told me – frightened!" gasped the old man, and pointed to the open study windows.

Dick walked quickly back, followed by Puttler. Drooping in his study chair was a plain-looking girl, wearing over her coarse nightdress a man's overcoat; her lank hair falling over her shoulders, she presented a sight which at any other time would have moved Dick Alford to laughter.

"Now, Alice, tell Mr Alford what you told me," said the old butler, beside himself with anxiety.

It was some time before she could speak coherently, and then she told her amazing story. She had gone to bed in the servants' quarters soon after eleven, with a sick headache. She had heard nothing of the scream, but at some time, which she placed with accuracy, having an alarm clock with a phosphorescent dial by her bedside, at 1.45, she heard "a terrible commotion" downstairs. Her room was immediately above Lord Chelford's. She heard shouts and screams, the smashing of glass and the sounds of a struggle.

"Hurry, hurry, woman!" said Dick, frantic with anxiety. "Downstairs, in his lordship's room – are you sure?"

"Yes, sir," whimpered the girl. "I simply dared not get up for fear I was murdered. I simply laid there and fainted and come to again."

Before she had finished, Dick was across the hall and running up the stairs two at a time. He tried the door of Harry's room, but it was bolted. He called him by name, and hammered on the panels, but there was no answer.

"We'd better break in the door," said Puttler. "Have you got an axe?"

Mr Glover went downstairs in search of the tool and returned with an axe and a case-opener. In a second the panel of the door was smashed and Dick peered in.

All the blinds save one were drawn, and the exception admitted sufficient light to enable him to examine the room. He gave one glance and his heart sank. The room was in hopeless confusion; the bedclothes were thrown on the floor, two mirrors, one a cheval glass, had been smashed; the uncurtained window was open. Dick put his hand through the hole in the panel and unbolted the door, and the two men rushed in.

There were signs as of a terrible struggle. The wreckage of two chairs lay scattered about the floor. The table which had held the medicines was overturned and the floor was littered with broken glass, and wet with the spilt medicines.

Puttler walked over to the bed. The mattress had been half dragged to the floor, but the pillows were still in their place, and one of these and a part of the under sheet were smothered with blood.

Dick examined the open window. Three or four of the leaded panes were broken, and the steel rod that kept the windows open was bent as though a heavy weight had rested upon it. The ground was about fifteen feet below, and immediately under the window a large rhododendron bush had been broken as though by some heavy weight dropped upon it. Without hesitation, Dick threw his legs across the window sill, poised himself a moment and dropped to the ground. There was blood on the leaves of the bush; he could find no footprints. Searching the ground, he came upon a smudge of blood against one of the buttresses of the wall.

By this time Puttler, who had chosen a more sedate method of descent, had joined him, and the two men went on, keeping to the paved path, and searched the ground for a further trail.

"This happened when we were in the grounds with the local police," said Puttler.

He had been full of self-reproaches all night, and now Dick silenced him.

"It can't be helped," he said. "The fault is as much mine as yours. I ought to have expected this, after the killing of Thomas. Knowing what I know, I should have gone up to his room and stayed there with him, or at least outside. Poor old Harry! Poor old boy!"

His voice broke, and for a second there were tears in his eyes.

"What is this?"

The paving ended abruptly and was continued by a rolled gravel path, and there were marks here of something heavy being dragged along. These ceased as suddenly as the paving.

"Wait," said Dick, as the solution dawned upon him.

He ran back along the wall of the wing, turned the corner, and stopped before the first of the library windows. It was open, and, drawing himself up, he dropped into the darkened room and pulled back the curtains. So far he had not examined the library; his practised eye, familiar with almost every book on the shelves, told him that somebody had been here. One section of the shelves had been almost cleared. A drawer in Harry's desk had been broken open, and on the floor he found an empty cash-box.

He made a brief and hurried survey, and, returning to the open by the window, he rejoined the detective and told him of his discovery.

Beyond the gravelled path and the dragging marks, all trace of Harry was lost. Ahead of them, at a distance of four or five hundred yards, was the river. To the left, and at this point out of sight, were the abbey ruins.

An hour's search brought them no nearer to discovery, and Dick went back to his room to find the first of the dishevelled reporters stepping from his hired car.

43

Mr Gilder rose at six o'clock that morning. He had spent a restless night and welcomed the dawn. The first post did not arrive until eight o'clock, and he met the postman at the door. There were half a dozen letters for him, and he carried them into his room and examined them eagerly. Only one bore a familiar postmark, and that was in a hand which he recognised. He tore it open and found a few scrawled lines.

If I don't see you again, thank you for your kindness, and don't think too badly of your old friend.

So Thomas had gone! With a curse he threw the letter into the fireplace and went back, accosting the postman as he descended from the upper floors of the apartments.

"No, sir, there's no other letter." The man went through his bundle carefully. "There is another post at half past nine. The country post doesn't usually get into town in time for the first delivery."

Gilder slammed the door and went back to sulk in his room. By this time his servants were about. At nine o'clock they called him to breakfast, but a glance at the contents of the dishes did not tempt him.

His newspapers were placed folded at his hand. He opened the first, and on the centre page a paragraph arrested his eye.

STRANGE HAPPENING AT HAUNTED MANOR HOUSE
By telephone, Chelfordbury, 2 a.m.

There has been a tragic sequel to the appearance of the Black Abbot in the grounds of Fossaway Manor. At eleven o'clock last night, Mr Richard Alford, hearing screams, ran out from the house and discovered the dead body of a man in the habit of a monk. He had been terribly injured, there being no less than nine wounds. The man has been identified as Thomas Luck, a former footman in the employ of the Earl of Chelford.

Gilder uttered an exclamation and put down the paper. Thomas! His first thought was for himself. Suppose it were known that this man was staying at his cottage, he would be dragged into the affair; inquiries would be made, and he would figure at a coroner's inquest, if not in a murder trial. Cold-bloodedly he cursed the dead man for his folly.

Gilder had no doubt in his mind what had occurred. Thomas had gone back to Fossaway Manor to get the remainder of the cash out of the box in Lord Chelford's room. And then – was Thomas the Black Abbot after all? It was quite possible that he had used this disguise on other occasions, and he was in a position very favourable to such a masquerade.

It was nine o'clock; the early editions would be out in an hour. He could, if he wished, have called up a tradesman he knew in Chelfordbury, but that would associate his name with the crime, and these villagers gossiped.

For the time being, all thought of the expected letter went out of his mind. But as the tragedy became familiar to him, his thoughts came back to Leslie Gine. The country post would bring the letter, and he would act generously, munificently. There should be no haggling, no bargaining, no balancing of accounts to the last penny. Her word would be sufficient. Overnight he had written his letter, prepared the grand gesture which should break down the last barrier of mental resistance; and, with his knowledge of women, he did not doubt what form the reaction would take.

He went into the little library where he did his work, opened a combination wall safe and took out the letter. He had read it again and again after it had been written, and with every reading he had the warm glow of complacency which men derive from the contemplation of their own generosity.

MY DEAR LESLIE,

Thank you for your letter. I did not doubt that you would keep your word. My answer you will find enclosed herewith − a blank cheque. I make no stipulations, I extract no conditions. Draw the cheque for as much money as your brother requires to clear himself from his dreadful situation. I have given instructions to the bank that the cheque is to be honoured without question.

FABRIAN.

It was characteristic of the man, who kept three banking accounts, that the cheque was drawn on a branch where his balance was exactly the amount required to liquidate Arthur Gine's liability. It would have been a simple matter to have filled in the form for the amount required, but there was a certain nobility, a magnificence, in the blank cheque. It was a carte blanche upon his fortune. He replaced the letter in the envelope, put it back in the safe and pushed the door closed as the telephone bell rang.

The caller was the man who had taken his place at the office. Had he heard anything about Gine?

"We haven't seen anything of him since you left, and the letters we have sent down for him to sign haven't been returned."

Gilder comforted the anxious man with the assurance that Arthur would put in an appearance some day that week. At the back of his mind there was still a great uneasiness about the tragedy at Chelfordbury. He sent a maid out to get a copy of the sporting editions, but they had not arrived at Regent's Park, and he decided to take a taxi to Piccadilly Circus, and, if necessary, to Fleet Street, to get an early copy. Such a journey would serve the purpose of filling in the time until the country post arrived.

It was at Oxford Circus that he saw the first newspaper contents bill. The first said "Terrible Tragedy in Sussex Village"; the second made him sit bolt upright in the car: "Well-known Earl Kidnapped and Murdered."

44

Gilder stopped the taxi and, springing out, grabbed at a paper. A flaring headline met his eye.

"LORD CHELFORD CARRIED OFF BY UN-KNOWN MURDERER. FEARED DOUBLE TRAGEDY IN A SUSSEX VILLAGE."

There were other sub-headings, but his eye ran down to the story.

At eleven o'clock last night screams were heard in the grounds of Fossaway Manor, the fine old Tudor mansion which has been the country seat of the Earls of Chelford for hundreds of years. The Hon. Richard Alford, the only brother of Lord Chelford, ran out, accompanied by Detective-Sergeant Puttler, who was staying at the Manor as Mr Alford's guest. They were horrified to discover, lying on the grass, the dead body of a man dressed in the habit of the famous Black Abbot. The local police were immediately called in, and hardly had their investigations begun when, unknown to them, a second tragedy occurred. A maid in the employ of the Earl of Chelford, Alice Barter, who sleeps in a room over that occupied by Lord Chelford, states that at one o'clock in the morning she heard sounds of a struggle in his lordship's room. In terror, she did not report the occurrence till four o'clock in the morning. Lord Chelford's door was broken open and a dreadful scene met the eyes of the police officers.

The room was in confusion; mirrors and furniture were smashed; and it was evident from the indications that a terrible struggle had taken place, and, either stunned or killed, Lord Chelford was pulled to the window and thrown out. A search of the grounds left no doubt that his body was dragged for some distance along the ground. At the moment of telephoning, says our correspondent, no trace of the body has been found, but from certain indications there can be little doubt that the unfortunate peer has been a victim of foul play. Certain of his property is missing, whilst a cash-box which he kept in the drawer of a desk in his library has been found empty. Detective-Sergeant Puttler of Scotland Yard is in charge of the case.

The newsboy was still waiting for payment. Mr Gilder put his hand in his pocket mechanically and, giving him a shilling, re-entered the cab.

"Drive me round the Outer Circle," he said. He wanted time to think.

In a dim, uneasy way he realised how deeply he was involved in this tragedy. Fabrian Gilder had a lawyer's mind. He saw the connection between Thomas, himself and Chelford. Thomas, a known thief, harboured in his cottage, goes out, with or without associates, and is killed. Chelford, lately engaged to the girl whom Gilder himself was pursuing, disappears in circumstances which leave no doubt as to his death.

Round and round the Regent's Park Circle the cab moved slowly, and all the time he was piecing together a version which would sound plausible. He had known Thomas; was aware that the man was dismissed, but did not know his criminal connections. The man had asked for shelter for a few days, and in charity Gilder had given it to him. He himself was in London when the crime was committed; had unchallengeable alibis if necessary.

Perhaps he was exaggerating the seriousness of the situation, he thought. Putting his head out of the window, he directed the driver to take him to Regency Mansions. He had forgotten his key; had to ring the bell, and the maid who opened the door handed him the post, which had arrived a few minutes before. He examined the three letters carefully: none was from Leslie. But at the moment he was too occupied with the happenings at Chelfordbury to be disappointed.

And then came a thunderbolt.

"Mr Arthur Gine is waiting for you in the library," said the girl.

"Mr Gine!" he said in astonishment. "When did he come?"

"Ten minutes ago, sir."

"Oh!" said Gilder blankly.

Had she sent her brother instead of a letter? Had she told him? Well, it was a situation that had to be faced.

He walked carelessly into the little library and found Arthur Gine sitting in one of the easiest chairs, a book in his hand, a half-smoked cigar between his teeth.

"Good morning, Gilder."

His voice was cheerful and almost amiable, and for a moment Mr Gilder's heart leapt. This was a friendly ambassador sent by the girl to make the necessary arrangements.

"I think we'd better forget all that's passed," said Arthur. "We both lost our tempers, and there's no sense in keeping the old trouble alive. You don't mind my smoking?"

He replaced the book he had taken from one of the shelves, dusted his knees carefully and then laughed.

"You're thinking of marrying Leslie, I understand?"

Gilder nodded, watching his visitor closely.

"Expecting a letter from her? Well, I'm afraid you won't get it."

"Why not?" asked the other, with a sudden tightening at his heart.

"Because friend Thomas, who spent the evening in wholesale robbery – incidentally, he stole a very ancient dagger from my hall, a silver teapot and a few other etceteras – added to his infamy by attempting to rob a letter box. He didn't succeed in opening the box, but he put the lock out of order."

Gilder breathed again.

"So there was no collection, eh?" he said huskily. "Well, that is rather a relief."

There was a quizzical smile in Arthur Gine's eyes; the discoloration on the left cheek had faded to a pale green.

"I understand you're going to help me?"

"I am going to get you out of your trouble, yes."

"It occurred to me" – Arthur leaned sideways and very carefully dusted the ash of his cigar into a silver tray on the library table – "it occurred to me that you might care to give me proof and evidence of your good feeling."

"I don't understand you," said Gilder.

Arthur hesitated.

"I wondered whether you would write me a letter, to the effect that you are lending me this very large sum. You see, Gilder, although you plan to marry my sister, I am vain enough to wish that it should not be regarded as a gift or the price – the price of her marriage – but as a loan to me." He laughed. "Don't look at me like that, my dear fellow. I am not asking you for money, I am seeking a salve to my conscience. I don't want people to say, 'Leslie Gine was sold for fifty thousand pounds.' I want to produce evidence that you did no more than lend me the money."

A slow smile dawned on Gilder's face.

"There's no objection to that," he said. "I'll give it to you now, if you like. Do you mind if I address you as 'Dear – Arthur'?"

"Charmed," murmured Arthur.

"One has to keep up the pretence of friendliness," said Gilder as he wrote rapidly; "and really I've no strong feeling against you, Gine. You've been a useful man to me."

"Damned useful," said Arthur, without heat.

The man blotted the letter, brought it across, and Arthur Gine read it carefully.

"Thank you," he said, folded and put it into his pocket. "You may think I'm rather weak – which of course I am – and vain: I'm afraid there's no doubt about that! You will hear from Leslie when the mailbox is cleared – that is, if the letters are intact. There is some suspicion that our friend Thomas, baffled in his attempt to open the box, and inspired with that instinct for destruction which is one of the characteristics of the unbalanced criminal, threw in a couple of lighted matches. I had the curiosity to smell at the letter slot, and I think it is very likely that the police theory is correct."

He rose, took up his silk hat and stifled a yawn.

"We've had rather an exciting night in my part of the world. You've probably read all about it in the newspapers?"

"Has Lord Chelford been found?"

Arthur shook his head.

"Not at the time I left," he said. "Unfortunately Leslie was a witness, if not to the murder, to the finding of the first body. The poor little girl was knocked all to pieces. Don't bother her for a day or two – do you mind?"

He held out his hand and Gilder took the soft, cool palm in his.

"I think we shall get on together, Gine."

"I'm sure we shall," said Arthur. "Do you mind showing me the way out? Your flat is rather like a box of tricks, and I'm never sure which is a door and which is a cupboard."

Arthur dispensed with his car. A taxicab took him into the City, and another cab to a small flat in Gray's Inn where he slept when he was in town. He changed into a plain blue suit, carefully and reluctantly shaved off his moustache, and took from his pocket a pair of newly purchased horn-rimmed pince-nez. Surveying himself in the glass with a certain amount of satisfaction, he sat down and wrote a letter to his sister, then, taking a final survey of the little flat where he had spent many a happy bachelor evening, he locked the door, went out and posted the letter in the Holborn post office.

Another taxicab took him to Croydon aerodrome, where he arrived in the early afternoon. He showed the officer his brand new passport.

"That's in order, Mr Steele," said the official. "Your taxi is waiting."

His "taxi" was a sturdy two-seater aeroplane. Five minutes after his arrival he was zooming up to the blue, and was soon a speck in the hazy sky, heading for France, possibly for Genoa, as likely as not, by an Italian liner, for Rio de Janeiro. Everything depended on how Mr Fabrian Gilder swallowed the pill which Arthur had administered.

45

"Burnt," said Dick, with considerable satisfaction.

"The poor brute did some good in his life – heaven forgive me for speaking ill of him. Where is your Arthur?"

"My Arthur went to town very early," said Leslie. "There is no news of Harry?"

He shook his head.

"None," he said.

He looked dreadfully tired and broken, she thought.

"I'm so sorry!"

He took her hand and patted it.

"I wish you would go away somewhere, Leslie," he said. "Couldn't you take a long voyage?"

"Why?" she asked.

"I want you out of the way. I don't exactly know why, but I'm rather worried about you. Get Arthur – "

He stopped. It was quite possible that Arthur would not be a free agent at the end of the week; and, reading his thoughts, she smiled sadly.

"What am I to do about Mr Gilder?"

"Let him write. He is hardly likely to leave you in peace. But you understand, of course, that until Harry is found there is no danger to your brother. Until he appears, no action can be taken."

She looked at him pityingly.

"Do you think he is alive?" she asked.

"Yes," he replied shortly. "Puttler doesn't think so, but I do. We are dragging the Ravensrill today, but it is not deep enough to hide – a body."

He covered his face with his hands.

"I wish I were a million miles away, perched on some solitary star," he said wearily.

She slipped her hand through the crook of his arm.

"You'd be very hot," she said, with a pathetic attempt at gaiety, "unless I have forgotten all my astronomy."

He put his arm about her shoulder and hugged her. It was an affectionate brotherly hug, and no more.

"You've got to go away, my dear. What about the prosaic Bournemouth? Or the vulgar but wholesome Margate?"

Again she shook her head.

"Or London, which I am told is a health resort?"

"You're very anxious for me to go, really?"

"Very," he said, with an emphasis that betrayed his concern.

She drew back from him and faced him.

"Dick, will you tell me something without any evasion?"

He nodded.

"Do you think that I am in any personal danger?"

"I am sure of it," he said. "It would be cruel not to tell you the truth. The shot that was fired the other day was intended for you. It was fired by a man who is as brilliant a shot as any in England, and the height of the bullet mark told us that it was aimed directly at your heart."

She listened, stupefied, unbelieving.

"But why?" she asked, bewildered. "I have no enemies, Dick; I have wronged nobody. Who could do such a wicked thing?"

"If I told you, you would perhaps be no wiser," he said. "There is a man in this world who hates you and hates me, and has good reason from his point of view. Now that I've told you the truth, will you go?"

She thought a while.

"I'll wait until Arthur comes back," she said, "and ask him to take me to London."

And with that he was satisfied.

He was leaving the house when Puttler's cycle swung into the drive.

"Anything wrong?" asked Dick quickly.

"I don't know. Look at this."

He took from his pocket a large sheet of foolscap paper; roughly printed in pencil were the words: "Lord Chelford is safe. Don't search for him, or he will be killed. The Black Abot."

The word "Abbot" was printed with one "b." The placard had been found hanging from the twig of a tree, the jagged hole at the top showing where the mystery man had threaded the paper.

"We found it halfway between the ruins and the house," said Puttler. "Curiously enough, we had been searching that part of the grounds only a quarter of an hour before."

Dick handed the warning back to him.

"Is that a bad joke or do you believe this paper?" asked Leslie anxiously. "And, Dick, couldn't I be some help? I know Fossaway Manor so well, and I am sure there must be places where the police haven't looked. Do you know there are tiny caves in the banks of the Ravensrill?"

"They've all been searched, and they're not big enough to hold a large-sized dog," said Dick. "If you want to be helpful you can come up to the Manor and put my correspondence in order. I am afraid it has been neglected in these days, and there are a lot of bills and things to be entered up."

He had no real need for her, he thought, but whilst she was in the neighbourhood he was anxious that she should be under his eye. She may have suspected something of this, but she gratefully accepted the offer.

"Drive up," he warned her; "keep to the main road and the main drive. Don't stop for anybody, however well you know them, and take no notice if you hear somebody shout at you."

In spite of her anxiety she laughed.

"How very alarming that sounds!"

After he had gone she busied herself with the affairs of the house, arranged the dinner for that night, and was on the point of leaving, when somebody rang the front-door bell. She was putting on her hat before the mirror in her bedroom when the maid came up.

"Miss Wenner?" cried Leslie, aghast, and only then did she remember that at Arthur's request she had written inviting the girl to spend the weekend with them.

Here was a complication she had not foreseen. And yet, in the space between her room and the hall, she had made up her mind that, if there was one thing she welcomed at this moment, it was the society of a woman.

Mary Wenner was in the hall and greeted her as effusively as if they had been bosom friends, though in truth Leslie scarcely knew the girl.

"My dear, I'm so glad to be back in this lovely old country!" she said. "I couldn't help thinking, as I was driving past dear old Fossaway Manor, how perfectly peaceful everything is!"

Leslie could have screamed! Peaceful!

"Perhaps it isn't quite as peaceful as it looks, Miss Wenner," she said dryly.

"Call me Mary," begged the girl. "I do so dislike formalism and standoffishness! It will be so awkward if Arthur calls me by my name and you call me Miss – I mean – ?"

"Well, I'll call you Mary with pleasure," said Leslie. "I think you know my name?"

"A beautiful name," said the ecstatic Miss Wenner. "The only thing against it is, you can't tell whether it's a boy's or a girl's, can you? Don't you sometimes find that very embarrassing?"

"I've never found it so yet," said the girl, leading the way up to her room.

She waited till Mary had taken off her hat before she gave her news.

"Arthur is in town, but he'll be back tonight," she said. "Have you seen the newspapers?"

Miss Wenner shook her head vigorously.

"I never read the newspapers," she said, reprovingly. "They're always full of lies, and after the way they roasted me over my breach – " She coughed.

For a moment Leslie had a wild idea that the reference was an indelicate one, and then the truth came to her.

"Did you ever have a breach of promise action?" she asked, in astonishment.

Mary was very red, and her embarrassment was painful to witness.

"I did have a little trouble with a young gentleman I went to business with," she admitted. "I was a mere girl at the time, young and silly as it were, and I must say that I felt that I had to stand up for my rights. A lot of people think it was unladylike, but I say that a girl who is an orphan without parents must look after herself. I got fifty pounds, and it wasn't worth the trouble and the nuisance."

There was something about the girl that Leslie liked. Unconsciously she was amusing, but there was a sterling value in her, she thought, and Leslie had an uncanny knowledge of women.

"No, I never read the papers, Leslie. After being told by the *Daily Megaphone* that I had a curious mentality – I shall never forget those words – I've given up the papers."

"Then you haven't heard what has happened at Fossaway Manor?" asked Leslie.

The startled girl listened, her mouth an O of amazement and horror.

"Thomas? Why, I was talking with him only the other day! You don't think Harry is killed?"

Leslie shook her head.

"I don't know what to think. Mr Alford is very confident that he is still alive, and they have just received a strange message which seems to bear that out."

The girl was shocked, and Leslie could not help feeling that she was hurt too.

"Harry Alford was the best fellow in the world," said Mary quietly. "He was a little irritable and difficult to get on with – you don't mind me talking about him?"

"No," said Leslie. "You probably do not know that our engagement was broken off?"

This seemed to be a greater shock still.

"Broken off? I'll bet that was Dick Alford's doing."

"Mr Alford had nothing to do with it," said Leslie, and Mary made a rapid re-estimation of Dick Alford's character; and she was eminently adjustable.

"Dick Alford is not a bad fellow really," she said diplomatically. "There is a great deal about him that I like. And he is so good-looking!"

She was a shrewd, discerning *gamine*, who had won through by her ability to adjust her views at a moment's notice. And in a fraction of a second she had realised that perfect harmony with Arthur Gine's sister could only be ensured if her views on Richard Alford underwent a very thorough reorganisation.

"I didn't get on very well with him; I used to think he was a bit overbearing. But it must have been rather a trial for him, poor fellow!" A pause, and then: "I seem to have come at a pretty bad time, Miss – Leslie. Would you like me to go back to London?"

"Wait," said her hostess, and, running downstairs, called Dick on the phone. He had just returned to the house as she rang.

"Surely," he said. "Bring her up. I think that would be rather a good idea. And, Leslie, perhaps you would like to stay here the night. Arthur can come along too – you might leave him a note or wire him."

The idea was so appealing that she put no obstacles in the way, and returned to carry Dick's invitation to her guest. Miss Wenner accepted with an alacrity that was almost indelicate.

"I may be able to be of some help," she said. "I know the ins and outs of that place, and all the nooks and crannies. It is the treasure that's done it all, Leslie! He was always after that silly Life Water, and I shouldn't be surprised if he hasn't got into bad company."

"But Harry never went out."

"Oh, yes, he did," was the surprising reply. "He often slipped off to London when Mr Alford was away. And there was something queer about it, because Harry made me promise I would never tell Mr Richard, as he called him."

"How often did that happen?" asked Leslie.

"Sometimes once a month, sometimes twice or three times a month. He never went to the front drive; he followed the field path through the cutting, and I used to arrange for a Horsham motor cab to meet him. He used to go from Horsham and come back the same way, and I've known him to ring me up before he came back, to ask me if Mr Richard had returned."

Leslie wondered if Dick knew this.

"I've known him to go as many as three times a week when Mr Richard was up in Yorkshire, looking after the Doncaster estate," added Mary, and, virtuously: "I hope I have not let any cats out of the bag: all young men are a bit wild."

46

The adaptability of Miss Wenner was never more strikingly illustrated than in her greeting of Dick Alford. There was a coyness, a shy friendliness, in her glance which might have deceived an uninitiated spectator into believing that they were old lovers, parted by cruel circumstances and meeting after an absence of years. Dick, weary and heartbroken as he was, found in her the first cause for amusement he had had in twenty-four hours.

He had had rooms prepared for them in the east wing, which was opposite to that in which his own room and Harry's were situated. There were two small apartments with a connecting door, which he had assigned to Leslie and her guest. The next room had been prepared for Arthur.

"I've moved Puttler to this wing, too," he explained, "though I don't suppose the poor fellow will get very much sleep for a night or two."

After he had shown them the rooms he took his departure, and Leslie followed him along the corridor and overtook him at the head of the stairs.

"There is really nothing I can do, I suppose, Dick?" For she had accepted the story of the disordered accounts as being a plausible excuse on his part to get her to Fossaway Manor.

To her surprise he said "Yes," and took her below to the study.

"Here are the estate accounts. I haven't touched them for three or four days. Do you know anything about figures?"

She nodded wisely.

"Will you start by checking these wages sheets? You'll find the books on the shelf, and you will be able to get the hang of my rather simple system."

He gave her instructions how to deal with the bills that had accumulated, and left her very contented. It was half an hour before she remembered that she had left Mary Wenner in her room, and hurried upstairs to apologise. She was to find Mary a very capable assistant, for not only was the girl efficient in her work, but she knew all the domestic mysteries of Fossaway Manor.

The two girls lunched alone, for Dick had sent a message to say that he would not be back in time.

"The place gives me the creeps," said Mary with a shudder, and her nervousness was not affectation. "The whole thing is frightful! Poor Thomas killed, and Harry taken away heaven knows where – oh!" She sprang to her feet, and her face had gone pale. "I know where Harry is," she said, quivering with excitement. "I know, I know!"

"Where?" asked the wondering Leslie.

The girl ran out of the room into the hall.

"Where is Mr Alford?" she asked quickly. "I must see him at once."

"He telephoned from Red Farm," said Leslie, who had followed her. "Perhaps we can get him."

She turned the handle of the old-fashioned instrument and gave the Red Farm number.

"Is that you, Dick? How lucky!"

"I expected it was you. Is anything wrong?" he asked anxiously.

"No; Mary Wenner has something she wants to tell you." She lowered her voice. "She thinks she knows where Harry is hidden."

There was a silence at the other end.

"She's not – "

"No, no, no." With Mary within earshot, it was impossible to assure Dick that the girl was not trying to make a sensation.

"I'll come over right away," he said.

They went out to the head of the drive to meet him, and Mary offered her theory.

"I must have been mad not to have told you about this before. I don't know where my wits have gone," she said. "After all my treasure-hunting and the horrible experience I had that night with Gilder, and not to think of it now, when I practically came down to show Mr Gine the place – well, I'm surprised at myself!"

Dick listened with growing impatience to this preliminary.

"Where do you think my brother is?"

"Where?" said Miss Wenner triumphantly. "Why under the abbey – that's where. I'll show you."

They walked side by side across the meadow, and as they went Miss Wenner related the startling story of her adventures after treasure.

"Of course, I always knew that it didn't belong to me, even if I found it," she said virtuously; "but Mr Gilder was so very pressing that I couldn't very well refuse him, especially after what he'd written in vanishing ink, though I've got the ink back again, as he'll find out one of these days."

Leslie listened, scarcely crediting her ears. Yet, unless Mary Wenner had an imagination of a particularly inventive nature, it was hardly likely that she could have made the story up.

Dick examined the great corner-stone of the tower. He stood by, watching curiously, whilst, with a pair of scissors which she took from her bag, the girl pressed back the catch and sent the corner-stone turning noisily on its invisible hinge.

The opening was between twelve and fifteen inches wide. A stout man could never have entered by that way, as Dick pointed out.

"You had better stay here; I'll go down," he said.

"You'll want a light," warned Mary.

There was a lamp in his pocket. He had spent the morning peering into impossible dark places. In a second he had disappeared down the moss-grown stairs, and Leslie waited with palpitating heart for his reappearance. Presently they heard his voice.

"Come down."

"Not me," said Mary hastily. "I've been there once, thank you!"

And Leslie went alone, guided by the light he showed from step to step.

Now she was standing with him in the vaulted room. He tried first one and then the other of the two doors leading from the ante-chamber, but neither yielded to his touch. It was pitch dark save for the fan-shaped ray of the lamp. He swept the light along wall and floor, and presently she saw the focus halt upon a broken flagstone.

"What is it?" she asked.

"Nothing," he said quickly. He had moved the light to the narrow entrance of the room. "Up you go; there is nothing here but mice and memories. I have always known there were underground vaults in the abbey. In fact, I think there was a report on them by one of my recent forbears."

Although he was immediately behind her, his voice seemed to come from a distance. She was walking, and he gave her no help with his lamp, so that she had to feel her way up. Turning her head, she saw that he was ascending the stairs backwards, keeping the light covering the stairs below.

"Hurry," he said tersely, and she stumbled up the remaining steps and emerged into the blessed daylight.

It was some time before he joined them, and when he came out she saw that he was white to the lips.

"What did you see, Dick?" she asked.

He shook his head.

"Nothing," he said, and slammed the stone door tight.

Of the little party, only Miss Wenner was unaffected by the atmosphere which Dick Alford brought from that vaulted room.

" – so far as Mr Gilder said – and I don't trust the man entirely, as you can well understand, Leslie – there were only pieces of music in lead cylinders – that was the word, 'cylinders.' To me they looked rather more like rolls. And this Black Abbot must have cleared them out whilst we had gone. Mr Gilder *was* disappointed. In fact, he was quite rude to me over the telephone. I do think a gentleman should keep his temper in all circumstances, don't you, dear?"

Leslie agreed mechanically.

What had Dick seen? What object was it that showed for a second in the light of his lamp?

Near to the house he made an excuse to them. He had to go back to Red Farm to finish his interview with the obstinate Mr Leonard; but he did not take his car. He said he would take the short cut, and Leslie thought it was not the moment to question him. She watched him until he disappeared in a fold of the ground. He was heading for the abbey. The other girl had gone in to finish her lunch, and Leslie hesitated. The thought of his going back to that dark room again filled her with blind panic. She wanted to call out to him and bring him back, but he was out of hearing now, and she obeyed an impulse and went after him.

He was not in sight until she climbed the second of the gentle slopes. Here she stopped; he might resent being overlooked, and she lay down on the grass, watching him. She saw him come to the square tower, pause at the corner, and disappear apparently into space. From such a distance the effect of his entry was eerie. The entrance was so small that he seemed to melt into the solid stonework. Ten minutes passed, a quarter of an hour, and then a long, interminable wait; she heard the village clock strike two. A lark in the blue was singing his passionate song; over by Red Farm a donkey was braying – a ludicrous accompaniment to what might be stark tragedy.

She was on the point of rising and running across to the ruins, to follow him into the depths, when he appeared again. He came slowly forth, turned and closed the stone door and leaned against it, his head on his arm, a picture of tragic despair.

She stopped and sank down on her knees, the better to escape observation, and presently he walked slowly away, and it was the gait of a broken man.

47

Hurrying back the way she had come, she joined Mary in the study. Puttler she had not seen since the early morning, when he cycled to Willow House to bring the notice he had found.

"My dear," said Mary, "I'm not so sure I shall stay here tonight. This place is full of shocks! I'd like to see your brother very much indeed, but you can tell him all about the room under the abbey, can't you? That's where the gold is – you mark my words!"

"The gold?" Leslie for a moment did not understand. "Oh, you mean the Chelford treasure?"

The horrible thing! It was behind all this misery; behind the killing of Thomas and the disappearance of Harry. She said as much, and Miss Wenner, not pausing in her typewriting, calmly expressed the view that it was very likely.

Shock followed shock indeed! At half past four Leslie's maid brought a letter which had come by special delivery. It was in Arthur's writing; she tore it open and read:

DEAR LESLIE,
You are under no circumstances to marry Gilder. I refuse to allow you to sacrifice yourself for me, now or at any time. I am going away to France for a few months, and will return when things have blown over.

Ordinarily quick-witted, it was a long time before Leslie could understand the significance of this message. When she did, she took the letter to Dick, and he read it without comment and handed it back to her.

"What does that mean, Dick?"

"It means that Arthur has taken the line of least resistance," he said. "To put it vulgarly, he has bolted!"

Her heart sank, and in that moment she felt terribly alone. As if he read her thoughts, he went on:

"He has certainly precipitated the crisis, but I don't see exactly how it will affect you. There was nothing else in the letter?"

She shook her head and opened the envelope, and then saw a slip of paper which she had overlooked. It was an authority to sell his business, drawn up in legal form, and had evidently been added as an afterthought.

"If there are no further defalcations, that ought to be worth something," said Dick. "I'll see what I can do."

But on this point she was firm.

"I think you've enough trouble without mine," she said quietly. "Did you find anything in the ruins?"

He started.

"Why – no," he said, a little unconvincingly. "Did you see me go back?"

"I'm afraid I spied on you," she said, with a pathetic little smile. "Dick, I'm so worried about you; I wish you wouldn't go into these places alone."

"There was nothing to fear," he said. "I thought I saw something on the floor which gave me a clue to Harry's fate, but it was nothing – nothing."

He changed the subject abruptly. She had a feeling that he was not telling her all that he had seen.

Mary and she had dinner alone, and Mr Glover, the butler, free from the restraining presence of Dick Alford, was inclined to be talkative.

"There's no doubt Mr Alford looks after the policemen. I have had to get a food basket ready – thermos flask and everything the heart can desire. Personally, miss, I don't believe in pampering the police.

They're only dissatisfied when they go back to their own homes. He won't have anybody take the basket down to them either. 'No,' he said, 'I'll take it myself. You have it ready at nine o'clock, put it just outside the servant's door.' My own opinion is that they'd be much more pleased with bread and cheese and a bottle of beer. What's the good of making chicken sandwiches for policemen? And having a bottle of the best wine up from the cellar! It's a waste of good food!"

Leslie listened, petrified. Now she understood!

The food was not for the police – it was for Harry! Harry, held prisoner in Chelford Abbey – by whom?

48

The bane of life that day had been the London reporters. The Red Lion Inn at Chelfordbury was already filled with them, and not an hour passed that one did not make his way to the house in a vain endeavour to interview the second son. One intercepted him in Elm Drive, and to him, as to the rest, he gave the same reply.

"You boys can't expect me to tell you any more than I already know," he said, at bay. "My brother has disappeared, but I believe he is still alive."

"Who do you think is responsible for these outrages, Mr Alford?" asked the reporter.

Dick shook his head.

"If I knew, it isn't reasonable to suppose that I should be discussing the matter with you."

"Is it the Black Abbot?"

"The Black Abbot has nothing whatever to do with this crime," said Dick shortly. "Unless I credit you with being so foolish as to believe in ghosts, it is unnecessary for me to tell you that there is no such thing as a Black Abbot, and the figure that has been seen in these grounds was somebody masquerading for his own purpose."

"A practical joke?" suggested the newspaper man.

Dick shook his head.

"I don't think it was a practical joke; indeed, I am sure there is something very serious behind it. But I can't tell you any more."

"Mr Alford," said the reporter, "I'm going to ask you a very delicate question, and I hope you won't think it an impertinence. If your brother is dead, then the title comes to you, does it not?"

"Yes," said Dick.

"You won't be offended if I tell you that there is a little talk in the village of some antagonism between your brother and you. I am told there have been frequent quarrels."

Dick mastered his anger with a great effort, realising that the reporter was not intending to be impertinent, but simply epitomising the gossip of the countryside.

"My brother was very nervous and quick-tempered," he said, "but I've never had a serious quarrel with him in my life."

"Is it true that Lord Chelford's fiancée, Miss Leslie Gine, recently broke off her engagement with your brother?"

"Perfectly true," said Dick, stifling his impatience.

"And yet she is staying at Fossaway Manor as your guest?" The keen eyes of the reporter were watching him closely. He saw the blood mount to his victim's cheeks and hastened to add: "I'm merely telling you what other people will tell you, Mr Alford. I have a much wider experience than you have of the uncharity and suspicion that surrounds every man associated with a crime like this. If you are annoyed with me I can understand it, but I can assure you that I only want to help you."

"That I quite believe," said Dick with a smile. "But you can understand just how embarrassing your questions are. I will tell you the truth and you may put it into your paper. I am satisfied there is a very terrible danger overhanging Miss Leslie Gine, and it is for that reason, and that reason alone, I have asked her to stay at the Manor, which is under police protection and where I know she will be safe. Her brother has gone abroad, and I cannot allow her to stay at Willow House alone."

"You mean she is in danger from the same person as killed Thomas the footman, and who is responsible for the disappearance of Lord Chelford?"

Dick nodded, and the newspaper man made a mental note.

"Thank you," he said. "You will find that this little talk has cleared the air. In cases like this, if you clear up the minor mysteries as you go along, it makes for everybody's comfort."

Dick, who had been trembling with anger through the interview, had to agree, in the calm moments which followed, that the reporter had taken a sane view of the matter. When he met Leslie a few minutes later, he told her of the interview. She was in the study alone, and had just finished writing a letter, which lay face downward on the blotting-pad. She saw him glance at the envelope and turned it up. It was addressed to Fabrian Gilder.

"What have you said?" he asked.

"I've told him that I've considered the matter, and I've decided that I could not marry him – in any circumstances it would be impossible now, so soon after Harry's disappearance."

He picked up the letter and, taking out his pocket-case, tore off a stamp and affixed it.

"I'll see that this goes," he said grimly. Then, seeing her tired face: "Poor old girl, you're having a bad time."

The pressure of her hand, the love and sympathy in her voice, were almost too much for him, and he had to set his teeth or he would have taken her in his arms and, in that place of tragedy and horror, told her of the love that was shaking him, and which had added a new and fearful burden to his overstrung nerves.

"Go to bed early," he said, with an effort at gaiety, "and rise with the dawn. I shall be busy till very late."

"The butler was telling me that you have ordered a basket of food for the policemen."

Not a muscle of his face moved.

"That is so; one or two men who are patrolling the cutting need a little light refreshment. They cannot get to the house and we haven't men to relieve them."

She was sensible enough not to pursue the subject.

It was only on her earnest entreaty that, as the night drew on, Mary Wenner remained. The girl was a bundle of nerves, started at every sound, paled and flushed with the opening of a door, and the sound of a falling plate in the servery whilst they were at dinner had made her scream.

"I can't help it, my dear; I'm naturally temperamental," she explained. "And this house has got me shivering! I can't leave another young lady without a chaperone, or I'd fly off to London before it got dark."

She had been in the library that afternoon, she told Leslie, and the sight of that familiar room with its empty chair had been almost the last straw.

"I had to have a good cry," she confessed, "and I'm not ashamed of it. Harry was one of the best – you don't mind me calling him Harry, do you, dear?" And, when Leslie shook her head: "I can't say that I was fond of him as a young girl ought to be fond of a man she loves, but he was very nice. He had his tempers, the same as the rest of us, but they were only his high spirits. I could never understand why he hated Mr Alford."

Leslie looked at her incredulously.

"Hated Mr Alford?" she repeated. "Surely you're mistaken? They were very good friends."

Mary shook her head.

"No, they weren't," she said. "It all arose out of her ladyship's picture."

"The late Lady Chelford?"

"That was the lady," nodded Mary. "It happened three years ago. Dick Alford suggested that the portrait should be moved to the gallery. I think he was silly to say it, knowing how Harry adored his mother, and when he said the picture was depressing – and that was the silliest thing of all – Harry got right up in the air! It was dreadful, the things he said to Mr Alford – and before me too! Dick Alford realised his mistake: I could see that, and he tried to pacify Harry, but for a fortnight they didn't speak."

Leslie was silent. Slowly the inner life of Fossaway Manor was beginning to reveal itself to her; she had seen nothing of these cross-currents, had not suspected, even dimly, the conflicting antagonism which must have been visible to Harry Alford's secretary.

"They were very friendly sometimes. You'd think that Harry was fond of him, and I think he was," Mary continued; "but the quarrels used to break out every now and then, once because Dick always stood with his back to the picture, and never looked at it at all. He hated it, I'm sure of that. Of course he never took me into his confidence. We were not what you might term good friends. I suppose it was foolish of me to take up Harry's quarrel, but I never liked Dick – you don't mind me calling him Dick? – after that."

She glanced nervously through the window. The sun had set, and dusk was creeping over the great park.

"If I get any sleep tonight I'll be lucky," she said. "Do you mind if I leave my door open and keep a light burning?"

"Why, of course not," smiled Leslie.

"There is a lock on the door, and I asked Glover to find me the key," Miss Wenner went on. "And I'll tell you frankly, Leslie, that if he hadn't found it I wouldn't have stayed, not for all the money in the world."

Leslie felt that it would be indiscreet to offer encouragement to a further discussion of this subject, for she was as reluctant to spend the night under that roof as her newfound friend.

49

Though she waited up till nearly eleven, she did not see Dick, and, in response to the repeated hints of the other girl, they went upstairs together.

The Manor was lighted by a power plant which was accommodated in a small shed midway between the house and the Ravensrill, and owed its installation to Dick's enterprise.

Harry always had candles in his room, Mary told her, but accepted the lighting of his library as a compromise.

"It's a very strange thing," said Mary from her inner room, "but Harry was afraid of electricity. In thunderstorms he always went down into the cellar and stayed there until they were over. He used to have a bed which was made every day in the summer, in case of a storm coming on in the night, and – "

At that moment all the lights in the room went out.

"Have you turned the lights off?" asked Mary's anxious voice.

"No, I haven't been near the switch; I expect a fuse has gone," said the girl.

There were matches and candles on the dressing-table, she remembered, and, groping her way to the table, she lit the two candles. Mary was standing in the doorway, very pale and wide-eyed.

"What was the meaning of that?" she asked, her voice sharp with fear, which was beginning to communicate itself to Leslie.

She forced a smile.

"That happens in the best-regulated houses," she said, with spurious gaiety. "The door is locked, so there's nothing to be afraid of."

And then she heard footsteps in the corridor; there was a knock at the door that made Mary jump.

"Are you there, Leslie?" It was Dick's voice. "Something has gone wrong with the lighting arrangements; we'll put it right in a minute or two."

"Are the lights out everywhere?" asked Mary, but he was gone.

Twenty minutes passed and again Leslie heard his footsteps approaching.

"I'm afraid we shan't be able to fix up the lights till the morning. Have you candles? Did Glover put a flashlight for you?"

"We've everything we want," said Leslie. "Don't worry about us: we shall be asleep in ten minutes."

"Not me," murmured Miss Wenner tremulously. "I shan't sleep a wink!"

By the light of her candle she had replaced most of the garments she had discarded when the lights went out.

"I knew I oughtn't to have stayed – there's somebody coming along the corridor!"

"It is only Mr Alford."

But her ears caught the sound of two pairs of feet, and presently Dick's voice spoke.

"Do you mind if I leave one of Puttler's men outside your door?" he asked. "Don't be alarmed if you hear him walking about in the night."

"Is anything wrong, Dick?"

"No, no, nothing wrong; only I knew Miss Wenner was rather nervous."

"I am," quavered Miss Wenner loudly. "It's very good of you, Mr Alford."

"You had better keep your windows fastened," said Dick. "There is a system of ventilation in the rooms, so you needn't be afraid of waking with a headache. Good night."

When he had gone, Mary Wenner looked solemnly at her companion.

"Did you hear what he said about keeping the windows shut?" she asked hollowly. "My Gawd!"

"Don't be silly, Mary."

The girl was past feeling comfortable, but she had need to set an example.

"Come along, I'll help you fasten the windows."

" 'Keep the windows fastened,' " repeated Mary Wenner. "There's something doing!"

They went from one to the other of the leaded windows, closed them and pressed down the catches. Suddenly Mary clutched the girl's arm fiercely.

"There's a man under my bed!" she gasped, staring wildly at the drooping counterpane.

With a fluttering heart Leslie lifted the cover, and pulled out a pair of riding boots, the soles of which the frightened girl had seen, and they both laughed hysterically.

"I wish I could bring my bed into your room." Mary looked helplessly at the heavy four-poster to which she had been assigned.

"You can come and sleep with me," said Leslie. "I've got a big bed." And this offer was most gratefully accepted.

"Have a look under your bed first," said Miss Wenner nervously, and not till this ritual had been observed did she commence very slowly to undress.

Down below in the library, Dick was in consultation with Puttler, who had just returned from a hasty visit to Scotland Yard.

"The batteries were smashed, and an attempt had been made to cut the main cable," reported Dick. "I got to the power house just after it happened, but I saw nobody."

Puttler pulled at his comic little nose and there was a look of trouble in his brown eyes.

"The Commissioner thinks you ought to have a dozen men down here and make a clean-up," he said. "I've brought three, and I think they all ought to be inside the house. One we've got in the east wing, another in the west, and a patrol in the hall. That will leave you and me and the local 'flatties' for the grounds. Though I think we might as well stay here – you want a battalion to patrol the estate properly. By the way, when I was looking round early this morning I found a great mound of earth in the north-east corner of the estate, near the river. One of your gamekeepers told me it was called Chelford Greed. What is the idea?"

Dick was not in an archaeological mood, but he explained.

"One of my ancestors – I don't know which one – planned and carried out a big steal. You probably know that the charter by which we received these lands from King Henry confines the northern boundary of the estate to the course of the Ravensrill, and the ingenious Chelford of the times had the idea of changing the course of the Ravensrill so that the estate would embrace another thousand acres. The Chelford Greed was the dam he built. The natural course of the Ravensrill runs through the Long Meadow. It was one of those clever little pieces of robbery that has made us landed proprietors what we are! As I say, I don't know which of the Chelfords planned this piece of larceny, because there is no written record, and the legend has come down from mouth to mouth, so to speak."

He looked up at the big portrait above the fireplace and shook his head.

"Lady," he said softly, "you've given me a lot of trouble!"

Puttler was interested.

"As how?" he asked.

"I'll tell you one of these days," said Dick. "I wonder if those girls are asleep?"

He stole quietly up the stairs. The man on duty in the corridor flashed a lamp upon him as he approached.

"No sound," he whispered, and Dick crept downstairs again.

It was arranged that he and Puttler should snatch a few hours' sleep in turn, the other patrolling round and round the block of buildings. At two o'clock in the morning Dick was aroused from a deep slumber to feel Puttler gently shaking at his shoulder.

"Nothing has happened," said the detective, eyeing with a friendly look the sofa from which Dick struggled. "I've warmed up some grub for you."

A spirit stove was burning on the desk and the kettle above was steaming. Dick poured the black coffee into a cup and scalded himself to wakefulness.

"One of the local men thought he saw somebody moving and challenged," reported Puttler, settling himself down with a luxurious sigh. "But it was probably only a bush. These birds are jumpy – they see a Black Abbot in every shadow!"

Dick sipped at the boiling fluid and broke a biscuit with his disengaged hand.

"Thank God this can't go on much longer!" he said. "By the way, did you bring those papers from London?"

"I gave them to you in the library: they were in the blue envelope."

Dick put down the glass.

"I'd better keep them in my safe," he said. "I don't want the servants to see them."

He crossed the hall, unlocked the door of the library and went in, mechanically switching on the light, and only then remembering that for the time being Fossaway Manor was denied the service of the little power house. He went back to the study and got his lamp and picked his way across the room to the desk. The envelope was where he had put it, and he slipped this into his pocket. As he did so, he was aware that a cold wind was blowing. He sent his light along the windows. That at the end was open; one of the curtains, which had been drawn across, lay in a heap on the floor.

He went to the door and called Puttler softly and the detective joined him.

"Somebody has been here," he said, and pointed to the curtain and the twisted pole that had supported it.

It was easy to see how the intruder had made his way into the library. Two of the panes near the iron handle which fastened one leaf of the window had been broken, and evidently the midnight visitor, in entering, must have fallen and, catching hold of the curtain to save himself, brought it to the ground, breaking away the pole, which was hanging drunkenly.

"I passed here ten minutes ago, and the window was shut then," said Puttler.

"He may have been inside at the moment," replied Dick thoughtfully. "I wonder what has been taken?"

He examined the desk. Evidently the intruder had not opened any of the drawers, though, if he had done so, his labours would have been in vain, since Dick had cleared every document out of the room early in the day. As they circled the room, Puttler stumbled over something.

"Where did this come from?" he asked.

It was a light ladder, and Dick recognised it as one of two that were part of the library furniture, and were employed to reach books from the top shelf of the lower tier.

"When I saw this last it was standing at the end of the room," he said.

He flashed his lamp up on to the shelves, looking for a gap in the long line of books. So doing, his lamp swept across that space intervening between the shelves which was covered by the portrait of the late Lady Chelford. He could see the big gold frame, caught a glimpse of one white hand hanging gracefully, and then something brought his lamp back. He heard the churchwarden detective swear softly. Himself, he was speechless. The light of his lamp focussed on the place where the woman's face had been, and where now was a black emptiness.

The face and shoulders of the picture had been cut from the frame, and the ragged strands of canvas told him that it had been cut by an unskilful hand.

50

Neither man spoke until they were back in the little study, and then Puttler looked gloomily at his companion.

"What do you make of that?"

"Heaven knows!" groaned Dick.

The study door was closed, and he had pulled across a dark curtain which had been hung that day for the purpose.

"I suppose I'd better get out, though I don't suppose I shall find anything."

"Wait until I've had the remainder of your coffee and I'll come with you," said Puttler. "No, Mr Alford, I never felt less like sleep. We shall have daylight in a couple of hours. Wait."

He turned down the oil lamp which had been requisitioned from the kitchen, blew down the glass chimney and the room was in darkness.

"Now you can pull open those curtains and go out," he said, "if that is your way."

Dick moved the curtains slightly and looked out. The world lay peaceful, silent, in the pallid light of the moon, and as he opened the door, the sweet scent of the earth and the cold morn greeted him fragrantly.

His foot was raised to step across the threshold when Puttler's big hand closed round his arm.

"Wait," he whispered again.

Dick stood motionless.

"I see nothing," he said in the same tone.

Still Puttler held him, his head bent, listening.

"All right," he said, released his grip and stepped out on to the little terrace before Dick.

He gave a swift glance left and right.

"What was it?" asked Dick, in surprise.

"Somebody breathing," was Puttler's astonishing reply. "You won't believe that I could hear a man breathing a dozen yards away, but I can. It's one of my many animal qualities."

He took a little run, cleared the gravel path in a bound and went noiselessly along the grass to the left. Presently Dick saw him returning at a jog-trot. The detective went past him and disappeared round the wing of the block. In a few minutes he returned.

"Hearing and scent are my two qualities. Can you smell anything?"

Dick sniffed the morning air.

"No," he confessed.

"Come along with me."

This time he walked softly across the path, explaining that he was afraid of waking the girls, who slept almost immediately above them.

They went to the end of the wing, and then the sergeant halted.

"Now do you smell anything?" he asked.

Dick sniffed again. There was a sweet odour in the air, the scent of some exotic flower that seemed familiar to him.

"Does anybody in this house smoke scented cigarettes?" asked the detective, and Dick went suddenly cold.

"Harry!"

"Your brother, eh?" Puttler's deep-set eyes surveyed him in the half-light. "That doesn't necessarily mean that he is smoking them. Where were they kept?"

"In the library as a rule."

Puttler began searching the ground with the aid of his lamp. He had not gone far before he saw something and picked it up. It was a half-smoked cigarette with a rose-leaf tip.

"Humph!" muttered Puttler, and continued his search – a search which yielded no further evidence.

Retracing their steps, they passed the study door, and Puttler, who was walking a little ahead, stumbled over something, and put his light to the ground.

"You keep rather a lot of ladders about here, Mr Alford," he said, in a low voice. "A library ladder outside? What's the great idea?"

The ladder was lying parallel with the gravel drive, and Puttler examined it rung by rung.

"That wasn't here last night, I'll take my oath," he said.

"No," said Dick, puzzled; "it usually hangs on two pegs near the garage."

He lifted it up. It was a long, light, triangular ladder tapering to a point at the top, and used by the staff for outside window cleaning.

"You had better have it chained up," was all Puttler said after he had finished his inspection. "The man who brought this here was the man who cut off your light supply, and, incidentally – "

Far away in the grounds came the faint sound of a man's voice, challenging in military fashion.

"Halt! Who goes there?"

"That's Renwick, a local man," said Puttler immediately.

They ran towards the sound of the voice, and presently saw the flicker of his lantern; and it was a badly scared man who challenged them a few minutes later. He had seen nothing, he said, but he had heard voices.

"One of them was laughing. I thought at first it was you, sergeant, but when I heard it again it was so wild that I got a little nervous."

"Did anybody answer your challenge?"

"No, but the voices stopped. I couldn't hear the woman's voice – "

"The woman's voice?" said Dick quickly. "Was it a woman? Surely you're mistaken?"

"I could swear to it," said the watcher. "It was the woman's voice I heard first, and the man who laughed. I think the voices must have stopped as soon as I put my lamp on."

"In what direction?"

The policeman pointed across Long Meadow, the shallow, valley-like depression which ran parallel with the rising ground on which the abbey stood. To the left there were a number of cottages, occupied in the main by people working on the estate, two gamekeepers, a carter and a groom. It was from one of these cottages that the Black Abbot had been seen and reported by a terrified gamekeeper.

"They sounded as if they were walking away from you over the Mound to the river – or to the ruins?" suggested Puttler.

"Well," confessed the man, "they might have been going that way: I can't be sure."

"That certainly beats the band," said the sergeant, as they were moving in the direction the man had indicated.

"He must have been mistaken," said Dick with emphasis. "They were walking away from him – "

"They," repeated Puttler significantly. "I don't think he was wrong at all."

"There is another possible solution," said Dick. "Sometimes the people at Chelfordbury avail themselves of a short cut across the park to a neighbouring village."

"At three o'clock in the morning?"

"There may have been a dance," suggested Dick lamely.

"A short cut through a park that's known to be haunted and where a murder was committed two nights ago?"

There was no answer to this.

They reached the bank and followed along the top till they were parallel with the abbey, but there was no sign of man or woman, and they turned back. In spite of his protestations of wakefulness, Sergeant Puttler did not resist the suggestion that he should take his sleep. Dick was left alone to his vigil.

By the time daylight came he was a very weary man. Twice in the night he had visited the two men posted in the corridors above, found them awake, but in each case with nothing to report.

"Thank goodness at any rate somebody's had some sleep!" he muttered, as he passed under the girls' window and glanced up.

The morning wind which stirred the trees and filled the world with the pleasant music of rustling leaves moved also the casement window of the room which he had assigned to Mary Wenner. The window swayed to and fro slowly, and he inwardly condemned the girl for not carrying out his instructions.

By six o'clock the first of the servants was stirring; smoke was crawling lazily from one of the big twisted chimneys. He was sitting in envious contemplation of Sergeant Puttler when the door of the study burst violently open and Mary Wenner came in. She was in her dressing gown; her untidy hair floated over her face.

"Mr Alford," she asked agitatedly, "have you seen Leslie?"

He was on his feet in an instant, and the movement woke the sleeping detective.

"No; she's with you, isn't she?"

"We went to bed together," said the girl, in a tremulous tone, "but when I woke up just now she was not in the room. I waited a while, thinking she was taking her bath, and then I went outside and asked the man you put there. He said she hadn't come out of the room!"

Puttler, listening, dragged himself erect.

"The ladder!" he said simply, and Dick reeled under the blow.

The Black Terror of Fossaway Manor had in his grip the woman for whom he would have given his soul and counted it no heavy price.

Running out on to the lawn, Puttler searched beneath the window. Yes, there were the marks of the ladder in the mould of a garden bed, and on the ladder itself he found confirmatory proof. Lifting it against the wall, he scrambled up, and came breast-high to the window sill on its topmost rung. Drawing himself up, he sprang into the room and looked round for some clue. By this time Mary Wenner, followed by Dick, had come through the door.

"Her dressing-gown isn't gone!" whimpered Mary, pointing to the hook where it hung. "But her shoes are. She must have dressed, and I didn't hear."

The tired man at the door had heard no sound in the night. A thick carpet covered the floor. Mary said that, when she woke, the door which communicated between the two rooms was closed.

She had heard no sound at all, and claimed that she was a light sleeper, which, in fact, she was not. When she had gone to sleep the candle was burning. Examining this, Dick saw that it could not have been alight for more than an hour. There were two burnt matches in the tray, which meant that the candle had been extinguished once and relit again.

"I wonder she didn't wake me; I'm usually a light sleeper."

Dick left the girl explaining to the watcher who had been on guard outside the door.

"It was her voice, of course, that the patrol man heard in the dark. I blame myself that I didn't jump at that idea."

"I'd like to keep all the blame!" said Dick bitterly. "Oh, God! it doesn't bear thinking about!"

He went away on a solitary search; none saw him slip through the back of the house, and he moved under cover of the river bank. When he returned, after an absence of two hours, Puttler told him that there was a message from the Home Office awaiting him. That institution had rung up twice. Dick got through after a wait, and learned that he was talking to an important under-secretary.

"Could you run up to London for an hour?"

"Is it necessary?" asked Dick, and he explained with all rapidity the happenings of the night.

"I'm afraid you had better see us as soon as you possibly can. In view of all the circumstances you cannot come too soon."

With a curse Dick hung up the receiver, and this time he took Harry's big two-seater, a car that his brother had only used a dozen times, but the use of which he had steadfastly refused to anybody else.

Just as he was leaving he recalled a resolution he had made in the night; he ran upstairs into his room, and, bolting the door, opened a locked drawer of his dressing chest and took out something which he put carefully in his bag. That must be removed from Fossaway Manor as soon as possible, he thought. He put the bag in the boot of the car and sent the machine flying down the drive.

Midway between Horsham and Dorking, a motorist, coming from the opposite direction by another route, shot at a fast pace from a forked road right across his path. Dick jammed on the brakes and the big car skidded halfway round, striking the concrete kerb with a thud, but no damage was done, and he went on, with a glare at the goggled driver of the machine at fault that was murderous.

He did not hear the cover of the dickey snap open, nor did he see the brown bag leap up and roll over on to the pavement. But the man in the other car saw all this through his big goggles, and, restarting his machine, brought it to the kerb.

And there and then, Fabrian Gilder discovered the secret of the Black Abbot!

51

At nine o'clock that morning Mr Fabrian Gilder had risen intending to make a hurried visit to his country cottage. The newspapers had been full of the Chelford tragedy, but no mention had been made of the fact that Thomas had been Mr Gilder's guest. Such a happening, he realised, being an intelligent man, must necessarily upset all arrangements and plans that the girl had made.

There was a lot about Fabrian Gilder that was admirable. To his servants he was a kind master; to all who knew him superficially, an excellent and even a generous friend. He was in truth no worse than the average man in point of desires, a little better in his fairness of dealing. Arthur Gine had been legitimate prey, but he had, he thought, treated him with scrupulous fairness. He had succeeded, by the exploitation of the lawyer's weakness, in amassing a very considerable fortune; but then, the city of London, and, for the matter of that, the city of New York, were filled with rich men who had founded their houses upon the cupidity or folly of men who were now almost penniless.

He glanced at the morning papers. There was nothing new reported from Chelford, except the little interview that one reporter had had with Dick, and that paragraph was, in many ways, very comforting to Gilder, for it explained why the girl – and then his eye caught sight of a line.

Mr Alford said he had asked Miss Leslie Gine to stay at Fossaway Manor whilst her brother was abroad…

Abroad? He frowned. If Arthur Gine had gone abroad he must have left very suddenly. He had seen him only a day or two before. But perhaps that was one of Dick Alford's lies to save the girl's face. Still, it was disquieting.

He was pondering this matter when the maid brought him his morning letters, and the first he saw was one in a well-known hand. It was from Leslie. He tore it open with trembling fingers, took out the half-sheet of paper and read the few lines. He read it not once but many times. So that was that! She had changed her mind.

It did not occur to him that she had not made any promise, but he was so sure of her, so satisfied in his mind that she would agree to his proposal, that he felt he had been tricked.

When the shock had worn off, his anger and resentment grew. Very well: if she could not keep her promise, he at least would keep his. He understood now, he thought. Arthur had bolted, and there was no necessity for the girl to make her sacrifice. He had been fooled, tricked. He pushed the chair back from the table, leaving his breakfast untouched, and, going into his library, turned the handle of the combination and pulled open the door of the safe with a savage jerk. There was the letter, all ready to post, and at the sight of it his heart grew hard and sour.

He took out the letter, made to tear it into fragments, and then remembered that inside was a blank cheque. He pulled out the sheet of notepaper and felt for the little pink slip that in his magnificence he had signed with a complacent flourish. It was not there!

Gilder peered into the envelope with a frown. Gone! He searched the safe: it might have fallen out, though how, he could not imagine; but there was no sign of the cheque. He unlocked his drawer and took out his cheque-book. There was the counterfoil, and, written across it, "For Leslie – " He had intended showing her that counterfoil one of these days, when she felt more kindly towards him.

With his head in his hands he tried to remember when he had last seen the cheque, and then he recalled that it was on the morning Arthur Gine had called to see him. At that thought he went white. Surely he had closed the safe? Again he struggled to remember, minute by minute, that fateful morning. He had been looking at the letter, he had put it away, he had closed the door, and then – the telephone bell had rung and he had forgotten to fasten the safe!

He pulled the phone towards him now and called furiously for a number. It was twenty past nine; most of the staff of the bank would be there. When the call was answered: "I am Mr Gilder," he said quickly. "Is the manager there?... No? Then the assistant manager will do. It is very urgent."

He waited whilst the clerk went to investigate. Presently he heard the voice of a man he knew – the manager himself.

"I just came in at this moment. Is anything wrong?"

"Fletcher, do you remember my telling you that I should be sending down a cheque for fifty thousand pounds and asking you to honour it?"

"Yes; I honoured it."

For a second Gilder was speechless.

"You honoured it? Who presented the cheque?"

"Arthur Gine – it was made out in his favour – payable to bearer. I notified you last night; didn't you get my letter?"

"I haven't opened all my post yet," said Gilder steadily. "Thank you."

He hung up the receiver, breathing heavily. For now he remembered clearly every event of the morning: the coming of Arthur Gine, and his seemingly absurd proposal, that Gilder should write a note expressing his willingness to lend the money. That was the trick of it! Not only had Arthur got the fifty thousand, but with that letter he had a complete answer to any charge of fraud.

He sat with clasped hands, every vein on his forehead swollen, and murder in his heart. Tricked! And she should know. She had been a party to the fraud – unwittingly perhaps, but nevertheless a party. She must have told him of this money.

Whatever else he was, Fabrian Gilder had the gift of clear thinking. Five minutes' riotous fury, and he was his cold self again. Of course she couldn't have helped in the fraud. It was the accident of leaving the safe unlocked, and Arthur Gine's known inquisitiveness – he could never resist reading even Gilder's private letters; Arthur had no sense of other people's privacy.

What could he do now? He thought the matter out. He must tell the girl, and perhaps she would regard herself as being under an obligation to him. If she had any sense of honour she must fulfil her promise, whatever she had written in her letter that morning.

He telephoned for his car to be brought round from the garage, and came back to his breakfast table and made an attempt to eat.

He would try Leslie first, telling her nothing about the letter he had given to her brother, and threaten him with a warrant for fraud. Perhaps this strengthened rather than weakened his position. He grew cheerful as the thought took shape.

He passed slowly out of London, for all the streets in the metropolis seemed to be "up," and at last struck the open country, avoiding the main roads and taking a more circuitous route which would bring him to the main Sussex road between Dorking and Horsham. With a clear road before him, he sent his car at full speed. He was not well acquainted with the road, but he knew that it joined the old Roman "street" at a gentle angle, and he did not slow down as he approached the principal thoroughfare.

Left of him, on the London side, the road was clear; to the right, the view was a little obstructed. He sounded his klaxon and came out on to the main thoroughfare at thirty miles an hour.

He saw the car just in time, jammed on his brakes and threw the machine into reverse. The big car ahead of him skidded round; he caught one malevolent gleam from Dick Alford's eyes, and then he saw the bag and, driving to the side of the road, picked it up. His first inclination was to leave it; he had no particular desire to help the second son; but there are certain innate decencies to be observed by motorists, even though they loathe each other, and he picked the little bag from the pavement and threw it into the back of his car.

As he did so, it opened, and, turning to fasten it, he saw something that made him change his mind. Getting out of the car, he lifted the bag to the pavement, opened it wide and pulled out – the sombre habit and cowl of the Black Abbot!

52

So Dick Alford was the Black Abbot! It was unbelievable; he could
hardly credit the importance of his find. Here, then, was the greatest
lever of all. Beside this, the threat of a charge against Leslie Gine's
brother faded to unimportance. He snapped the lock, put the bag
carefully back in the car, and, restarting his engine, moved at a slower
pace towards Chelfordbury.

He stopped in the village, where he was recognised, and heard at
first hand from the innkeeper the story of the strange happenings at
the "big house."

"They do say that something's happened to the young lady from
Willow House."

"What!" Gilder almost shouted the word. "You don't mean Miss
Gine?"

"Yes, Miss Gine," nodded the landlord. "I haven't got the rights of
it yet, it's only a rumour down here, but, Lord bless your heart, Mr
Gilder, there's never been so many rumours in this village since I came
to live here forty-eight years ago. Some say that his lordship's been
murdered" – he lowered his voice and looked round – "by his brother!
Mr Alford is a very hard man, though the people who work for him
have got nothing to say against him, but that doesn't seem possible
to me."

Gilder's mind was in a whirl. He did not want to know anything
about Dick Alford or his reputation.

"Who told you this story about Miss Gine?" he asked, and the landlord, looking round the group that had formed outside the Red Lion, pointed to a man.

"He's a carter up at the big house," he said.

"Fetch him here," said Gilder.

When the carter arrived: "What is this story about Miss Gine?"

The man looked a little sheepish to find himself the centre of interest.

"I don't know nowt about it," he said. "It's only what I heerd that monkey-faced gentleman saying to Mr Richard. He says, 'I don't think any harm's come to her.' And one of the maids says that that young lady who used to be his lordship's secretary – "

"Miss Wenner? Is she there?" asked Gilder quickly.

"Yes, she come up last night."

"What about her?" asked Gilder.

"They say she's been crying her eyes out all the morning. That's all I know about it. They do say something bad happened to the young lady early this morning, and the way Mr Richard has been running about and him looking as ill as death – "

"I hope something's going to be done about this Black Abbot," interjected the innkeeper. "My womenfolk are so frightened they want to sit up half the night."

Gilder looked at him with a queer expression.

"You needn't be afraid of the Black Abbot," he said. "I am going to lay that ghost today."

"You, Mr Gilder?" said the man, in surprise.

But it was not the occasion for confidences, and Gilder, getting back into his car, turned it about and went up the road till he came to the lodge gates. Here a policeman on duty would have barred his progress, but fortunately he was a local man who knew the lawyer.

"Mr Alford's away, sir. Do you want to see Sergeant Puttler?"

"Is that the man who has been staying at the Manor? What is he – a policeman?"

"A Scotland Yard man, sir," said the Sussex policeman, with a certain pride. "Though I don't know they're much better than our own detectives. You'll tell him you saw me, will you, and I asked you not to go to the house unless you had business?"

Evidently these were the policeman's instructions; Gilder promised faithfully to supply this exoneration, and continued up the drive. There was nobody to meet him when he pulled up before the old carved porch, but he had hardly alighted when a long-armed, queer-faced man came from nowhere.

"Good morning," said the visitor.

"Good morning, Mr Gilder," said Puttler. "Mr Alford has had to go to town."

"I want to see Miss Gine," said Gilder, watching the man closely.

If he had expected an experienced detective-sergeant to betray himself, he was to be disappointed. Puttler did no more than fix him with his melancholy eyes.

"Want to see Miss Gine, do you? I'm afraid she's not at home either."

"Then perhaps I could see Miss Wenner?"

The sergeant scratched his chin.

"She's not very well," he said; "in fact, she's lying down, and the doctor says she's not to be disturbed."

"Is there anything wrong with her?"

"No, there's nothing very much wrong with her. At the same time," said Puttler juridically, "there's nothing very much right with her! It has rather got on her nerves sleeping in this place, and I can't very well blame her."

"Do you know where Miss Gine has gone?"

Puttler shook his head.

"No," he said, truthfully, "I can't tell you that; she didn't tell me."

"Perhaps you will answer this question," said the exasperated man: "has anything happened to her?"

"So far as I know," said the imperturbable officer, "nothing whatever has happened to her. Are you a friend of hers?"

"I am her fiancé," said Gilder, on the spur of the moment.

Here he had the satisfaction of seeing that the sergeant was startled.

"Oh, yes, of course, you're the gentleman she isn't going to marry."

It was said in all innocence, without any trace of impertinence, but Mr Gilder went red and white.

"You see, Mr Gilder," the sergeant went on, "I've heard quite a lot about – affairs in this neighbourhood; in fact, I'm an authority upon all the gossip and scandal for the past twenty years. And I'm very glad you came, because there are one or two questions I wanted to ask you. For example, I wanted to know how it came about that you placed your cottage at the disposal of an ex-convict, Thomas Luck – so called."

But here Gilder was ready with his answer.

"I had no idea the man was an ex-convict," he said. "He told me he had been discharged from the Manor, and as I wanted a caretaker, and he offered to come for a very small sum, I employed him. I was terribly surprised and shocked to hear of his death, but even more shocked to learn of his character."

Puttler was politely interested. But if he thought that he was going to get rid of Gilder so easily, it was because he did not know the man's pertinacity.

"I think I must see Miss Wenner before I go," he said. "At any rate, I'd be glad if you'd send up my name – "

Puttler shook his head.

"It can't be done, Mr Gilder," he said, almost cheerfully. "Just now I'm a combination of the Earl of Chelford and the family doctor. In other words, I'm in charge during Mr Alford's absence. If you care to wait until he comes back, the drawing-room is at your disposal, but you understand, Mr Gilder, that you are not in any circumstances to question the servants. I am a great admirer of amateur detectives in my leisure moments, but this is one of my busy days, and I can't afford to have any interference in this case, however well-meant it may be."

Gilder had to accept this invitation. He was determined not to leave the house until he had learned the truth about Leslie Gine. The detective conducted him to the drawing-room, the long windows of which were open.

"I'll ask you not to leave here until Mr Alford arrives," he said. "If you require anything, perhaps you will ring?" And, seeing the light in

Gilder's eyes, he added: "One of my men, who is a first-class footman, will attend to you."

He had not long to wait, as it happened. Dick, who had torn up to town, breaking every speed rule, and so intent upon the object of his visit that he had forgotten even that he had put the bag in the dickey, was lucky enough to get through with his interview in a quarter of an hour. It was a very important interview: one on which his own future very largely depended; and there were too many things to think about for him to give a thought to the bag and its contents. His car, white with dust, sped up the drive and came to a halt in the wide space before the porch. He identified the other car and recognised it as the machine that had nearly brought about a nasty accident that morning.

"Gilder, is it?" he said, as he got down.

"Gilder it is, and full of interrogation marks. You saw the Secretary?"

Dick nodded.

"Yes. He was very kind, but rather vague. He has given me twelve hours to find Harry, dead or alive."

"Did you tell him about Miss Gine?"

"He wasn't even interested," said Dick, with a hard laugh. "Harry, the estate, the title – everything except Leslie! That was the burden of his conversation. In twelve hours I must find him – and believe me, Puttler, in twelve hours I will!"

He went into the drawing-room and greeted Gilder curtly.

"You wanted to see me?"

"I wanted to know what has happened to Leslie Gine," said Gilder.

"I wish to God I knew!" said Dick.

The man stared at him.

"Nothing bad has happened?" he asked in a low voice, and Dick forgave him everything for the sincerity of his concern.

"I'm afraid it is something very unpleasant," he said, and told the story.

As he did so, he saw the man's face change and a sceptical smile curved his lips.

"I've got something to say to you, and I'd like to say it before a witness, Alford."

"To me?" said Dick, in surprise, and called over his shoulder to Puttler, who was passing the door. "Mr Gilder has something he wants to say – I presume it's something of an unpleasant character," he said. "Perhaps you had better listen to this, Puttler."

"Alford has just told me that Miss Gine has disappeared, and the inference is, of course, that the Black Abbot has spirited her away. I think that is extremely likely, because the Black Abbot has every interest in holding fast to that young lady."

"Sensation," murmured the detective, but Gilder did not notice the interruption.

"For some time past there's been a queer spook haunting this countryside, an object of terror to Lord Chelford, designed, if anything, to cover the series of outrages which have recently been committed. Chelford's a weakling – you know that, Alford – but weaklings have children, and once a child is born to Harry Alford your hope of succession would go like that!" He snapped his fingers.

"What are you suggesting?" asked Dick steadily.

"I'm suggesting that you are the Black Abbot!"

Not by so much as a flicker of his eyelid did Dick betray himself.

"I not only suggest it, but I'm prepared to prove it. On your way to town this morning you nearly collided ·with my car. As you skidded, your bag fell out of the dickey. I picked it up, threw it in the car and found it was open. In that bag was the robe of the Black Abbot, well worn, often used! Do you deny that?"

"You've got to bring proof of this." It was Puttler who spoke.

"Proof!" cried the other triumphantly. "I'll give you proof!"

He walked rapidly through the hall to where his car was, the two men following him. He had left the bag under a rug at the back of the car.

"There is the bag," he said, as he pulled the rug from its place. "And here" – he snapped open the bag –

It was empty!

"And here?" said Puttler encouragingly.

"It was there a few minutes ago. I saw it before I came into the grounds. Somebody has taken it. You!" he accused Dick.

Dick smiled.

"Sergeant Puttler will testify that I came straight from my car into your august presence," he said sarcastically.

"Why don't you accuse me?" asked Puttler. "I was out here all the time."

The baffled man looked from one to the other. It was impossible to believe that these two were in league. He knew Puttler by name to be one of the best officers Scotland Yard had ever had. He shrugged his shoulders and dropped his hands to his sides.

"You've beaten me, Alford," he said, "for the time being. But I'm satisfied the girl is within a mile of this house, and I'm not going to rest until she is found. Heaven knows why you've done it – she's fond of you, and there was no need – "

"Don't be a fool, Gilder," said Dick roughly. "If you want to help, help! But you're not going to help by thinking that I've raised my hand against Leslie Gine. I don't care whether you're a friend or whether you're an enemy, but if you can help us to bring her back safely I will go on my knees to you!"

Dick's voice was trembling, vibrant; there was a look in his eyes which not even Gilder, for all his prejudice, could mistake. He held out his hand and Dick Alford took it in a grip that made him wince.

53

Despite all her gloomy prognostications as to her sleepless night, the head of Miss Wenner had hardly touched the pillow than her breathing became regular and even noticeable. Leslie Gine smiled to herself as she turned over and stealthily extinguished the candle. She had not been lying ten minutes before she realised, from past experience, that many a weary hour would pass before her eyes closed in sleep.

She had the alternative of relighting the candle and reading, or counting myriads of sheep, and the first plan was somewhat hampered in its achievement by the fact that there was nothing in the room to read, and she dare not disturb the sentry, because that would probably wake Mary. So she lay perfectly still, overcoming a mad desire to turn every few minutes, trying to make her mind an absolute blank.

With so much to occupy her thoughts, with the past twenty-four hours and all the terrible shocks they had brought, her effort to turn her mind into a cabbage was a hopeless failure.

She heard a distant village clock striking the half-hours and the hours, and was grateful when one o'clock chimed, for she felt she had turned the hill of the night and was approaching the blessed day. There were queer creaks and noises in this old house; strange, stealthy footsteps that seemed very real; fingers brushing along wainscotings, queer little chatterings as of laughter. In spite of her courage, Leslie got up and lit the candle again and felt happier.

She lay on her back, gazing at the ceiling, striving to concentrate upon one little crack that ran from corner to corner; and it seemed as though, as she looked, the room went perceptibly darker, and was filled with a strange unearthly light.

And then she saw behind the door a great steel clothes hook that she did not remember having seen before; and attached was a cord and a shapeless something that hung with terrible limpness – a woman! She opened her eyes wide, almost screamed, but put her hand before her mouth in time.

She had been dreaming, she realised, and she reached out for her handkerchief to wipe her damp face. There was no hook behind the door – nothing. She shivered and turned on her side, looked for the twentieth time at her watch. Twenty-five minutes past one.

Tap, tap!

That was distinct enough. It came from the room which Mary Wenner was to have occupied.

A silence, and then the unmistakable sound of gravel being thrown against a window. Perhaps it was Dick and he wanted to see her. She slipped out of bed, pulled a dressing-gown about her, opened the door of the dark room and went in. The windows were closed, but as she entered the room she was startled by a third handful of gravel that sounded with terrifying distinctness.

With trembling hands she pulled up the catch and pushed the casement open. A man was standing down below, and for a second she did not recognise him. And then everything went round; she had to grip the window ledge for support.

It was Harry Alford!

"Is that you, my dear?" His voice was little above a whisper, but remarkably clear.

She managed to answer: "Yes."

She was so dumbfounded that she could not ask one of the thousand questions which crowded to her lips.

Harry! And alive!

"You are in terrible danger," he said. "Will you come down? I can get a ladder."

Before she could answer he had disappeared, and presently he came back, carrying a triangular-shaped ladder, and planted it against the side of the house. The top came within a foot of the window ledge.

"I can't come, Harry; I'm not dressed. Besides, Miss Wenner is here."

He raised his finger to his lips.

"Don't wake her," he said.

He had a little roll of something in his hand, and she noticed that he was bareheaded.

"Can't you dress? I must see you."

"Shall I call Dick?"

"No, no." In his energy he almost raised his voice, and looked back over his shoulder. "That would spoil everything, and it would endanger his life. Dress quickly, my dear."

What should she do? Her first instinct was to run to the door and tell the guard what she had seen; her second was to obey him. His earnestness and the terror in his voice made her yield to his suggestion. Quickly she dressed by candlelight, hoping and praying that Mary Wenner would wake up. Once she knocked against the bed, but Miss Wenner slept peacefully, a seraphic smile on her good-looking face, and the only notice she took of the disturbance was to murmur "Dick!"

It needed that ludicrous interlude to restore Leslie's courage; for she could not be amused and afraid at the same time.

Perhaps Dick was waiting below, she thought, and, swinging herself over the sill, she reached out her foot, found the top rung of the ladder and came down. Harry was standing on the grass-plot, curiously alert and watchful.

"What is it, Harry?" she asked in a low voice, but he put his finger to his lips again and led her, not, as she expected, towards the front of the house, but by a wide circuit, keeping to the shadow of the trees, until they went past the rosery and near to the stables.

A dog barked as they passed in silence.

"I can't go any farther, Harry."

"You must, you must!" His voice was urgent, compelling. "I tell you that not only my life, but your own is in danger."

"But what of Miss Wenner?" She drew back.

"They will not touch her. My mother's spirit will watch that poor girl – she died in that room."

Leslie gasped.

"Your mother?" she asked, in an awe-stricken whisper.

"Come!" He was impatient, caught her by the arm and led her farther down, until she saw near at hand the gleam of the Ravensrill.

"But, Harry, I can't go any farther." She stopped resolutely. "I'm sure you're mistaken. Where have you been all this time? Everybody has been looking for you, and Dick has been terribly worried."

He laughed. (It was the laugh that the policeman heard.)

"Dick is worried? That is rich!"

And now, as the challenge of a distant voice came to her, she saw his face in the moonlight. He was unshaven, unkempt, grimy of face and hands; he wore no collar, and stood a collarless man in a long frock-coat with a wild appearance. Slowly she drew back, dread and fear on her face, and then he clutched her by the wrists.

"If you scream I will throw you into the river and kneel on you until you are dead," he whispered in so calm and matter-of-fact a tone that she could not believe he was serious.

And yet she had an extra sense which told her that he was not only serious, but that she was in deadly peril. He kept hold of her wrist, or she would have taken to flight, though she would have had little chance of escaping one who in his schooldays was a noted sprinter. She remembered something else now and felt sick. Harry Alford had captained his public school team at Bisley and had carried everything before him. This pale anaemic youth was the greatest shot of his time. The greatest shot! She remembered the bullet that was meant for her, and he felt her dragging on his hand, but said no word. She must not lose her nerve at this moment of crisis.

They were making for the ruins. Near the edge of the cutting, Puttler had told her, were stationed two men; they must see her soon.

But Harry went no farther than the broken tower, and here he paused and pulled the block of stone aside.

Now she knew; they were going down to that dreadful underground cavern where Dick had taken her. Dick Alford knew his brother was there! She knew this long before she saw the basket, still filled with food, that stood at the bottom of the steps.

54

Harry had lit a candle, and, guided by this, she went down the steep circular stairway.

"He brought me that food – the devil!" He pointed his shaking finger to the basket.

"Dick brought it?" she faltered.

He nodded.

"Poisoned," he said. "But he didn't catch me. Poisoned, every bit of it!"

He carefully unwrapped a white napkin and showed a dainty pile of sandwiches, took one and opened it.

"You can see the crystals glittering on the meat," he said, in so calm and matter-of-fact a tone that she almost thought she saw something glitter on the white flesh.

Then he lifted the bottle and looked at it with a smile. "It was too childish. Nobody but a fool would have dreamt I could be deceived." He put the bottle and sandwiches back again carefully and covered them with the napkin that had been over the basket.

"Come," he said, and they went farther into the apartment.

She saw a big gap in the floor and a stone standing straight up from the centre.

"I have a lamp below. I prepared this place a very long time ago against such an emergency. Light and food – and all the water you want. Will you go first?"

He was very courteous and polite, took her hand to guide her, and held the light so that she could see the stairs, and came down immediately after, stopping to swing the stone into place.

"Will you hold the candle?" he asked.

She was trembling so violently that her fingers were soon covered with hot grease, but she did not feel the smart of the boiling wax; her eyes were fixed upon the man, fascinated.

He was lighting a new storm lantern which burnt, she guessed, paraffin gas, and it took some time before a brilliant bright light illuminated the room in which she found herself. It was twice the size of the apartment above, and neither the walls nor the floor had fallen into decay. It was almost as new-looking as it had been when the Norman builders had handed it to the Black Fathers of Chelfordbury.

The first unusual things she saw were two sporting rifles that stood in a corner of the room. Following her eyes, he smiled.

"I shall not sell my life without a struggle," he said firmly.

The furniture consisted of a very old refectory table, the top of which must have been at least four inches in thickness, a long form and a high chair that looked like a bishop's throne. There were no visible windows, but the ceiling did not quite reach the wall, and there seemed a space all round the room where air was admitted.

"Excuse me," he said.

He took the thing he had been carrying, unrolled it, and, to her astonishment, kissed it passionately before he carried it to a truckle bed that she had not noticed before, and tacked it to a beam which showed between the stone courses and was in truth the only wood she had seen in the building.

She looked in amazement, and knew the picture instantly. It was the head of his mother.

"How lovely!" he sighed. "How wonderful! Do you know, I feel that nothing matters now, Leslie!"

He smiled at her, and looked at that moment so happy that she could have cried.

"Richard hated her," he went on. "He never lost an opportunity of speaking ill of her. I am told that in my absence he used to bring the servants into the library, and together they would laugh and gibe at this beautiful martyr."

"How absurd, Harry! You know Dick would do no such thing," she said, stirred to his defence.

But he was neither angry nor did he show any resentment at her championship.

"You don't know Dick," he said simply. "Dick, of course, is the Black Abbot. I only found it out a week or two ago, when I went into his room and discovered the costume in a box. He had forgotten to put it away."

She did not believe the only truth he had told her so far, but she felt that it would be undiplomatic, to say the least, to argue with him.

"Harry, I can't stay here, you know," she said. "There is only one room, and I have a weakness for a daily bath – "

He walked across the room and pulled aside a sacking that hid one corner, and pointed dramatically.

"You will find everything you require here," he said. "This room is yours. I shall sleep upstairs, only coming below at the first hint of danger, either to you or to me. The position calls for courage and patience, and I know that my wife-to-be has those qualities to excess."

He was his old, smiling, genial self.

"By the way, there are plenty of books to read – I brought some away from the house. They were rather heavy and I had to drag them a little bit, but thank heaven I got just what I wanted."

She noticed them now for the first time, piled at one end of the refectory table. He took up a volume and turned the leaves lovingly.

"You do not read German? I think you told me that before. It is a pity, because this is a very fascinating narrative, told by an outsider, of the Chelfords of the period. You will be pleased to learn that I have located the treasure. It was not difficult. I knew all the time that it was behind the second door in the room above."

"Have you known this place for long?"

He nodded.

"For six years," he said. "I found it on the twenty-first anniversary of my dear mother's death. I think I ought to say 'murder,' for there is no doubt that my father, who had all the worst qualities of Dick, killed her – hanged her."

Her face contorted with horror.

"In that room?" she said, in a strained voice. "Behind the door?"

He nodded.

"The thing was hushed up. My clever father was too great a man to be put on trial for his life, and the story was circulated that she had died by her own hand."

Every word he said was a lie, as she knew, but he believed it. He explained quite rationally how the light was worked; showed her the little wash-place with the stream of water running from the raw rock through a cavity into some invisible deeps; even gave her a short résumé of the history of the place. It had been built by the Black Abbot himself for his own especial purpose.

"My first idea was that there was another exit here, or rather an entrance for those peculiar friends of his, but that I have failed to discover."

He took up one of the rifles, shot back the bolt with the air of an expert, and, going up two steps, unfastened the heavy oaken bar that kept the stone in place.

The slab pivoted round, and she had a wild idea that when it was closed she would fasten it; but he was evidently prepared for this, for she heard him drag a paving-stone to the edge of the hole and place it so that the trap could not close.

"Good night, Leslie," he said, peering down at her through his spectacles. "You will not mind my light? I want to read a chapter before I sleep."

For a quarter of an hour no sound broke the silence. She sat on the bed, her hands clasped on her knees. And then she heard him move and her breath came faster, but he had only a question to ask.

"Tell me, Leslie, did Thomas leave any relations? I should like to provide for them. The man annoyed me, and I really do not regret killing him. But I should not like to feel that his relatives were suffering through my act of justice."

She shook her head.

"I don't know," she said, and it did not seem to be her voice.

55

It seemed an interminable time before his light went out. Was he sleeping? Should she attempt to escape past him? From where she sat she could see his hand, which lay over the edge of the pit, and she remembered Dick telling her how light a sleeper he was. Systematically, and without moving, she searched the place with her eyes, foot by foot. In one corner of the room square tins of every shape were piled. She supposed they were preserved provisions and she wondered how he got rid of the debris. She examined the wash-place, cupped her hands and drank of the cool, refreshing water, afterwards bathing her face. The touch of the cold spring water refreshed and invigorated her.

How long she sat there motionless she could not tell. She was in a kind of coma, paralysed by a sense of helplessness. It must have been hours before she heard him move and, his blanket over his arm and rifle in hand, he crept down the steps and fastened the slab.

"What is it?" she asked.

"Don't speak – it is he!" he whispered, and sat down by her side, his hand on her shoulder.

She heard the sound of footsteps above.

Dick!

She had to bite her lip to prevent the cry that came. Harry was watching her – a scream and she would be dead. Dick could never break open that trap in time, even if he could locate the sound. Presently the footsteps went away and she felt the hand on her shoulder relax.

"Sorry to disturb you."

He picked up blanket and rifle and ascended the steps; she watched him pull the paving-stone forward, and after a while there was quietness.

There must be some exit, if the legend of the disreputable Black Abbot was true. She took off her shoes and walked noiselessly over the even floor, examining it stone by stone. The walls were obviously impenetrable; the vaulted ceiling was decorated with the lines of a St Andrew's Cross that met in a great stone rosette in the centre.

He had left a box of matches and a candle on the table. This she lit and carried it into the tiny cavern where the water ran. She could see no roof; she guessed it stretched up the full height of the tower, and that somewhere above was the edge of the circular staircase that had brought her down to the first cavern.

Holding the light above her head, she strained her eyes upward, and presently she saw great iron D-shaped projections fixed at intervals of a foot; they reached to the top, and, most blessed sight of all, she saw above her head a star.

And yet she was puzzled. The Abbot had a reputation for gallantry, and it was hardly likely that the visitors who shared his solitude would make their entrance by so precarious a means. She reached up, but her hand was three feet from the nearest rung, and there was nothing in the room on which she could stand. She went back to her bed noiselessly and pulled out one of the sheets; she took the remaining rifle and, by dint of great exertion, managed to push one end of the sheet through the nearest rung. After ten minutes' work the end came down and she had a rope. She knotted together the sheets at the end, and tested her weight. The staple held, and, springing up, she climbed hand over hand to the lowest rung. Her arms were almost pulled from their sockets; she was breathless, but she held on, and, reaching up, caught the third rung and pulled herself up until her feet rested on the first. She waited a little while to gain breath and began to climb. Higher and higher, and then her heart sank. Above her she saw a steel grille, fixed immovably across the exit. It was impossible even to put her arm through, the meshes were so small, and with a bitter sense of disappointment she descended again and slid down the sheet to the floor.

There was no escape this way. She unknotted the sheet and replaced it in her bed, stained with rust and torn at the edges. She brought the rifle back with her. She was an enthusiastic miniature target shot and knew the mechanism of the weapon. Pulling out the magazine, she found it loaded to its full capacity. Here, then, was something; her confidence grew, though she prayed she might never have to use this weapon upon the madman who slept so quietly above. The rifle might be used to terrify him in an emergency.

She went back to the wash-place and looked up. Day was breaking, and she took a sudden resolve. The man had been almost his normal self, as she had known him, and she guessed that this was but an interlude and that there were periods when she must shoot to save her life. Stealthily she crept up the stairs, rifle in hand, and she heard him stir, and presently his shrill voice asked: "Where are you going? Stay where you are, you vixen!"

She brought up the butt of the rifle and smashed past the paving-stone that prevented the trap from closing. The stone thudded down, and instantly she swung round the heavy bar that kept it in place. She heard him stamping and screaming above; heard, with a shivering horror, the threats that, as she thought, no human tongue could frame; staggering down the steps, she fell.

56

A high official from Scotland Yard had arrived and was interviewing Dick in the library.

"I am wholly responsible. I have always known my brother was queer, and about a year ago I was certain that the horrible taint of madness which his poor mother transmitted to him was developing in a way which could only have one end. I begged of him to see a medical man, but he hated doctors. I brought down the best alienists from London in various guises, sometimes as bailiffs, and occasionally as prospective buyers of our property, but in their presence he behaved so rationally that it was impossible that I could get a certificate.

"My own position was a very delicate one. I am, as you know, the heir to the property. Any step I took meant that the estate came into my hands, and that eventually, when poor Harry died, as one doctor told me he must die in a few years, I should be branded with the stigma of having put him away, and I was anxious to save the family name. My chief anxiety was that he should never marry."

"Wasn't it easy enough to take the girl into your confidence?"

Dick was silent for a while.

"Not in this case. There were reasons why – "

And the official, dimly understanding, changed the subject.

"Then you were the Black Abbot?"

"Mostly," confessed Dick. "My brother was terrified of the Abbot and would never go out if there was a rumour that the Black Abbot was about. I was especially anxious to keep him in the house, where, under my eye, there was no chance for him to indulge in these extraordinary paroxysms that have really alarmed the countryside. The man whom the villagers feared and whom they call the Black Abbot is really Harry. I was a very silent Black Abbot," he smiled faintly, "and I had no other purpose than to keep Harry indoors. I'm going to say I did not always succeed."

"I'm afraid the truth will have to come out now," said the official, shaking his head.

"I wish it had come out last week," replied Dick bitterly.

"Do you think your brother is responsible for the disappearance of Miss Gine?"

"Undoubtedly. He must have attracted her to the window, and persuaded her to come down into the grounds. He was very plausible; no man would dream that he was not sane, only I, who have seen" – he drew a long breath – "what I have seen. I'll tell you this, Colonel," he said, with sudden vehemence, "not all the lordship of Chelford, not all the estates, not even the Chelford treasure, would make me live again my life of the past five years! There are times," he said, his voice trembling with passion, "when I feel I would like to dig up the abbey and scatter its stones in the dust, raze this house to the ground, and turn the place into a public park." He laughed at his own excess. "I am talking like an idiot. This place belongs to a family that knows not Harry. He is just a terrible accident. My dear mother often told me how worried my father was about Harry, his queer, secretive ways. And yet in a way he is a sportsman, one of the best shots in England as a boy, a great runner, and a wonderful fellow over the country, until about eight years ago, when this treasure bug got into his brain and he shut himself away from us all and gave his mind and his soul to this wild chase."

"The gold?"

Dick shook his head.

"No," he said. "If it were only the gold, that would have been an intelligent interest in life."

He described Harry's search for the elixir, the famous Life Water of which the ancient Chelford had written in his diary.

"It is probably no more than a flask of a native wine – arrack or the like," said Dick. "Poor Harry!"

Miss Wenner had intended leaving by the early morning train but had changed her mind. Possibly the arrival of Fabrian Gilder had been a factor. She had one solution for Leslie's disappearance.

"Have you searched the abbey?" she asked, not once but a dozen times.

Dick was weary; the abbey had been his first thought. He had suspected this was Harry's hiding-place, and with his own hands had taken a basket of provisions for him, but this, he saw, was untouched.

There was one possibility about the underground cavern, and that was the second door, and he had ordered the blacksmith and his assistant to be at the stone tower at two o'clock that afternoon with instruments, one of which had to be procured from London.

The presence of Miss Wenner was not as distasteful to Gilder as he thought it would have been. To use a phrase of childhood, she was "on his side." In very truth, Miss Wenner was on anybody's side if they happened to be agreeable to her.

They were walking through the rosery before lunch, and certainly the trend of Mary Wenner's remarks was very comforting to a man who had been so badly rebuffed.

"If I had my way, Fabrian dear" (she assumed all the rights and privileges of an engagement which was somewhat illusory, and he made only a feeble resistance), "if I had my way I'd put you in charge of this case. After all, you are the very man to solve this mystery, and I must say you could have knocked me down with a feather when you told me you were fifty – you don't look a day more than thirty – and you've got experience, you're a lawyer, you're up to all kinds of artfulness."

"Not to all kinds," said Gilder, with a grim recollection of a certain blank cheque.

"Well, to most kinds," conceded Miss Wenner. "And what are they all doing? This Dick Alford and this so-called detective? They're just standing around, scratching their heads, whilst you could go, as it were, to the real heart of the mystery. Don't deny it – I'm sure you could, Fabe."

"Don't call me Fabe, Mary," he asked gently. "If you want to call me by my Christian name, let us have all the three syllables."

"You're a man of the world, Fabrian" (she accentuated the word as she would have done "Mary Ann"). "You understand the ins and outs of everything. Why don't they come to you like men and say, 'Mr Gilder, what is your opinion of this mystery?' Instead of which, they don't so much as ask you if you've got a mouth!"

"Perhaps they know that," said Gilder in good humour. He lifted his head suddenly, a frown on his face. He had heard a shot; more than a shot, the whirr and whine of a bullet.

"What – "

Something fell at his feet with a "plop!" He saw a little hole, and, stooping, dug out a bullet with his fingers.

"Where on earth did that come from?"

He looked up at the sky, but the aeroplane which was later to make an appearance, and which had nothing to do with this mysterious shooting, was not yet in sight.

Dick had heard the shot and was running across the lawn.

"Did you – " he began.

Plop!

They heard it again, and presently Dick saw leaves fall from a laurel bush and heard the thud of an impact. One of the police who were still patrolling the grounds shouted to him, but he could not hear what he was saying, and raced across to him. Nearer at hand he saw that the man was pointing to the ruins.

"It came from there," shouted the constable, and Dick changed direction.

He was flying up the slope when the third shot sounded, and this time he located it with fair accuracy. Somebody was shooting from the tower.

Happily he had made preparations for the blacksmith's visit, and there was an assortment of lanterns near the entrance. He stopped long enough to light one, and, slipping back the catch with his knife, he pushed aside the stone corner-piece and ran down the stairs. The room was empty. He tried the mystery door; that too was closed. Somebody shouted his name from the landing above and he answered: "Come down, Gilder. There's nobody here."

Gilder descended the steps gingerly and looked round with his keen, shrewd eyes. And then he remembered and pointed to the slab.

"Have you tried that? I meant to tell you before."

"What is it?"

"I don't know, but I rather think that the stone turns on a pivot. If that is the case, there are pretty stout supports underneath that will want cutting through."

Gilder sprawled flat on the floor, his ear to the crack.

"There's nothing there that is audible," he said. "Can't you smell anything?"

He put his nose to the crack.

"There's a petrol light burning down there, or else it has been burning recently."

Flat on his face, Dick sniffed.

"Yes," he said, and called: "Leslie!"

There was no answer. He called again, with a like result.

Gilder went up the stairs and searched amongst the tools that had been brought in readiness for the afternoon's investigation. He selected two saws and a second lantern, and, lighting this, he descended to Dick's side.

"It is pretty sure to be an oaken support; these old builders seldom used iron," he said.

Throwing off his coat, he rolled up his sleeves. The thin blade of the saw worked down between the stones, and after a while he began sawing gingerly.

"It's wood," he said. "You'll find yours is the same."

They both worked at one end, for, as he pointed out, there would be only one bar, the other end of the stone being bevelled to meet the edge of the floor. The wood was like rock, and both men were perspiring before they had sawn half through the support. Presently Dick drew out his saw. It had gone through the oak and he had heard

266

the loose end fall below. A few seconds later, Gilder's saw passed through the last obstruction. Gingerly he put his foot on the edge and pressed down, and the stone trap swung open.

They looked down into a dark vault; and now the smell of the burning lamp was very pungent. Dick lowered the lantern and peered down. He could see no sign of human life. He caught a view of the end of a bed, a table, and, on the floor, a rifle. He reached the bottom and, swinging his lantern round, called:"Leslie!"

A mocking echo came back to him from the little cavern at the far end of the apartment. The place was empty; the man and woman who, five minutes before, had fought in a grim struggle had disappeared.

57

"Leslie!"

He called again, his voice hoarse with anxiety. He had seen two little shoes by the side of the bed. Her hat was on the floor, crushed into a shapeless mass. Picking up the rifle, he felt the barrel; it was still warm, and under the tower there were four empty cartridge cases. And then, holding his lantern high, he saw the rungs in the rough face of the wall, and jumped to the conclusion that she had escaped that way. Within a minute he leapt up, caught the lower rung and ran up the ladder to the top, oblivious to one or two ominous cracks as his weight came upon the old ironwork. The grille at the top stopped him. He had seen it, but thought it might be movable.

"They couldn't have gone that way," he said breathlessly as he came down to the ground.

Gilder rubbed his grey hair.

"Then where on earth have they gone?" he asked irritably.

They searched every inch of the long room, pulled the bed from the wall, but beneath was solid stone pavement. The table seemed fastened to the floor; they could not move it.

"Do you notice anything about this floor?" Gilder asked suddenly. "It is not level."

And when Dick looked, he saw this was true. The floor sloped gradually down from the wash cavern to the wall behind the steps. Gilder went in search of a hammer, and the two, now reinforced by Puttler and the Scotland Yard man, went over every inch of the wall and flooring, tapping and sounding. They struck no hollow place. The four men took hold of the side of the table and tried to drag it from its foundations, but they might as well have tried to move the wall itself. It had a thick oaken base, from which ran three pillars supporting the enormously heavy top.

It was very clear to Dick what had happened. The girl had been attacked, and, having discovered this opening to the sky, had procured a rifle by some means and had fired up the shaft to attract attention. Then she had been overcome and – what?

The water ran down through a crevice in the solid rock about six or eight inches wide. It was impossible that any human being could have gone down that narrow slit, but, to make sure, he had the edges of the water-worn rock broken away. The blacksmith by this time was waiting above. Dick had asked him to bring his tools; the second door might yield some sort of solution.

For half an hour they worked with jacks and levers, and presently, with a deafening crack, the lock parted and the door was pushed open. There was revealed a room similar in shape and size to that which Mary Wenner had discovered; with this exception, that there were no stone benches, and in the centre of the apartment was a circular hole. Dick knelt by the side and held down his lantern; he heard the faint "clug" of water, and saw the light reflected at a considerable depth.

"A well," he said. "All these old places have an interior well. There's one in the Tower of London, in the centre of the dungeon."

This room had been used as a prison at a distant period. At intervals along the walls hung rusted chains, with leg-irons attached. In one corner he saw a heap of rags, glimpsed a milk-white bone and shuddered. What was the history of this poor wretch who had been shut away from the light of God's sunshine, to die miserably in this dark and dreadful place?

"Well, there's nothing there," said Gilder, peering over. Dick tied his lantern to the end of a cord and let it slowly down to the depths. Thirty feet below, as near as he could judge, the bottom of the lantern touched water. The old builders had built splendidly. The green, weed-grown sides of the well seemed intact. And then his heart almost stood still. A hand was thrust out, seemingly from the solid brickwork of the well, a white hand on which flashed and sparkled a single diamond that he knew well. And from below he heard a muffled voice; and in his agitation the cord which held the lantern slipped from his hand into the water.

He cursed aloud in his rage at his own criminal carelessness.

"Give me the other lantern!" he called, and pulling the other hand over hand, he untied it and flung it aside, fastening in its place the lighted storm lamp that Puttler handed to him. "And get a rope – quickly."

But there was no rope nearer than Fossaway Manor, and he fumed in his impatience and would have made an attempt to slip down the treacherous sides of the well if Puttler had not restrained him.

After an eternity one of the detectives came running back carrying a rope, and, dropping one end, they fastened the other to a crowbar and placed this across the open doorway. Dick slipped down the rope, the handle of the lantern between his teeth. The sides were wet and slimy, and presently he came to the place where he had seen the girl's hand.

It was a small air-hole about six inches by four. He tried to look through with the aid of his lamp, but he could see nothing but a rough rock wall. He called the girl by name, but no answer came, and the word "Leslie" came echoing back from the interior.

And now he saw that these little apertures occurred at regular intervals. The first two were hidden by overhanging water weeds, but from below they were visible. Some sort of natural stone gallery existed on the other side of this stonework, and he remembered having heard at some remote period that the abbey had been built upon an early English catacomb. In all probability each of those apertures represented a distinct "landing," or a place where some natural winding staircase touched the wall in its revolutions.

He had made a rough loop for his foot, and they passed him down a crowbar at the end of a cord. With this he attacked the hole in the wall, but found himself engaged in an impossible task. Nothing short of an explosive could blow these holes larger. He was almost exhausted by his efforts, and they had to haul him to the top for a rest. Puttler was anxious to go down, but Dick insisted upon being lowered again. This time he took with him a rod, to the end of which a small electric bulb had been attached. The flex ran along the rod, which was a bamboo cane, and terminated in a small battery in his pocket. He switched on the light and pushed the bulb through the opening. He could see now that the wall, which he had thought was natural rock, had been roughly hewn, but he could not see the floor nor more than a foot in either direction. Withdrawing the rod, he put in his hand and felt around, but could touch nothing but the outer facing of the well.

"Look out!"

The warning shout was Gilder's and came from above. He drew out his hand quickly.

"Away from the wall – push with your feet!" yelled Gilder.

He had a glimpse of a grimy hand thrust out from one of the square air-holes, saw the flicker of steel and felt the rope giving as strand after strand was slashed. Then, with a crack, the rope parted, and he went down, down, until the bitterly cold waters engulfed him.

He struck the bottom with his feet and paddled up to the surface again. He was instantly chilled to the marrow. He saw the lantern come down towards him, and heard Gilder say: "Hold to the cord just enough to keep you afloat."

Dumbly he obeyed. His eyes were fixed on the air-hole. So too were the eyes of Puttler, who, flat on the ground, his head and shoulders over the edge, covered with his revolver the place where the hand had emerged.

The cut end of the rope was passed down to him. By reaching up he could just grip it, but not sufficiently to obtain a sure purchase. Cramp had attacked his legs. The paralysing coldness of the water was astounding, and in one moment of fear it seemed that his life was to end miserably in this dark hole. There was no foothold on either side, and unless help came quickly he knew he could no longer keep his senses.

Almost within reach was the lowest of the small apertures, but it did not seem worthwhile to reach for that. The cord of the lantern served to keep him afloat, the warmth of the burning wick was the only comfort he had.

"Dick!" He heard his name whispered with a fierce intensity. "Dick, take my hand!"

It came out of the lower air-hole, and with an effort he reached and found his wrist gripped. And then his senses left him.

When he came to himself he was lying in the open air; the warmth of the sun's rays made him sleepy.

"Where is Leslie?" he asked, struggling up on his elbow. They looked at him blankly, thinking that he was in a delirium.

"How did I get out?"

"Gilder went down for you when he saw you drop."

"But Leslie caught me by the wrist," he said wildly. "She was there – didn't you see her, Puttler?"

Puttler shook his head.

"I saw you holding on to the side just as the new rope came, and Gilder went down for you."

Dick was ghastly.

"You didn't see her? You didn't hear her?" Struggling to his feet, he passed his hand wearily across his forehead. Had he been dreaming? Was that part of the delirium of the death that nearly overtook him? But he was sure, as positive as of any human experience he had had. Leslie's hand had come out from the wall and caught him by the wrist. He had seen the diamond scintillate in the light of the lantern and then he could remember nothing more. But it had been Leslie. He could still feel the pressure of her fingers about his wrist. He had not been dreaming. Somewhere in the deeps of the earth was the woman he loved, and he was helpless to save her. He covered his face with his hands and for a while his shoulders heaved.

58

Leslie had no doubt that the wooden bar would hold. She could afford to sit, covering her ears to shut out the hideous noise above, until his paroxysm had subsided. It must have been in such a mad fury as this, after the killing of Thomas, that he had wreaked destruction upon his room before, in a sudden fit of panic, he had got out of the window and, taking his books from the library (she saw the torn and soiled pillowcase in which he had packed them), had escaped to this lair of his. She took her hand from her ears; he was moaning dreadfully, but somehow she could endure that. Fortunately, she had put on her wristwatch when she dressed, and this marked the passage of the hours. Noon came; there would be people about the estate now, though it was not likely that Dick would come again to the ruins unless he was attracted there.

The plan she had made she now proceeded to put into execution. Standing under the shaft, she fired a round into the air. The third shot struck the iron grille, and ricocheted with an angry buzz that sounded like the drone of a bee. No sound came from the room above. If she could only attract Dick to the ruins, she could indicate her position. But Harry had a rifle! She went cold at the thought. She may have lured him to his death.

For one mad moment she thought of opening the trap and forcing her way out at the point of the rifle. But it was too late now. And then she heard his voice, sounding hollowly and faintly.

"Leslie!"

She went up one of the steps so that she could hear him better.

"They're coming, Leslie. You will tell them I haven't hurt you, won't you?"

"Yes, yes," she replied eagerly.

He said nothing after that, until there came a shuffling and stamping of feet above her head, and then she heard him say:

"Hullo, Dick, old man! I hope I haven't given you any trouble."

From below she heard a deep rumble of sound which might have been a voice, but in her eagerness she was tugging at the oaken support, and in another second the stone fell behind her and she scrambled up through the trap. She could see nothing; the place was in darkness.

"Dick!" she called.

And then a hand gripped her, and she realised with horror that all the shufflings of feet and the conversation had been so much acting on his part.

She was still holding the rifle, but before she could raise it he had gripped the stock and wrenched it from her hand. She heard it fall with a clatter on the stone floor below.

Half swooning in her fear and terror, her struggles grew weaker. He was holding her in his arms, and his strength was surprising.

"We are going below, my sweet," he whispered in her ear. "At last I know the truth! So it was Dick you wanted! Dear Dick!"

He was chuckling softly to himself as he carried her to the top of the steps.

"Will you walk down, or must I throw you?" he asked, in a tone so even and rational that he might have been uttering some commonplace of everyday life.

With trembling knees she walked down the steps into the lighted room, and he followed, pausing to close the trap and secure it firmly.

"Sit down." He pointed to the settle by the table and immediately she sat down. Her face was ghastly; her last reserves of courage were almost sapped. "You have hurt me beyond forgiveness, Leslie," he said, his solemn eyes fixed on hers. "Do you realise what you have done? You have treated with contempt Harry Alford, eighteenth Earl of Chelford, Viscount of Carberry, Baron Alford."

With the solemnity of a child reciting a lesson he repeated the titles he held, even to a remote barony of Aquitaine which the Chelfords had held in the dim past. She had a queer feeling that she was standing before a judge, listening to an indictment of some hideous crime she had committed.

"You have attempted to endanger my life; you have conspired with those who hate me; you have treacherously held communication with and given comfort to my enemies."

There were other charges, that would have sounded ludicrous at other times, would have roused her to fury, but she listened now, husbanding all her strength for the coming struggle.

His rifle leant against the steps, but he barred her way effectively. Looking round for some weapon, she saw nothing but the lamp, and that was too heavy for use.

"For you," he said, in tones of deepest gravity, "there can be only one punishment – death!"

His voice trembled. She felt that, in his queer, crazy way, he was sorry for her, and regretted the necessity. She tried to rise, but her limbs refused her office. She put out an appealing hand and then, with a sudden leap, he was on her. His hand closed about her throat, strangling the scream. And then, up above, there was the unmistakable sound of footsteps and a deep voice. It was Dick. She tried to call out, but he held her tight. With one hand he reached over and extinguished the lamp; and now, in a final desperation of fear, she threw him backward and for a second he released his hold.

But before her tortured throat could utter a sound he was at her again, pressing her back against the edge of the table. She tore at his hand, but it was immovable. This was death! A loud ringing in her ears, a fiery light before her eyes; she was losing consciousness. And then she felt the table move, at first slowly and then so rapidly that she lost her balance. The big refectory table was sliding lengthways towards the end wall. His grip relaxed, and in that instant he dropped away from her, and, reaching out her hand, she could feel nothing. She heard a thud and a groan and stepped forward – into space. She did not see the yawning cavern before her. One desperate effort she made to recover her balance, caught at the hard edge of the floor as she fell and went slipping and sliding down stairs that cracked and broke beneath her, until her feet struck something soft and yielding. Overhead there was a deep rumbling sound, a soft thud, and silence.

59

Harry was unconscious. She felt his face, and her fingers touched something warm and wet.

She could see nothing; the darkness was impenetrable. No sound came from the room from which she had fallen. The floor was thick, the heavy oaken base of the refectory table gliding – she guessed on rollers that worked as truly as they had when, hundreds of years before, the Black Abbot found this exit so valuable – had slipped back into its place. If she only had some sort of light! It occurred to her to search the unfortunate Harry. Presently she found a silver box containing matches. She struck one and looked around. They were lying at the foot of what had once been a wooden stair. The treads were broken, the heavily carved handrail had rotted, leaving two wide gaps. Half the treads had vanished, the other half were now broken by her fall.

Harry was lying in a recess carved from the solid rock, and left and right ran a narrow passage streaming with water. She left the alcove and struck another match. The passage curved and twisted so that only a few feet in either direction were visible. Pools of still water filled the hollows of the floor; long bunches of grey fungus, grape-like in its formation, hung from the roof. Yet the air was sweet enough. She felt a gentle draught coming from the left-hand passage, but as yet she could not explore and she returned to Harry.

His eyes were closed, his lips bloodless, and through the grime his face was grey. With a gasp of horror she thought he was dead, but when she put her hand under his waistcoat she could feel the faint flutter of his heart. He had an electric torch somewhere in his pocket, he had told her, and she began to search. It necessitated moving him slightly, and as she did so he groaned. The lamp was in the tail pocket of his frock-coat, a square, flat lamp, of a type usually to be found in every room of Fossaway Manor.

She thought at first that the unconscious man carried two, but found that the second package was a spare battery. Switching on the light, she examined the roof above the broken stairs. She saw it was the underside of a slab of wood. From here she could see the rollers on which the table ran; stout things of wood. Near the head of the stairs two large wooden grips projected downwards, rather like the butts of huge Browning pistols, and she guessed that by this means the table was drawn back from below.

When she looked at Harry again he was staring upward with wondering eyes.

"What happened?" he asked.

"We must have fallen through a trap," she said. "Do you think you could reach those handles?" She pointed to them.

He rose unsteadily to his feet, replaced his spectacles, which had been knocked off in his fall, and looked at the butts. Only two of the treads remained intact. He tried one, but it broke under his feet and the supporting posts were sagging.

"I can't reach that," he said. "It must be twelve feet high."

Then she noticed his wound and made him sit down while she dressed it with a strip of silk torn from her skirt.

"How on earth did we get into this beastly place?" he asked, wondering. "Where are we?"

"We're under the abbey," she said, and his frown ended in a grimace of pain.

"Where is Dick?" he asked.

"He is up there, I think," she said.

And yet why should Dick be there? He would not know his way into the lower chamber, she thought, with a sinking heart.

"Do you think you can walk?"

He looked round in dismay.

"I can walk all right, but whither?"

"Let us try the left-hand passage first," she suggested, and he was agreeable.

The left-hand passage, they found, was a steep ascent which turned continuously to the left. It was like one of those corkscrew tunnels through which she had travelled in Switzerland, where the train burrows its way upwards in the heart of the solid rock. Was it above Montreux or on Pilatus? She was too tired to think.

At the first turn she stopped. She had seen a glimmer of light, and, making an inspection, she found a square hole, cut apparently in the rock; the further end was covered with hanging weeds, and through these she saw the light distinctly, a faint yellow glow. They continued their climb, and presently came to another small opening. Here, then, was one of the sources of air supply, though little came this way, for when she lit a match before it the flame scarcely wavered.

"How much farther are we going?" asked Harry faintly. "I'm nearly all in."

"We must go on," she said. "This probably brings us to the open air somewhere."

He put his hand on her shoulder, and, walking slowly, they made another complete turn of the winding passage, and this time they found an air-hole that was not weed-covered. The light was stronger now, and, looking through, she thought she saw a swaying cord. And she heard something too – voices. It was not an illusion; somebody was talking at an immense distance away, it seemed. She looked again. The cord seemed very near, but when she thrust her hand through the opening and tried to grasp it, she knew that she had been the victim of an optical illusion. She called out, but there was no answer. She must have imagined the voices.

And then she heard a faint shout and the yellow light which had shone through the entrance went out.

"I can't go any farther." Harry collapsed against the wall and slid down into a sitting position, his head on his breast.

"Do you mind if I leave you in the dark?" she asked.

He shook his head wearily, and, leaving him, she continued the climb, and presently found herself in a straight, narrow passage. At some period an attempt had been made to dress the sides with stone slabs. The wall was littered with crumbling fragments of stone, and gaps showed where age and the action of the damp had detached the dressing from the walls. As near as she could judge, she was moving away from the abbey in the direction of Fossaway Manor.

This latter was a guess. It was impossible that it could lead towards the cut road to the north of the estate. Then the explanation came to her; she was passing under the Mound, the high bank that fringed the Ravensrill. What light feet had trodden this way? she wondered. What fears or hopes, desire or despair, had sped along this rough stone floor? Unconsciously she was reconstructing an ancient cause and effect. The effect brought her to a standstill. Right across the passage a wall had been built; a solid barrier of masonry which checked all further progress.

Though she did not know and could not guess, here was the obstacle that the revengeful Lord of Chelford had set up after his assassin had gone forth to slay the man who had dishonoured him. No more would the light steps of frail womanhood trip along this secret passage, and since Yvonne of Chelford had died of a broken heart no woman's foot had stirred this dust.

Leslie turned back, her courage failing. Approaching the spot where she had left Harry, she heard his soft chuckle and her skin crept.

"Leslie, Leslie!" he whispered eagerly. "You have no idea what a bit of good luck I've had!"

And when he came into the light of her lamp he was his old exalted self.

"What do you think happened?"

She was conscious now of voices. She heard somebody shout and a faint answer, but faint as it was, she recognised the voice. It was Dick's.

"What has happened?" she asked quickly.

He doubled up with silent laughter and could not speak for a minute, and then he showed her a knife.

"With that," he said complacently. "I saw him go down – and then the rope came near – I could have touched it. Then I remembered I had my knife, and I reached through, and before they could pull it away I'd cut it."

She gazed at him in horror.

"Was somebody on the rope?" she gasped.

He nodded gravely.

"The arch-enemy of the human race," he said in a sober tone. "Richard Alford."

Petrified with terror, she put her ear to the hole and heard Dick speaking. Then without a word she fled down the slope. Round and round the circular passage she went until she was almost dizzy. Presently she reached the lower air-hole, put through her hand and tore away the veiling weeds.

"Dick, Dick!" she called.

She could see him now for the air-hole was just above water level. His face was grey and drawn.

"Dick!"

She thrust out her hand and presently closed it about his ice-cold wrist, and at that moment Harry's hand fell on her shoulder and she was dragged backwards. She felt the wrist slip, she heard the splash of water as Dick Alford fell, and fainted.

60

She woke, and it was so dark she could not believe her eyes were open until she felt the lids. There was no sound. She was lying on the hard, uneven floor where she had fallen, she thought, but when she put out her hand to feel for the air-hole, her fingers touched rough rock. Groping round for the flash-lamp, she found nothing. Presently, however, she touched a smooth, cold surface. It was Harry's knife, a long-bladed clasp knife.

And then she remembered clearly. Dick was in the water, drowning. She struggled to her feet, trembling in every limb.

Dead perhaps. She staggered blindly forward and came in contact with the wall. Gripping her hands till the nails cut the palms she strove to regain her self-control. He would be rescued; there were men with him, she told herself, and became calmer and again sat down, so that her back was to the wall, and waited, the open knife on her lap. Feeling in her pocket for a handkerchief, her hand touched the matchbox, and she took it out with a sense of gratitude.

She was weary to the point of exhaustion. The rough flooring had slashed the soles of her silk stockings to ribbons and her feet were terribly sore. She waited for some time before she struck her first match, for the box was already half empty. She saw that she was in a part of this underground system which was unfamiliar to her. The roof was higher; the walls bulged in like the sides of an hourglass, and the floor had been roughly paved. At intervals there seemed to be niches, alcoves in the wall, and again she thought of the Swiss tunnels with their safety niches. There was no sign of the lamp; evidently Harry had carried that with him when he had gone off. It was not like him to leave her; even in his delirium he would not have done that, she thought.

As the match burnt out she heard halting footsteps re-echoing down the passage, and, closing the knife, she slipped it into her jacket pocket and waited. He must have been a long way from her when she first heard him; the passage acting as a huge speaking-tube.

"Are you all right, Leslie?" He was normal again. "I'm sorry I had to leave you, but this place rather rattles me, and I had to go along and see if I could find an exit."

"Where are we?" she asked.

"I don't know. I carried you down that wretched circular arrangement, and you were fearfully heavy," he added, so naïvely that the girl laughed for the first time in that period of horror. "Do you know, Leslie" – he squatted down on the floor by her side – "I have an idea. Do you remember those holes we looked through?"

"Yes, I remember them," she said, wondering what was coming next.

"Do you know that they are placed in the side of a well of some kind?"

Not a word about Dick. He had forgotten the rope-cutting and the horror that followed.

"Has it occurred to you," he went on, "that the treasure may be at the bottom of that well? It only struck me a few minutes ago. If we could get out and have a talk with Dick, he's such an ingenious devil that I'm sure he would find the opening of the well, which may be inside the old abbey itself. Most of these mediaeval buildings had a well in the centre and kept their water supply enclosed."

"You didn't find an exit?" she asked.

"No," he said. "I got into a sort of labyrinth and I thought I should never get out again. Good heavens! Look at your feet!"

They were indeed in a sorry plight, swollen and bleeding. In an instant he had pulled off his own shoes.

"Put them on," he said authoritatively, and when she demurred, he seized her foot and slipped her toes into the shoe. "I was a great runner in my day," he said, with a hint of pride, "and barefooted running was my speciality – to use a horrible theatrical word."

The shoes were much too big for her, but the comfort of them after walking barefooted on that rough floor!

"There's one place I haven't explored, and that is the little side passage to the left. There has been some sort of a fall there and the rock looks rotten. I didn't like to attempt an exploration. By the way, what made you faint?" he asked suddenly.

"I don't know – nerves, I suppose," she said.

It was useless and even dangerous to tell him of what had happened by the wall of the well.

"I thought it might be that," he said. "If you feel fitter now we'll go along."

He walked ahead, switching his lamp on and off at intervals. He wanted to economise his batteries, he told her, which had shown signs of running out. All the time he kept up an incessant chatter. He had plans about the future of the abbey and grew enthusiastic when he expounded his scheme.

"This is not even a Saxon-English burrow, but probably goes back to the days of the original inhabitants of Britain," he said. "We are walking in paths that were originally cut by cavemen. Doesn't that thrill you, Leslie?"

"Terribly," she said, with unconscious irony.

"I'll have the place wired and lit; it will be necessary to increase the electric supply, but Dick will see to that. I may present it to the nation or to the Ecclesiastical Commissioners – I'm not certain which. There is no doubt from an archaeological point of view – "

So he talked on and she followed him, sometimes listening, sometimes her mind occupied with the agony of thought. Was Dick safe? She was sure that he was not alone; there were men at the top of the well, and they would save him. It was not possible that Dick Alford should die in that dark place, that his splendid life should be ended so tragically. The walking was tiring, for they were climbing all the time.

They must have covered about a quarter of a mile when he stopped.

"Here is the side passage," he said, and warned her: "Don't go into it; the stones are still falling."

He put his light into the hole – it was no more – and she saw a great heap of fallen rock in the middle of the path. There was just room between the top of the heap and the roof to crawl through. But what she noticed instantly was the strong current of air that fanned her cheeks when she stopped to look through the aperture.

"This must be the way, Harry," she said instantly; "can't you feel the air?"

"I noticed that," he agreed, but was reluctant to enter this unpromising byway.

"We must go, Harry. There's no other way out," she said. "We are getting farther and farther down, away from the abbey, and, as you say, beyond here is only a labyrinth that brings you back to the place from where you started."

"All right," he agreed, with evident distaste. "I had better go first."

He crawled gingerly over the pile of stones and slid down on the other side.

She heard his voice.

"It is all right here," he said, and then the light of his lamp showed and she followed him.

The passage was very high; it was a natural fissure in the rock. Yet the hand of man must have been here, for the floor had been levelled, and there was evidence of animal life. A long black shape scudded across the path and disappeared through a hole. The girl gave a little scream and shrank back.

"It is only a weasel," said Harry calmly. "Where a weasel can get, we can get."

The passage had widened, and now the work of man became evident. They were in a square chamber: the roof was of vaulted stone that seemed to bulge downwards, as if it supported a weight beyond its capacity, but this was hidden by the long stalactites that flashed in the light of the lantern. And she shivered. It was extraordinarily cold, almost as if they had come into an ice-house.

"No door and no doorway. I wonder what the idea of this place was."

It was the first man-made chamber they had seen. The walls were running with water, wet and shining; the roof dripped incessantly, but only one small pool of water gathered on the floor; the rest ran off in a central chamber and apparently into the solid rock.

"The dripping of water wears away stone," quoted Harry, and pointed to the floor with its tiny saucer-shaped depression.

There was no sign of a door at either entrance, and he went ahead of her through the arched entrance, covered a few yards, and stopped, looking upwards.

"Daylight!" he said.

The first thing of which she was conscious was that, away from the little room, she was warm again.

The shaft that worked upwards was a natural fissure. They could see the rough edges of rock jutting out at intervals. In some places it was wide enough to hold a full-sized man; in other places it was so narrow that only an arm could have reached through. But there it was, the clear, uninterrupted view of the sky, and the girl beheld a phenomenon with which miners are familiar, the view of a white, winking star, in broad daylight.

"That is where the air comes from," said Harry. "Now we'll try where this passage leads."

It led to a blank wall of solid rock, he found. They stared at one another in the darkness.

"We must try back," said Harry.

Hardly were the words out of his mouth than there was a distant rumble and roar, the ground beneath their feet shook, and down the passageway through which they had reached the Cold Room swept a cloud of flying dust.

"Wait," he said, and flew along the passage.

He was gone a few minutes before he returned. She could not see his face except from the reflected light he threw upon the floor to guide him on his way.

"The roof has fallen in," he said, and there was a tremor in his voice. "I am afraid, Leslie, we are finished!"

61

A hot bath and a meal, though every morsel seemed to choke him, restored Dick Alford to something like himself. There was hope – faint indeed, but still hope. He had despatched his bailiff in search of explosives, but explosives cannot be bought over the counter like cheese and bacon. He had a telephone message from the man to say that he was on his way to London and would return with the necessary apparatus. Dick's plan was simple; even then a derrick was being rigged over the well; his plan was to dynamite the wall of the well and to get into the gallery.

"For a long time I've been suspicious that the rock on which the abbey was built was honeycombed with passages. My father told me something about it, and I've seen an old plan that shows an elaborate system of corridors, though the family has always thought this was largely imaginative on the part of the artist."

"Have you the plan now?" asked Gilder.

Dick shook his head.

"Harry took everything of that nature away with him the night he left the house."

"It is not amongst the books you found in the underground room?" said Puttler, and a search was made of the library, but without success.

They were on their way to the ruins when Puttler saw the aeroplane in the sky. It circled twice and then began to dip steeply.

"I believe that fellow is coming here," he said.

And so it proved. The machine roared its progress for a hundred yards or more, and then dropped. Presently they saw a man get down. Though he wore an airman's helmet, Dick recognised him. It was Arthur Gine.

He met Gilder's scowl with a little laugh.

"I've got some money of yours, Gilder," he said, and dragged with some difficulty a huge packet from the pocket of his leather coat. "That is more or less the amount I owe you, unless the franc has depreciated in value since I left Paris. And now you can do your damnedest!"

Gilder took the packet without a word and Arthur turned to Dick Alford.

"I read about Leslie in the French papers," he said simply, "and so I came back. Has she been found?"

Dick shook his head.

"Have you any idea where she is?"

Dick told him all that had happened that afternoon, and Arthur Gine listened in silence. When Dick came to speak of his plan, he shook his head.

"I had my early training as an engineer before I went into the law," he said, "and I tell you, from my elementary knowledge of the science, that you're likely to blow in the whole well, and if there's anybody on the other side, God help them!"

He accompanied them to the lower room and was swung down on the derrick to make an inspection. When he returned to the surface his report was not very promising.

"So far as I can see," he said, "whilst you may enlarge the opening of any of these air-holes, you may also bring about a fall of the rock inside. You're dealing with surfaces which have been exposed to the chemical action of the air."

He went down and made an inspection of the lower room, which was new to him, and, as they had done, tried to pull the table aside. And then he did what they had not attempted; he pushed at the table at one end and felt it move, at first slowly and then quickly, as though he had set in motion a counterweight. He had just time to swing himself on the table and grip its edge when the aperture appeared under his feet.

Dick saw the broken stair, and, sitting on the edge of the hole, dropped through to the rocky floor just as the table slid into its place. They pushed it back again and propped it, and Arthur and Gilder joined him below, carrying lanterns. He saw a piece of something dark on the floor and picked it up. It was a strip of silk.

"This is the way," he said quietly. "I'll work to the left; you go to the right, Gilder."

Arthur made a rapid mental calculation.

"The left passage will lead you to the well, and unless I'm very much mistaken you will find the air-holes on your right-hand side. If you don't mind, I'll go with you."

The men ascended the treacherous slope and came to the first of the air-holes, continued up until they reached the straight passage down which Leslie had made her fruitless journey. They too were brought to a halt by the wall barrier, and returned the way they had come. There was no sign of Leslie or Harry, but when Dick passed the alcove down which he had dropped from the Abbot's room he found a burnt match-stalk.

He ascended again, a long, steady climb.

"We're near the surface of the ground," said Arthur.

Ahead of them the star lamp of Gilder showed. He was coming back to meet them.

"This passage ends in a sort of maze," he reported. "There is a side passage, but that's entirely blocked by stone."

They went back with him to the place and Arthur Gine examined the debris.

"The roof has fallen in here," he said. "How long ago it is impossible to tell. This stone is old, but I should think that the fall has been going on for years."

They returned dispirited, and accompanied Gilder on his exploration of the maze. Though they tried passage after passage, they invariably found themselves back at the place where they had started. Dick made another inspection of the fallen roof. It had collapsed a few feet from the entrance; and, though he did not know this, there were twenty yards of crumbled rock between him and the little chamber where Leslie Gine was waiting for death.

Dick came out into the light of the setting sun, his haggard face white with dust. Arthur sat on a stone, his head in his hands, the picture of despair. Even Gilder was shaken from his habitual calm, could do no more than stare tragically at the ruin which hid so much. The broken arch of the window, red in the light of the setting sun, was more than ever like a query mark. There was something devilish about it, something which epitomised the spirit that leered and mocked at them.

"Come back to the house," said Dick steadily, and, to the bailiff who approached him: "No, I shan't want the dynamite – yet."

They walked dispiritedly along the Mound, Arthur Gine, the most dejected of all, walking in the rear. Suddenly they heard him shout and turned. He was pointing across the river.

"What is it?" asked Dick, hurrying back to him.

"The wishing well – have you thought of that?" gasped Arthur.

"The wishing well?"

And then Dick remembered that rendezvous of the country swains, the unfathomable crevice in the earth down which, as a boy, he had dropped stones, listening to hear them strike from rock to rock until they grew fainter.

"That reaches somewhere," said Arthur excitedly. "We can but try it."

Dick ran down to the bank, plunged into the water and waded through to the other side. The two men followed him, and something whispered in Dick Alford's heart that this was his last hope.

62

"What time is it?" asked Harry.

He had not spoken for two hours, but had sat, clasping his knees, his head thrust forward, engaged with his wild thoughts.

"Lend me the lantern."

She passed the lamp back to him.

"A quarter to seven," she said. "Harry I feel so hungry."

"Do you?" he asked in surprise. "I don't feel hungry. I feel – I don't know."

Presently he spoke again.

"How did we get here?" he asked. "I know the roof fell in, but how did we come into this beastly place?"

"You've been very ill," she said gently. "You came here whilst you were sick."

"Did I really?" He seemed amazed at her reply and did not speak again for fully five minutes. "I seem to remember now that I have been ill. I sleep so badly and have such horrible dreams. Poor old Dick was always ragging me about my patent medicines – queer bird, old Dick, but one of the very best."

He spoke so heartily, with such enthusiasm, that her heart ached for some unknown reason.

"We shall have to get out of here," he said.

She did not answer him.

For the tenth time he turned on the light of his lamp and examined the roof.

"It is vaulted," he muttered. "I hope nothing happens here."

She felt him shivering.

"Nothing is going to happen, Harry," she said soothingly. "We're going to get out and we're going to have a big dinner to celebrate our rescue."

He chuckled softly.

"We shall never get out of here," he said cheerfully. "This is the end of the House of Chelford." He thought a while. "By Jove, no! Of course, Dick will inherit the estate. Isn't it queer, Leslie, that he never wanted me to marry? That's the only thing about Dick I cannot understand, because he's not a jealous man or an envious man, but a good, big-hearted fellow – and yet he didn't want me to marry. Doesn't that seem strange to you?"

"I don't think you're right, Harry," she temporised. "Only he didn't want you to marry the wrong woman."

"But he didn't want me to marry you," said Harry in a tone of indignation. "And if there's a better girl in the world than you, I'd like to find her! Of course I'm a terrible slacker, but – "

"Hullo!"

The booming voice seemed to come from somebody in the chamber. She felt him start, and again his frail body quavered in a fit of trembling.

"What was that?" he asked huskily.

"Hullo!"

The voice came again. She seized the lamp from his hand and ran out of the cavern to the place where she had seen daylight.

"Is that you, Dick?" she called at the top of her voice, and heard a husky "Thank God!"

And then from the Cold Room came a burst of demoniacal laughter. There was yet the gravest danger of all to overcome. She was alone with a madman!

63

She could see no daylight, and thought that night must have fallen, until a patch of golden red appeared high above her.

"Is Harry with you?"

"Yes," she replied. "One moment."

She went back to find him cowering against the wall, and gripped him by the shoulders.

"Harry," she said pleadingly, "they have found us!"

He scowled up at her.

"Who have found us?"

"Dick – everybody. We shan't have long to wait now."

He licked his lips.

"Dick and everybody," he said dully. "That is strange – found us!"

She flew back to the little shaft.

"Are you hungry?" boomed the voice. "Very," she answered. "But that doesn't matter – I can live without food for another twelve hours. We're in a sort of underground room. The roof of the passage has fallen in."

"How long is the passage?" asked Dick quickly.

She thought a moment.

"About forty yards, I think. It cannot be much less."

"How far from your end is it blocked?" and when she told him, she heard him groan.

"Leslie."

"Yes?"

"I'm sending something down to you at the end of a string. It is a pocket compass. Will you tell me exactly the bearings?"

It reached her at last, battered, its glass broken. She put the little instrument on the floor.

"Put it where I can see it," he said. "Have you a light?"

She flashed the lamp upon it.

"Where is the north? Just touch the place with your finger. Wait, I will send for field-glasses."

Ten minutes passed, and then he said again: "Now show me." And when she had indicated the north, he asked her where the cavern was.

"Exactly west," she said with tremulous triumph. "Will it be a long time before you reach us?"

He made no answer to this.

"Tell me how many paces you are from the compass," and when she had paced it off and had told him, he groaned.

By this time the consulting engineer to whom he had telephoned in the afternoon was on the spot.

"The cavern is exactly under the bed of the river," said that official.

"Could we enlarge this hole?" asked Dick.

The surveyor shook his head.

"Impossible. It would take you the best part of a month to blast a way down. There's a long fault in the rock here which accounts for the river's course," he added. "Both banks are solid; I can assure you on that point, because my predecessor bored for water for your respected father."

Dick groaned. He could keep the girl alive for a month, but the strain of it would kill her. Then there flashed simultaneously to two minds a solution.

"Why not break the dam of the Ravensrill?" he said, and Puttler, who had the words on his lips, nodded.

"That's the idea," he said. "Undo the work of your ancestor! Turn the course of the river to the Long Meadow – there's a natural bed for it!"

Ten minutes later the telephone at Fossaway Manor was busy, and here Mary Wenner was a heaven-sent helper. Every great contractor within twenty miles had his instructions, and within an hour charabancs, motorcars, omnibuses, crowded with horny-handed workmen, were lumbering up the drive. Car succeeded car, and disgorged the fustian-clad navvies. They had been taken from ale-houses, from their homes, from workmen's clubs, drawn even from the cinemas of distant Brighton, and every hour the number swelled, until there were a thousand men working by the light of naphtha flares on the great dump behind Fossaway Manor.

At ten o'clock the omnibuses and lorries were still rolling up the drive; trolleys laden with wheelbarrows and tools were being rapidly unloaded at the side of the dump. All southern Sussex worked to cut the dam of the Ravensrill, and the big dump grew smaller and smaller. Presently, as the water rose, it spilled into the bed that it had left for hundreds of years and flowed its irregular course, sweeping aside barns that had been hastily evacuated, lapping the walls of one cottage, the inhabitants of which had been removed in time. Little by little the water in the old bed sank and sank until it was a dark mass of weeds and silvery shapes that leapt up and down *in extremis*. Water voles, trout, pike were shovelled to the bank, and the bed of the river attacked by men who worked at fever pace, being relieved every half-hour.

"If there is rock there," said the surveyor, "we are dished! My own belief is that there's nothing but sand."

"And shingle?" suggested Puttler.

"No, sir, there's no shingle. It is a curious fact that we've never found shingle in the Ravensrill. They've struck the sand now," he said, looking down into the hole, which the men were shoring with logs of timber. "And I'm glad there is no shingle – sand is much easier to work."

He had hardly spoken the words before the foreman shouted: "We've struck shingle here, governor!"

"Shingle?" The surveyor went down the ladder into the hole.

"It is only a layer," he said when he came back, "but even that is rather surprising. It opens up all sorts of possibilities."

Dick did not listen. The value of shingle to a county surveyor was of no more interest to him than the value of sand to a grocer.

The work was now heavier. A derrick and windlass had to be rigged to move the heavy loads from the cutting, and that took a considerable time, during which he paid frequent visits to the "wishing well."

It was after the shingle had been discovered that Harry's voice answered him.

"Is that you, Dick? What are you fellows doing up there?"

The voice held all the old irritation and fretfulness. Briefly Dick described what was happening.

"Couldn't you send me something down so that I could work below?" asked Harry. "I'm perfectly sure I could make it much easier for you."

To humour him, Dick Alford found a light crowbar and with great difficulty lowered it. Because of its shape and size, the operation was a painfully slow one, and Harry fretted and fumed below.

"Hurry, for heaven's sake," he shouted. "You don't suppose I want to stay down here, do you? I've a tremendous lot of work to do – you know that, Dick, very well."

Dick did not answer, but his anxiety increased. He knew Harry and his symptoms all too well to be under any illusion as to what would follow if his irritation grew beyond the power of restraint, and it was with a sigh of thankfulness that he felt the crowbar caught in the eager hands of his brother.

"Be very careful how you use this," he called. "The men are working from above and you may have a fall unless you take the greatest care."

But he was talking to the air. Harry had gone and it was Leslie who answered him.

"How long will you be, Dick?" she asked.

"I don't know, my dear. A few hours, not longer. Are you all right?"

A little hesitation.m

"Yes, I'm all right."

"Is Harry?"

A longer pause.

"I think so. Is it possible to send something down that he could take?"

Earlier in the evening Dick had tried to pass the end of a thin rubber tube to the imprisoned pair, but the attempt had been futile.

"I'll try," he said, and went in search of one of the two doctors who had been summoned.

From him he obtained two small brown pellets, and these, wrapped in paper and weighted, were dropped into the wishing well.

"Thank you," said her low voice. "I don't know how I can use them, and for the moment he is very busy."

64

There was no question as to Harry's activity. He had rolled a heavy boulder from the debris in the passage, and, placing it in the centre of the floor, he could reach the stone roof, which was in six petal-shaped sectors. The lens of his lamp had been removed so that the light was diffused, and Leslie had a better view of the room.

There were little holes at intervals that looked as if they had once held hat-pegs, though why anybody should come into these depths to hang up their hats she could not imagine. And then the real value of this peculiar chamber occurred to her. She found against the wall a long, rusty hook, so thin that she could break it. This had been the meat store of the abbey, the mediaeval equivalent to a refrigerator. The atmosphere was deathly cold. It seemed a very long way from the abbey, but in reality it was not more than a hundred and fifty yards. The old monks had found this cavern, had dressed and strengthened it, had lined and converted it to their own use. That explained why this chamber, so far distant from the main building, had received the ancient architects' attention.

Harry was in his shirtsleeves, which were rolled up, revealing his thin but sinewy arms. He had managed to get the claw of the crowbar between two of the stones, and was working at them gradually, talking the while to himself in an undertone. Her anxiety increased. The paroxysm, when it came, would be short, but what would be the end of it? Her mouth went dry and she felt for the knife she had put in her pocket, and stealthily opening the blade, thrust it through the lining to keep it in place.

Presently Harry paused, wiped the perspiration from his forehead with his arm and looked down at her. His horn-rimmed spectacles had slipped down his nose and he stopped to adjust them.

"Dick has no intention whatever of rescuing us. I think that you ought to know that."

"I'm sure you're mistaken, Harry," she said.

But opposition only made him worse and he snapped down at her: "You're a fool! All women are fools! I tell you it is a plot. Dick has no more intention of rescuing us – "

He stopped suddenly and passed his hand across his eyes.

"I wish I had brought the picture," he muttered, and glared at her. "But for you I should have taken it with me, and now I've left it behind for that swine to jeer at!"

She looked up at the roof.

"You're doing splendidly, Harry," and, his attention distracted, he attacked the roof again.

"You can trust me, Leslie," he said. "I am the only person in the world you can trust. You have no enemies. The Black Abbot is dead! I killed him, and I am very proud of the fact. Every Chelford should kill at least one Black Abbot, and I have had the approval of my illustrious ancestor."

By this time the claw of the crowbar had been worked deep into the crevice he had made, and he began to lever slowly. As she watched him she saw the stone move. It dropped suddenly an eighth of an inch, and he raised an excited shout.

"You see, you see!" he said, in his shrill voice. "Dick never dreamt I would be able to do that, or he would not have allowed me to use this crowbar."

He got down from the stone, scooped up two handfuls of water from the worn channel and drank, dashing the remainder of the water into his face before he leapt again on the stone and went to work with renewed vigour. Backward and forward he levered the crowbar, and again the stone dropped, until it was perceptibly out of place.

"You must be careful Harry," she warned him. "That may come down with a rush and hurt you."

He was sensible enough to see this, changed the position of the stone and worked from the other angle. And then, without warning, all that she had predicted happened. He leapt aside into the open doorway as with a crash the sector fell and broke into fragments on the stone pavement.

"You see, you see!" he screamed. "I've done it!"

A steady shower of shingle was falling. He struck upwards with the point of his crowbar, and the shower increased until it made a heap on the ground.

And then he saw the edge of a box.

"Look, look, look!"

His trembling hands could scarcely hold the tool. With the energy of dementia he dug away at the shingle beneath it, and presently, gripping it by the edge, he pulled it clear. It was a tin chest, a miniature of those she had seen at Fossaway Manor, six inches, in length, four inches broad and as deep. With his crowbar he prised open the lid and the rusted iron hasp parted with a snap. Inside was what appeared to be a bundle of discoloured cloth. He lifted it out.

"There's something heavy here," he said hoarsely, and his hands shook so that in pity she came forward and helped unwrap the thing that the box held. Presently it came to light; a long flask containing a colourless fluid. The bottle was heavily sealed at the top.

He snatched it from her hand, a frenzied gleam in the staring eyes.

"The Elixir!" he croaked. "The Life Water! Oh, God be thanked!"

She tried to take it from him, but he snarled round on her like an angry dog.

"You devil!" he screamed. "You're in league with Dick! You're trying to rob me of life! But you shan't, you shan't!"

The flask was corked with a piece of wood that had swollen. He dragged at it with his teeth and presently extracted the stopper.

"I shall live eternally! But you shall die! He shall find you here dead, and realise – "

He put the flask to his lips and drank. She covered her eyes with her hands, then, as he moved, gripped the knife.

And then she heard something drop with a heavy crash to the floor and looked. The shingle was still sliding down like sand in an hour-glass, but now something big and heavy thudded to the ground. It looked ludicrously like a yellow candle, but its weight was such that the first bar struck the pavement and the impact bent it hook-shaped. Another followed. She watched, fascinated as they came, first slowly, then in a stream, from the triangular space in the roof – scores, hundreds of yellow candles thundering down in twos and threes amidst the flow of shingle.

"The gold, the gold!" screamed Harry. "But he shall never have it!"

He lifted the lamp, but as his arm rose she stooped swiftly. The crash of the lamp as it struck the wall came to her and she crouched back towards the wishing well. She heard a loud crash in the chamber; a sector of the roof had given under the strain, and now, with a hiss and a rush, shingle and ingots were falling until they almost filled the room. They flowed about her feet like a heavy stream. She struggled to get it underfoot and became more and more engulfed.

"Dick, Dick!" she screamed, but he did not hear her.

He had reached the broken roof of the Cold Room and was slipping and sliding down the heap of shingle under which lay a man who was dead before the torrent of stone was loosened. Later they found him, gripping a crystal flask in his hand. What it had contained no man ever knew.

65

When Leslie Gine woke, the sunlight was peeping round the edges of the drawn blinds. She sat up suddenly and her head went round and round. And then she remembered and her eyes closed, as if to shut out some horrible sight.

"Oh, you *are* awake?" said Mary Wenner, bustling in. "Dick sent me up to see how you were. Everybody's most fearfully anxious about you – even Fab, though I'm not of a jealous disposition, as everybody knows."

"What is the time?"

Then, with a shiver she remembered that somebody else had asked her that. How long ago? An eternity!

"Twelve thirty-five," said Miss Wenner, consulting her watch. "I've been out looking at the workmen. Really, my dear, it's more like a Desirable Residential Estate than the grounds of Fossaway Manor. Wheelbarrows and navvies and goodness knows what! They say it's cost his lordship twenty thousand pounds."

Leslie looked at her in wonder.

"His lordship?" she said in a hushed voice.

"I mean Dick," said the calm Miss Wenner. "The King is dead, long live the King! That's my motto every time." And then, in a more sober tone – and rather ashamed of herself for her heartlessness: "Poor boy! It was a mercy for him. Fabe's gone back to London."

"Who is Fabe? Oh, Mr Gilder!" said the girl, smiling faintly.

Miss Wenner dropped her eyes modestly.

"We are engaged. It was all his idea, because, as you know, Leslie darling, I'm not the sort of girl to throw myself at any man's head. But he's persuaded me." She sighed heavily. "I suppose I'd better. I'm getting on in years, and a girl can't always be pretty."

Leslie brought her feet to the floor and stood up. She was still a little unsteady, and the pain in her feet was atrocious, in spite of the dressing that the doctor had applied.

"I must say that Arthur took it very well," said Miss Wenner as she assisted the girl to dress. "It was naturally a great blow to him."

"What was?" Leslie was a little dazed.

"My engagement," said Mary. "You didn't know." She sighed. "Arthur was very fond of me, I'll admit it. But in the circumstances I don't think it would be nice to marry a gentleman who's bad friends with my fiancé; do you, Leslie?"

"I had no idea that there was anything between Arthur and you," said Leslie truthfully.

Again Miss Wenner sighed.

"Very few people knew anything about it. Perhaps it is all for the best. Arthur thinks so. It isn't as though I'd thrown myself at him, so there's no harm done one way or the other."

Leslie was wearing a pair of men's slippers when she came down the broad stairs. Dick's study door was open, and she saw him sitting in a deep cane chair on the lawn outside, a pipe between his teeth, a heap of documents on his knees which he was examining slowly one by one. He looked round, rising from his chair at the sound of her voice. She saw his face and was shocked.

"Dick, you look a hundred years old!"

"I feel a thousand," he said, and guided her to the chair. "Sit down. Well, that's the end, Leslie – and the beginning."

She nodded.

"I think we've managed to keep the ugliest part of it out of the newspapers. Poor old Harry!" There were tears in his eyes which he did not attempt to hide. "Poor old victim!"

"Victim of what?"

"Of his mother," said Dick. "There never was a time when she was sane. My poor father did not discover this until after the child was born, and her death removed one of the greatest sorrows from his life. The other was – Harry! Well, now you know the secrets of us all, what do you think, Leslie?"

"Who was the Black Abbot?" she asked, and then, to her amazement:

"I was," he replied quietly, and told her all he had told Gilder.

"The queer thing was that he must have seen the gold before he died. What fools we were! The diary told us as plainly as anything could that the old Lord Chelford who hid his treasure chose the bed of the river. It was a year of drought, the river was quite dry, and probably he found a deep hole in its bed, hid the gold and covered it with shingle that would not wash away."

"You are very rich now, Dick?"

He nodded slowly.

"Yes – I suppose I am. There are a few minor trials and troubles for us, Leslie dear," he said, "but when those are all over and everything is settled we will go abroad for a year and forget all about these ghastly days and nights."

She took his hand between her two palms.

EDGAR WALLACE

BIG FOOT

Footprints and a dead woman bring together Superintendent Minton and the amateur sleuth Mr Cardew. Who is the man in the shrubbery? Who is the singer of the haunting Moorish tune? Why is Hannah Shaw so determined to go to Pawsy, 'a dog lonely place' she had previously detested? Death lurks in the dark and someone must solve the mystery before BIG FOOT strikes again, in a yet more fiendish manner.

BONES IN LONDON

The new Managing Director of Schemes Ltd has an elegant London office and a theatrically dressed assistant – however, Bones, as he is better known, is bored. Luckily there is a slump in the shipping market and it is not long before Joe and Fred Pole pay Bones a visit. They are totally unprepared for Bones' unnerving style of doing business, unprepared for his unique style of innocent and endearing mischief.

EDGAR WALLACE

BONES OF THE RIVER

'Taking the little paper from the pigeon's leg, Hamilton saw it was from Sanders and marked URGENT. *Send Bones instantly to Lujamalababa… Arrest and bring to headquarters the witch doctor.*'

It is a time when the world's most powerful nations are vying for colonial honour, a time of trading steamers and tribal chiefs. In the mysterious African territories administered by Commissioner Sanders, Bones persistently manages to create his own unique style of innocent and endearing mischief.

THE DAFFODIL MYSTERY

When Mr Thomas Lyne, poet, poseur and owner of Lyne's Emporium insults a cashier, Odette Rider, she resigns. Having summoned detective Jack Tarling to investigate another employee, Mr Milburgh, Lyne now changes his plans. Tarling and his Chinese companion refuse to become involved. They pay a visit to Odette's flat and in the hall Tarling meets Sam, convicted felon and protégé of Lyne. Next morning Tarling discovers a body. The hands are crossed on the breast, adorned with a handful of daffodils.

EDGAR WALLACE

THE JOKER
(USA: THE COLOSSUS)

While the millionaire Stratford Harlow is in Princetown, not only does he meet with his lawyer Mr Ellenbury but he gets his first glimpse of the beautiful Aileen Rivers, niece of the actor and convicted felon Arthur Ingle. When Aileen is involved in a car accident on the Thames Embankment, the driver is James Carlton of Scotland Yard. Later that evening Carlton gets a call. It is Aileen. She needs help.

THE SQUARE EMERALD
(USA: THE GIRL FROM SCOTLAND YARD)

'Suicide on the left,' says Chief Inspector Coldwell pleasantly, as he and Leslie Maughan stride along the Thames Embankment during a brutally cold night. A gaunt figure is sprawled across the parapet. But Coldwell soon discovers that Peter Dawlish, fresh out of prison for forgery, is not considering suicide but murder. Coldwell suspects Druze as the intended victim. Maughan disagrees. If Druze dies, she says, 'It will be because he does not love children!'

OTHER TITLES BY EDGAR WALLACE AVAILABLE DIRECT
FROM HOUSE OF STRATUS

Quantity		£	$(US)	$(CAN)	€
	THE ADMIRABLE CARFEW	6.99	12.95	19.95	13.50
	THE ANGEL OF TERROR	6.99	12.95	19.95	13.50
	THE AVENGER (USA: THE HAIRY ARM)	6.99	12.95	19.95	13.50
	BARBARA ON HER OWN	6.99	12.95	19.95	13.50
	BIG FOOT	6.99	12.95	19.95	13.50
	BONES	6.99	12.95	19.95	13.50
	BONES IN LONDON	6.99	12.95	19.95	13.50
	BONES OF THE RIVER	6.99	12.95	19.95	13.50
	THE CLUE OF THE NEW PIN	6.99	12.95	19.95	13.50
	THE CLUE OF THE SILVER KEY	6.99	12.95	19.95	13.50
	THE CLUE OF THE TWISTED CANDLE	6.99	12.95	19.95	13.50
	THE COAT OF ARMS				
	(USA: THE ARRANWAYS MYSTERY)	6.99	12.95	19.95	13.50
	THE COUNCIL OF JUSTICE	6.99	12.95	19.95	13.50
	THE CRIMSON CIRCLE	6.99	12.95	19.95	13.50
	THE DAFFODIL MYSTERY	6.99	12.95	19.95	13.50
	THE DARK EYES OF LONDON				
	(USA: THE CROAKERS)	6.99	12.95	19.95	13.50
	THE DAUGHTERS OF THE NIGHT	6.99	12.95	19.95	13.50
	A DEBT DISCHARGED	6.99	12.95	19.95	13.50
	THE DEVIL MAN	6.99	12.95	19.95	13.50
	THE DOOR WITH SEVEN LOCKS	6.99	12.95	19.95	13.50
	THE DUKE IN THE SUBURBS	6.99	12.95	19.95	13.50
	THE FACE IN THE NIGHT	6.99	12.95	19.95	13.50
	THE FEATHERED SERPENT	6.99	12.95	19.95	13.50
	THE FLYING SQUAD	6.99	12.95	19.95	13.50
	THE FORGER (USA: THE CLEVER ONE)	6.99	12.95	19.95	13.50
	THE FOUR JUST MEN	6.99	12.95	19.95	13.50
	FOUR SQUARE JANE	6.99	12.95	19.95	13.50
	THE FOURTH PLAGUE	6.99	12.95	19.95	13.50

ALL HOUSE OF STRATUS BOOKS ARE AVAILABLE FROM GOOD BOOKSHOPS
OR DIRECT FROM THE PUBLISHER:

Internet: www.houseofstratus.com including synopses and features.

Email: sales@houseofstratus.com
             info@houseofstratus.com
             (please quote author, title and credit card details.)

OTHER TITLES BY EDGAR WALLACE AVAILABLE DIRECT
FROM HOUSE OF STRATUS

Quantity		£	$(US)	$(CAN)	€
	The Frightened Lady	6.99	12.95	19.95	13.50
	Good Evans	6.99	12.95	19.95	13.50
	The Hand of Power	6.99	12.95	19.95	13.50
	The Iron Grip	6.99	12.95	19.95	13.50
	The Joker (USA: The Colossus)	6.99	12.95	19.95	13.50
	The Just Men of Cordova	6.99	12.95	19.95	13.50
	The Keepers of the King's Peace	6.99	12.95	19.95	13.50
	The Law of the Four Just Men	6.99	12.95	19.95	13.50
	The Lone House Mystery	6.99	12.95	19.95	13.50
	The Man Who Bought London	6.99	12.95	19.95	13.50
	The Man Who Knew	6.99	12.95	19.95	13.50
	The Man Who Was Nobody	6.99	12.95	19.95	13.50
	The Mind of Mr J G Reeder				
	(USA: The Murder Book of J G Reeder)	6.99	12.95	19.95	13.50
	More Educated Evans	6.99	12.95	19.95	13.50
	Mr J G Reeder Returns				
	(USA: Mr Reeder Returns)	6.99	12.95	19.95	13.50
	Mr Justice Maxell	6.99	12.95	19.95	13.50
	Red Aces	6.99	12.95	19.95	13.50
	Room 13	6.99	12.95	19.95	13.50
	Sanders	6.99	12.95	19.95	13.50
	Sanders of the River	6.99	12.95	19.95	13.50
	The Sinister Man	6.99	12.95	19.95	13.50
	The Square Emerald				
	(USA: The Girl From Scotland Yard)	6.99	12.95	19.95	13.50
	The Three Just Men	6.99	12.95	19.95	13.50
	The Three Oak Mystery	6.99	12.95	19.95	13.50
	The Traitor's Gate	6.99	12.95	19.95	13.50
	When the Gangs Came to London	6.99	12.95	19.95	13.50

Tel:	Order Line 0800 169 1780 (UK) International +44 (0) 1845 527700 (UK)
Fax:	+44 (0) 1845 527711 (UK) (please quote author, title and credit card details.)
Send to:	House of Stratus Sales Department Thirsk Industrial Park York Road, Thirsk North Yorkshire, YO7 3BX UK

PAYMENT

Please tick currency you wish to use:

☐ £ (Sterling)　　☐ $ (US)　　☐ $ (CAN)　　☐ € (Euros)

Allow for shipping costs charged per order plus an amount per book as set out in the tables below:

CURRENCY/DESTINATION

	£(Sterling)	$(US)	$(CAN)	€ (Euros)
Cost per order				
UK	1.50	2.25	3.50	2.50
Europe	3.00	4.50	6.75	5.00
North America	3.00	3.50	5.25	5.00
Rest of World	3.00	4.50	6.75	5.00
Additional cost per book				
UK	0.50	0.75	1.15	0.85
Europe	1.00	1.50	2.25	1.70
North America	1.00	1.00	1.50	1.70
Rest of World	1.50	2.25	3.50	3.00

PLEASE SEND CHEQUE OR INTERNATIONAL MONEY ORDER
payable to: HOUSE OF STRATUS LTD or card payment as indicated

STERLING EXAMPLE

Cost of book(s):..................... Example: 3 x books at £6.99 each: £20.97
Cost of order:...................... Example: £1.50 (Delivery to UK address)
Additional cost per book:.............. Example: 3 x £0.50: £1.50
Order total including shipping:.......... Example: £23.97

VISA, MASTERCARD, SWITCH, AMEX:

☐☐☐☐☐☐☐☐☐☐☐☐☐☐☐☐☐☐☐☐

Issue number (Switch only):

☐☐☐

Start Date:　　　　　　　**Expiry Date:**

☐☐/ ☐☐　　　　　　　☐☐/ ☐☐

Signature: _____

NAME: _____

ADDRESS: _____

COUNTRY: _____

ZIP/POSTCODE: _____

Please allow 28 days for delivery. Despatch normally within 48 hours.

Prices subject to change without notice.
Please tick box if you do not wish to receive any additional information. ☐

House of Stratus publishes many other titles in this genre; please check our website (**www.houseofstratus.com**) for more details.